Lindsay Simpson is the author of six works of non-fiction. She spent twelve years as an investigative journalist with *The Sydney Morning Herald* and in 1999 was the founding member of the Journalism and Media Studies program at the University of Tasmania. She lectures in journalism and writing at James Cook University and lives on Magnetic Island with her husband, Grant Lewis. They have five children. *The Curer of Souls* is her first novel.

Also by Lindsay Simpson

Brothers in Arms (co-authored with Sandra Harvey)
My Husband My Killer (co-authored with Sandra Harvey)
The Killer Next Door (co-authored with Sandra Harvey)
The Australian Geographic Guide to Tasmania
More Than One: twins and multiples, and how to survive them
(co-authored with Andiee Paviour)
To Have and to Hold: a modern love story cut short
(co-authored with Walter Mikac)

THE
CURER *of*
SOULS

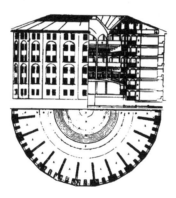

Lindsay Simpson

VINTAGE BOOKS
Australia

A Vintage Book
Published by
Random House Australia Pty Ltd
20 Alfred Street, Milsons Point, NSW 2061
http://www.randomhouse.com.au

Sydney   New York   Toronto
London   Auckland   Johannesburg

National Library of Australia
Cataloguing-in-Publication Entry

Simpson, Lindsay.
The curer of souls.

ISBN 978 1 74166 107 1.

ISBN 1 74166 107 2.

I. Title.

A823.4

Cover photography by Getty Images, Australian Picture Library and
Photolibrary.com
Cover and internal design by Greendot Design
Typeset in Bembo 12.5/15 point by Midland Typesetters, Australia
Printed and bound by Griffin Press, South Australia

10 9 8 7 6 5 4 3 2 1

'History . . . is certainly the most erudite, the most aware, the most conscious, and possibly the most cluttered area of our memory; but it is equally the depths from which all beings emerge into their precarious, glittering existence.'

Michel Foucault, *The Order of Things*

'I hold this slow and daily tampering with the mysteries of the brain to be immeasurably worse than torture of the body, because its ghastly signs and tokens are not so palpable to the eye and sense of touch as scars upon the flesh, because its wounds are not upon the surface, and it exhorts few cries that human ears can hear.'

American Notes, for General Circulation by Charles Dickens, 1842, quoted on a plaque at the Female Factory Historical Site, Hobart

To Grant, my
soulmate on a
sea of possibilities

CHAPTER ONE

London
March 1865

Lydia imagined her parents in heaven, twin figureheads, their carved expressions gazing confidently seaward. She had dressed her stepmother's body in her hand-crocheted wedding dress. The fine cloth hung around Jane's wasted flesh. Her face was sallow and sunken, the skin stretched across prominent cheekbones; her mouth loose, not how she would have liked. The white cotton bonnet around her head made her features look uncharacteristically witch-like. Her eyelids had the translucency of the leaves that rustled outside Lydia's bedroom window. Lydia could feel no connection between the body lying in the coffin and the woman with whom she had spent most of her life.

Jane had always cared about her appearance and Lydia felt her wedding dress was appropriate apparel to wear to her final resting place. The bonnet jarred with the dress but, now it was in place, it seemed too much effort to remove it. Besides, Jane had always told her it was where the soul went after death that was important.

Now both Lydia's parents were dead. Jane had chosen to be buried in a country grave in a churchyard in Wiltshire, next to her forebears rather than next to the empty coffin of her husband. At the funeral each scrape of the shovel resonated, as though ending a chapter. Clods of earth fell on the coffin, a muffled sound pierced by the cries of gulls under a leaden sky. There was only a handful of people. Charles Darwin, the grey-haired evolutionary, came in a wheelchair, along with other elderly gentlemen Lydia recognised – lords of some sort – and a few family members. They stayed for the requisite time and then escaped in small clutches. The clipped hooves of their horses and the rumble of wooden wheels echoed off the low stone walls that surrounded the country cemetery as they disappeared out of Lydia's life forever. At forty-one years of age, she was alone.

One morning after the funeral Lydia awoke to sunshine in the family's London house in Bedford Place, Russell Square. She had been half listening to the familiar noises that denoted the beginning of the day – the grate being dragged away from the fireplace as the maid prepared to lay the coal, doors banged, the heavy curtains opened, the great clock in the hallway striking the hour – and waiting for the tinkle of the bell to summon her for service; Jane's voice commanding her to read, to adjust her pillows, to have a game of draughts, to administer her medicine, or to simply sit in a chair and listen to her talk.

Lydia felt separate from the cloistered world below. No one disturbed her. She did not go down to breakfast, nor did she ring to explain her absence. Instead, as the ordinary morning street sounds clattered outside, she sat in the study and wrote letters to her stepmother's relatives.

Each day since the funeral she had been delaying the inevitable. Jane's death had not been unexpected, but now it had finally happened she felt paralysed by indecision. She was unaccustomed to taking control. Besides, her future was decided. She imagined her relatives' sympathy clinging unspoken between them as they discussed her letter. How would she cope without Jane? They had been erstwhile companions, inseparable until death. Lydia was a spinster, alone with no direction and no real purpose in life.

Nobody wanted the house in Russell Square. It was expected that it would be sold, having been emptied of the furniture of generations of Griffins, Jane's family. Then Lydia would begin her new life by moving to the family's small country cottage in Wiltshire, near Jane's grave.

Twenty-one Bedford Place had been Lydia's home since they returned from Van Diemen's Land in 1843. It was a five-storey Georgian house in Russell Square within walking distance of the British Museum and Covent Garden, where the gaslights still bore the name of the Duke of Bedford from whose estate the suburb had been born. As a child, Jane told her there were so many windows on each floor she used them to help her to learn how to count.

Before Lydia moved she had to dispense with the staff – at one guinea per servant she could not afford any of them: the maid, the footman, the hall porter or the steward's room boy. In the past few years of Jane's illness they had rarely entertained.

The servants had been an unnecessary luxury. The cost of their livery alone amounted to a princely sum and they expected new suits once a year, not to mention their board. After summoning the footman to take the letter, Lydia moved into the morning room and sat staring at the large green ledger on the desk.

She had already decided she would sell the silver and put her stepmother's exotica up for auction. The house was also full of memorabilia from her father's two trips to the Arctic. Jane had wanted her husband's study left the way it was when he had sailed for the last time all those years ago. In it there were the reindeer tongues he had given Jane on their wedding day and three pairs of shoes from the snow people, which he had brought back for Lydia. Then there were his dusty paintings, large Arctic horizons with the sun a watery smudge and the Eskimos' faces yellowed, harsh and uncompromising. When she was a young child the large canvases had given her nightmares: the ghost of a ship trapped in the ice, its mast like a dead branch from a tree rising from whiteness, the ship a foreign object in the natural surroundings. Later, they reminded her of her father's death. She imagined him in a soundless land carpeted with snow.

Eleanor, Lydia's mother, had only been dead for three years when her father married Jane. Jane had been Eleanor's friend. Jane had known her mother whereas Lydia could not remember her. Her father had one portrait of Eleanor: the girl in the painting was in her teens, her hands clasped in front of her lavender dress – not like a mother at all. Lydia came to think of her as an older playmate who never aged, her eyes solemn and almond-shaped, spaced far apart, her hair dark like Lydia's.

Her father had first brought Jane home from a trip to the Continent when Lydia was about four years old. Her new stepmother had brought her two porcelain dolls that were cool to touch and had fixed glassy smiles. She remembered waking to their shadowy stares and her stepmother's irritation when she perceived her gift had been rejected. Her father, hovering, had tried to bind them together – the two girls he loved.

It was Jane who had told Lydia that Eleanor had died when her father was on one of his trips to the Arctic. Eleanor had told him to go, Jane said, even though she had been sick and was left with their baby daughter. Lydia did not want to ask her father whether this story was true. Her father did not like to speak of Eleanor and Lydia shirked from the idea of asking Jane more. It was not Jane's place to be revealing things her father had chosen not to tell her. Nor did she want Jane reminding her that as a toddler she too had lost her mother. That did not make them the same. Nothing made them the same.

By then, Sir John Frankland was already knighted, a hero after two trips, including one successfully charting much of the mythical North-West Passage. His book about his adventures in the Arctic had been a bestseller. Jane listened to the same stories Lydia had listened to: the blistering winters he had endured; eating a man's leather boots to survive; the stabbing pain of frostbite. Watching her stepmother, it appeared to Lydia she was a consummate manipulator, supporting her husband only for her own ends. To Lydia, Jane seemed to be incapable of real affection for anyone. Nevertheless, she knew he was happy so she tolerated Jane. Lydia never had the sort of conversations with Jane that she imagined having with her real mother. Her transition to womanhood was a solitary journey.

When they had bidden Sir John farewell at Southampton on the voyage that was to be his last, Lydia was twenty-one. Jane had grasped her hand in a rare show of affection, which united them in their love for this man, and as they were alone Lydia knew this was not for anyone's benefit. The gesture touched her because of this. A dove had settled on the mast of the ship. It was a sign, Jane had said. He would return to them soon.

But he never had. They had delayed his funeral for so many years and they still did not know the truth. Jane had been wrong, but Lydia had believed her. She tried to gain comfort by imagining that her father was preserved under so much ice, frozen for posterity, but instead, she would see his corpse frostbitten, his mouth hollow from lack of food and love. Jane never gave up hope, until she finally conceded in her dying moments that his coffin would never be filled and she would be apart from him in death as she had been in life.

Now Lydia was left to journey on alone. She tried to enjoy the unfolding of each new, uneventful day until one morning she arose early, having decided she could procrastinate no longer. She pulled back the heavy maroon curtains in Jane's study that adjoined her bedroom to let in some of the foggy city sunshine. Jane had spent her last two years bedridden. The room had the feeling of being unoccupied for some time. Dust had settled, in spite of the parlour maid's efforts.

Lydia surveyed the scene in front of her, unsure where to begin. Her stepmother had charged her with cataloguing her belongings. On a table in the corner of the room she noticed some large bulky shapes under a heavy canvas. Her curiosity aroused, she picked up the canvas and, struggling with the weight of the cloth, pulled it along the table. Particles of dust floated in the sunshine, a shower of diamonds. She peered into the blackness. As her eyes adjusted, she saw the yawning mouth of a Tasmanian devil. The taxidermist's handiwork had survived for nearly thirty years. Teeth yellowing with age, the creature snarled at her as though protesting at being awoken so suddenly. It looked ferocious and real. Lydia closed her eyes. She was smelling the whale oil at the wharves on an island at the end of the Earth; the fresh chilled breeze as it came off the Derwent River; the soft blowing sound of whales at night off Battery Point; the musty smell of the shops that sold kangaroo and possum skins. The devil was a relic from Van Diemen's Land. Lydia had almost forgotten about her stepmother's collection from that wild colonial outpost where she had spent much of her childhood. During the winters in Van Diemen's Land the clouds would circle Mount Wellington threatening a storm and only its jagged dolerite peaks would be visible. She would bury her head in her father's greatcoat as they strolled through the Government House gardens and he told her more of his Arctic adventures.

'Come and see the Tasmanian emu,' he would say. 'My little Lydia, what a place we live in. Giant birds and convicts – we are in an island jail and I am the jailer.' And he would laugh his loud, comfortable laugh.

She saw his black frock coat buttoned to his neck, a white bob rising above the crown of his black beaver hat, a belt and a sword in a glittering scabbard around his ample waist, a red seam down the outside of his trousers. More than half of the population were convicts when her father arrived to govern the colony. Her fondest memories of that time were walking in the garden with her father where the lawns ran down to the river. After his marriage to Jane, her stepmother took up the space she had once inhabited, but during those early morning or evening walks, she had the opportunity to speak with him alone. He would take her hand in his and watch her lips sounding the words. There was much that he missed in conversation due to his deafness. He had told her it was the legacy of an old battle wound from Trafalgar, when he had stood too close to a cannon firing. He wanted to know if he spoke too loudly and he was always happier away from a crowd.

When they first arrived in the colony and trumpeters blazoned a welcome, the crowds had lined the streets, waving their hats. Sir John's cheeks, usually pink, had shone even more than usual that first night at dinner in Government House with the glory of it all. She had imagined him in the hubbub on the deck of the ship in full battle. Her father, the Arctic hero who ate men's boots, who had defended the old country at sea, who had charted the coast of Australia, would now show he was capable of leading a colony, of deciding the fate of criminals, of succeeding as a leader of men. She watched Jane bask in the reflected glory. As he settled into the role of governor, Lydia suppressed her need to see him as more and more often his position took him on journeys around the colony. She and Jane were left to their own devices and Jane had taken up collecting as a hobby.

No doubt the Royal Society would be interested in the Tasmanian devil. With some excitement now, Lydia lifted the canvas off the other boxes, coughing into the dust. Finally, the creatures stood on the table, imprisoned in their glass cages, a silent zoo awaiting her direction. Her favourite was the platypus, a creature that laid eggs, had furred skin like an otter and a beak like a duck. On impulse, she pushed her fingers against the glass lid of the cage, a child again, tempted by the forbidden. Her stepmother had always been protective of her boudoir of stuffed animals. Was the platypus's fur coarse or soft? It looked so sleek.

She pulled across a small footstool from underneath the piano and stepped gingerly onto it. It seemed to bear her weight. Now she could reach inside the cage. The fur felt smooth and dry. The animal's webbed feet seemed incongruous with its furred body and she hesitated before touching the feet, wondering if they would crumble with the stress of time. Wedged between the wooden stand on which the creature was mounted was what looked like a crease of butter. Forgetting her original intention, Lydia began to prise at the object with her fingernails. It was a document of some sort. She searched the study and found an old ivory letter opener, but it was not strong enough. Impatiently, she pulled at the folded pages with the nails of her thumb and forefinger. She heard a rip and drew breath, but the pages were intact, yellowed with age. How long had they been there? She moved through into Jane's boudoir to her walnut writing desk where the light was better and opened them.

The letter was addressed, 'My dearest Louis', and the handwriting belonged to her stepmother. Blinking, she thought the light was playing a trick. Louis? An early suitor perhaps? She hesitated, confronted by the thought that she was prying. There had been so many men in Jane's life: geologists from Poland with unpronounceable names, botanists who specialised in grasses from the Falkland Islands, amateur natural historians with an insatiable appetite for the new and unclassified.

Then she remembered. Louis – a keen natural historian from Port Arthur, an amateur painter. Jane had introduced him during one of her Tasmanian Society dinners. Lydia recalled he had his own museum at the penal settlement, but she could remember little else about him. Jane had kept some of his paintings, she thought.

Marlborough
March, 1842

My dearest Louis,

I leave this arid township to venture into a wild land with quartz peaks and streams of ice.

You are already spoken for, as am I, yet from the day you showed me the southern boobook and spoke of Cuvier, of Lyell, and I saw your passion and curiosity for life, you seemed at once familiar and shocking to me. Love is the domain of Coleridge and Keats. I have studied their verse yet I have never understood it. Everything I read now speaks the same as my heart.

I may never return from this journey and never speak of what is between us. The deputy surveyor-general, Calder, has prepared the first fifty miles of our route. He tells me it is frightening terrain, like that of Milton's *Paradise Lost*, with horizontal trees that grow outward and fallen branches, which will hamper our path. All around there are craggy mountains clothed in mist. Beyond is Transylvania, where few white men have been and to my knowledge no woman.

Of course, my mind runs away with me. The trip has been meticulously planned and Calder seems an able man. But even as a seasoned traveller, I confess to being alarmed.

The canvas flaps so strongly in the gale outside. I wonder if I will have the courage to send this to you? Committing it to paper is so dangerous.

Oh, my love. There. I have written it. I imagine your hair falling across your brow, reading those words. What will your expression be?

It is time to write of secrets so long kept, the heresy we have talked of. I have battled with myself for thinking these things, but I am writing to you to say that as each day passes I know there is truth in Mr Darwin's hypotheses, though he may feel as though he's confessing to a murder. In his last letter he told me that his young wife, Emma Wedgwood, has been counselling him not to shut out the truth of religion. Why, she asked him, did he want to constantly prove things?

Mr Darwin challenges all of us — and not without proof — to accept his theory that species are not immutable. Louis, we have been placed in this savage outpost at the end of the earth, where we have examples of strange creatures adapting to their habitat: the platypus — part bird, part mammal — the Tasmanian tiger with a body and jaws like a hyena. Is it heresy to believe they adapt to where they live? I want to take this opportunity in case I have no other to tell you that I believe it is not heresy.

Darwin writes that he was in the Regent's Park Zoo when he came across a baby orangutan that had the same expressions he had seen in human babes. 'Man from monkeys?' he asks. I cannot yet make that leap, yet I am entranced by his logic.

Are you still recording the tides on the Isle de Mort? I think of your quill scratching across the page as you sit in the storeroom writing your meteorological register. The Royal Society will accept your records — they must. Your curiosity matches mine. You will have a place among scientists as a hydrographer of world renown. You deserve this, no matter what happens.

I must ask. What happened to the boy? I still dream of him and ponder his fate. I know of your compassion for him. I attempted to intervene with Sir John as you asked me to. Alas, an exception cannot be made for a boy who has already been transported across the seas, particularly as his crime is murder and one so brutal. I realise you may not agree. You, a curer of souls. Do we have a right, I hear you ask, to take a young man's soul?

Perhaps had I not been on this journey I may never have had the courage to tell you any of this. God be willing we shall meet when I return to Hobart Town. If you feel moved to finish my portrait, I can only acquiesce to your request. Do not reply to me at Government House, I beg of you, for it is not safe.

Yours,
Jane

CHAPTER TWO

Lydia stared at the inlaid cockleshell on the face of the bureau that she had admired as a child. Jane had sat here almost every day for the past twenty years, except when she and Lydia had travelled on the Continent. The view through the window revealed hansom cabs on the cobbled streets below. Her gaze alighted on a mail coach piled high, the sheen of its black and mauve doors reflecting dappled leaves. She looked back at the desk and wondered briefly whether the letter had been planted there as a bizarre hoax, but there were too many accurate references to the past. Transylvania – on the west coast of Van Diemen's Land. Lydia had been eighteen when her parents had undertaken the journey there. She remembered anxiously waiting for letters each day, imagining herself an orphan if they had perished in the wilderness. But after Marlborough, the township Jane had mentioned in the letter, none came. Her parents had underestimated the force of the remorseless west-coast weather. It was reminiscent of the ice age, and the land that they crossed utterly devoid of humans.

Lydia looked up at the portrait of her father hanging opposite the desk: beatific, serene. He'd sat for the painting just before he set sail for the last time. His balding head and cheeks had been lightened with gouache so they had the smooth-ness of peaches. Lydia looked into those untroubled eyes that gazed across the room, past the bed and out of the window. She considered destroying the pages, destroying this person, Louis, whoever he was. Had her father known that his wife had felt this way for another man? Jane's letter mocked from the grave. It showed an entirely different woman to the step-mother she knew. Jane, who attended church every Sabbath; who devoted so much of her time counselling female pris-oners about God; who said her prayers each night and who had spent most of her fortune sending ships to search for her husband in the Arctic. This letter challenged all that. Jane had a lover, or had desired a lover. She had deceived her husband. Worst of all – and this shocked Lydia most – she couldn't ask her to explain any of it.

Her thoughts scattered, a kaleidoscope of possibilities. Looking at her father's portrait again, she felt pain reopen in her heart. The finality of his death – she had never said goodbye properly. After all these years she wanted to be reas-sured that he had not died in pain. She walked over to the fireplace, avoiding the portrait's eyes.

And the boy? There were boys, she remembered, at the penal settlement in Port Arthur. There was the boy on the ship. A face appeared before her then vanished like the image on the silver-coated plate of the new daguerreotypes she had seen on the Strand. Lydia stood up and stared out of the window.

The day had become chilly. Her breath was a cloud on the windowpane. The under housemaid had already lit the coal fire in the grate, but the warmth hadn't entered the room. She had declined morning tea and breakfast. The servants presumably thought her lack of appetite was brought on by her state of mourning.

She felt paralysed with indecision: to destroy the letter or undertake some course of action? As the gaslights gradually went off in the square, she decided. She would begin a search. If anyone was able to unravel Lady Jane Frankland's life, Lydia could. She would begin with the diaries.

Feeling better, she walked through from the boudoir to Jane's bedroom. Her eyes travelled to the four-poster bed, accustomed to seeing Jane's diminutive figure under the bedclothes, but the rose-patterned coverlet was smoothed flat. Lydia was in charge now. Outdated Regency furniture Jane had kept from the days of her marriage sat gathering dust. A china washbasin stood in the corner. Her books were against one wall. Lydia opened the wardrobe. Clothes, mostly unworn for years, were hanging amidst a musty smell of mothballs. She walked around the room, searching for . . . what?

She found the picture of a kangaroo rat in a dark corner beside the wardrobe. She lit another oil lamp and carried it across to the canvas, lowering the light. In the flickering flame, the creature's fur was luminous. She held the candle closer until she could make out the signature on the bottom right-hand corner of the frame. Louis Lemprière. She glanced behind her at the bed where Jane's prone form had always lain, accusing, but there was no one there. She placed the canvas back where she had found it.

Lydia was sure now this was the same Louis that she had

met at Jane's Tasmanian Society dinners. Her father would have known him too. She thought of her stepmother with a suitor in their midst in the large dining room at Government House. She wondered whether Jane had publicly humiliated her father. Had she openly flirted with this man? Distracted and entering adolescence, Lydia may not have noticed. This was the same woman who had once been received by the Pope as the devoted widow of Sir John Frankland. Her stepmother's devotion now had a different complexion.

She saw the bedside table under the window. Jane might have hidden other documents in it. Now she felt like a detective, the torpor from the beginning of the day replaced with a feverish desire to know more. She slid open the drawer. Here was the small maroon book her stepmother had been writing in the days before she died. The words crawled across the page.

3rd February, 1865

Today I am a sulphur-crested cockatoo, wings wide, sweeping the air white before me in the vast reassurance of the sky.

Far below is the church with its wooden spire, standing on the edge of the bay. Coal fires are crackling inside the whitewashed houses of the penal settlement and there are the comforting rituals of home: backgammon and afternoon tea. I can see people on the deck of a visiting ship dancing a quadrille, whirling in tightly controlled circles, engaged in a parody of manner, a show from the British Empire. What an empire we think it is.

The clanking sound of irons echoes on the afternoon breeze. The curtains protect us from their view, but we cannot mistake the unwashed smell and the stench of the putrid abscess where steel has rubbed against flesh. The convicts have the same fascination for me as a captive bear I once saw in a Chinese marketplace. Or maybe the slaves I saw in Ecuador. Linked by chains, they move as one like a gross living creature; a centipede. They have become as much part of the settlement as the quadrilles and the daffodils that sprout amongst the vegetables, and the young orange trees planted from seed from Sydney Town.

I can smell that odour as if it were yesterday, assisted by old age and the way it sharpens memories. I am standing in the pew smelling, too, old mildewed cloth, wet shoe leather and sweat, the wooden railing hard against my knees, listening to the sermon. But the man who addresses me is not a minister. I can see hot and yellow lights, dancing. Are they candles or eyes? They have become giant felines waiting in the dark, prancing, watching for me to stumble. I am weighed down by velvet drapes and the sombre walls. The words I speak come from underneath their fabric.

Then the voice speaks. I am back before my inquisitor in the witness box.

Senile rantings. Her dying stepmother had been prone to reveries. Talk of the courtroom had become commonplace with her towards the end. Lydia had long ago given up trying to work out what witness box she was talking about, what trial. At other times, as Jane spoke, Lydia would catch entertaining glimpses of a life long ago: helping to make a blancmange in the shape of a ship for a dinner party in honour of Queen Victoria's ascent to the throne. Fancy-dress balls and extravagant costumes. Sending a white kangaroo as a present to the new queen. Then darker times, when Jane's words were like a draught blowing through an open door. A fragmented mind in its dotage. Near death she had paid even less heed to others. Her stepmother's words would become jumbled, unintelligible, or full of hate and venom. Lydia would watch the dried cracked lips of the old woman lying on the bed and wish her dead. Before opening the diary again, Lydia glanced back at the bed for reassurance. Jane was definitely gone and her secrets with her.

Later, discarding a half-eaten supper, she ordered the flustered chambermaid to find her a ladder. The trunks containing Jane's papers were in the attic. Lydia had never shown an interest in her stepmother's writing, but now she felt compelled to uncover some answers. She knew Jane would never have thrown anything out, as she was proud of the record of her life.

Lydia braced herself. She would not shy away from the unorthodox; perhaps Jane had taught her that. An image of Jane in her bloomers being lowered down a volcano in South America when she was in her sixties came into her head and she almost laughed out loud. These journeys were the highlight of Lydia's time with her stepmother. Jane was the most inspiring of travelling companions, always seeking the most out of every experience, even when Lydia, twenty years her junior, was exhausted. Lydia was inured to the continual attention they received on their many trips to the Continent, America and their most recent trip in Spain on donkeys. At first she thought Jane was travelling to forget her husband, but as the years passed, she continued to journey. Even as she aged, Jane shirked the idea of popular destinations, choosing instead the more intrepid. Lydia had no choice but to accompany her. Fellow travellers took up the task of entertaining and listening to her stepmother as she relived her adventures, and told and retold the story of her widowhood.

However, Jane's tiresome appeals for sympathy at her status as a widow never extended to sympathy for Lydia as a spinster. Lydia knew her spinsterhood was inevitable. She couldn't look at her reflection without seeing the faint jagged line across the left side of her face that had cursed her youth and for which she blamed her stepmother. The scar ran along the bridge of her nose before splintering off into her cheek. Jane had introduced her to flaky lead-based skin powder in her teens to hide the worst of it. Never once had she claimed responsibility for what had happened. Throughout her life Lydia had struggled with her fear of not being able to find a husband, of going to her grave without ever having experienced intimacy. After the accident, she had felt doubly damned.

The gas they had laid throughout most of the house did not yet reach the attic, but later, using the light of a candle and wearing her thickest tweed cloak, Lydia unearthed a dozen small hard-covered books from one of the large trunks up there. The books did not appear in order of date. Some seemed quite old, others appeared to be government records, ledgers of some sort.

Jane had begun keeping diaries when she was seventeen. In her old age, she had rejected a Van Diemen's Land publisher's request to publish her account of the colony, although Lydia knew she was secretly flattered. Her journals, she would tell Lydia, were like the hypomnemata used in Ancient Greece; a notebook to record her encounters through her life for herself and her family. Lydia surely had every right to read them.

Her stepmother's life was laid out before her. The youthful pledges to 'better herself', studying a new subject every week – three hours on Latin and a determination to come to grips with physics, 'which I hate'. In some of the diaries she found withered sprigs of blue forget-me-not, still preserved from Jane's youth. In others, she found blotting paper once pressed on the now faded ink. Lydia had not expected to become so absorbed.

The later books were slightly larger in form and Jane's hand more assured. She was surprised to find little about her wedding. Finally, she reached 1836 – the year they all sailed to Van Diemen's Land. Lydia recalled the exhilaration of the adventure: sailing across the ocean to the other end of the Earth. She had never been on a ship before. The first night after they left Southampton she could not sleep because of quacking ducks and other poultry on board, then the clanking of buckets in the early morning as the decks were washed. She remembered her first meal – boiled cabbage and some sort of meat – and her queasiness from the rocking of the ship. There were some days when the violence of the storms kept her from sleeping, as furniture was hurled about in the cabins and had to be lashed down. Schoolwork was largely abandoned since her governess, the ineffectual Miss Williamson, suffered from seasickness throughout the voyage. One of Lydia's favourite memories was the hours spent stretched out on cushions on the deck, reading.

She had attended Sunday school with a group of other children while Jane organised soirées and held audiences on 'important' topics, often insisting Lydia attend to improve her education. Her father would appear proud of his indefatigable wife as she presided over the discussions. Lydia would listen wide-eyed to accounts of a man in Sicily born with a tail, and lots of discussion about the age of the Earth and the perils of Satan.

Each evening the family shared a meal in the dining room, their places reserved for the duration of the voyage. Once, during a violent storm, the archdeacon slipped and banged his head against a buffet in the dining room, where he lay for some time, lifeless. Lydia had been convinced the devil himself had visited them, but the archdeacon had recovered.

Lydia saw more of her father on the ship than she had in her lifetime, although Jane was usually by his side. During the five-month voyage to the colonies, she and Jane had learnt to live with each other, both aware of their shared responsibility to Sir John. Were they ever friends? Lydia shivered, knowing that in spite of the decades they had spent together, she had never thought of her stepmother as someone who understood her. If there was a friendship, it was conditional. Did that count?

Her eyes scanned the pages, looking for further reminders of a life lived long ago. The octopus they had caught with tentacles the size of a man's wrists which sprawled on the deck; the shark's dissection. As an eleven-year-old girl she remembered gazing up at the spectacle of a creature from the deep dangling from a large iron hook in front of her, his tail thrashing before the sailor's knife. She remembered the taste the next morning at breakfast – rich and oily, not unlike the taste of eel – but most of all she remembered that its tail was dismembered while the creature was still alive. It was the first death she had encountered.

15th October, 1836

The shark cursed me in death. Its blood leaked out over the poop deck and sprayed on my Balmoral petticoat. Dr Richardson, the ship's naturalist, was much taken with the sucking fish attached to its back. He thought it might be the same one the amateur historian Bennett spoke of during his wanderings in New South Wales, but he'd never seen it attach to a blue shark like this one. He didn't even know its biological name. The jaw was his trophy. The backbone was divided up among the forward passengers and the skin was stretched over a hoop and transformed into a tambourine. It was used for the rest of the voyage to summon passengers to meals, a hollow drumming uncannily like the beat of my pulse.

Lydia kept reading. Jane declared that she was now a collector as she began to record the creatures she and Dr Richardson plucked from the sea's depths. There was another sucking fish that had stayed alive for some time in spite of being kept in formaldehyde. There were several entries about the days they spent in Cape Town at the house of the astronomer John Herschel, and Jane's journey to the top of Table Mountain. Lydia remembered sunshine and vineyards and the towering mountain that looked as though it was sheered across the top, it was so flat. Then her eye alighted on a passage further on.

24th October

I was taking my customary stroll on the foredeck and had strayed below, curious to find out more about our cargo. If I write the truth, I am committed to that, but I blush even now as I do so. The sight of intimacy. The sound of pleasure, discordant to my ears. And a boy? I examine my thoughts, like Dr Richardson would a specimen. Why did I keep watching? I was shocked. The boy was in danger and I stood there, transfixed, unable to accept what my eyes recorded. I have relived that scene many times. I did not see the boy's face immediately, just the side of his buttocks and the other man's trousers around his ankles, his hands gripping the boy's shoulders, his dark hair across his features as he half crouched against the railing. Most of all I remember the urgency of the way the older man thrust – his hair matted and stripes across his back – like an animal; like the two dogs I once saw copulating in an alleyway. I must have cried out. The eyes of Satan turned towards me. And the boy? His hair was dark and in curls, his eyes wide when they turned to face me. But by then the soldiers had come running.

The boy. The ship. Lydia felt unnerved. This was not the voyage out to Van Diemen's Land as she remembered it. Several days passed with no entries.

28th October

My husband interrogated me this morning. It was extremely difficult to talk to him. He seemed ashamed for me and I felt, ridiculously, complicit. I told him I had not realised we were transporting boys. After all, this boy was not much older than Lydia. He hadn't thought it important to tell me, he said. When I asked to see the boy, Sir John seemed surprised, but not disagreeable.

There's so much I do not know. He speaks of our cargo as if they are the sucking fish on the back of that shark, not men. But then, he has to control them or we shall perish.

On my wedding day, I thought I was the strings of a newly tuned instrument, vibrating when plucked, striving to produce the best of notes, delicate, restless and strong; my husband a bassoon, deep, resonating and dependable: Sir John Frankland, captain in the Royal Navy and Knight of the Guelphic Order of Hanover.

29th October

I will stop wearing my hair à l'anglaise. By parting it down the middle and flattening it to the shape of my skull, it accentuates the grey. Besides, it's coming out in handfuls and becoming finer every year. I detest the cap, but it conceals a multitude of sins. When I look at my reflection in the bright daylight, flooding in from the porthole, I have fine wrinkles around my eyes where the skin is becoming translucent. My skin is ageing quickest around my neck.

The boy appeared before me and Lydia, an hour before the evening meal. A lad in his early teens. His clothes hang awkwardly, rough woollen fabric, and his shoes are made from coarse leather, yet they cannot hide his beauty. His neck is long, his chin firm and his nose finely boned. His hair is dark and less curly than I remembered, but his eyes are the same – coals staring straight at me from a pallid face. His most alluring feature. Then, as I looked at him I remembered the other man's eyes, mocking, his passion spent. And the boy? He had shown no fear. Perhaps he was inured to it?

I asked him his name, trying to muster a distance between us. His wrists were in irons but I could see signs of breeding in the hands folded in front of him – long-fingered, belonging to a piano player, not a convict. He told me his name was Henry Belfield. He sounded educated. He is being taken to Point Puer, where they send the young male prisoners – boys. His voice was soothing. I wanted him to stay, to talk to me.

He was polite when he answered my questions and said he had always enjoyed literature. His grandfather founded the first bank in Cambridge and became mayor of that town. Some of his father's friends were dukes, and so was his uncle.

I had no idea someone of his stature was in the the hold with common criminals. Words competed with the silence. We shared an episode of which neither of us can speak. He looks like a young gentleman in spite of his garb, with lips plump as a choirboy. His manners, his appearance, those hands, are confronting. He shows something like arrogance, certainly a sense of surety. I left him standing there to prove I could trust him and went to find a book in the ship's library for him to read.

The memory now had immediacy and clarity, as though it had happened yesterday. In this part of the house the damp had seeped in under the eaves and leaked through the wallpaper. The attic smelt of mildew and neglect. Long shadows flickered on the sloping ceiling until they became large, black menacing clouds and distorted faces. A boy's face, not much older than she had been. She remembered the large wooden table with Jane's writing implements. The boy pushing her against the wall, her head hitting the timber panelling, his mouth on hers, his hands in irons, groping at her bodice. Her stepmother return-ing to the cabin – how long afterwards? She was holding a book. The boy's eyes fixed on the wall, expressionless. Lydia had pulled her shawl tightly around her shoulders, covering her shame, and rushed past her stepmother. Later, she saw the flat denial in his eyes. He knew that she would tell no one.

Searching surreptitiously in Jane's embroidery box for lilac thread to stitch her torn dress, Lydia interrogated herself to find meaning in what had happened. The swollen shame, the bruise on her head, her exposed breast, but, most confusing of all, a peculiar sense of awakening. She had glimpsed desire in his eyes, but did not understand from where it came. His raw need for her had terrified and intoxicated her at the same time.

The candle flickered and she left the illusory world, hearing the noise of rats in the silence. She returned the diaries to the chest and hastily descended the ladder, holding her skirts with one hand and the candle in the other. Downstairs, she found an oil lamp had been left burning. Within minutes she was back in her room, in familiar territory once more, undressing for bed and sitting before her mirror. The maid had long since retired.

Unrolling her braided hair, greying at the temples, she brushed it rhythmically in long slow strokes until her scalp glowed. Her father had always commented on how her hair was like Eleanor's. The face that looked back at her was drawn and pale and there were dark shadows under her eyes. She was middle-aged, around the same age Jane had been when she sailed to Van Diemen's Land.

That night she read Dickens's latest tome, now in one volume, *Great Expectations*. In her dreams, instead of Pip she saw the boy, Henry, dark-haired, eyes alluring, beckoning her from her bed. Images conjured up by the diaries, ghosts, all of them. She was being hurled back into the past when her life should have a new beginning. Jane was controlling her again, from the grave, leaving enough clues to challenge Lydia's happiness, so she could not be at peace.

The next morning the maid transported the diaries in boxes to Jane's study and Lydia began the laborious task of cataloguing them into years before she returned to reading them. Many were missing. Where were they? It didn't make sense that Jane, the diligent diary-keeper, had destroyed any. Like Pandora, Lydia delayed opening the ones in front of her, clinging to the security of the present, fearing to continue to tap hidden secrets.

25th November, 1836

After the storms, I rallied and climbed up to the foredeck for my first glimpse at the cargo. Twice a day they are brought up in groups, about fifty of them, from their layers below deck, a sea of indistinguishable faces. I searched for Henry Belfield, but I couldn't see him.

What makes a man commit a crime? One convict stood apart from the rest, leaning against the ship's mast. I watched him for some time. Could he have killed someone?

When I was nineteen, I breathed the same rank air as eight hundred men in the hold of a prison ship under a roof where they could not stand upright. We were touring Plymouth and I was bored with our chaperone's idea of fun – the rural sports of donkey racing, jumping in sacks – and convinced her to allow us to visit the prison ships. They were political prisoners, not convicts like our cargo, and our visit below deck was greeted with silence.

A year later, in Toulon, I saw six hundred galley slaves. Those guilty of murder were chained to benches, their backs shining with sweat. They reminded me of so many pigs awaiting the slaughter-house.

So many years later, I am a governor's wife sailing into the unknown on a ship with human cargo. Dining on dissected shark and octopus curry, breathing the same fetid air of unwashed bodies like the ones I remember from the hulk at Plymouth. To travel is to throw oneself over the abyss. To be exposed to the universal truth of life.

This morning when I questioned my husband about the boy prisoners, he told me there were pickpockets clogging the streets of London, Bristol and Manchester – criminals in training, he called them. These boys were learning about crime and they needed to be taken away from such evil influences and taught trades. We were simply benefactors, feeding them, clothing them and educating them. In the new colony they would learn skills to take the world, whereas in the old country he said their mothers had practically given birth to them underground while pulling along carts of coal. I asked how old the youngest was and he told me nine years old. I suggested that we might be turning them into slaves, breeding carpenters or shoemakers to build our empire for us. Transportation was not slavery, he said, in spite of those who opposed it, and I saw I had irritated him. These men and boys were misguided. Take Henry Belfield, he said, the nephew of the Duke of Guernsey. He was being transported because he had killed his uncle in cold blood. I had a murderer in my cabin, albeit chained. Think what might have happened.

Lydia shivered and stopped reading, transfixed by the oval clock on the mantelpiece above the fireplace, soothed by its rhythmic sound, thinking of his hands on her, the hands that had killed someone. Jane had not protected her from harm. She had not registered that the murderer had been left alone with her stepdaughter.

It was some time before she returned to the diaries. Then she read late into the afternoon, delving uneasily into memories, shackled to the words on the page in the same way she was once bound by Jane's voice when she was commanded to her bedside. She dreaded reading more about Henry Belfield. As night fell, she began looking for references to Louis. Surely he would have been mentioned after they reached Van Diemen's Land? How soon had Jane made his acquaintance?

25th January, 1837

This morning we entered the Derwent River and five months after leaving Southhampton reached Hobart Town. We arrived into a fog that reminded me of the 'jerries' on the Thames. We were enveloped in its mist. The sounds were hollow. Our sails flapped ominously and the mast disappeared in clouds as we headed northward. Since we began this journey one man has fallen overboard and there have been several burials at sea. Three children are now orphans, the youngest only seven months old. I thought of the other children in the hold. In spite of the fact it is summer, the day was chilly. This is the closest I have ever been to the South Pole.

My husband is here to punish and to rule; to become the leader of a colony. And what will my role be? I will be the governor's wife with the colony watching. In this land, I can be whomever I choose. I have no reputation to sustain. I am no beauty: my forehead is too wide, my mouth too small, but my husband does not see it. The physical is superficial, he told me once. He draws on my opinions on matters outside of the home, encourages me to take an interest in his affairs. He has already suggested I might busy myself with the convict women. And he has told me he wants me to accompany him to the Port Arthur settlement.

What about the child convicts at Point Puer? Surely their moral development is as important as the women's? He told me the man I saw with Henry on the deck died from the flogging. They 'went slow' he said, for the maximum pain. When I asked what that meant, he said they waited for the skin to redden and inflame before inflicting the next blow. He watched my lips to see if I would respond. Learn by example, my husband told me by way of assurance, although I said nothing. We are not going to cast his body to the deep. We are too close to the end of our journey. I told my husband the land seemed more cultivated than I had imagined, but I was thinking at the same time that he was responsible for a man's death.

Round-shouldered hills covered in the dull green of eucalypts came into view. As an adolescent, I paid sixpence on the Strand to see a panorama of the most southerly town in the British Empire. Six watercolours stretched a long way. Now, I am here. There are cottages surrounded by orchards and the odd steeple of a church. A mountain like a giant watchtower. The patchwork quilt of civilised farming land among the native trees.

I looked at the grey sky and the woodlands sweeping past on the shore, more and more visible now the mist has thinned. Dark and light green, but little other colour. Dappled light played on the water, shafting through darkened clouds. I felt like a diver reaching the end of the shelf, below which unknown life lurks, the seafloor so far down it is invisible. The shore seemed like a mirage, it dazzled me.

When the ship came closer to the wharf, I was surprised to see how many people were gathered to greet us. I retired to my cabin to prepare and awaited orders to disembark. We are here after many months at sea.

The following morning, Lydia travelled alone by coach to Westminster Abbey. She felt clogged with words and her eyes hurt from deciphering Jane's untidy handwriting. When she closed them she saw spidery forms rushing across the page, and when she opened them the words crisscrossed the ashen London clouds. Conversations flooded back to Lydia from her past, mingled with the words she had read. Snippets of Jane's concern for Henry's moral education. Visits her stepmother had made to Point Puer. Lydia could not help but compare her stepmother's concern for the young criminals to her concern for her stepdaughter. And the tone Jane used when writing about her father seemed to Lydia proof that Jane may never have loved him. Perhaps on their wedding day, when she had written of how protective her knight would be – 'resonating and dependable' – but then ... What had happened?

Had her stepmother considered anyone would read her diaries? She may have declared they were written for her family and she had certainly not hidden them, but had she meant them to be found? Sir John would never have pried into her writing and Lydia had never shown an interest.

The coach had become snarled in traffic at Ludgate Hill at the foot of St Paul's, pedestrians jostling for a foothold on overcrowded pavements. London had tripled in size since Lydia was a girl. Looming soot-blackened chimneys eroded by factory fumes towered above the smaller artisans' shops. New warehouses and old spires leant over the streets. Horses clattered past, dogs barked. Drays competed with carriages. She watched as a young girl was pushed into the muddied embankment, wedged between a set of horses pulling a wagon and a man carrying a pig's carcass high above his head. She drew the curtains. She thought of the blue skies and the empty wide roads of Hobart Town.

Half an hour later she reached Westminster. After entering the abbey through the large wooden door, Lydia was immediately embraced by the silent stone walls. She stepped softly on to the black-and-white-checked marble floor shaped in a Latin cross. The vaulted roof was three hundred years old.

She looked up past the rich stained-glass windows to the belfry and was immediately reassured. As a child she'd imagined the souls of those buried there soaring upwards. The hand of God was with her. Her father would laugh at her pronunciation of the son of God: 'cheeses'.

It was quiet for a Sunday, there were a few other visitors. She had felt consumed with a need to see her father, even if his presence was as a marble effigy, to spend some time alone with him away from the diaries; to reach out to him for some words of advice – surely he would hear her? His favourite poet, John Dryden, had a memorial here, and other men of words lay in state in Poets' Corner. Kings and queens had been crowned and buried here. Lydia walked softly on the checkered floor until she was on the quieter side of the abbey. Sir John's bust stood in the window facing the mall. The light coming from the cloisters softened his expression.

She rarely visited this place. Her father's bust, it seemed to her, was a concession to the failure of never having found his body. The marble was not the flesh of the man she loved. Lydia's vision blurred through tears. Had he ever known the thoughts of the woman he had married?

'Should I go to Van Diemen's Land?' she whispered, aware of other people behind her. As she voiced her thoughts, she realised that this had been her plan since the night in the attic.

His lips curved and his hollowed eyes sparkled through her tears. Checking she was not being observed, she placed the palm of her hands on those cool cheeks and read aloud the words on the epitaph.

'I will pursue the truth as befitting a man who was a hero to all men,' she whispered. Glancing around again, she pressed her lips to his, willing warmth into the marble.

CHAPTER THREE

The Old Sessions House was the centre of criminal jurisdiction for Great Britain. Its entrance was an ancient archway of gargoyle lions and dragons etched in stone. Lydia joined the top hats, frock coats, dress coats and overcoats mounting the steps and entered the darkened chambers of the library, which housed colonial convict records. She stood in front of the high bench, unsure whether to discreetly rap on the counter or to wait until the clerk saw her.

After days of reading the diaries, she wanted something external to confirm Jane's words. Perhaps her stepmother was making it all up, a joke at Lydia's expense? Lydia knew this was fanciful, but the journey to the Old Sessions House, like the journey to the abbey, took her away from the stifling atmosphere of Bedford Place. Here in the outside world she could be the self-proclaimed adventuress, discarding accomplishments such as needlework, or painting insipid water-colours, or strumming at the piano or the harp. Two weeks ago she would not have had the confidence to make such an outing, but her discoveries had awakened a new person in her. This was the second time she had ventured out in central London unaccompanied. Besides, she had ambitious plans. She would leave England and the feigned concern of relatives; she would be as Jane had been – a woman unknown with 'no reputation to sustain'. She would invent her past before it invented her. Besides, and perhaps most importantly, now she knew her father would have wished her to make this journey.

The house in Russell Square would be sold and when she returned she would move to the country. Until then she had means to support herself. She would book a comfortable cabin on a ship to Van Diemen's Land, where she would search the government offices in Hobart to find out whether Jane had left any other papers. She need consult no one. There was no one to consult. Jane would no longer dictate her movements; she had kept her much as a husband keeps a wife.

She heard her stepmother's voice, rueful, reciting Tennyson:

When the man wants weight, the woman takes it up,
And topples down the scales; but this is fixt
As are the roots of earth and base of all . . .

Jane would have insisted on accompanying her, and then it would not have been Lydia's journey but her stepmother's.

'Convict records?' The clerk appeared before her suddenly. 'An ancestor?'

Lydia shook her head.

'You have a ship number, Madam? Full name?'

'A name, that's all.'

She watched his eyebrows become a frown.
'And what name?'

Man for the field and woman for the hearth:
Man for the sword and for the needle she:
Man with the head and woman with the heart:
Man to command and woman to obey:
All else confusion.

Man copulating with man.

Lydia blushed. The image of Belfield and the other convict below the deck of the ship appeared unbidden. Suddenly, she was unsure why she'd come. She could feel the clerk's eyes upon her, exasperated, challenging her. Lydia had never before been alone in such a place. Jane would often take her to lectures, but she never went unaccompanied. Who would protect her when she was so far away from home? She knew no one in Van Diemen's Land. It was Jane who had booked hotels, passages on boats, trains and other modes of transport. Lydia had allowed her to take control. She breathed deeply.

'Belfield. Henry Belfield.'

'And he was a convict where? Madam, we need more details than a name.'

'Of course. Van Diemen's Land.'

'When?'

'1836. I have the name of the ship. It was the *Fairlie*.'

'But no transportation number. Identification of any sort? Did he have a tattoo?'

'No. I don't know . . .'

The boy's long-fingered hands in irons appeared before her and she felt nauseated.

The clerk was showing her some small wooden drawers.

'These are alphabetical. You may be lucky, but if it's to do with the colonies we don't always keep everything here.'

The cards were filled with tiny cramped inked writing, not unlike Jane's. Lydia began sorting through: Bell, Bells, Belfield. John, Henry.

She approached the desk, having written down the number. The clerk disappeared. When he returned he directed her to a table by the window. An oak tree blocked out the light, but she could make out some sky between the newly formed spring leaves which brightened the gloom of the library.

She opened the folder. The writing was elegant copperplate style, as if it had been copied many times to achieve perfection. The ink was deep blue and the effect final.

An Inquisition taken for our Sovereign Lady the Queen at Port Arthur, Tasman's Peninsula, within the island of Van Diemen's Land, this third day of March in the year of Our Lord, 1842, and in the fifth year of reign of our sovereign, Lady Victoria, by the grace of God of the United Kingdom of Great Britain and Ireland, the said island its dependencies. On view of the body of seventeen-year-old Thomas Boardman then and there lying dead at Her Majesty's Colonial Hospital Port Arthur upon the oath of David Hoy, Henry John Goulden, Henry Poole, Thomas Atkins, Robert Filch, Daniel Newman, Frederick Myers, good and lawful men of the said island and duly chosen and charged to enquire for our said Lady the Queen, when, where, how and after what manner the said Thomas Boardman came to his death. They say that Thomas Boardman came to his death in consequence of the wounds and bruises occasioned on the head and upper body. They are of the opinion there is strong presumptive proof that the prisoner Henry Belfield committed the murder.

Lydia's fingers were ice cold. She stared at the mottled trunk of the oak tree. The words had sapped her of warmth. In seeking confirmation of Jane's words she had been led unwittingly to more horror. Henry Belfield had killed another boy as well as his uncle. So brutally. And she had been alone with him. She closed her eyes, but he became even more real to her and she imagined being suffocated. She wanted to bury him in the darkened archives of the Old Sessions House, relegate him to the entombed life he deserved. Now she had started this journey, she knew this could never be, that she could not simply discard what she did not want to know. She had begun poking among ghosts and now the die was cast. She had to follow this course. Besides, she had an increasing sense of curiosity, as though awakening from a long sleep.

There was a pencilled reference on the file: CSO 22/83/1714. Feeling far less bold than she perhaps appeared, Lydia approached the counter again. The ageing clerk smiled toothily. 'You must fill out one of these sheets, giving us your details, and the file will be retrieved for you this afternoon.'

Outside, the brick-dust seller dispensed his product from sacks carried on the back of a donkey. Several women, sleeves rolled up exposing fleshy arms, were collecting the dust, used to clean knives. There were vendors selling horseflesh, bullocks' livers and tripe cuttings. 'Chairs to mend,' came a loud voice carrying a bolt of rushes in his arms. Around her were live rabbits in cages, doormats, rat-traps, baskets, fish and ice from the fishmonger. Everyone was selling something. Girls carried wicker baskets selling jellied eels and pea soup. In the midst of the crush of people on foot, a wagon rolled past displaying hieroglyphics and colourful portraits of cats, some exotic Egyptian gods and an announcement that a superb panorama of Egypt was now on view. The whirl of colour and the stench gave her an extraordinary sense of purpose. Usually, Lydia shopped in sanitised specialist stores or ordered the maid to purchase items from the tradesmen who entered at the back door of Bedford Place.

Lydia whiled away some time in a teahouse in one of the new department stores. About an hour later, she was back at the Old Sessions House. The clerk smiled at her as she approached the desk.

'We have the file you requested, Madam.'

It contained only two sheets of paper.

4th March, 1842

To: John Montagu, colonial secretary
From: Charles O'Mara Hawkins, commandant of the Port Arthur settlement

I regret to report the proceedings of a coroner's inquest held on the unfortunate deceased named in the margin Thomas Boardman under the following circumstance. The deceased was reported absent from his gang on 19th February and was supposed to have absconded on that day. The poor youth was found in the bush about half a mile from the settlement bruised about the head in a most dreadful manner and at the back of his neck a knife inserted left sticking in nearly an inch beyond the blade, altogether about four inches, which was, with difficulty, extricated. The deceased when brought into the hospital was perfectly sensible, though suffering much. He died some hours later. I am happy to say, however, that as soon as his wounds were dressed I immediately took a deposition on oath. Nothing could be clearer than his evidence about who gave him these mortal wounds. No cause appears to have induced the commission of the act. It is appalling to contemplate the wretch who perpetrated the act was the very man who reported the deceased as having absconded. During the examination of the evidence the perpetrator of the matter, as before the inquest, appeared perfectly indifferent.

I have, therefore, considering the evidence before me, committed Henry Belfield for the wilful murder of Thomas Boardman.

A further letter to the colonial secretary was stamped and dated ten days later, on 14th March, 1842.

This reports that Henry Belfield 2362 stands fully committed for the wilful murder of Thomas Boardman 3155 and proceeds this day to Hobart Town on Her Majesty's colonial brig, *Tamar.*

Lydia spent the afternoon looking for evidence from the trial, but there was nothing. On the homeward journey, in spite of the stench outside, she opened the window of the coach. Each time she closed her eyes she saw the knife embedded into the victim's neck.

That evening, she returned to the diaries. This earlier life of which she had once been part had become for the moment more important to her than the present. The ghosts were beckoning. Soon she was immersed in the daily routine of Government House, that weatherboard mansion on the slopes of the Derwent; in Jane's trips with Lydia to visit the convict women in the Female Factory in South Hobart, the bleak prison at the foothills of Mount Wellington. Jane cast herself in the role of moral saviour to these women, in spite of the fact that she recorded during one official visit that the women had raised their skirts, turned around and bared their bottoms at the official party. Lydia stifled a giggle. Jane wrote of her grandiose plans to begin the first scientific society outside London 'such as has never before been seen in the colonies'.

I have already decided to collect as many animals as I can and send them back as specimens to England, particularly marsupials, who give birth to their young in their pouches. I shall keep Europe informed of our discoveries.

Then she reached Jane's description of the Franklands' first visit to Port Arthur, shortly after reaching Van Diemen's Land.

5th March, 1837

Port Arthur is more like a town or a village of antiquity planted in the Australian bush than a jail. The wood smoke that hovers in the valley and the chill of the evening reminds me of home. High woods form a natural barrier all around so the penal settlement seems to be in the middle of an amphitheatre. It is some eight hours by ship south-east from Hobart Town.

Young oak trees have been planted down to the waterfront from the partly built church. Everything here is familiar and reassuring, not in any way how I had pictured it. The lawns are vibrant green and the autumn colours so European. Fields of vegetables crowd up the hill until they reach the encroaching bush that surrounds the settlement, a reminder of the wilder roots of this colony. When we arrived yesterday, the sun was shining.

Lydia remembered the village materialising at the bow of the ship, a mirage after many hours at sea – cultivated, charming, belying its purpose until they came closer to land and she saw, for the first time, 'the centipede': the convicts in single file, resembling a huge lumbering insect carrying giant eucalypts from the forest. The red jackets of the military. The beasts of burden, men instead of horses drawing carts full of coal between the houses. She had wanted protection from the men's blank stares, as though by avoiding them neither of them could be contaminated. Once, she had seen a convict stumble and become almost crushed under the weight of the log. Lydia realised she had observed their suffering as though watching a play.

And then when she least expected it, she stumbled upon Louis Lemprière.

On the jetty was a bewhiskered man in a short frock coat with tight sleeves. He was carrying a hat and had a proprietorial hand on a woman's arm. She was wearing redingote and a large hat ornamented with flowers and ribbons, both decidedly out of date. She was attractive in a dark, Spanish kind of way, in spite of her old-fashioned apparel. In her right hand she carried a parasol.

I asked Commandant Hawkins who they were. Monsieur Louis Lemprière, the deputy-assistant commissariat, and his wife, Charlotte, he said. The man doffed his hat as we pulled closer and said, 'Enchantez, Madame.' He released his wife's arm and reached forward, the first to assist me to dry land. He spoke English with a strong French accent. His wife, I later found out, is English but she speaks French well.

Inside the shipyard several convicts sat around with thimbles, swiftly stitching at yards of canvas. In rows behind were sewing needles and twine. In another area, the carpenters worked. There was much sawing and hammering. Large barrels of tar and pitch filled the air with a smell that made me cough.

My husband fingered the rough canvas of a whaleboat and ran his palm over it, caressingly its smooth underbelly. My gaze settled on Louis Lemprière. I noted the way he took leave of his wife, tenderly, as though they were to embark on a lengthy separation. He had the same expression my husband bestowed upon the boat. I watched his gaze following his wife up the hill from the wharf. A match borne out of love. Hawkins told me later they have been married for some time.

Strange disconnected memories flooded Lydia's mind. The acrid smell of tar in the shipyards, the unfamiliarity of it. Hawkins had taken them to his cottage for an inspection. Lydia remembered walking up the steps to his verandah and seeing several small wooden boats there like stranded fish out of water. The Franklands were told later that the boats were seized after aborted escape attempts by the boys from Point Puer. Hawkins clearly saw them as his trophies.

Her father had told her that Hawkins flogged the convicts in front of an audience as he saw blood as a deterrent. He appeared to Lydia even then as a man devoid of compassion. She remembered his red uniform and shiny gold buttons, the smile that never reached his eyes, a hooked nose. His hands, when he unfolded his arms, were too small for his size. He was a bachelor, a smooth and feminine man; his eyebrows looked plucked to ensure tidiness. He was proud of his inventions: the semaphore behind the house – if there was an escaped prisoner, on a clear day, Jane wrote, it took half an hour to get a message up to Hobart Town – and the model of the human-powered convict railway he had designed on nights spent alone in his cottage.

6th March

Today Hawkins showed me more of his boys' collection: dollars coined by their small hands; knives made with a stamp of crown on them. When I asked him how the boys fared so far from their parents, he said that they were better off out here, away from the streets of London, or those rat-infested industrial holes. He showed me, as though to dispel my illusions, sticks of tar that the boys used to bribe the overseers. The tar was meant to resemble sticks of tobacco. He described the boys as 'crafty, cunning depraved little felons'. His words were quietly venomous. Perhaps it is the increasing number in his care that challenges him. There were sixty-eight in number back in the early thirties but now it appears there are closer to four hundred. I told him about Henry Belfield and asked if I could visit him. He appeared surprised and wanted to know the details of my acquaintance. I gave him the merest sketch.

He spent the rest of the visit describing his modes of punishment, as though to impress me as wife of the governor that he is never lenient. As magistrate he can mete out prompt punishment for misdemeanours. He told me that it was more difficult to maintain control now the law restricts him to handing out thirty-six lashes instead of a hundred. The job, however, pleases him.

He showed us his portrait above the fireplace. The Frenchman Lemprière painted it. He wanted to know if I liked it. I could not help thinking he resembled a bird of prey with his uncomfortably hawk-like nose. His jacket epaulettes and expression fix him in the way of the military. His wide-set dark brown eyes peer out from underneath straight, narrow eyebrows, and his side-whiskers are almost level with his mouth. The artist has captured the coldness in his eyes particularly well.

Lemprière, apparently, also has an interest in natural history and is a collector. He is an amateur architect and the convict chaplain. He speaks five languages and plays a tough game of chess. A man of many talents. I might be able to see his museum.

Then Hawkins became unnecessarily bawdy, making reference to the fact that Madame Lemprière had been confined almost every year since they have been at the settlement and that they had more than eight children – obviously 'not enough to occupy themselves at night', he said, laughing heartily. Was he married, I asked? He told me his dogs were good enough company, even though he had to continually drown his whippet's unwanted litters. When I asked him about Point Puer and the boys' moral education, he said they had yet to find many 'decent' overseers. I will take care not to be left alone with him in future. He is a strange man, indeed.

Sir John and Lemprière finally joined us. We chatted over tea and cake in the parlour. I asked Lemprière if he was a collector. He raised his head, startled, as if he had momentarily forgotten I was there, so I asked again, adding 'of natural history'. I spoke in French. His eyes smiled recognition. They were dark sepia, I noticed, like the brown pigment used in monochrome drawings. He came here from the Channel Islands and is obviously well read. I listened to him speak in that captivating inflection that only the French have. I told him Papa loved languages.

Since deciding to start collecting I have been on the look-out for men like Lemprière. We discussed our geographical position – at the end of the world on this little island – and agreed that there is much to discover, so much we do not know. I asked him if he had heard of Mr John Gould, the British ornithologist, and Mr Ronald Campbell Gunn, the naturalist. He said he knew them personally and told me with some pride that he had just discovered a new species of Ostracion, which is known at Port Arthur as pig-fish. As English is not his native tongue, he considered his words before he spoke, or perhaps he was wary. Before we took our leave I asked if he would collect for me. He has agreed to do so.

In our room the small grate was empty and the place was damp and cold. Sir John expressed pleasure that Hawkins had received our signal from Hobart Town telling him I disliked heated rooms. Alas, no separate quarters for me as the cottage is too small.

So Lemprière had a wife and family and he shared her stepmother's passion for collecting. Lydia reread the entry more closely. A bewhiskered man in a short frock coat with tight sleeves. What had later transpired between them to stir such passionate declarations from her stepmother? Jane had met more bachelors than most married women might encounter in a lifetime. Lydia thought back to Jane's trip to Government House in Sydney, where she had invited herself to stay with the New South Wales governor, Sir George Gipps. She had returned reeling off exotic names like Count Strzelecki – 'a bright star in my galaxy of worthies'. Then there was the German geologist Johann Menge and the French explorers Dumont d'Urville and Cyrille Laplace. In spite of so many male acquaintances, Lydia had never doubted her stepmother's loyalty to her father. After enjoying the company of so many esteemed scientists, government officials and explorers, a storekeeper who was far beneath her station, as well as married, made no sense.

Now that she'd transported the diaries downstairs, Lydia was less dependent on light from candles. She had been working through the journals methodically, but tonight she felt tired and distracted. If only she was able to intervene in the past in the same way a writer might decide on a plot for a novel, her father might be alive today. She went through to his study, imagining him sitting in the leather armchair he had once inhabited, his face still smooth in spite of his age, spinning tales of the land of snow and ice. She sipped on some madeira from the cocktail cabinet, a present given to Jane.

On the wall was the Union Jack that Jane had stitched to accompany Sir John on his last voyage. He had left it behind. There was a collection of objects from a previous voyage — silver spoons with a coat of arms, a seal's tooth, his bestselling book on his journeys to the North Pole. And in an alcove, out of sight, hung a painting of a dark child in a red dress and white shoes: Mathinna. In Hobart Town Jane had adopted the Aboriginal girl with her crimped dark hair and haunting wide-spaced eyes the colour of treacle. She had been an orphan from Flinders Island, north of Van Diemen's Land — that ironbound island in Bass Strait where the indigenous people were unceremoniously offloaded by George Robinson, who had been appointed by her father's predecessor to round them up and relocate them away from their homeland. Why hadn't the Franklands brought her back to England? Lydia remembered Mathinna's face at the wharf when they left Van Diemen's Land for the last time, inscrutable as always, her arms folded in front of her in the way she had been taught, a bonnet covering her head.

She had introduced Lydia to life outside the weatherboard walls of Government House; had shown her cider gum, the hard chewy substance that oozed out of some of the native trees and tasted like toffee – the memory of the taste was so clear Lydia's mouth watered – and the emu in the Government House gardens, who would talk to Mathinna, his head on one side, brown eyes larger than hers.

Mathinna had been her playmate. They had connected without language, united in their childish appreciation of the natural world beyond the stuffy parlours and dining rooms of Government House. Mathinna had shown her some of the wonders of the wild island, its windswept she-oaks and the native berries. In turn, Lydia had secreted chocolates and almond bon-bons from Jane's newly arrived supplies from England.

Lydia remembered the way sadness clung to Mathinna's clothes, was present in her gestures, in those large eyes that never seemed to close or blink. The silent way she responded to Jane, watching, but not speaking, submitting to Jane's desire to dress her as a young woman, to cultivate manners. Once she had heard Jane discussing the colour of Mathinna's skin with Sir John; that surely it had whitened since she had come to live in Government House, a sign of her being more civilised.

The girl was never sullen; her resistance was the silence of pathos, and the sight of her dressed so neatly never failed to impress the visitors at Government House, which pleased Jane greatly. Attempts at conversation, however, usually floundered. Jane had taken Mathinna to several doctors to see what was amiss, but even the top medical practitioners in Hobart could not tell what was wrong, why she did not like to speak.

Lydia and Mathinna were co-conspirators against Jane. Lydia's tactics were less successful because she had more to lose, always performing a balancing act, aware that she might upset her father if Jane's instructions were not followed. Together they observed the adults. They would sit on the hill on top of the Domain and watch the square-rigged vessels dock at Sullivan's Cove, relics of a civilised world, and Lydia would try to explain to her silent companion about her life in Bedford Place, the house with so many windows, the Duke's name in gold under the gas lights. Mathinna became her confidante, as she spoke of her father, her stepmother, her governess and, above all, of her loneliness.

Looking back, Lydia realised the square-rigged ships on the Derwent were symbols that had changed Mathinna's life forever. When the Franklands had sailed from Van Diemen's Land, Mathinna would have been in her early teens. Lydia had tried warning her they were leaving, but Mathinna had looked at her, nonplussed. Jane cited the girl's bad chest as her justification for abandoning her, saying that the doctors told her Mathinna would not survive in their homeland. As much as Lydia tried to discourage it, Mathinna had been placed in an orphanage. Jane had lost contact with her adopted daughter after she was old enough to leave the orphanage. In fact, Jane had shown little interest in finding out about Mathinna's welfare after they left the island. It was almost as though Mathinna had never existed. But Jane had never had children of her own. Sometimes she had taken Lydia to visit the Factory nursery. She could still hear the cries of the motherless red-faced screaming infants, the silent wet-nurses going through the motions of motherhood, propped against the damp sandstone of the large walls. The chill of the place seeped through to her bones. She was always glad when the visits came to an end. Had Jane considered the mothers of these babies?

Over the years, Lydia had often thought about her dark-skinned companion. She tried to imagine an older Mathinna, perhaps with children and an Aboriginal husband. The orphanage might have records. She could not imagine how they would react to each other after more than twenty years.

7th March

Charlotte Lemprière is dark like a Creole, with a fresh healthy complexion and red cheeks. She sat in the parlour opposite me this morning, her hands folded in her lap, with three other women.

I was unsure how these women viewed me, was conscious I was being judged. I felt my old fear of inadequacy return but, since there was silence, I asked the questions. Charlotte told me she had been here fourteen years. She said she had come over with her mother and five sisters and that her father had been lieutenant quartermaster in the West Indies, but he had died when she was a baby. When I asked her if she had met her future husband on the voyage, she smiled at me and nodded with an honest, proud smile. Her pale blue eyes had nothing to hide. She said her sisters had also all married in the colony.

I had an irrational desire to ask her how she managed to be so happy. On her lap a toddler sat staring at me, his eyes also unfaltering. Their complacency seemed unshakeable.

One by one I met them all. Mrs Turner, the wife of the booming Methodist preacher, her hair tied back severely so none shows below her bonnet. The chief police magistrate's wife, Mrs Forster, a plump lady of plain countenance, and Miss Wood, governess to the Lemprières' children, a young slip of a thing in a light muslin dress. Charlotte is by far the most intelligent, I think.

I was thankful when the tea-sipping and the plum cake, served by Hawkins' manservant, came to an end.

I told her I was going to see her husband's collection and she said he would be most honoured. I asked her to let him know I would visit tomorrow after we had been to the penitentiary.

Such devotion, I thought, as I watched the small party walk between the ornamentally arranged lupins and the marigolds.

8th March

Today I visited Point Puer, the collection of houses on the promontory opposite the main prison. Here there is a much more relaxed atmosphere, although the military is still present. Apparently there is a line halfway across the promontory which the boys are not permitted to cross. We landed at the jetty. As we walked up the hill to the main group of houses, boys were hard at work, sawing some of the young eucalypts that were growing up the hill. Some of the more trusted work in the shipyards.

Commandant Hawkins organised my visit through the superintendent, who told me that I would find Henry working in the bakery. After visiting the school room, which doubled as their dormitory, the superintendent took me to a bricked-in room built into the side of a hill. I had to stoop to enter. Inside, it was dusty and hot. A man was discernible in the gloom and after my eyes adjusted, I saw it was Henry holding a tray of newly baked bread. I was surprised he was not wearing irons. He put the tray down on a flattened area and wiped his brow with the back of his hand, bowing but in a mocking way. He accepted my books as if he had expected them — Milton's *Paradise Lost* and one of Dickens', *Sketches by Boz*. He looked shabbier somehow, dustier with all that flour, but his eyes were still the same – unfathomable. He told me he was comfortable, but said little else.

Strange that I should feel sympathy for this young man who has committed murder. Perhaps it is because he is not anonymous, like the other boys toiling in the gardens and the school room – I have made some connection with him, albeit from distasteful beginnings. Surely he will see the error of his ways, particularly if he is educated and is protected from evil influences. After exchanging the books we had little to say to each other and I bid him farewell.

Next I visited Monsieur Lemprière. He was inside the chapel sorting out some prayer books and here was a surprise – as I approached he appeared to be distressed. I do not know the man well and perhaps he hadn't intended to be so forthcoming but he opened one of the books that he was sorting into piles and showed me some heart-rending prayers written by the boys.

'Dear Lord, please deliver me from my bondage. Even if it be by death that I might join you in a better place.'

The words in large childlike scribble touched me. I asked him why they had written this – was it because they were missing home? He told me there was some cant among the boys and he wasn't sure where it had come from. Some boys appear to believe it is a sin to laugh and play, and that if they are caught in this way they will be punished. He said they seemed obsessed by God. He is obviously concerned for their welfare, poor man. According to him, the escape vessels I saw on Hawkins' verandah are commonplace. One poor lad made his escape craft in the shape of a coffin and drowned trying to get away. Another apparently tied a log around his leg and waded into the water to meet his maker. There was talk, Lemprière said, of two boys jumping off the cliffs on the southern side of the promontory. I have made a note to speak with Sir John about these incidents since he continually assures me this incarceration is for the boys' good. Perhaps he can take up the matter with Commandant Hawkins.

As I took my leave of Monsieur Lemprière and the prison of boys, I could not help but think that beneath the civilised orderliness and manners of this place so reminiscent of the old country, something sinister lurks. There have been a series of apparently 'motiveless' murders at the settlement. The latest, Commandant Hawkins informed us, involves a man being attacked with a pickaxe while digging the foundations of the church inside the settlement. Of course, this is a prison and there is bound to be violence, but I still feel uneasy.

Hawkins apparently rules his kingdom, the Tasman peninsula, his jail – for that is the way he thinks of it – with vigour. Sir John tells me he collects the skulls of those hanged for murder. These prisoners are not permitted a burial like other Christians, and often he dissects their bodies. He is apparently engaged in some scientific exploration of mankind.

Lydia shuddered, thinking of Hawkins' soft manicured hands cradling a skull. She imagined him welcoming a hanging, thinking of how he could add the unfortunate to his collection. Jane had never mentioned any of these misgivings about Hawkins to Lydia.

Her stepmother had visited Henry, presumably driven by the same moral righteousness that motivated her to try to reform the convict women. Unable or not permitted to become involved in the governing of the colony, she still wanted to have influence. Her stepmother seemed to be more preoccupied with causes than individuals. Henry was an exception: he was an aristocrat and therefore deserved her sympathy. Jane had been prepared to put her stepdaughter in danger while she appeased the educational appetite of a criminal. She had always been more comfortable in the public arena than the domestic. Her diary entries discussed penal reform, transportation. Her reading list included works on ladies' prison societies. How little time she had spent with Lydia, except in the matters of her education.

Lydia drank the madeira and poured herself another glass. What had happened to Henry Belfield? What of the penal settlement? Was it still in use or abandoned? Lydia knew little of the politics of the colony twenty years later. Transportation had ceased, of that she was aware. How did the colony fare without its workforce? Jane's most recent diary entries sharpened her desire to travel to the land where she had lived so long ago. It was a matter now of booking her passage.

CHAPTER FOUR

There were no more diaries. At the bottom of a chest Lydia found more of Jane's letters, browned with age, wrapped in faded green ribbon. Most were to her husband, in order of date, written from the first days of their acquaintance. They were usually addressed: 'My dearest love'. In those early days after their marriage Jane wrote to Sir John frequently. Due to his naval duties, usually commanding ships in the Mediterranean, they were often apart. These were dutiful wifely letters. Lydia spent the next few days reading them, taking refuge in their ordinariness. They soothed her, memories tumbling out of the boxes as she grasped at one, then another. Snatches of a life past and more memories: her father picking her up from her bed before setting sail from Portsmouth to command a twenty-eight-gun frigate, his face comforting in the dawn light, deflecting the pain of another farewell.

In those years Lydia had been sent to stay with her Aunt Lily Cracroft and her cousins under the vast skies, undulating hills and salty marshlands in the wolds and fens of Lincolnshire. Lily Cracroft, with her greying red hair and face peppered with freckles, carried the same serene air as her father. Lydia felt much more affection for her aunt than for the woman her father had decreed after his wedding day should be known as 'Mamma'.

Jane, meanwhile, continued to travel on the Continent. She became an increasingly distant figure in Lydia's life, returning to regale her with tales of her adventures: her visit to North Africa and 'the snow-white city of Tetuan', sidestepping bandits in Spain, and eating sweetmeats in a harem, a term that for Lydia conjured up the exotic, although she knew little of its actual meaning. She must have been about ten years old when her extended visits to Aunt Lily came to an end and she moved back into Bedford Place with Jane. Her earliest memories of that time were Jane with a poker in hand in the entrance hall after a deliveryman was discovered by the butler pocketing silver spoons from the dining room. Lydia also remembered being presented to King William IV in Brighton, her stepmother dressed in white crepe over satin with a deep border of silver grapes and green leaves, a headdress of an ostrich plume and a necklace of pearls and diamonds. Lydia's dress was a simpler affair and in her dark hair, which hung loose, were garlands of tiny white rosebuds. Her father, as usual, was absent. Those were the pleasant memories.

Reading the letters, however, reminded her of Jane's preoccupation with Lydia's inadequacies. She would be greeted with exclamations that she was 'an undersized child', she'd be chided by Jane that she was prone to being naughty, and reminded that she was 'as little like her father as a child can well be'. Lydia came across one letter to Sir John that Jane had written when Lydia was about eleven years old:

Your countenance is open and mild, full of benignity and candour; hers is full of the acutest vivacity. This is not to my mind the belle ideal of the female countenance or mind, but we must work upon the materials we find and strive to mould them to our purpose.

As she grew older, Lydia became increasingly emotionally unconnected to experiences, responding like the trained monkey her father had taken on his last voyage to the Arctic. Nobody seemed to notice the change. Predictable Lydia. As she passed through her teens into her womanhood, continuing to live by Jane's side – though she had long since stopped calling her Mamma – Lydia became more like the shadow of her dominating stepmother.

She remembered the day everything changed. Lydia had been in the middle of a piano lesson when her father had burst in through the front door. She had not even heard the sound of carriage wheels. His face was flushed and he was unusually animated, talking of a wild island he was to visit, full of romance. He made the shape of a telescope with his hands and twirled his arms around in a semi-circle. He boasted that it was his friendship with King William that had secured him a position of governor of this island.

'Don't worry, my darling Lydia. I will still work for the Admiralty and your papa shall still go to sea in full uniform.'

He had taken her to his study and pointed to the atlas, drawing a long line from the tiny island of Britain out to the end of the opposite page. She took some while to understand that she was to be invited too. He pulled her down on his knee.

'We will go there together, my Lydia.'

'And Mamma, too?'

Sir John had slapped the opposite knee on which she sat and laughed. It seemed to her now a gesture to hide his discomfiture.

There were long letters from Jane on the voyage on the *Fairlie* to her sister, Mary Simpkinson, probably returned to Jane when Mary died. Amusing anecdotes about personalities on board and more serious matters: how they had narrowly escaped being run down by a whaler; their three weeks at the Cape of Good Hope. Then, after their arrival, there were letters from the colony about Jane's role as governor's wife and her journeys to Flinders Island, the east coast at Swansea and that early trip to Port Arthur.

Here was a letter about the expedition they had made to Mount Wellington, the four-thousand-foot mountain that towered above Hobart Town. Early one morning in summer, when Lydia was about fourteen, they had boarded a midnight-blue spring cart in the circular driveway of Government House. Lydia remembered the hot breath from the horses, the scrub past the cleared lawn in the lights of the lanterns and the dark shapes of the men waiting in the shadows in the pre-dawn light, ready to ride escort by the ladies' side.

After a solid two days' walking, they had pitched their tents close to the summit at the foot of the organ pipes. Before dawn the next morning they reached the top while it was still dark. A huge sea of sleeping cloud obscured almost everything from view. Every now and then, between the clouds, she could see a piece of sea, or a chunk of land, or a waterway glinting in the moonlight. Jane told her the only other woman who had made it to the summit was a newly-wed widow who had wanted to see for herself where her husband had drowned.

The following day they had eaten a picnic lunch: roast fowl, cold tongue, a loaf of bread and a bottle of claret, which made Lydia's head spin; then, later, a drink of sugar and ginger mixed with the cold mountain spring water. After the meal she had lain with Jane on a couch, with awnings to shade them from the sun. They had both stared at the view through the handle of the teapot in a rare moment of intimacy. Later, they netted shrimps in a delicious brook of water and after selecting another good site, set up camp for the night, before heading back down the mountain the following morning.

These were welcome escapes from the draughty wooden building that was Government House; from the routine of embroidery, French lessons and elocution. Jane supervised Lydia's learning and she would sometimes put her to work on one or other of her new schemes. Once Lydia was to record in a big ledger the number of snakes brought into police stations around the colony, including the date they were received. Jane paid a shilling for every snake's head and many a convict took up the opportunity to earn money. In one season Jane had spent £600, which to Lydia appeared an enormous sum. After six years of living in Van Diemen's Land, the scheme did nothing to rid the colony of snakes. Lydia remembered one being discovered wrapped around the wheel of a government coach.

Another threat for the newcomers was bushrangers. Her father's secretary, usually at his side, always carried a sword in his umbrella case. One evening, Lydia had been getting ready for bed when Jane appeared in the doorway demanding she put on her cloak and make for the river immediately where a boat was waiting. Jane rebuked the maid for wasting time collecting her mistress's pillows and limewater on the way down to the river. As they stepped off the shore, Jane told her that bushrangers had been sighted nearby and Lydia remembered cowering in the bottom of the small rowing boat, expecting at any moment bullets to be fired on them.

Even though she had been half expecting it, Lydia felt unprepared for the account of their trip from Melbourne to Sydney. Jane and she had been the first white women to travel overland between the two cities. They had journeyed for six weeks in a carriage and carts across roads so rutted and boggy that once the maid was thrown from the box of the carriage. They had stayed with squatters, proprietors of rough grog shanties and had met Aborigines living in wretched conditions on pastoral stations. Lydia's fingers trembled as she turned the pages. Here it was. The field of maize. The maize and the accident were intertwined in her memory. The letter to Mary had been posted during their journey.

It was the tallest maize I ever saw, much of it twelve feet high, but cobs now well filled. Lydia had never seen it before – she admired its rich glowing ears, the careful manner in which it is sheathed and enveloped in dry leaves, the bunch of hairy filament-like tassels, the bunches of dried flowers perfect for the plume of a straw bonnet.

Closing her eyes, Lydia saw the field of yellow, and blood. She saw Captain, the large black stallion, bolting; her hands clutching the reins, her legs squeezing hard to stay on. The world had been bathed in red and then black and she remembered a blinding white light that seared her vision, and a high-pitched ringing in her ears. Jane was saying her nose had saved her head and she was lucky to be alive. She was carried on a stretcher to the camp. Blood had gushed all over her riding cloak. A doctor had been in attendance, but his medications had been ineffectual. He had been unable to stitch the wound that ran across the bridge of her nose and on to her cheek. Stitches would have made it more prominent, he said. It was a snake that had caused Captain to rear, so perhaps Jane had been right to wage war on them, after all.

This chance encounter had caused her disfigurement, a line like a tentative pencil sketch that could never be erased. After the accident Lydia had lain in the tent, her head thundering in pain. Now, try as she might, she couldn't remember Jane comforting her.

Up until the accident, Lydia had taken her appearance for granted. Visitors would sometimes comment that she was pretty. Her father always called her his 'beautiful girl'. Perhaps she had not been beautiful after all, but her looks had never presented any particular reason to stare.

Still en route to Sydney, they had finally reached a small town where the doctor redressed the bandage. She had searched his eyes for confirmation that the gash was not as bad as she had feared. For months after the accident she refused to look at her reflection. Each morning on waking, her fingers would reach for the bandages and she would know that it was indeed a reality. It was only some weeks after the scar had healed that she plucked up enough courage to pick up a mirror. Gasping at the jagged line that ran across her cheek, she burst into tears. Although the scar gradually faded, in her mind Lydia was marked for life, branded an outcast.

It was all so long ago. She took time off to walk in Hyde Park and watch the ducks skittering across the pond, trying to focus on her life now. Eventually she returned to Jane's letters and this time she found them easier to bear. There was more about the politics of Van Diemen's Land; Jane's *conversazione* parties that Lydia remembered well, evenings during which free settlers listened to lectures on the flora and fauna of Van Diemen's Land, or a piece played on the harpsichord.

Then, in the midst of this domesticity, came another letter, separate from the rest. Lydia was contemplating going to bed, but when she saw to whom it was addressed, her drowsiness vanished. There was no date.

Dear Monsieur Lemprière,

I am writing to thank you for the time you spent as our host during our recent visit to Port Arthur. I want to express my gratitude and to ask whether you had made any headway with the watercolours of the beautiful surroundings at Port Arthur that I had the boldness to request. You may remember my wish to hang these in the halls of Government House, which are altogether too dreary for my liking.

I trust you have considered my proposal to come up to Hobart Town. Our next meeting of the newly formed Tasmanian Society falls next month, in three weeks' time. Please let me know if you can attend and whether you can present a short lecture on the drawings you have made of the fish you have observed at Port Arthur. I have written to the commandant to ask him whether you can be available. I hope you do not think this presumptuous of me.

I have received a letter from Mr Charles Darwin, a ship's naturalist on board the *Beagle*, one of His Majesty's surveying vessels.

He spent five years travelling around the world. Mr Darwin spent time with John Stevens Henslow, the famous botanist, with whom I'm sure you will be acquainted. He is also a keen admirer of astronomer John Herschel, whose charting of the southern skies has so assisted us in understanding the universe. I was fortunate enough to meet Mr Herschel in Cape Town, en route to Van Diemen's Land.

Lydia remembered Herschel's house in the wood in Cape Town, with its garden divided by three avenues. One seemed to stretch all the way to Table Mountain, which towered at its end. Lady Herschel had shown them her collection of flowers and some paintings of native flora while Jane climbed Table Mountain, arriving back with flowers she had picked for her hostess. Lydia remembered seeing drawings of the forty-foot telescope designed by Herschel's father, William, who discovered the planet Uranus. By then John Herschel had become as famous as his father by identifying so many of the stars in the southern sky. The marvel of the heavens and their celestial offerings had always fascinated Jane. Perhaps there was a similar attraction with Louis Lemprière – their shared love of collecting. But was this enough for any other sort of relationship to flourish; for Jane to risk all that she had with Sir John – her entire life?

The *Beagle* spent some time on the Galápagos Islands off the western coast of South America, near the equator, where Mr Darwin continued his collection. He visited Hobart Town last year and collected some geological specimens. My sister, Mary, tells me Mr Darwin recently arrived home in England with his crates of specimens. I dispatched a letter to him requesting that we present some of his findings at our next meeting, since he left notes with one of the naturalists. I hope he will agree.

Captain Hawkins tells me that the man responsible for that dreadful murder at the church has been sentenced to be hanged. It is a fitting end for such a scoundrel and should be a resounding message to those who might follow his example.

I trust your charming wife and children are well and protected from living in such a confronting abode.

Yours respectfully,

Lady Frankland

Charles Darwin. Lydia thought back to the launch of *The Origin of Species*. It was inside one of the hothouses at the Regent's Park Zoo. Cold north-easterlies had brought blizzards from Siberia to England in 1859 and the whole nation was huddled indoors. She and Jane had dressed in warm winter cloaks with fur around the collar – matching olive green and plum – although inside the hothouse it was warm, the rain drumming gently on the roof, the atmosphere simulating tropical heat.

Looking back now, Lydia had never sought an explanation as to why her stepmother had seemed preoccupied that evening. They had left inexplicably shortly after the great man himself arrived, as though Jane didn't want to be seen by him. She remembered Darwin's voice, neither loud nor soft, but assured. He was serious and middle-aged, with an unfashionable beard, a rather flat boxer's nose and hooded eyelids, and was shabbily dressed in a faded Regency-style frock coat with brass buttons and a high black stock collar. He cared little for fashion, it was clear.

There had been talk of man coming from monkeys. The air had been raw with cigar smoke and insults. She had not seen him again until the day of Jane's funeral. By then he was famous. Why had Jane behaved so oddly at the launch? Had she fallen out with the great man? But if that was so, why had he attended her funeral, an honour indeed?

That evening Lydia decided to take a bath. On impulse she sprinkled rose crystals into the tub and watched the water flush pink. At least the water was real and it made her feel real too. This was the present. She felt the sensation of warmth on her toes. But, as she lowered herself, shivering, into the bathtub, an image of Henry appeared, quickly followed by that of another man, Captain Ross, who had visited Van Diemen's Land in 1840 in search of the south magnetic pole.

As a child, Lydia had imagined a silver vaulting pole protruding from the ocean, swaying from side to side in the manner of bamboo. Jane had laughed at her, explaining how Captain Ross used a small compass to look for the terrestrial magnetic force while sailing to the Antarctic. He was the husband Lydia had imagined she would have – teeth strong and regular, eyes warm and beckoning, a hand that was firm and steady. He had once rocked her hammock when they had sailed in rough seas out of Storm Bay at the mouth of the Derwent, lulling her until her heartbeat slowed to sleep. She remembered afterwards that she had had unfulfilled adolescent dreams of desire and would blush when she encountered him at mealtimes. Jane had deemed him a worthy catch, but a proposal never eventuated. By then, Lydia was scarred and inured to disappointment.

She closed her eyes, the warm water caressing her, and slowly submerged her head, knowing her hair would take more than an hour to dry before the fire. Jane would have greatly disapproved. She'd always feared chills. Now, Lydia had time to sit before the fire if she needed to, to luxuriate in its heat. Daringly, she swirled her hair around the bath water, feeling deliciously free. Fourteen years her senior, perhaps Captain Ross had desired her in her youth. Would he desire her now? Gradually, revelling in the warmth of the water, Lydia became aware of her body. Long ago, she had suppressed its presence under a multitude of clothing and the overwhelming pressures of daily existence; the Christian verses preaching chastity with which she and Jane surrounded themselves. For so long she had been consumed with these beliefs that washing herself was simply a bodily function to be dispensed with. An unmarried woman, with no possibility of conceiving a child, should repulse any thoughts of temptation. These were reserved for the low-class women in Rotten Row who worked for the devil. She had read Dr William Acton's pronouncement that it was abnormal for women to be troubled by sexual feelings of any kind, but James Copland's *Dictionary of Medical Practice* stated women could only conceive if they reached orgasm. Pleasure was clearly in the domain of married women. These issues she never discussed with anyone, certainly not Jane.

Half-submerged, she blinked the water out of her eyes and began slowly washing between each toe, under her arms, across her belly, her breasts, delighting in the silken feeling of her skin, succumbing to the warmth of the water. She felt a sense of abandonment, but at the same time, empowerment. Her fingers strayed between her legs and her breathing quickened. Her life was before her. She knew later she would feel guilt and would consult her Bible to repent. The cry, when it came, emerged from deep within, echoing around the hollow chambers of the bathroom. Lydia was shocked at the animal sound — it was as though it did not belong to her.

Later, she sat in her bedroom, giddy. She towelled herself dry, inhaling deeply the perfume of rosewater from her body. She felt invigorated, that she had regained her senses. Both she and the world were new and alluring. Why not use the mystery of the past to take charge of her destiny?

She thought again of Ross and his descriptions of the night canopies of sky near the South Pole. His animated exchanges with her father, her hand on his arm as they strolled to the Rossbank observatory near what was now the new Government House, where they had all studied the stars in the crisp night air with the colony's first telescope — she had had to stand on tiptoes to reach the eyepiece. What was Van Diemen's Land like now it was no longer a jail? Had it become a true colony? Then another thought occurred to her. Ross would have known Louis Lemprière.

She discarded the cotton nightdress that she always wore, laid out on the bed, and instead slipped into a heavy indigo satin kimono from one of Jane's trips to the Orient. She shivered at the sensation of the fabric. She summoned the maid with unaccustomed authority in her voice and asked that the footman find Captain Ross's whereabouts.

The following morning she woke early, and chose a morning dress worn close to her throat, trimmed with chocolate-coloured velvet, the sleeves loose and revealing ivory lace. She felt defiant as she strolled across the park, chilly with winter and the sky scudding snowclouds like those in

Van Diemen's Land. When she was home, she summoned her coach for another public outing, this time to the docks to secure her passage.

A fortnight later, Lydia entered the hallowed waiting room of the Royal Society in London. Captain Ross was sitting on a leather armchair, his chin resting on his cupped hand, his posture strong, handsome still. She felt a familiar sense of shame and excitement. As he looked up, his eyes rested on her face. She felt like a young girl, once again looking up at his jaw, square and resolute, her face not yet disfigured. She blushed, remembering her feelings in the bath. Back then she had desperately wanted him to welcome her to adulthood. She positioned herself intentionally, so that the scarred side of her face was towards the books that lined the walls. His eyes were still the same, a light brown with dark flecks.

'Captain Ross,' she recovered herself. 'I mean, Sir James.'

He had been knighted, of course, since those days of her adolescence, and married. For many years he had shown great dedication to finding her father. He had known the terrain and had spent many months moored in the ice searching for him, to no avail.

'Miss Frankland,' he lowered his head so his lips hovered, breathily warm, over her proffered hand. 'You are little changed. You are lucky to find me in England. In spite of my increasing years I still spend time at sea, although since I retired, mostly for pleasure. I think the last time we met was when I set sail for the Arctic on board the *Fox*, looking for your father?'

'Yes, of course.'

'And I was sorry to not be able to attend your mamma's funeral. My condolences, I hope, were conveyed by letter.'

They talked of mutual acquaintances and the house at Bedford Place where he had been a guest at so many dinners. Lydia was remembering the last time she had seen him on board the *Fox*. Her father had been on Ross's former ship, the *Erebus*, when he disappeared. Jane had not been well at the time. Lydia remembered her consulting a clairvoyant in Grosvenor Square, who saw a ship in the ice and several men on board, one 'rather short and stout with a nice face'. The woman had been unable to tell which way the ship was moving but she had described a man who fitted Captain Ross's description on board another ship. When she tried to see if the two would meet, however, a cloud had come down.

Lydia looked at the man in front of her, surprised she was affected by their reunion after such a long time. He had been a presence in the family for most of her life and, in spite of some criticism that he had turned back too soon in the search, she knew he had cared deeply about her father.

She wanted to know then and there whether he knew of the affair.

'My stepmother mentioned in one of her diaries a man named Louis. He worked on tides at the Port Arthur penal settlement. I think he might have been the storekeeper.'

He seemed surprised at the sudden change of subject.

'I had thought your late stepmother told me you had no interest in her collections.'

So, he had thought her vacuous. All the while she had been flattered by his attention, but, just as her anger flared, she considered his statement. Perhaps he was right. Reading the diaries had made her realise how little she did know about Jane's interests. Perhaps her stepmother despaired of her lack of curiosity, her acceptance of life; a personality so different from her own. She wondered what her mother had been like, whether her acquiescence towards her husband's travels was something Lydia had inherited – a complacency that caused her to accept her predicament. What had Ross thought about her? Was he simply her father's friend behaving in a gentlemanly fashion, while she deluded herself that there was more about the way he felt for her.

'I . . .' She hadn't been expecting interrogation. 'I am collecting information about Lady Frankland's life. Perhaps a biography.'

'A worthy topic,' he said.

He was treating her as if she was the fifteen-year-old girl he last knew in Hobart Town, not a woman of forty-one. It was time to prove him wrong, and to prove the others wrong, too, before it was too late. After all, she was also her father's daughter.

'Louis Lemprière,' he was saying. 'Yes, I know him. At least I knew him. He died years ago, in Aden or some such place, I seem to remember. His tidal charts are still in use. They're kept at the old Royal Society rooms in Argyle Street in Hobart Town, along with some of the convict records that survived a couple of fires at Port Arthur.'

'What did he do at Port Arthur?'

'He was commissariat, a storekeeper, and for a number of years too. Hawkins thought much of him. They used to play backgammon together. I joined them for a game or two. Had a museum that began in the storeroom – all sorts of strange stuffed animals, you know, platypus, kangaroo rats. Peculiar fellow, but most congenial. Come to think of it, he published some sort of work on the penal settlements. He had been commissariat at three of them, so his work might prove interesting to read. Not sure if it was ever published here. Always thought he was far too educated for his position – feeding the prisoners. I seem to remember it wasn't his choice. That he ended up in a bit of a predicament because he and his father were bankrupt when they got to Van Diemen's Land. I helped him instal the tidal gauge in front of the store, his museum, at the penal settlement. Lovely fellow though, most helpful for no recompense. Always wanted to be a hydrographer, to have his records taken seriously by the Royal Society. He had children aplenty.'

'Did he collect for Lady Frankland?'

'Well, I know Monsieur Lemprière was a collector. He may have, I suppose. I have some hazy memory he painted her portrait. He thought himself as something of a dilettante. There were many of them, you know – amateur natural historians. He did visit Government House to see Ancanthe, your mamma's museum, remember? The one just out of Hobart Town. Come to think of it, your mamma's papers relating to that collection are housed in Van Diemen's Land, too, I believe. It's now called Tasmania, of course. Your stepmother would have approved. It was she who proposed the name change.'

Lydia wondered, not for the first time, whether her father had minded Jane's constant meddling in the affairs of the colony, whether he had ever reprimanded his wife in private about her continuing involvement in the affairs of state. Certainly, he did not seem to be concerned about her interest in the boys' prison. Perhaps that was his way of keeping her busy.

Ross went on to talk about the south magnetic pole.

'You thought it was a vaulting pole sticking out of the ocean,' he said, looking at her. He did remember something about her after all. He spoke of the observatory, the wide streets of Hobart Town, the carts and horses, the men in chain gangs and afternoon tea at Reverend Knopwood's. She was silent as he conjured up this world they had both shared, thinking of those marble lips and the promise to her father.

'If I am to document her life, I suppose I must go there.'

'To Van Diemen's Land?' He was looking at her with renewed interest. 'It is a long voyage – months at sea, as you know.'

'Captain Ross, I have little else to occupy me.'

She did not invite his sympathy, although he made a series of perfunctory noises, she guessed through a sense of duty. She looked at him again. Perhaps he had good cause to have considered her life a waste.

She was smiling.

'I am sorry I cannot help you further,' Ross said.

'Oh, you have helped me more than you know.'

Lydia was already rolling on her gloves, as though Ross himself had thrown down the gauntlet. Jane's voice from the grave felt suddenly a source of liberation, not containment. Besides, she had already discovered more about her step-mother's secret. For once, Jane would not get the better of her.

CHAPTER FIVE

Lydia arrived in Hobart Town relieved to reach her destination after being plagued by seasickness during the voyage. In a small, dark green box in the bottom of her trunk were Jane's diaries and letters, which she had read and reread until she could almost recite each line. Now she was here: nearly at her journey's end. Van Diemen's Land. She couldn't get used to its new name: Tasmania.

The familiar sight of the town where she had reached womanhood at once reassured her. It was busier than the Hobart Town of the 1840s. There was the rivulet that ran into the small harbour, once a sparkling stream, now a filthy trickle with people crowding its shores. Ships of all sizes, cranes lading and unlading merchandise, filled the harbour. There was a far greater sense of vitality – the town had shaken off its convict roots and become a place of free settlers, with the verdure of affluence clinging to its branches. Lydia identified the change immediately – no lines of shuffling men with vacant stares shackled together.

Hobart had changed from a wild frontier town to a colonial outpost. The island had been renamed Tasmania in 1856, and given a constitution and permission to form an elected government. Gracious buildings had been constructed: a customs house, law courts, ordnance stores. The military barracks stood where she remembered, and the burial ground too. The muddy footpaths on which she once tripped and slid had been replaced with flagged sidepaths. Gas pipes were in the process of being laid and there were construction sites everywhere. Yet the architecture of the town still bore the convicts' marks: pockmarked indentations from their picks showed on the sandstone of most of the buildings; land had been cleared and roads had been built by the gangs.

She would return here, but for now Port Arthur beckoned, central in so many ways to the unfolding story of her past: the home of the storekeeper and the boys' prison, which she had never before visited. So, three days after her arrival on the island, she boarded a vessel bound for the settlement.

The old penal colony bore little resemblance to Lydia's adolescent memories. In those days the place had been bristling with order, punctuated with shouts to attention from the parading military. Now, it was filled with holidaymakers. Vegetables grew in neat rows up the side of the hills on which houses sat like comfortable seaside cottages, their chimneys plumed with smoke, their gardens filled with English shrubs, eucalypts and she-oaks.

Lydia found lodgings in the same house she had stayed in as a girl – the old commandant's house that had once belonged to Hawkins – and the following morning she hired the whaleboat to visit the boys' prison.

A lone figure on the jetty, staring seaward at the approaching whaleboat, she clutched at her cloak in a gust of wind. The next land mass south, apart from an island or two, was Antarctica.

On the way to Point Puer they passed some cliffs, a fortress of stone.

'See where that there arrow's painted?' The ferryman pointed through the choppy seas. 'That's where they threw themselves off, those boys. Can't blame them, poor mites.'

Lydia looked at the cold, dark rock face, which cast a shadow across the waves in front of them. Where the surf broke the clear water gleamed a shining white. In between the heaving swell she gazed down at the sandy bottom littered with rocks, the spikes of sea urchins and the flat-leathered arms of kelp, which flapped below the surface like the tentacles of giant brown octopi.

'Most of them couldn't swim,' the ferryman was saying. 'Cap'n Hawkins, 'e was the commandant here. Kept their escape vessels on his verandah like trophies. Flogged two out of three of them over the years. The shop 'ere, it's got some fings for sale from the boys' prison. The bad uns 'd sit in dog kennels, tiny wooden huts, for up to a month at a time. Some of them as young as nine years old. Hard to believe there was once seven hundred of 'em on this tiny piece of land.'

He whistled to lend a bit of theatre to his dialogue.

Lydia changed the subject.

'Do you know of a Louis Lemprière? He was the commissariat here. He kept records of the tide somewhere on the Isle of the Dead, I think.'

'No, Miss, that I don't. That be Dead Island over there, where all the convicts who died 'ere at Port Arthur were buried, God rest their souls.'

He crossed himself.

'Some of them went mad locked away at the end of the earth. One poor old soul's 'einous crime had been to throw stones at the king. He refused to eat and died of starvation – they treated 'im that bad. The Point Puer boys was buried alongside the men.' He paused. 'Wellard in the old shop's got some stuff about the boys, if you want to find out more, Miss.'

'Point Puer,' she said softly into the waves.

'Funny name, ain't it? Latin for "boy".'

He said it with pride, as though she would not expect him to know this.

'Them buildings are wood, yer see. Not much of them left now.'

He deposited her on the dilapidated jetty. As she disembarked some of her hair escaped from her bonnet and flew across her face. With a splash of the oars he left, without any apparent curiosity as to why a woman of her status would want to visit an isolated, craggy windswept peninsula a whole day's sailing from Hobart Town.

The boys' chapel stood alone in the middle of the promontory before an arc of blue sky scudded with clouds. The wooden building was on a flattened grass plain, its peeling white timber stark against the yellow grass. A cross in silhouette, at the peak of its shingled roof, was etched on the windswept sky, as if to announce an omnipresent God.

She felt a sense of futility as she walked up a long, sloping hill towards the southern part of the land, but in the silence, she slowly became aware of the beauty of the place.

The promontory was wedge-shaped and there was a thick forest of eucalyptus gums to the south. Across the choppy water, to the west, she could see the adult penitentiary nestled in the bay, a much bigger affair, surrounded by the dark hills and sandstone buildings glowing the colour of honey. When she was level with the chapel, she looked across at the main settlement again. There was the church with its burnt-out spire lit like a prop in a theatre, the ambient light through the clouds proclaiming God's wrath. The ferryman had told her that two bushfires had almost decimated the place, but the church had been worst affected. As she looked across the bay she noticed that it was directly opposite the chapel. Lydia felt as though the heavens might open and a crack of lightning reach out to claim her.

Immediately to her left she saw a pristine beach, the sand alabaster, small waves lapping at the shore. Tiny pearl shells littered the sand, some silver, some green and blue – the shell of muttonfish. Weathered driftwood lay at odd angles. God was showing her that what He created was beautiful. She looked out to sea again, to the tiny island with the cemetery. She watched the waves dashing against the cliffs, drawn by their fury, thinking of her ferryman's chatter.

'One day them bones'll be shaken out of that there graves and they'll remind us what horrors happened in this Godforsaken place, for God has forsaken those of us who still have the misfortune to live here. Those fortunate enough to have gravestones'll find them smashed to smithereens but those others, poor varmint criminals buried in little humps in rows, their bones'll lie on the surface for them crows to pick at.'

Lydia wished that his words would stop feeding her growing fear of being abandoned here. The splash of the oars sounded in her head and she shook herself. All around her was ocean. Henry had been on this isthmus; had gazed through these trees towards freedom, or perhaps plotted to commit further crimes here. As she looked around her, she was drawn by the landscape. In a way, she was glad to be alone. She'd forgotten the subtle colours of the Australian bush, the gums with their stringy bark, layers peeled back to reveal the colour of the trunk – apricot and pale ash, slashed with charcoal from sporadic fires.

She was standing on a flattened area next to the workshops. The ferryman had told her it was the muster ground. The boys had been mustered here five times a day, to count their numbers to check whether any had escaped, he'd said. She imagined them, heads bowed, perhaps scuffing the dirt, submissive in a place of such beauty, where the land soaked up their cheerlessness. They had been taught it was a sin to laugh and play.

For seventeen years the boys' prison had been closed. They'd chopped down the trees for surveillance, the ferryman had told her, so any boy stupid enough to try to escape would stand out like an ant on a white tablecloth. The chapel had somehow withstood the ravages of the weather that whipped across the naked promontory. The convict overseers had supervised the felling of the woods. The timber structures had rotted away. Stumps and some foundations were the only reminders of the past.

The chapel stood between the barracks on the western side and the jails on the east, the punishment side of the promontory. Lydia headed there. The promontory sloped upwards through a new eucalypt forest. There were the remains of an overgrown trail, which helped her to get her bearings. She came to the fortress of cliffs that she'd seen from the boat while they bobbed around in the swell, where, according to the ferryman, the boys had jumped off. Jane had also written about this in her diaries, something Lemprière had told her. Grasping an old she-oak, she peered cautiously over the abyss. There was a wide rocky ledge, with seams of iron dividing it up like icing on a cake scored with a knife. Across the waves, the view was out to the heads where the water surged, like a boiling vat, pulled along in a giant tidal suction, to threaten even the strongest swimmer. They would have had no chance of escape, especially in the flimsily built vessels Hawkins had kept on his verandah. It was as though they'd had a death wish. At the southern end of the promontory the military had a line that was patrolled day and night, the furthest distance from the barracks. She sat down at the foot of a she-oak, listening to the waves crashing on the cliffs, imagining a boy's limp body floating like flotsam.

After a while she left the cliffs, picking her way carefully through the tree ferns that grew in abundance under the young eucalypts. This was the windy side of the land and although it wasn't the height of summer Lydia was terrified at the prospect of seeing the cool black body of a tiger snake lying across the path. Jane and her accident had imbued her with this neurosis. Today, though, she saw none.

She was about to return to the jetty when her riding boot struck rock in a muddy clearing. Large stone blocks were underfoot, surely man-made. Lydia scraped away the soil with the heel of her boot and a large stick until, almost ten minutes later, she'd cleared away the surface mud to reveal a small square foundation. A cell – for what else could it be? Scrabbling among the ferns, she realised she was in the midst of them – a whole series of solitary cells, not big enough for anyone to lie in. Most had been destroyed by the weather, but when she walked deeper into the forest, she found one that stood with its walls, roof and door intact, though the door was off its hinges. Lydia entered. She closed the rickety door as best she could, her heart beating so she could almost hear it in the darkness, imagining the night sounds – the hoot of owls, the growl of Tasmanian tigers, the snarling calls of devils and the crunch of their teeth on the bones of dead wallabies. She imagined boys' cries, then a soundless menace: a snake coiled up in the wooden rafters of one of the tiny cells, and a boy waiting helplessly. She shivered with fear and cold.

When the ferryman returned an hour later, no amount of his cajoling Cockney sense of humour could penetrate her mood. The adult penitentiary loomed suddenly in sight with its charred empty buildings, eerily suspended above the choppy sea, an unexpected vision of civilisation after the untamed bushland.

Lydia wondered what Jane would think if she had been alive to see this place, so clear in her memories as she approached death. The penal settlement crowded around the small bay into which they headed. Lush green ivy smothered the walls of the sandstone church. Daisies grew in clumps to relieve the monotony of the green. The sandstone pillars, which once stood at the entrance to the government gardens, now stood strangely askew as if they'd fallen from the heavens.

The ferryman was right. God had forsaken this place. He told her now that a small earthquake, between the fires, had uprooted the pillars. A series of disasters had continued to shake the settlement: the old asylum, used to house prisoners who became insane after incarceration, was claimed by fire. A second fire, which swept through three years after the first, hadn't deterred those who sensed money could be made from the convict remains, although many of the old documents, she was told, had been burnt. Perhaps the past was best left buried, Lydia thought, as they pulled up at a small dilapidated jetty at the foot of what had been Hawkins' cottage. She stood on the jetty looking back at the settlement.

The place had the false gaiety of a carnival now. It was reminiscent of a small country town, except for the five-storeyed brick penitentiary that stood in the centre. A small group was playing cricket on the lawn, the men in felt hats, checked shirts and waistcoats. In the distance some women toiled over lawn tennis in long skirts. Lydia passed a sign written with elaborate flourish: 'Amateur theatrical performance, Port Arthur. This evening will be performed the laughable and amusing farce of *The Silent Woman.*' Splashes of rose-coloured taffeta dresses fluttered across the lawns like tropical butterflies as people strolled past a cascading fountain. Lydia found their light-heartedness jarring after the misery of the boys' prison. The tranquil gardens had replaced the human centipede, which only a few decades ago had lumbered across this same land. She avoided the guides who strolled around, buttons bursting over their girth, stories from the past spilling out of their mouths to entertain the visitors. The earth was stained with blood.

'There's always some 'un who wants to put a quantity of dynamite or gunpowder under the Model Prison to blow it up,' one told her, displaying a row of fetid gums as he laughed.

Unlike the boys' prison, many of the stone buildings here were still standing. The commandant's house above the jetty, which she remembered as an austere, unostentatious white-washed building, was now a hotel. Wicker armchairs had replaced the boys' escape boats and the verandah was patronised by the governor and the admiral of the fleet. Tiered thickly iced cakes and tea in china cups were served to patrons, as they looked out to sea and the Isle of the Dead.

Lydia sat on one of the chairs and ordered tea and scones. She watched as a steamer arrived at the wharf with a new batch of holidaymakers. The formal garden she remembered

Hawkins showing them was now overgrown with geraniums. Lupins, probably the original plants described by Jane in her diaries, ran riot. There were the remains of an old sundial. She was joined by an elderly couple from Devon, who told her they were amazed at such an English vista in the middle of a wild colonial island.

'The willows, those English trees, the church spire, the little wooden bridges – who would have thought those bad old varmints, those incorrigibles, were kept in such a place of beauty,' the man said, winking at his wife. 'And then there were all those nutters in the asylum – the old country dumping all their offal.'

Lydia looked with distaste at their careful appearances, the wife's powdered hair and the husband's carefully starched shirt. She did not tell them that it was her father who had introduced the oaks, elms and ash trees that had thrived so well over the years. Nor did she join in their mirth.

Later, she walked past a brass band and across the small piece of land between the wharf and the penitentiary. A guide had told her the penitentiary had been a flourmill before it was transformed into tiny cells to house the prisoners. Lydia joined some of the other visitors inside. At one end was a lofty, handsome entrance hall and on the second tier, a kerosene chandelier. Kerosene lamps hung in the corridors. A wide staircase led to a spacious dining room, with rows and rows of columns. On the right of the landing was the pantry, which contained tin plates and pannikins from occupants long since departed. To the left was a library. Lydia found a lift that had been used to haul food from the kitchen below. She imagined the penitentiary's occupants on the top floor. The visitors' book placed on a table at the top of the stairs said this floor housed no less than 604 bunks in three tiers. It reminded Lydia of the convict-hold on the ship. The bunks, which were railed off from each other, were so close together it would have been impossible to sit up.

Chased out by ghosts, she left, walking as quickly as she could back down the stairs to the ground-floor lobby, past a drinking fountain built by the convicts, through the exercise yards, underneath a large clock and out into the fresh air.

A placard told her the land she was standing on was newly reclaimed and now formed the head of the bay. A wall had been built to prevent the sea washing at the foundations of the building. The salt air and sound of the waves was comforting after the damp interior. In front of her was a canal that led to the sea. She followed groups of visitors back towards the commandant's cottage, but instead of climbing the steps at the end of the wharf, she headed for the long building facing the sea on the southern side of the penitentiary. Two warehouses were at either end and, in the middle, a small cottage. She noticed the pulleys above the large doors on both warehouses.

There were no holidaymakers here, but the door to the small cottage opened when she pushed it. Her feet echoed on the wooden floors as she walked through the empty space, lifting her skirts above the small clouds of dust. This was the commissariat, she was sure of it – although, unlike some of the other buildings, there was no sign to tell her so and she had no memory from that earlier visit to Lemprière's abode. It would make sense, however, that the storeroom would have been built near the wharf to offload the wares. The room smelt of aged sawdust and the sickly sweet, damp smell of rodents. She could make out remnants of flour on the floor. In the far left of the room she saw a door. It was locked. Perhaps this was Lemprière's museum? She imagined him behind the high counter that stood abandoned in the centre, counting the stores, dispensing rations; the incongruous collection of stuffed animals Ross had described behind him. A curer of souls, Jane had said in the letter. She had been prepared to put her life as governor's wife in jeopardy for him, and to risk the possibility of destroying her husband's life.

Peering through a grimy window full of cobwebs, Lydia could just make out some shelves. There was no sign of the taxidermist's wares. Opposite the shelves was a large window, with the glass broken as though someone had thrown a cricket ball through it. It was boarded up with wood. There were no other signs of occupancy. Lydia had half expected she would find something tangible to signal Louis's presence; that he had existed.

She returned to the commandant's cottage and went straight to her lodgings, avoiding the dining room and the couple from Devon. There was the sound of voices coming from the parlour and the tinkling of a piano but the hall was empty. She saw a tall bookcase and skimmed its contents: cookbooks, government regulations, a book entitled *Varieties of Vice-Regal Life*. Then she noticed another – *The Model Prison: Control of Criminals*. Her father's name on the spine jumped out at her and, opening the book, she recognised his flourish of a signature underneath the preface.

Lydia took the book back to her room. Outside was a fig tree that she'd been told had been planted by Charles O'Mara Hawkins. In the afternoons it made the room dark, but in the mornings the sun filtered through onto the counterpane, leaving a patch of sun on the armchair next to the large window. Perhaps the room had been Hawkins' office?

She settled down in the armchair and opened the volume. It was a slim book, written presumably by some government official. The pages were hard to open as though no one ever read it.

Her father had established in Port Arthur the Model, or Separate Prison, as it was sometimes known, which operated like Pentonville Prison in London. Unlike the old system of the penitentiary, which relied on flogging for punishment, the men in the Model Prison were to be kept separate and in complete silence from each other, even when they exercised or attended the chapel housed inside the jail. Fifty separate stalls were built. The lack of contact with fellow prisoners was to encourage them to reflect on their criminal behaviour and lead more moral lives.

No one prisoner can recognise another. All prisoners must be masked when they walk to chapel on Sunday. Only once inside the cell can the mask be removed. Speaking to the prisoner must never be permitted. He can never read aloud, sing, whistle or dance and this must be part of the regulation. Nor should he hear the sound of footsteps, even his own. Cloth must be used to cover all footwear so that his steps make no sound.

A dumb cell will be used for the incorrigibles. Prisoners sentenced to this cell must be deprived of light and touch and should remain in this state to consider their offences for a period of up to a month. Only when they are reduced to babbling like babes can we have an effect on their minds.

For other punishments, confine the men in strict solitude for periods varying from a year to eighteen months. Using this system, I anticipate relieving the colony of a permanent class of offenders — men who have no sooner paid the penalty of one crime than they are sure to commit another. This must be seen as <u>a place worse than death,</u> otherwise we have failed.

Lydia closed the book quickly. She thought of the marble bust of her father, his serene features. She had been vaguely aware of this project of his, but she had imagined model prisoners – prisoners who were on their best behaviour – not a jail that operated on such inhumane terms of mental deprivation. He had been responsible for the introduction of this cruelty. The man who had been found with Henry on the *Fairlie* was flogged to death at her father's command. Lydia shuddered. In adolescence she had not questioned what he did. She had understood it was his job and that he was in charge of an island of felons, but how much had she really known?

She had seen him as benevolent, caring. She thought of him talking confidently about how the convicts would come to understand that his way was right, that it was necessary for reform. He had told her he did not like them being flogged. She had believed him. Walking around the boys' prison, she knew she had begun to doubt him. Reading these words seemed to confirm her thoughts. Instead of inflicting wounds on their bodies, his system had scarred their minds.

The next day Lydia visited the Model Prison on the hill behind the penitentiary. The prison was set back from the other buildings on the road into the settlement, which was lined with old elms, probably donated by her father. She had not seen it, having arrived by boat like the other sightseers at the opposite end of the settlement.

The jail was a single-storeyed affair with a wall around it. She joined a small group of early visitors and entered through the wooden door in the middle of a solid stone wall. The guide waited inside a long, dank corridor. On either side were cells as far as the eye could see. Open fires had been placed at each end of the corridor, their grates now devoid of ash. The guide explained how cold it would have been in winter. Lydia shivered, imagining hooded prisoners with cloth around their shoes. Even the staff had been slippered, walking these corridors like members of a bizarre monastic cult. She imagined the prisoners deprived of sound and sight, not permitted even to whistle, even when they were back in their cells. If she closed her eyes they slipped past her, silent ghosts, heads bowed in defeat.

All the darkened corridors led to a central room, a wide airy hall where a glass dome ceiling spread light into the dingy corners. Fifty cells, arranged in three wings, radiated from this central hall. A small flight of stairs led to a door above them and the guide ushered them up these stairs and pushed the door, which opened into a large amphitheatre. They were taken down some narrow steep wooden steps, flanked on either side by shutters. They entered one by one onto a wooden stage and stood next to a pulpit. Once they were all on the stage, they looked back at the room.

Lydia couldn't believe the sight that met her eyes: stalls, wooden pens, the sort made to house pigs, rows and rows of them, empty all the way from the front row back up to the door where they had entered. She imagined eyes staring straight ahead at the reverend delivering the sermon, unable to see the man standing next to them. The guide opened one of the stalls with a theatrical air and stood looking back at them as if about to deliver a soliloquy.

'Once inside their stalls, the prisoners were permitted to remove their masks.' He smiled. 'The idea was that they never saw a friend or foe walking to and from the chapel. Once inside the chapel, they could only see the reverend. Being cunning varmints, however, we know they used a code – they rapped on the wall and the number of raps represented the corresponding letter from the alphabet.'

After five minutes, which seemed like an eternity, Lydia was glad to escape again to the airy central hall.

'Here was where the inspector sat.' The guide pointed to the centre where all lines converged. 'From here he could watch the prisoners. He could see, and knew everything that went on in this jail.'

Lydia glanced up and down the corridors that intersected the room with such precision. Instead of prisoners, she saw perfumed women dressed in finery leaning on men's arms and peering into the dank, moss-covered cells, their bustles preventing them from fitting through the cell doors. Parasols twirling, they looked as though they were at the opening of the Crystal Palace in London, not within the austere surroundings of the Model Prison in Port Arthur. Lydia presumed they were from Hobart Town, perhaps drawn by macabre curiosity.

When the tour was finished, the guide bade them farewell and Lydia was about to leave when a man with a monocle and a small bowler hat approached. He was dressed in a black suit and had a large turquoise cravat folded inside his jacket pocket. His eyebrows were arched and groomed like pencil lines curved around the top of his eyes, giving him a comic expression. He reminded Lydia of a clown. In his hand he clutched a journal she recognised: *The Harbinger of Light*. He must be one of those spiritualists, claiming to offer scientific and rational explanations for ghostly phenomena. She thought of Jane dabbling in the occult. Two of the younger women left abruptly and soon the rest of the group also vanished as though, Lydia thought later, into thin air.

'Séances are held here. Madam, could I interest you in taking part in a séance?'

Lydia realised he was addressing her.

'See that clock there?' He pointed to a large wooden box, standing upright. At the top, inside the glass, was a shiny brass clock with roman numerals, but instead of hands to show the time, it had small spines like the back of a hedgehog around the perimeter and, above, a small peg.

'The inspector turned that striker which pushed that peg down every hour to prove he was on duty, that he was vigilant at all times. As the inspector had to see all, everything.'

His vinegary breath smelt of onions. He spoke in a clipped voice with an accent from the Continent.

'The inspector had his job cut out for him. A man called Quigley was in one of these cells, an insane highwayman, considered a dangerous lunatic,' he said. 'Cell number thirteen and fourteen were his. Six or seven men were needed to handle him.'

She was looking for somewhere to escape, but she was alone with him in this empty glass domed hall.

'His dementia came from a skull fracture, a scuffle during a highway robbery. Quigley's Cage was actually two cells converted into one: he needed more space because he was always going berserk.'

His pupils were large, dilated.

Lydia's eyes fixed on his to show she was not scared. She felt ethereal, floating.

'You must join us. That's where we will have the séance.'

He paused.

'I take you to be a person of great intelligence. You must know that the essential self, the soul or spirit, resides within the body. It's a vehicle of expression on the mundane plane. You are connecting with some of these tortured souls allowing them to talk to you, to lay them to rest. That is your destiny.'

His eyes shone blue. As Lydia watched, they converged into one.

'But, you are also on a journey in this life to discover intimacy. You will find out soon enough.'

She felt the man's hand on her arm and struggled for breath. The stuff of the place was seeping into her bones. She looked upwards. The glass dome was like the centre of a web, its octagonal beams spreading outwards. Beyond, she saw blue sky and clouds. As she watched, a white cockatoo flew slowly over the pane.

An image came to her then of the inspector sitting, like a spider spinning a web for his victims, and a man pinned to the gossamer. For a brief moment, the stranger became the inspector, one eye shimmering. Lydia felt giddy. She was in an open space with nowhere to sit down.

The voice continued.

'In the darkness, in the dumb cell, do you know how they tried to remain sane? They would throw a button in their cell and spend hours, days even, trying to find it. You see they were kept for a month at a time without light or human contact. When all is black and there is no light, there are only spirits.'

His voice droned on.

Her eyes became heavy listening to his cloying words. She felt as though she had been drugged.

How did she get back to the commandant's cottage? She had a vague recollection of walking down the long corridor, past the rows and rows of cells and then she was back inside the lobby of her hotel. Approaching the reception desk for the key to her room, she found it hard to speak.

'Madam, we have other attractions, too, while you are staying with us. A horse-drawn tourist coach that will take you to marvel at the railway line once powered by humans.'

The lodgekeeper's face blurred into the man with the monocle.

The convict railway. An invention of Hawkins, but another punishment introduced by her father. She remembered the sound of the chains chinking and clanking; the convicts' wet bodies drenched in sweat, their perspiration running like rivers down their forearms. It had never occurred to her until now to wonder how they felt as they pushed such a weight up the incline. She could still feel the air buffeting her face as she hurtled into the darkened bush once they started the descent. Her stomach had churned like a child visiting a fair. She remembered Jane telling her to stop shouting, but she had been terrified. The odour of the men who sat squashed against her in the tiny carriage assailed her. Her father would sit near the front. What was his expression? A faint smile perhaps? For the first time she saw that she had been complicit in the cruelty. Dressed in her Sunday best, with tight-fitting shoes and frills, she had been oblivious to everyone but herself.

'If you don't wish to take the horse-drawn carriage, Madam, I am afraid that the ship won't be sailing for some time, due to the inclement weather. Madam, are you feeling all right? Can I get you a chair? We have smelling salts, Madam. I will be with you directly.'

CHAPTER SIX

Lydia spent some of the afternoon resting, resolving to book her passage back to Hobart Town on the steamer. As she lay there unable to sleep, she remembered the ferryman telling her the peninsula's store had souvenirs on sale from the boys' prison. Perhaps it might also sell other documentation, some references to the storekeeper's museum?

She headed down to the grocery store on the other side of the penitentiary to the commissariat. Snakey Wellard was a smiling, leathery-faced man with a large nose and ears. He had been a prison warden, then a guide. Shortly after the convict settlement was closed, he'd begun displaying relics of those days. He was doing quite a trade, but it was the convict collection of which he was most proud.

She had not expected so much material. Wellard stood at an old bench at the front of the shop. Behind him were shelves containing books, and it was here Lydia made her discovery. She was idly flipping through a prayer book, a softbound gold-leaf affair she'd taken from high up on a shelf, one of a collection from Point Puer, when she noticed some writing in the back, a few verses in large scrawl referring to God striking down an overseer.

But Lord, to thee I cry'd; my prayer at morn prevent shall thee.
Why Lord, dost thou cast off my soul,
and hid'st thy face from Me?
Distressed am I and from my youth
I ready am to die;
Thy terrors I have borne, and am distracted fearfully.

There was no author. She had the eerie feeling again of the boys' presence, which she had first experienced on the promontory. Voices from so long ago had occupied her since reading the inquest papers at the Old Sessions House. Their fate seemed somehow bound up with hers. She had been on board the ship that had transported the first of them to the island jail. She now felt complicit in her contribution to their pain, although at the time she had thought nothing their plight. She was but a child herself.

Maybe this was Henry or Thomas Boardman speaking to her from the grave. She peered into the darkened room. Behind the sacks of flour, vats of butter and crates of apples there were more shelves of books, mostly unsorted in untidy piles.

'They found 'em in the chapel. Boys' prayer books, I believe,' Wellard told her. 'You see, Miss, the boys, they was taught 'ow to read and write and they was allowed pencils and paper, unlike the adults. Part of their education for a trade, like. Part of their learnin'.'

Lydia had been considering whether or not to show the writing to the shopkeeper in case he seized it back, knowing its value.

'I'd enjoy looking through them, if I may. I'm most interested in the teaching of children.'

He looked at her.

'They'll be 'ere for many years to come, m' lady.'

She postponed her trip back to Hobart and decided to spend the next few days searching the dusty books at the back of the store, trying to decipher cryptic notes in bad handwriting.

The following day Wellard was more forthcoming – she sensed he was intrigued by her and was probably wondering why she was there. She chatted with him when she arrived. As if reading her thoughts he said: 'Most in these parts, don't stay long. But there's plenty 'ere to see when you're lookin' like you are, Miss. Interested in the boys, are you? Not many know the little mites was sent out 'ere so far away from their families, though there was brats too.'

'Did any of them commit murder?'

'Now, there's a funny question.' Wellard's eyes narrowed in his weatherbeaten face. 'What would you be asking that for?' He paused. 'Matter of fact there was a couple of murders. Overseer met his end one night. Crownin' the overseers, they called it. Know what that means, eh?' He winked and Lydia played along, shaking her head.

'Putting the night soil up at the top of the door so when he walked in, it fell all over him,' Wellard laughed far too uproariously.

'How did they kill him?'

'Oh, Miss, I don't think you want to know that. Sufficient

to say, it weren't pretty. They never did work out who did it, either.'

She saw blood spattered on the walls and a man, his head battered, gasping for breath.

'And the other murder? You mentioned others.'

'That were nasty, too. Two boys, like, one killed the other.'

'You know the boys' names?'

'Both began with 'B'. Can't remember . . . Browning . . . Bingham . . .'

'Belfield?'

'Not sure. Why? Do you know someone by that name?'

Lydia sat down on the chair next to the cash register but did not answer. Instead she asked:

'What happened?'

'Oh, 'oo knows in this place, my dear, what 'appened. Much of the papers was destroyed in the fire on the main settlement 'ere. They say there was some papers from the boys' prison, if you got the time to look. Problem is, Miss, I don't get time, what with all the folk lookin' for trophies. No one's really dug around in that back room. Stuff got dumped 'ere when they cleared out the chapel.'

That night, Lydia battled with a desire to leave. Wellard was probably wrong. Besides, what was she was looking for? It was becoming increasingly difficult to get to the books on the back shelves in Wellard's store and what more information could she expect to find? Rusty farm hoes and ploughs were piled up against the wall, sets of cutlery scattered out of boxes. There was an old scythe, glassware, and tin trunks weathered with age, leg irons dulled with time, leather shoes with holes in the soles, and an old yardarm from the days of mustering. Wellard had moved some of the larger stuff aside, but she had already cut her finger on a rusty implement. She had returned to her lodgings covered in decades of dirt, but she knew something would draw her back to Wellard's store the following day. That night, alone in bed, she saw those words again – religious verses and some heartfelt pleas to Jesus. She had glimpsed raw fear in the childish fervour of their words.

Lord Jesus, think on me,
That, when the flood is past,
I may the eternal brightness see,
And share Thy joy at last.
May God forgive thee.

'The boys,' she asked Wellard the next day. 'They had religious instruction?'

She was perched on a small stool next to his cash register again, for there was no room amongst the dark clutter and dust of the store.

'Oh, they was very religious, Miss.'

He had persisted in calling her that from the first, as if he had assessed her marital state. It sounded to her like a taunt. She had considered having a wedding ring made before leaving England and now wished she had.

'Who gave them the religious instruction?'

'A number of the clergymen, Miss. Cap'n 'Awkins, 'e was always concerned about their souls. Now, that man Lemprière, the storekeeper, the curer of souls . . .'

Of course, he would know Lemprière. She had been focusing on the boys so much she hadn't thought to ask him.

'You know him, Miss?'

'I didn't. I mean, I don't think I ever met him.'

Wellard looked at her in that piercing way of his.

'So you were 'ere too, Miss. What, a long time ago?'

'Yes, I was . . . with my parents.'

She had no intention of revealing her true identity to this man. He did not persist, but she knew, the gossip he was, that he would try to find out.

' 'E were known by boys and men alike.'

'What do you mean by that?'

'Lemprière . . . the convict chaplain. Kind man, he was s'posed to be. 'E fed their stomachs and their minds, looked after their souls, like. 'E used to give sermons from the chapel at Point Puer, try to turn some of those rascals to the way of the Lord. Twern't an easy task. Those that went to the gallows, they confessed to 'im so their souls'd be saved. Don't know about those 'oo threw themselves off those cliffs.'

The following day in the store Wellard handed her some pages, as though she were a novice earning entry into a world hitherto secret. He had found them, he said casually, hidden in the binding of one of the prayer books: 'Smoothed down, 'idden, like. The murder we talked about – the prayer books came down from 'Obart Town, from the Tench, where they 'anged the poor bastards, sorry Miss, men. They never 'anged any of them 'ere at Port Arthur, you see.'

Her heart beat quickly as she felt the crackle of the paper beneath the tips of her fingers.

'I slit open the binding of one of those books one day. Felt a bit strange, like. 'Oose to know what they contain?'

'Would I be able to purchase these?'

Wellard looked up at the ceiling.

'Oh, I don't know if they're for sale.'

'How much?' she asked.

'One yellowboy.'

Lydia knew the sum was preposterous but she handed him the guinea.

She waited until she was back in her room next to the fig tree, until the evening light had almost faded. In the damp air she drew her shawl around her, then she sat staring at the pages, unsure suddenly whether she wanted to read them or not. Under the sheen of the whale oil lamp she unfolded the pages, taking care not to tear them.

15th March, 1842

This is my letter to you, though you will never read it. My only bedding on the ship was the stones the brig carried as ballast. I've no eye for the beautiful, but to be under that deck estranged from the health-giving breezes, the sylvan glades and you . . .

I feel nothing. Without leg irons I'm strangely light and disoriented. How long now since I walked unfettered? Months, years? To think I once counted my life as though each day was significant.

Reverend Bedford took my measurements this morning with a cloth tape and I shrank into the dank wall of the cell away from his teeth which are yellow and his breath which is cloying and smells of sweetmeats and brandy. We always dig a hole for the tall ones, he said.

To join you in that place of which we dreamt. It will be like the tomb where I spent a month in eternal darkness when they tried to crush me through punishment and I longed for salvation.

Sedgewick's evidence was the most damning. They said you named me as the murderer. At first I was angry. I'm still more afraid of the end than you were, you see. That probably surprises you.

The man who sent me to my fate is Judge Stephens, all eyebrows and nostril whiskers. He's a young man for the job he carries out. I saw the menace in his eyes as he wheeled above me. He would have me hanged. I must say, I didn't think Dr Casey would be agin me.

I don't believe you are mouldering in the grave, but when I try to remember your face, you have no features. Yesterday I awoke screaming, but I know in the darkest black I can make the light grow.

Hawkins will cut me after death. He is waiting for that moment of revenge. And then? I will end up under one of those mounds on Dead Island that we imagined for such a long time.

In the room next to the fig tree the smell of the muttonbird feathers in Lydia's pillow mingled with images of creatures and devils and Henry Belfield. She saw again clasped hands, linked together with steel. What had the other boy meant to him?

There was nothing to say the letter was from Belfield, but the dates and facts fitted exactly. In her stepmother's letter to Lemprière from Transylvania in March, 1842, Jane had referred to the boy and this murder. When Lydia checked her notes, the date on the inquest papers matched the date on this letter, and Wellard had said the pages came from Hobart Town where the prisoners were hanged.

The letter seemed to confirm all her misgivings about the place. She remembered Jane writing about its subterranean nature, and that she felt something lurked beneath the surface. Later, in the guests' lounge, Lydia stood in front of the oil painting above the fireplace. Hawkins' epaulettes were strangely pronounced, as if they had landed on his shoulders. His brass buttons shone. His head looked as though it was balanced precariously on top of the jacket, as if it had been placed as an afterthought, but it was his eyes that Lydia found most confronting. Cruel, hawk-like, they followed her around the room as if challenging her to discard her quest. He had called the boys 'depraved little felons'.

'Hawkins will cut me.' Why would Hawkins want to dissect a young man? But someone who had designed a train to be pulled by humans was bound to be hard to fathom. Lydia could not imagine who could have given him permission to perform such a macabre act. It was as though, by committing the act of murder, the perpetrators gave up the right to be treated as human beings.

'What place was this, your kingdom?' she whispered quietly. 'And what happened to those who lived within it?'

The following morning, Snakey Wellard eyed her with cunning.

'I've found more. All sorts of little treasures.'

'I see. But I think I've paid you more than enough. Besides, I'm not interested.'

'How much for the rest?'

'Mr Wellard, I think you have read my position incorrectly. I am not in a position to continue to pay you absurd sums of money for this material.'

At the same time, her breathing quickened.

He smiled as he handed her a box from underneath the counter.

'I can't part with these, Miss. I mean, they're priceless. Original letters and diaries of the boys. They're 'istory, like.'

'Well, perhaps you should keep them here, then.'

Wellard sighed.

'Now, Miss, I know you're interested. Not many in these parts'd understand. I'm not askin' for much, but there's nuffin' else like this anywhere that I know.'

Wellard was a master salesman and as Lydia handed over more coins, she could tell by his eyes that he was expecting her to have haggled with him. She felt suddenly tired. She had a small allowance left by Jane and would inherit a share in the house in Russell Square. She'd already spent a considerable sum travelling to the end of the world.

'I want unlimited access to the rest of those books.'

'Yes, Miss, of course, Miss. Anything I can help you with, I will.'

He waited until she was at the door. Then, he spoke again.

'I should tell you, Miss . . . that boy Belfield you mentioned. 'E was up to no good. 'E was a bender, that's what 'e was. Not that it's my place to tell you these things.'

'What things?'

She was already angry for parting so readily with the money and had no idea what he was talking about.

''E ran a racket, Miss. D'ye know what I mean?'

'A racket?'

'Boys, Miss. 'E traded in boys.'

Lydia blushed, at the same time registering Wellard's delight at her discomfort. But she no longer cared what he thought. She was thinking of Henry Belfield's face close to hers, the dull pain of her head hitting the wall of the ship's cabin. His mouth closing on hers.

CHAPTER SEVEN

Lydia left Port Arthur the following day, watching the sails fill with a fresh nor' westerly to deliver her away from this place defined by its past, where frivolity had replaced despair. She had decided if Wellard had more documents she was not going to be lured into buying them. Money would not last the way she was spending it. She was fulfilling Jane's prophecies that she could not cope alone and was incapable of making sensible decisions. This journey had begun with the chance discovery of a letter from her stepmother to a storekeeper. Now she was embroiled in an entire story that was barely her own. She had had an encounter with a convict boy on a ship many years ago that she had chosen to forget. Why, then, remind herself of his existence? She was drowning in the ocean of the past with no point of reference.

That night the ship pitched mercilessly under a moonless sky. In her dreams, they were all there rewriting her history: her father at the pulpit in the Model Prison dispensing punishment in the name of God; Jane flirting openly with the storekeeper in the musty backroom of the commissariat; Hawkins, his epaulettes askew, cutting up the dead; the boy Henry preying on other boys. Why had she made this journey? She had paid all that money for words written by someone who had molested her, for what reason? To be reminded of pain? And what did she expect to uncover about her stepmother's love for the storekeeper? Thrown from one side of her bed to the other, in the confusion of her senses Lydia felt more alone than she had ever felt.

The next morning the storm had abated. She walked up to the foredeck in time to see the peaks of Mount Wellington bathed in early morning light. The distant mountain – glowing, ever watchful – looked like a slumbering giant above the town. Clouds drifted across the summit. She found lodgings in a pleasant Georgian hotel not far from the wharves in Cromwell Street, Battery Point, which smelt of polish and leather, and she slept soundly.

On her second day in Hobart Town she walked along Murray Street, following a path trodden long ago. The town had grown up, as she had done. The streets were wider than she remembered, with more shops advertising wares. She turned right into Macquarie Street. Walking towards what had been the shoreline, she stopped abruptly. The house where she had spent six years of her life was no more. In her heart she knew she had been waiting to see it. Government House had gone, with its tall chimneys – the highest almost as tall as the old elm in the garden – the wide verandah that travelled around the perimeter of the long narrow house, the outbuildings and the lawn which ran down to the water, the peacocks grooming themselves, bringing their own exotica to the scene.

She stared in disbelief. There was no water. The old weather-board buildings had been replaced with new sandstone ones. A sign proclaimed the building housed historical archives and government records. Her home had been erased. They must have reclaimed the land the way they had done at Port Arthur. Timber did not have the longevity of stone, and like the buildings at Point Puer, it was as if the house had never existed. She could make out the old fence, now hanging askew around what had been the field that housed the emu.

Mathinna came to her then, as clearly as if she were standing next to her. She imagined passing her by in the street without recognising her old playmate. And if there was such an encounter? They might have an even bigger chasm to cross than the yawning gap that opened up as, bound for England, they had left her standing on the wharf.

Thus occupied, she was unprepared for what she saw in the cleared area where the house had been: a statue of her father, less portly than she remembered, and younger. His face was carved in bronze, his expression was sterner than in the portrait at Bedford Place. She had hardly recognised him. He held a book in front of him protectively; behind him she could see the wharves. Lydia knew such a memorial would have been important to him but she hadn't expected to find him so honoured. There had been many other governors to replace him in the colony, yet no other statue claimed the same significance in this square. He must have looked down on Hobartians young and old during the years she and Jane had sent ships to the Arctic waiting for him to come home.

The bronzed figure touched her deeply and cheered her. It seemed to be a sign from her father that she had chosen well in coming to visit the island of her childhood. Earlier thoughts about his treatment of the convicts vanished. She felt ashamed of doubting him.

After the months cooped up at sea and the days in the cramped confines of the store at Port Arthur, Lydia was enjoying the feeling of the earth beneath her feet. Declining a coach, she headed for the newly planted Royal Society's Botanical Gardens, which stretched along the hillside and down to the river near the new Government House on the road out to the Queen's Domain – a new macadamised road which led to the country town of New Norfolk. The home of the present governor was perched high up on the banks, about a mile out of town, and was resplendent with Tudor-Gothic turrets and military grandeur. With three towers capped by monstrous gargoyles, it had been built in a baronial style that reminded Lydia of country houses on the Scottish border. Jane would have been impressed – she had spent much time writing home to her sister for books on architecture to build a new home, but it had never eventuated.

Gardens had been planted behind the mansion. Plum and apple trees, pomegranates, apricots and nectarines grew along-side the spiky beauty of antipodean plants. A newly painted sign stated that members of the Royal Society, another legacy of her parents, had planted them. Couples strolled along the paths, arm in arm. In the distance, Lydia saw a regimental band playing on one of the lawns. This had nothing to do with her childhood and she was glad that she did not feel part of it.

At the entrance to the new Government House, next to some sandstone pillars, a sign proclaimed that thirty thousand people had been through the gates since the opening. It was here she rested, spreading out her riding cloak and loosening her boots. Her feet ached from all the walking. She could see the Derwent widen as it flowed closer to the ocean. Beaches had formed on its banks and white-crested waves splashed on them as though on the seashore. The river was no longer plied by the spiky masts of wooden ships like the one in which she had sailed as a child. Then, the port had been crowded with whaling ships and tea clippers. Now, steamships made out of iron with heavy hulls weighing several hundred tons lumbered up the river. She had seen some of them being constructed along Battery Point.

Lydia drank it all in. The whaling ships had begun to disappear when the industry, like the convicts, vanished. The familiar stench of blubber was absent from the wharves – the houses were now lit by coal gas. Cows grazed in a nearby paddock and beyond, at the water's edge, light played across the river's surface while she reminisced. No one could take this landscape from her, not even the ghosts of her past.

Her father had laid the foundation stone here for a new Government House, but they had returned to England before any building had commenced. She remembered her step-mother complaining about the draughty dining room in the old Government House, with its high plastered ceilings and open fires that emitted no warmth; her complaints about the convicts she was forced to employ as chefs, who tried to concoct blancmange castles designed for cool European summers, not the fierce Australian summer heat. The creations had melted before they'd even reached the table. Suddenly Lydia was a child again, a starched apron around her waist, crestfallen as Jane chastised her for her attempt at nutmeg biscuits: 'You can't possibly give these to Papa, my dear. They are simply not good enough.'

A phaeton pulled up at the gate, accompanied by horsemen. Was the new governor in the carriage? Lydia toyed with the idea of leaving a card, imagining the introduction – 'The former governor's daughter, Miss Lydia Frankland' – but dismissed it. Half an hour passed and, feeling rested, she continued her walk, firmly tying her bonnet and smoothing her skirts.

She passed the Rossbank Observatory, constructed by convict labourers in 1840 for Captain Ross, who was en route to find the south magnetic pole. It had begun to crumble from lack of use. The telescope it had once housed had been the first in the colony, a present from Jane's friend John Herschel. Lydia remembered their collective pride when it arrived at the wharf. Jane had been convinced that its purchase would be another way to ensure she left her mark on the colony.

Pangs of hunger eventually drove her back to her lodgings at Battery Point where she dined on cod and rice and sipped a small brandy. The next morning she looked at the box on her dresser, opened then closed it again. The box from Wellard was somehow tainted. She needed time to stave off the demons, to retain a sense of self, like the child who wanted to preserve the fairytale, to remember the happy ending.

Wellard was probably illiterate. He was capable of falsehoods. Those eyes with their appearance of concern and friendliness; his lower lip drooping slightly as he delivered the words that awoke the memories she had carefully buried. She was looking for distractions, something to keep her in the present. Besides, she was enjoying being a sightseer, unencumbered by the past.

She spent another day in Hobart Town, breathing lungfuls of spring air, savouring the blossoms fizzing with pollination, freshly cut hay and the crisp air from the mountain, before venturing back to the site of her former home, this time to visit the new sandstone buildings which, she had been told by her landlady, contained the correspondence from the colonial secretary and the attorney-general's records. Here, she might get a better sense of her father. She knew so little of his official life. The book at the Model Prison might have been an aberration. She wanted desperately to be assured that was the case.

The man behind the desk seemed nonplussed when she announced her name and her connection with the former governor.

'Of course, we have much of your father's writings. Legislative council papers, colonial secretaries' office correspondence, that kind of thing. After all, he was governor for six years and you would have seen his statue,' he said. 'We still have the barque named after your stepmother sailing in the harbour. Where would you like to begin? There are the duplicate despatches of Van Diemen's Land, the letter-books of the governors of Van Diemen's Land, the minutes of the executive council.'

For the next two days Lydia ploughed through the language of warfare and discipline, reading about the island jail, a world – she increasingly realised – from which she had been excluded. Letters upon letters, most of them deathly dull, all signed with her father's flourishing hand. Each day she hoped she would find something different, a memory to connect her with the man she had known. Her father was a warm, tender person who cared deeply for those he loved. He had been at sea most of his life. He had fought in the Battle of Copenhagen at the age of fifteen and at seventeen had surveyed the Great Bight and the Gulf of Carpenteria. He'd seen more fighting in the Battle of Trafalgar, where many men were wounded. Lydia remembered the battle stories he would tell her, of his conquests and his mapping of the great world at different points of the globe. He was a devoutly religious man who often read to her from the Bible whenever he was at home on a Sunday.

But away from the hearth, he was barely recognisable. In the large hardback books, instead of reassurance, Lydia encountered some of the reasons he was feared. The words seemed to come from a different man: ruthless, indifferent to the suffering of others; a man she had never been invited to see, the same man, undoubtedly, who had implemented the inhumanity of the Model Prison. In six years, he had left an indelible stamp on this colony.

Letter to the Home Secretary
15th February, 1839

My experience daily shows me how essential classification is to effect the ends of transportation, and my attention therefore has been long devoted to rendering the scale as complete as possible. It must be used to counteract the spread of wickedness.

Criminals are the scum of the earth, an economic burden to the Mother Country, an aberration of mankind in a world of exile, a mutant society.

And in another letter to the same home secretary:

It is not the crime that we should punish, but the habits and inclinations of prisoners, so they must be sorted, much in the same way plants and animals are sorted according to their genus. It is more important, therefore, in my view that we classify, not according to the crime, but according to conduct and character. I have therefore taken the liberty of collecting as much minutiae of detail to allow us to properly categorise these criminals. My dear Home Secretary, I can only hint that this knowledge was bequeathed to me by the dear Lord himself. I am but his humble servant and cannot claim to be responsible for such an insightful notion.

She had always known her father was a religious man, but she was shocked by his fervour. To see himself as God's servant imbued him with the authority to dispense orders, end lives, send men to the gallows. He wrote that he could convert vagabonds, useless in one hemisphere, into active citizens in another. As governor, he would not simply act as jailer, but be able to give birth to a new and splendid country – a grand centre of civilisation.

Among the papers, one document stood out. Her father had written to the colonial secretary with a proposal to be put to parliament without delay. His writing sloped even more strongly in obvious haste.

Linnaeus set out the documents of species, a static model to reassure us of the orderliness of existence. Order is above all what the colony needs. I have devised a scale for these men under my charge. Put most simply, at one end is freedom, at the other, the scaffold. Here is my scale:

1. Holding a ticket of leave
2. Assignment to a settler
3. Labour on public works
4. Labour on the roads near civilisation in the settled districts
5. Work in a chain gang
6. Banishment to the penal settlements
7. Penal settlement labour in chains.

I have begun to classify my specimens by instituting my own set of Black Books, leatherbound tomes three feet high where every aspect of them will be described. Tattoos, descriptions of countenance, every minute part of their body so they can be identified. There is no doubt that a different species should emerge from the criminal transported across the seas.

Her father had treated men as scientists treat plants and animals, to be categorised at will. There was no room, in such a model, to allow for human beings and their individuality. Lydia was confused. She felt robbed, having no pathway through to the man she loved. He had undoubtedly cared for her and Jane. An image of him playing with her hair, patting her on the shoulder; those eyes, serene, caring. Then, almost immediately, she remembered Jane's remark that he had left Eleanor knowing she was ill. When he returned, she was dead. Lydia had closed her eyes to this idea, preferring to believe her stepmother was jealous. One night, though, she had come across him at his desk in his study. Looking sharply at her, his eyes had hardened. She thought she had done some wrong. Just as suddenly, his expression softened. She had run to him, placing her hand on his cheek. What had he been thinking about? How many times had others seen such an expression?

For the rest of the day, Lydia read about a man who was far more delusional and conceited than she had ever understood him to be. Transportation had been a simple but ill-thought solution to the overcrowding of prisoners in the old country. After a Select Committee's inquiry, and following a public outcry, it was seen by some as akin to slavery. Her father appointed himself to oversee all sort of travesties far away from the prying eyes of the abolitionists.

His experiments involved prisons where inmates were mentally tortured, accused men were dissected after death and convicts were seen as dispensable – guinea pigs in the name of science. All this was supposed to reinstate a moral conscience into the mind of criminals. His thinking saw individuals as an obstacle to be removed or sacrificed for some haphazard scheme of purification.

After some time sitting at the desk in the archives, staring blankly in front of her, Lydia made her inquiry. The librarian confirmed that the Black Books were kept in the archives. He needed assistance carrying them to the table. He dispensed orders to an assistant to dust down the worn leather covers, creased through use.

Lydia turned the large pages slowly, her eyes running down the columns, holding her breath at the calculation of it all. Inside were the physical descriptions – including tattoos – sentence, details of transportation and assignment, jail and surgeon's reports, punishment and conduct records.

In the margin was her father's handwriting.

I believe crime is a sickness. The mob will run out of control. Look what happened in France when the king was executed. At all costs, we must keep them under control.

Lydia pushed her knuckles into her eyes, suddenly weary. The image of her father signing convicts' petitions swam before her. Or was it death warrants? Jane had once accused him of being a fundamentalist, she remembered, but Lydia had been too young to understand what it meant. Her father was always citing God's words. She had not known, however, that he had seen himself as God's appointee, in control of his brethren to correct 'the contamination of the criminal classes'. By classifying men, he could control them. She said the words out loud to herself: 'My father was responsible for suffering.' Had she submerged this knowledge all along? She tried to retrieve memories that would reassure her. His laugh, a vision of him patting the long neck of the emu as he leant over the picket fence. His concern for her. He had always managed to convince her she was important to him.

You are always in my thoughts and always in my heart, he had written once when she was in her early teens, leaving the words on a folded sheet on her pillow. She had kept them until the paper on which they were written had disintegrated.

She walked down to Salamanca Place and the warehouses along the foreshore. The weather matched her mood, unsettled, turbulent – spring weather, warm bursts of sunshine and gusts of wind that whipped up sheets of spray on the Derwent. The gum trees, growing near the river's edge, were angry black silhouettes against a dark sky.

Salamanca Place was no place for a lady but Lydia had walked almost to the Sailors' Rest before she was even conscious of her surroundings. As she approached the public house, she turned quickly in the opposite direction and walked towards the jetty on the new wharf. Looking out to sea, she remembered the time when she was nearly sixteen and she'd partnered her father at a ball on board the *Erebus* after Captain Ross and Crozier had visited on their journey to the Antarctic, shortly before the opening of the observatory. Mirrors hanging around the sides of the ship reflected the lights onshore. She had walked on her father's arm, taking care not to slip in her new satin slippers on the makeshift bridge covered in boughs and flags.

She had danced with Captain Ross until five o'clock in the morning. Then some of the young officers had asked her to breakfast with them. One brought her albatross eggs and specimens of granite from the east coast of the island and told her that her hair was the colour of a raven. Lydia felt a quiet aching for what might have been. It began like a persistent pain in her chest until it oppressed her. That was the last time she had appeared in public unscarred.

She walked back up to town, through the bustle of the crowds in the fishmarkets. At the first intersection, she found St David's Cathedral. After narrowly avoiding the carts, men on horseback and carriages, she arrived at the door of the sandstone church. It was empty. She knelt at the pew in front of the carved wooden pulpit, praying silently. But, instead of finding peace, she was thinking of the house in Russell Square where she had lived for so many years protected from all of this. Oil-painted faces of the Eskimos came to her, the Arctic paintings, the shoes her father had brought back which had sat on her mantelpiece for all these years. The reindeer tongues he had given to Jane. Those marble lips that had sent her on this mission. Her mother had died while he had sought to become a hero.

CHAPTER EIGHT

In Hobart Town, Lydia was touched by ghostly presences. They entered her dreams, competing for attention, offering disturbing images: knife wounds, headless torsos and shapes with fish-like eyes at the side of their face. She was sucked into a vortex of words that competed with the life that existed around her: the clacking of the wooden wheels of the coaches on the gravel outside her lodgings' window, the insistent clinking of the workers' tools across the road, improving the convict-built tunnel sewers. She had a choice of standing on the edge or teetering on the brink, not wanting to freefall into a world she did not know. The dead were arrayed before her at a dining table while she stood at the door waiting to be seated. If it were not for the discovery of that letter, she could have followed Jane to the grave, unaware of her father's conviction of his moral right to treat men like beasts. Lydia was still unsure of Jane's position on all this: the new bride, accompanying her husband on the *Fairlie*. She had shown sympathy for Henry and had expressed abhorrence at some of the practices she had found in the prison colony. Perhaps that was why she had been drawn to Lemprière? Perhaps she had also discovered a different man to the person she believed she had married. But she had sent so many ships to find Sir John when he disappeared. There was a multitude of unanswered questions.

Lydia no longer wanted to read about her father. The spring weather was gusty, blossoms from the cherry tree sprinkled the lawn like confetti. Wellard's papers lay untouched in the box, forbidden fruit. But rather than read more about Henry and the boys of Point Puer, Lydia felt compelled to find out what Jane knew about her husband's methods of punishment.

Ross had told her that some of her stepmother's papers were here in Hobart Town, probably as part of the collection of the Royal Society of Tasmania, which was housed among the museum collection since much of its material was on natural history. That morning she engaged a chaise to take her to this museum in Argyle Street. It stood on reclaimed land below the site of the old Government House, a new building with a plaque inside the entrance that gave its potted history. The Royal Society's rooms were further proof of her father's legacy. She noticed his name and Jane's, too, on the plaque. Public donations, Lydia read, had led to the rehousing of the natural history collection to this site only a few months before. She entered through some heavy swing doors. Inside were four rooms, surprisingly ill-lit and full of old taxidermy: a Tasmanian devil like the one at Russell Square, two platypuses, a kangaroo rat. In the library the walls were lined with books.

The curator glared at her. He had pursed lips and thick greying hair swept back from his face. Lydia faltered in her request and he stood looking at her.

'My father was Sir John Frankland . . .'

Since being manipulated by Wellard, she had found reserves of strength. Why not use her father's name to assist her in her quest? The announcement brought a marked change in the man's demeanour. Lydia felt herself grow stronger.

'I had no idea . . .' He smiled, bowing his head slightly.

'No, of course,' she replied, forcing a smile. 'Perhaps I should introduce myself more fully. My name is Lydia Frankland. Both my parents – my father and Lady Frankland – were keen Society members. Indeed, I believe it was due to them that the Society was formed, or so it says on your information in the hallway.'

'Yes.'

'I am looking for my stepmother's papers, and I believe that some are housed here.'

His tone was at once conciliatory. 'Miss Frankland, there is some loose correspondence from Lady Frankland at the museum. Personal and private papers that were part of a bequest.'

Lydia wondered whether he would have told her had she not been so forceful. She was learning that these librarians and curators seemed to mete out knowledge at their own discretion.

The curator now sounded apologetic. 'Lady Frankland's letters and papers are all in order.'

'Thank you. I would like to see them,' she said.

'A matter of identification . . .' he mumbled.

'Certainly.'

Lydia produced her passport out of a leather pouch and he glanced at it briefly.

Inside the files he brought were newspapers clippings and pages of letters Jane had sent to the *Van Diemen's Land*

Chronicle. She was unprepared for further revelations. They were documents relating to her father's dismissal. In 1843 he had been unceremoniously dumped as governor by the British government and she had had no idea. The newspaper editorials were also scathing about her stepmother; how she had meddled with the governing of the colony.

Jane herself had written about her views on the convicts at the Female Factory; advice on their punishment of picking oakum; advice on what to do with all their unwanted offspring. And much about how to improve mortality rates in the dank, dark valley in the foothills of Mount Wellington where they had built the Female Factory. The Orphan School where Mathinna had been sent after they left the colony was overflowing even though, Jane bemoaned, there were never any worthwhile servants to choose when the girls came of age. Lydia soon tired of reading her stepmother's opinionated outbursts.

She found some torn pages in Jane's handwriting, folded several times, their sides ripped as though hastily torn from a book. They were undated.

He was speaking of the paper nautilus, a genus of the Argonaut washed up on these shores and found in the Bass Strait Islands off the north coast of the colony. Caught up in the stories, he thumbed through books and papers. I watched him push his hair away from his forehead then turn to a blank sheet of paper set up on an easel near his collection. The mollusc floated in a tumbler full of water, sunlight dancing through the glass like so many fractured rays. He told me he would attempt to draw it in sepia and that sepia was from the black fluid of cuttlefish. I watched as he used the brush to size his subject. Sepia was the colour I thought of when I first noticed his eyes. He seemed oblivious to my presence.

I chatted about his work. He told that he had recently painted the first swallows of the season. Their beauty, he said, made him forget the purpose of him being here. We were fortunate to be visitors in this part of the world, he said. We chatted about the birdlife, the wedge-tailed eagles and the native hens and the black swan. Then he showed me a platypus he had had stuffed by a taxidermist in Wapping. Like me, he is unsure whether the creature is a reptile or a mammal, and we talked off how, in the old country, they still believed it was a scientific hoax.

He is a well-read man. He knows John Gould and he was most interested to find that Mr Gould and Elizabeth are living here in the colony while Gould completes his synopsis on the birds of Australia.

I told him he would be a valuable contributor to our new society and I urged him to come to dinner. He told me he did not think Captain Hawkins would see fit for him to visit Hobart Town because of his increased responsibilities as convict chaplain, but I told him I would organise it.

Then he suggested a walk on the beach to the forest at Stewart's Bay, where he said the heath flower was in abundance, so he could show me some of these creatures. I must confess I experienced a strange thrill at the unorthodox nature of his proposal. My maid had taken to her bed with illness, which he could not have known. Perhaps he was expecting we would be chaperoned or indeed accompanied by Sir John. But I knew my husband would be occupied with the convicts' petitions in the afternoon.

Outside the large window I saw the sun valiantly struggling behind the clouds and then a shaft of light cutting through the dark sky and the black ocean, bathing the Isle of the Dead in golden light. I shivered, thinking of the dead souls I visited this morning. The wind buffeted the wooden building.

He asked me if I was cold and I told him I wasn't and that the light reminded me of Tuscany. I said it was as though the Lord was casting light He had created for us to feast upon.

Before we left he had one more surprise. Reminding me of a magician conjuring up his best trick, he pursed his lips and whistled. From high up in the rafters a silent shape flew past and fanned my cheek with an almost imperceptible whoosh of its wings. It was a bird, the colour of dark brown earth. It landed on his arm and had a peculiar, primeval face. He told me he had found it in the church one evening with a broken wing. I thought it looked like an owl but he said it was a southern boobook and that its beautiful falsetto voice was often heard at dusk. He said it hooted continuously much like our cuckoo. As he was talking, the bird blinked and he described how its membrane closed over its eyes.

He has other injured raptors at his house: a white goshawk, *Accipiter novaehollandiae*, which he'd raised from a chick and up until recently, a young wedge-tailed eagle.

I felt curiously elated. I had been struggling for some time with a sense of oppression, a darkness I could not fix upon, problems with no solutions. But it was hard not to be captivated by his enthusiasm. I asked him when the walk might be and he replied if the weather held we would go after lunch.

The blue-lined paper on which the words were written was at once familiar. Jane had torn these pages from her diary and tried to hide them. There was no other explanation. Perhaps she had worried that they were incriminating, but had forgotten to destroy them? Other than the letter inside the platypus cage, they were the only proof Lydia had found of the interest her stepmother had in the storekeeper. They had walked together unchaperoned in a forest. It was the day her stepmother had fallen in love – Jane had said so in the letter she wrote to him from Transylvania. Lydia, weighed down with the preoccupations of any adolescent, had been oblivious to other people's affairs around her. Even if there had been a change in Jane's demeanour, she probably would not have noticed. What had happened in the forest? She imagined her stepmother in uncharted waters, for once unable to manipulate an outcome.

Lydia flicked through some more correspondence but her mind was no longer on the governing of the colony, nor even her father's governance.

'Yes, I believe we do have some of Monsieur Lemprière's papers,' the curator said an hour later when she inquired at the desk. 'But I cannot allow you to see them without the permission of his wife.'

Lydia was surprised. So Charlotte was still alive.

'His wife?'

'Yes, Madam, his wife. Mrs Lemprière has kindly donated his written words to our museum because of her husband's scientific contributions to our small society. They are, however, rarely consulted by the members of the Royal Society . . .'

Lydia thought that he had probably never consulted any of the works himself.

'May I suggest you approach Mrs Lemprière. She lives in Bellerive, across the water on the *Kangaroo* ferry. You could explain your interest . . . your parents' interest in the Royal Society. Well, they were the founders, weren't they?'

Back at the guest house, Lydia composed a short note to Charlotte, unsure whether this was the right course of action; but that afternoon, to her surprise, Charlotte replied, agreeing to her request for a meeting.

The following day Lydia caught the ferry to the opposite side of the river. The heavens opened as she disembarked and contemplated the steep hill up to the house. There were no coaches in sight.

On this side of the river, the houses were more makeshift and the footpaths crude, more like the old Hobart Town she remembered. She had no choice but to walk under a parasol, and she arrived outside Charlotte's small cottage on the bluff with her skirts dripping wet, still unresolved as to how to tackle this meeting. What was she going to say to this woman? On the tiny red ferry called *Kangaroo* that plied the river she had rehearsed the words, thinking of every conceivable falsehood. But all she could think of were Jane's words in the diary: *Charlotte Lemprière is dark like a Creole*. They ran like a mantra inside her head.

The house was modest with a shingle roof. It had a neat garden, if a little bedraggled with the sudden change of weather. Roses bloomed along the path – noisettes, Lydia's favourite.

When she knocked at the door a large-boned woman with teeth like a row of piano keys answered, holding the door against the buffeting wind, peering at her.

Lydia followed the woman down a narrow hallway into a parlour. Charlotte was sitting beside a cosy fire, in semi-darkness. It took some time for Lydia's eyes to adjust to the gloom. Charlotte's hair was grey now, but still neat. Her eyes were large and they stared at Lydia the same way she was sure they had once stared at her stepmother. Charlotte did not rise to greet her, but simply bowed her head. The housekeeper motioned Lydia to sit on a small sofa.

She could see at once that Charlotte had been attractive. She was petite, like a Spanish bride. Her small hands lay still in her lap on some needlework. She was dressed in an alabaster silk dress with a high cream collar and small pearl buttons at the front of the bodice. The garment looked well worn. Her silence and fixed gaze unnerved Lydia, who looked around the room, patting her damp hair and trying not to appear rude. On the walls were paintings. Lydia recognised Port Arthur – the penal settlement, the spire of the church, the penitentiary she had visited weeks before. She recognised some of the portraiture – the odd way Lemprière had of capturing his sitter, deftly painted but strangely discordant, with the head of his subjects appearing to float above their torsos.

'I have just come from there.' She nodded towards one of the scenes of the penal settlement.

Her words, voiced in this parlour full of memories, seemed false and small.

She thought of the words Jane had written so long ago: *Like a Madonna with child . . .*

'You are Lady Frankland's daughter?'

Jane had been jealous of this woman. Perhaps in the same way, Lydia suddenly realised, Jane had been jealous of her – the daughter she would never have, her own flesh and blood.

'Stepdaughter, Madame Lemprière. My mother died when I was an infant.'

Silence. Lydia was regretting she had come. What could she say? What right did she have to Charlotte's dead husband's words?

'What brings you here?'

'I . . .'

All the imaginary conversations Lydia had rehearsed as she walked through the rain vanished. On the wall behind Charlotte, she noticed for the first time a detailed painting of a kangaroo rat, its eyes luminous, the fur softened in a shaft of light. It was almost identical to the one she had found in her stepmother's wardrobe. She noticed Charlotte watching her. She had not answered the question.

'Your husband was a collector?' she asked.

'So was your stepmother.'

In that instant, Lydia knew that the other woman knew. She had been granted an interview for the same reason Lydia wanted to meet her. Curiosity. Somehow, the discovery made her task a little easier.

'How did he . . . ?'

'He died, in Aden, of a fever, suddenly.'

'I must . . . express my condolences. How long ago?'

'Too long ago.'

'My stepmother mentioned Monsieur Lemprière in her letters.'

Charlotte's large eyes never left hers.

'And? I cannot see where this is leading.'

'There was a murder involving two boys at the settlement,' Lydia said suddenly, not sure why.

Some emotion flickered across Charlotte's face and was gone again as quickly as it had come.

'*Pauvres garçons.* There were many murders. No one knew the truth except Louis.'

Again, Lydia was sure Charlotte knew more, but she was unsure of what to ask. Distrust settled between them. After a pause Charlotte asked her: 'And what business is it of yours?'

Henry's face, the sense of him, came before her. She blushed.

'None. None at all.' Yet it had everything to do with her. 'There was so much I did not know . . . I was a child.'

'And you think my husband's papers will tell you more, Miss Frankland? It is Miss, I presume?'

'Yes.' Lydia remained composed but she bristled at Charlotte's tone.

'Your stepmother thought children could be collected and then discarded, did she not? That Aboriginal girl, Mathinna, whom she paraded around town. A sorry predicament for a child to be taken away from her real mother and father. I remember reading a newspaper report quoting your stepmother as saying Mathinna was becoming lighter, more copper-coloured, because she had spent so much time in civilisation. What sort of comment is that? Mathinna died, you know, drank herself to death. Not that Lady Frankland probably ever knew. She never had children of her own, did she?'

Lydia felt a sharp stab of pain. In all her imagining about Mathinna, it had never occurred to her that she might be dead. Tears sprang to her eyes mingled with anger at Charlotte's words. They had deserted Mathinna. Jane had deserted her.

Charlotte's next question seemed softer.

'You did not know? How old were you when Lady Frankland began managing your affairs?'

'I was twelve, just before we came out to Van Diemen's Land.'

'Can you remember your real mother?'

Lydia was now the one being interrogated. Questions probing, opening wounds. If Eleanor had lived she would have been loved in the way she had never been loved. She would not have been treated as an unwanted being as Jane treated her. Mathinna had no mother, and what sort of friend had Lydia really been to her? Had she insisted they take Mathinna to England, or had she ignored what her plight might be in an overcrowded orphanage, having been plucked from her family? Lydia fumbled for her handkerchief and rose from the sofa.

'You are quite right, Madam Lemprière.' Her voice was small, choked with emotion. 'I have no right to intrude.'

She pulled her cloak around her and walked towards the door, bumping into the arm of the sofa, in her haste to escape. She had reached the small door to the hallway when Charlotte spoke again.

'I see no harm in you reading those diaries. They were to be made available to the public after my death. He would have wanted it that way. Indeed, he asked that they be left here in Hobart Town among his scientific papers. I was not ready yet for them to be perused, but soon I will be gone so why should I care? They will be of no use to me then.' She laughed bitterly. 'I will dispatch a note to the librarian.'

Lydia forced a smile of thanks. She did not trust herself to speak. The housekeeper appeared silently at the doorway to usher her out. Outside the parlour they walked down the hallway past more framed paintings and a seaweed collection: large leathery arms of kelp like those she remembered seeing in the water off the boys' prison. At the end of the hallway was a large oil painting of a man. A self-portrait. As she approached, his eyes seemed to be upon her. She was sure it was him, yet could not bring herself to ask the servant.

She willed his image to her memory. Jane had described his eyes as sepia. Lydia thought they were more like the colour of a running brook. Friendly, generous eyes, with crow's feet emphasised by the smile; a small nose, side-whiskers, and a forelock of greying dark hair. All of this she took in, but it was the absurd air of welcome emanating from the painting, the warm sense of the man – his humanity – that was unexpected.

She had thought she would resent him. She was conscious of her stays, compressing her lungs, fastened too tight for her emotional state as she stared at the painting. In spite of the brooding presence of the woman behind her, she paused at the door. No matter how she tried, she could not picture Jane with such a man.

Standing by the white gate outside the cottage next to the roses dripping with rain, she gulped fresh cold air. The colony was awash with rain. In spite of her emotional state, Lydia was convinced she had confirmed some sort of truth. She had been treated with disdain because Charlotte knew something. What had she meant when she said there would be no harm looking at 'those' diaries, as though there were more that she wouldn't be allowed to see?

She began her hasty descent back to the ferry beneath darker gathering storm clouds. Looking back, she was sure she saw the curtains in the small cottage moving.

CHAPTER NINE

Each evening, Lydia would deliberately leave the heavy velvet curtains in her room open so she would awaken to the sun's rays. She would eat an early breakfast of fresh damper, Irish butter and tea. Anna, the owner of the guest house, was a plump middle-aged lady with scroll-like plaits that reminded Lydia of the apple strudels in her favourite continental pâtisserie back in London. Anna had emigrated as a free settler in search of land, but her husband had died shortly after they arrived in the colony. 'I must eat,' she had said to Lydia in her guttural German accent, 'so I must work.'

She showed little interest in Lydia's pursuits, fussing over her without trespassing on her space, for which Lydia was grateful. Sometimes Lydia would return for lunch, especially if the weather was good, and she always felt welcome.

Two days after seeing Charlotte, Lydia went back to the museum. The curator had obviously received Charlotte's note since, at her request, he delivered Lemprière's files without a word. Strange, she thought, how the writings of her step-mother and this man had been kept side by side in the museum long after they were dead, their individual legacies left here for posterity.

Lydia sat at the back of the museum library, well out of the way of other visitors. To begin with she found it difficult to decipher Lemprière's handwriting, but soon the letters became familiar. She immediately noticed the difference between the words of this dilettante, who had died in anonymity in spite of his dedication to natural history, and her father's official bureaucratese prose. It occurred to her that he had been a servant of her father's. Ross had mentioned that Lemprière was too well qualified for his role as storekeeper, but having been left destitute he had no other choice but to seek such work.

Lemprière's first entry was more like official prose:

Deputy-assistant commissariat general to the forces and a magistrate for the territory of Van Diemen's Land, Louis Lemprière humbly craves for his work the indulgence in general kindly afforded to an author's first essay.

From then on, however, his writing became more personal. Lydia began looking for any reference to her stepmother.

30th November, 1836

I don't like leaving Charlotte and the children for a trip to Hobart Town. I always fret about them when I am away. Charlotte needs someone to care for her. Am I strong enough to do so? She is with child again. At least I have provided her with a home, even though it is cramped with our children. Each evening I ensure they listen to a reading of the Scriptures. If I'm unsure of an answer to something, I find it in between the well-thumbed pages of the book I have brought with me from Guernsey. When my mother died, my father stopped going to church. He stopped believing in God. Perhaps that was why he took his own life.

I have been sketching the Lemprière coat of arms as a transparency: the two symmetrical knights in resplendent steel, their masks pushed skyward revealing waxed-stiffened moustaches. The knight in the centre is holding our coat of arms. Each haystack, each lion, each cross and blackbird has to be painstakingly recreated. *'Timor Dei Nobilitas'*. I have copied the family motto on the flurry of ribbons at the bottom of the sketch, although I'm still not pleased with it. The colours aren't good enough and the knight's expression too sweet.

I have grown up with a belief I am capable of grand things, that life holds a secret in store for me that will commit me to the same history books as my forebears. From when I was a small boy my father, the merchant banker, told me tales of our richly embroidered past.

John de Lemprière was one of the barons of the third Crusade under Richard the Lionheart in 1191. Lemprière came from 'emperor' from the house of L'Empereur de Morfontaine of the provinces of Champagne and Brie. My father recited these connections often enough.

The storekeeper was descended from noble men who had lived for centuries serving royalty. He had been transported across the seas to such an ordinary occupation. This was not what Lydia had expected to find at all. When he was not writing about his past, Lemprière wrote about the world around him and his family: he had made a trip with his son Edward to Eaglehawk Neck, the small isthmus that linked the rest of Tasmania to Port Arthur.

15th December, 1836

We took four hours to reach Norfolk Bay, arriving at the flats about nine o'clock. Long-legged tidal birds stabbed like seamstresses on the ribbed sand. As we approached the small township, the sea spray merged with the sky. The gusts of wind and vista conspired to take my breath away as they always do. Pirates Bay. Turquoise, white-crested waves, alabaster sand. Magnifique. Such a beach could never even be imagined in Guernsey, where the air is stale and the skies are dull, deadening one's sensibilities.

Lemprière had shown Edward 'the slobbering beasts', eleven mastiff dogs that patrolled the isthmus to stop convicts from escaping. And he described Edward's antics, scampering across driftwood, running full pelt at a group of sooty oyster-catchers. 'In a year or two, he'll be a man.'

They had searched for rocks with pieces of quartz and the fossil remains of gorgonia shells. Lemprière had named one the butterfly shell.

Lydia could not help comparing their relationship to the one she had had with her own father. She and Sir John had never shared this sort of adventure. Palaeontology would have been a new science back then. Edward must have learnt so much from his father's wisdom.

4th February, 1837

This afternoon, I went down to Safety Cove to fossick. I was reciting one of my favourite verses when my prayers were answered. I bent down to view more closely the rock my spade struck, curious at the pale colour and strange markings. Grasping my pick, I coaxed a piece out of the earth and chipped back the igneous rock until I uncovered the wood I could see buried inside. Silicified wood, the colour of agate, fossilised remains of what looks like a species of beech; a relic of ancient times here at the other end of the world. I have read about the forces of wind, rain and frost, the erosion and sedimentation that worked on the Earth's ever-changing surface in Charles Lyell's volume of *The Principles of Geology*. What mysteries life holds. If the Earth is indeed that old, how trivial is life; how meaningless our lives are.

I am troubled, only a little, by what Lyell states – that our planet is aeons old. Most believe the Earth is not that old: I have read the landing of Noah's ark on Ararat was supposed to be 4,179 years ago. The Scriptures tell of this one catastrophe: the flood that Noah escaped. Yet Lyell seems to suggest there was much more; that there were many floods, perhaps separated by thousands of centuries. A fresh creation might have followed each although Genesis tells of only one flood.

I returned to my digging with renewed vigour. The Lord will always produce questions. I am on this Earth for a purpose, as God's servant.

17th February

I watched Doctor Casey amputate a convict's arm yesterday. I wanted to learn how to wield the knife with the minimum of disruption so I can learn the art of taxidermy. But this poor man was alive. Apart from a swig of whisky and the fact that he passed out, he had no means of escape. Hawkins was in the front row. Everyone clapped politely as though they were at the theatre. It seems we have forgotten that these are men, not performing animals.

Lydia became engrossed in Lemprière's intimate observations on family life: how he planned to bring Charlotte 'an elegant bonnet' as a gift from Hobart Town, or a pair of kid boots; his unashamed love for her; his love for his children; his favourite book, Bishop William Paley's *A View of the Evidences of Christianity*, in which he suggested that God exists as an intelligent designer of all things.

She soaked up his words, convinced he would not be the sort of man to have been tempted to risk his marriage for an affair with any woman, especially not her stepmother. He wrote of the mundane: faulty scales, an argument about missing flour bags and eternal correspondence about weevils in the rice. Beneath these pedestrian concerns was a compassion for life, for the men to whom he doled out rations, providing succour to their stomachs as well as their souls.

The word 'murder' in the midst of these deliberations ambushed her senses. Lemprière had been describing another journey to Hobart Town in late February 1837 to fetch further supplies of formaldehyde. After reaching Eaglehawk Neck, a constable had ridden up on horseback, ordering him to return to the settlement. Hawkins needed his assistance: there had been a murder involving two convicts who were digging the foundations in the church. Lydia remembered then that Jane had mentioned this tragedy. Lemprière was deeply troubled that it had happened in a place of worship, the church he had helped to design. He had returned straightaway. The victim had lived long enough to name his attacker. There were witnesses. Lydia found no other reference to the murder at the church, except a passing oblique note about the killer's confession.

I try to serve God as I know I must as His appointed servant. It is my duty to remain silent in this task, to speak of their confessions to no one, not even Charlotte. I take solace, instead, from my collection at the museum.

Charlotte had told her that only Louis knew the truth of what had happened at the settlement involving the murders. Wellard, too, had said that Lemprière as convict chaplain knew much of what went on in the prisoners' hearts. Then, further on in the diary, when her mind was occupied with the murders, she found the entry she had been searching for. The word Frankland jumped out at her. The entry was dated 15th March, 1837, around the time of their journey to Port Arthur.

Perhaps one day my sketch of the settlement will hang in more elaborate hallways than my humble abode. Charlotte thought Lady Frankland's interest might lead to further recognition of my talents. She and the governor have been visiting during the past few days with their daughter. Charlotte thought it chivalrous that I lent Lady Frankland my cloak in the forest. Why, then, did I not mention the other encounter I had with her Ladyship – in the storeroom? She asked me what it felt like to be handcuffed. Why did I even agree to such a thing? And what embarrassment, being caught by her husband and Captain Hawkins. She seems to exude a certain mischievous innocence, paradoxical with her persona as a poised woman of society.

There was nothing in what he had written that referred to anything improper between him and her stepmother, but the episode in the storeroom struck Lydia as odd, though knowing Jane, she could imagine her engineering such an incident.

There followed pages of detailed entries about Lemprière's discoveries in the museum and his dissections. Lydia was struck by the contradictions he grappled with. His obsession with Paley meant he believed that God had created the Earth and the animals upon it. Yet Lydia saw that he would often make observations about a particular species without realising how close he was to discovering that some characteristics surely could not be explained as God's creations.

28th April

This morning I dissected a small kangaroo rat shot by the good Doctor Casey on one of his hunting expeditions. Before dissection I set up my canvas and painted it. The tiny creature has hind legs like a kangaroo but the face of a rat, with a longish snout, short ears and a long tail with a white tip. It only weighed four and a half pounds. I laid it carefully on its back and examined it. I was surprised to find a young one inside its pouch. The sun shone on its coarse brown-grey fur – surprisingly soft – so I had a good view inside the pouch.

I have spent hours pondering the question of the pouch. Is that why the young are born so prematurely – because the pouch is a perambulator, a portable nest, and a place to carry them rather than leaving them in the burrow? Why have animals across the other side of the world not got a pouch? Perhaps it has been designed to help animals here to cope with the long periods of drought on this continent? I marvel, again, at God's prowess in design, God, who creates all things, who has an answer for everything.

I carefully removed the baby, cradling it in the palm of my hand. Its eyes were closed, only its lower lip was formed and its mouth was open. It had no hair at all. It must have been new indeed, but without succour from its mother, it had died.

I searched for my surgical instruments: a fine scalpel, tweezers and some strong antiseptic. I began work on the mother's stomach and intestines.

I know now more about the physiology of the kangaroo rat's nervous system, as well as its respiration. It reminds me of some of the cold-blooded animals I have dissected. I have read, now I come to think of it, that young marsupials can live even after being immersed in spirits for a day.

When I heard the bell for the lunchtime muster I cleaned my bloodied scalpel on a piece of rag and covered the morning's work with a sheet. My poor wife secretly hopes this is a passing phase. When she first discovered a partially skinned black cockatoo in the kitchen sink she could not look at me. And the entrails of a wombat on the kitchen table . . . She did not even ask to which creature they belonged. My obsession with these dissections of animals, is, I know, repugnant to her. She would prefer I used a sable brush and dabble in paints instead of a knife to dissect. She does not understand my interest. The make-up of living creatures for some reason fascinates me.

Lemprière was clearly unfazed by the dissection. Perhaps his passion for hunting, of which he had also written, meant that he could look upon such a pursuit dispassionately. Besides, he was in pursuit of science and had a thirst for knowledge. She sympathised with Charlotte as Lydia had never quite become accustomed to Jane's obsession with dissection. She remembered the five-course Tasmanian Society dinner Jane had held when one of the first microscopes was brought into the colony. Had Lemprière been present? An experiment had been conducted after dessert to compare the cells from a blue-tongued lizard with blood from a platypus. Afterwards, Lydia had watched her father stroke the quiet marsupial's smooth fur, then release the animal into the creek that ran into the Derwent, where the water was rusty from the tannery upriver. She had been convinced the animal would die. Jane took such clinical detachment in her stride and Lydia could see what Lemprière and her stepmother would have in common: a sense of discovery as scientists, as collectors, as amateur taxidermists probing the unknown; ideas foreign to both their spouses.

Lydia read on, imagining the games of backgammon at Hawkins' house which Lemprière had described. She recognised many of the buildings he wrote of at Port Arthur. She read of the children's French lessons in the old schoolroom; his visits to Point Puer. He was obviously fond of the boys. He knew their routine as well as he knew his own children's: how they would rise at five o'clock, roll up and stow away their hammocks, assemble for a reading of the Scriptures and then be inspected for personal cleanliness. Breakfast, he wrote, consisted of ten ounces of bread and one pint of gruel made from two ounces of flour.

1st May

I have begun a self-portrait. My right hand looks stiff and awkward, but I'm pleased with my expression. Charlotte tells me it is a good likeness, though the paint is hardly dry.

She thought of the painting in Charlotte's cottage. Lemprière had a vanity that was more endearing than offensive. She read the next sentence and paused. He had written that he was pleased Hawkins had not been available to sit for his portrait as he did not want to risk being interrogated. Interrogated about what? Lydia wondered. Further down the page, she found the answer.

Hawkins is convinced these men are performing unnatural acts with each other. I've told him I have discovered nothing from the men's confessions, but he seems not to believe me.

12th May

Another murder and still none of them explained. It is my job to speak to those who face their maker. How can I stand back and let these killings continue? How could they believe God would condone such acts? I have vowed to serve the Lord all my days, to uphold His assertions and to never again transgress His word. I cannot, however, reveal to anyone what these men have told me.

Lydia looked out of the museum window. Outside it was windy. The gutters were filled with leaflets left by pamphleteers who had been addressing crowds outside the Town Hall. She saw people scurrying about their business and longed momentarily to be one of them; to be lost in a mundane routine, not confronting such unsavoury words. What had these men told Lemprière? Whatever it was, it seemed to trouble his domestic harmony.

28th May

This afternoon, I fell asleep at my desk inside the museum. I had the same dream again. I could smell heather and the chill from the ponds on the moors; salty. The world was full of shapes and, later, shadows of light and dark, such as when I was a child stricken down by blindness from the pox and lighting a candle did not lighten the darkness.

I will always associate the feeling of warm saline water with regaining my sight again: opening my eyes carefully, the water at the Scarborough spa rushing to reach them, my father's voice – this time he has not abandoned me. After a few bathings the world returned to me in grey shapes and I knew what I saw was not imagined but real shadows; that between the grey were discernible images. God had given me back my sight.

When I awoke I lit an oil lamp and set it up on the large table in the centre of the room. The devil, tiger cat, black cockatoo and kangaroo rat smile from their glass cages. I wrote up some more of my findings from the kangaroo rat dissection, but I had not the heart to finish it. When I returned I found a bowl of cold mutton stew on the stove. Charlotte was already in bed. A dark tendril of hair lies across her cheek. She trusts me so completely.

25th August

This morning I rose early after an uneventful night, dressed quietly and closed the front door behind me. Charlotte and the children were still asleep. The sun had not risen above the large gums at the entrance to the bay. The sky was laundered clean and the bay sparkled again after the violence of the storm two days before. As I opened the heavy wooden door that leads to the outside world, the wind caught at the papers I carried and blew them hither and thither. I scurried after the sheets. At any other time it might have been comical, but I was seized with desperation. My efforts to come to grips with this place are in vain. I feel worthless and unworthy.

I pulled out a set of keys from my pocket and let myself into the side door of the museum, expecting to find my collection shattered on the floor, the same fate that once confronted Cuvier. It would demonstrate God's wrath for the blasphemous thoughts that plague me. But everything was as I left it. Then there was a loud knocking at the door. A young clerk stood on the doorstep, wide-eyed and staring. He said there had been another murder and that I must come at once.

9th December

Late this afternoon I decided to stroll across to Safety Cove. I reached the beach and crossed to the high-tide mark, then climbed the embankment, throwing my spade up first and clinging to a grass tree before hauling myself up. I scraped my shin on a rock and felt a small trickle of blood run down my leg inside my trousers.

I began to dig again, my spade striking rock underneath clay. How many more will die? These thoughts tear at my conscience. I raise my eyes to heaven.

Jesus, Saviour, pilot me
Over life's tempestuous sea.

Lydia felt the agony from the words on the page. He would not commit himself to paper — as God's servant he was sworn to secrecy. Then there was the matter of his dissections, his increasing unease about his questioning of God. She felt strangely comforted that he too grappled with life's trials, recognising in him her own vulnerability and insecurities.

'Has Madame Lemprière read all of these diaries?' Lydia asked the question innocently enough, but the blank expression of the curator confirmed that it was an inappropriate one.

'It was Madame Lemprière, of course, who supplied the diaries to the archives in the first place, but she said she had no wish to read them herself. That is her prerogative.'

Lydia returned to her desk. Her eyes were drawn from where she had stopped reading to the paragraph at the top of the next page and she was reminded of Arthur Conan Doyle's wolfish books:

I saw the bloodied towel under the victim's leather cap. Could I have prevented more murders from being committed?

She put down the diary and stared at the desk in front of her. A series of murders cropped up in all the diaries. Charlotte had said only that her husband knew the truth. Henry had been convicted of murder. What was the truth?

CHAPTER TEN

The box she'd bought from Snakey Wellard was wooden, scuffed with age, with stiff brass clasps. Lydia spent almost half an hour patiently coaxing it open, determined now to read its contents. Inside, she found bundles of loose-leafed pages, some with drawings – childlike renditions of the boys' prison, the wooden fence with the sharpened edges, the barracks where the boys slept and some sketches of solitary cells. There were official documents, too. She recognised one signature immediately: Charles O'Mara Hawkins.

She sorted the bundles into personal and official and began with what looked like diaries. Again, they were loose pages, none of them numbered, and there were two school exercise books. She compared the writing in those books with the letter she had read from the prisoner on his way to the gallows. It was the same. Lydia began to read with trepidation, unsure how close she wanted to come to any kind of truth about Henry Belfield.

September, 1841

We were playing a game of marbles. Thomas was spinning a marble across the ground when I heard boots contact bone and skin, then the scream; Bundock's heavy leather boots had crushed his fingers. The other boys were watching. Boardman, he said quietly, had pretty golden curls but it was a shame about his soft white hands and how they'd got all dirty. Then he grabbed Thomas's hand and thrust his own fat finger in it, wiggling it slowly. No one said anything. I knew he was doing it for my benefit.

He was crooning to Thomas and began to stroke his hand. Looking at me, he told him he would strip him off to make sure he was clean. His fleshy head with its bulbous nose was so close to Thomas; those wet lips and his tongue like one of those giant lizards that crawl around the rocks.

He always starts with harassment. Then he uses the conduct record: disobedience of orders; then solitary confinement. After that, he takes the boys away. But this boy was mine. He grabbed Thomas by the shirt, patted his cheek as a mother to her child, then he slapped him hard across the face. Thomas was sobbing now. Bundock pushed him towards the water tank and he stumbled and tripped heavily on the ground. Get up, get up, get up, I willed him. He staggered to his feet and at the tank splashed water on his face. I wanted to run to him, hold him, but I could not. Bundock watched me all the time, smiling.

I saw fear in his eyes that evening at muster. That's the way Bundock likes them — lily-livered, fearful, under his control. I told him quickly about the night-tubs and how we'd crown Bundock one night.

Thomas Boardman, who had come to a dreadful end. The name she had read all those months ago in London at the Old Sessions House.

The pages were in Indian ink, easily decipherable, as though they had been folded and rarely opened. These were Henry's words, she was sure. Lydia knew she wanted to be reassured that Henry Belfield was innocent of the charges laid; to know that he had been wrongfully charged with murder. If that was the case, she had been reasoning deep down, then perhaps she had only imagined what had happened to her in her stepmother's cabin? Why had she willed the episode from her memory? Was it because she wanted him to be worthy of desiring her, or had she enjoyed his hunger for her? Had his actions aroused her? She was shocked by this thought. He was devious, that much was clear.

Her gaze left the page and travelled to the wide river mouth leading to the southern Antarctic oceans. She felt devastated by what she had read. Jane said that Henry, unlike the other boys, was educated, related to a duke, perhaps transported for a crime he did not commit so he would certainly have been literate. None of the other boys would have been so eloquent, nor been able to write, even if they did have the materials to do so.

She remained seated at the bureau. Her eye was drawn to a line of soldiers as they marched down the hill from the nearby church at Battery Point towards the water. Their faces were illuminated in the murky yellowish light of the late afternoon storm. The river was like a boiling vat against a brooding sky. Gusts of wind pushed white breakers that threatened to swamp the wharf, where the steamers were disembarking their wares. She returned to her reading.

26th September

Yesterday as we folded our hammocks I told Thomas about Bundock's cat. Before I did, I swore him to secrecy.

I told him one of my favourite stories, about the great cat massacre – a group of printing apprentices in France who tortured and killed the cats who made their life a misery. I was a child when I first read the story – 'La Grise', the cat that belonged to the master's wife. There were twenty-six cats who lived there, all thrown into sacks half alive and bludgeoned with bars. I had his full attention, then. I said we'd get Bundock's, but he looked worried. I had to remind him that now he was one of Bundock's pretty boys and told him about the favours the man would expect. After Bundock finished with him, he would never be the same. He looked frightened. But it's true – Bundock's tactics are to make them believe he is all-seeing. Then they are putty in his hands.

He has beautiful lips. I hate to think of him in Bundock's clutches. I urged him to get in first. Get him where it hurts. We're both at the bakery this week and we'll have freedom. If we don't do it now, we might not have another chance.

God was on my side. At lunchtime in the half hour we had off from working the ovens, as we went behind the brick building to the vegetable gardens, we saw movement in the turnip patch.

I crept around to the room behind the bakery, came back with an empty sack and a foul-smelling piece of rancid meat and told him to stand guard. I returned to the turnip patch, where I lay on my belly.

The cat was so close I looked straight into its eyes – narrow and greedy. Then I had him by the scruff of the neck. I called for Thomas and we pushed it, howling and scratching, into the sack.

I lifted the sack easily over my shoulder, even though it was putting up a hell of a fight, and motioned Thomas to follow. When I started beating the bag he pleaded with me not to kill it. But I closed my ears. What would he want from a cat who was fed better than us? He looked at me strangely. I picked up the sack. Blood oozed out of the cloth. We hid it behind the gum tree and ran back to the bakery.

As he stoked the furnace under the bread oven his blond hair was sticky with beads of sweat on his temples. He was trembling. I placed my hand on his shoulder, my fingers straying to his neck. He did not resist. His face was turned away but he let me touch him. I returned to the shovel and raked the charcoal. Take things slowly. There's plenty of time. But I wanted him before Bundock had him.

Later in the darkened dormitory, I reminded him again how Bundock saved the choicest scraps for his cat — we got less than an animal. He said it wasn't the cat's fault, but I asked him why it was that witches used to make themselves into cats to cast spells. There was only one way to protect yourself from sorcery, mutilate a cat: cut its tail, clips its ears, smash one of its legs, tear or burn its fur and you would stop its malevolent power. God would have wanted us to punish Bundock, I said. I thought he had understood. Then he asked me if I thought it was still alive.

29th September

As a boy, I saw Christ's blood scarlet in the sunlight when it flooded the stained-glass windows in the church. I knew then He would look after me always. God had sent us here. We must endure it. Suffering means redemption. Jesus taught us that.

The lines from John Donne's *Divine Poems*, my schoolmaster's favourite verse. I will copy it out to give to him.

Or like a thief, which till death's doom be read,
Wisheth himself delivered from prison;
But damned and haled to execution,
Wisheth that still he might be imprisoned . . .
And red with blushing, as thou art with sin;
Or wash thee in Christ's blood, which hath this might
That being red, it dyes red souls to white.

He asked me why God treated him this way. I told him it was not our place to ask. He said he'd dreamt about me last night – I was on a throne dressed as an angel.

We hanged Old Tom from a gum tree after I asked him whether he confessed. As the dumb critter clawed in the air, I said we'd get some salt to put on the roasted meat and reminded Thomas of how good the wallaby tasted, which one of the convicts snared when we were out laying tracks for Hawkins' railway line. I saw him lick the imagined taste of the meat from around his lips.

CHAPTER ELEVEN

Lydia walked along Nutgrove Beach, past remnants of Aboriginal middens thickly layered with scallops and oyster shells embedded into the sand. She crunched through silken shells the colour of alabaster, which littered the beach like an exotic carpet. Whipped by the wind, the sand was a live beast, rippling towards her. Across the river in her little cottage, Charlotte was alone with that housekeeper, her children grown up, knowing that her husband had harboured feelings for another.

The land mocked her intrusion and she saw too that it mocked her ancestors who had travelled across the seas to set up their experiment: an island jail.

Henry's damaged behaviour contaminated everything she saw. The boy who seemed to taint all of them; the boy who tortured animals, who manipulated others, who wanted to commit an offence in the eyes of God, who had pushed her against the wall of the cabin, then discarded her to her memories.

She had left Wellard's box on her dresser, not wishing to read any more, seriously considering dumping it somewhere, burning it, perhaps in the dunes near Nutgrove Beach. She sighed, pulling her skirts around her, keeping her eyes half-closed against the flying sand. She had visited this beach as a child. Had she come here to be comforted, for nostalgia, to renew a sense of happiness? Her father had held an annual regatta here, introducing a public holiday to celebrate it. In this bay the colonial boys rowed against the newcomers. The Tasman Prize of thirty sovereigns presented by Sir John went to the winner of the whaleboat race. She remembered the regatta emblem with its blue ribbon, and how everyone waved their wattles at the craft in Sullivans Cove. Her father had donated beer and cheese. But the second time the regatta was held, twice postponed because of inclement weather, people had become drunk and disorderly and fights had broken out. That same undercurrent of violence seemed to tarnish the happiest of occasions on this island.

Lydia, try as she might, could not shake a deepening sense of misery. Images of the cat and Henry scheming beset her. If Jane had known about his real nature on board the *Fairlie*, would she have shown such sympathy? He cared about Thomas, in his perverted way, so why had he killed him? Or had he?

She was dabbling among contradictory ghosts, looking for solutions to her questions. It was far better, Jane had always said, to expect nothing from life, yet she had lived in complete contradiction to her advice: she had expected too much and wanted nothing for anyone else. Lydia realised now that any suitor for her threatened Jane, because, after her father died, it would have meant Jane facing widowhood alone. Suitors, at any rate, had been few and far between after Captain Ross. Instead, Lydia was a recipient, an empty vessel for all Jane's trivia, and a replacement for her heroic husband. Now, she was a recipient of her past.

She walked on, a solitary figure on the beach, until the sun disappeared on the other side of the river and the large white branches of the gum trees clawing at the breeze grew dark and menacing. There were farmhouses around, but as darkness fell she realised how far she was from civilisation, some miles south of Hobart Town. On Sandy Bay Road she was lucky enough to flag down a coach.

The day after her walk she returned to the museum to consult Lemprière's diaries again. There was no one there when she arrived. It wasn't until she stood at the attendant's desk asking for the diaries, staring vacantly out of the window while mulling over Henry and the overseer and Thomas, that she registered a man's presence. He did not look like the usual kind of visitor to the archives – the elderly or odd; jovial women dressed like bags of washing; or furtive men with eyeglasses who hobbled with walking sticks, like aged flamingos.

He was engrossed in whatever he was reading and did not notice she was staring at him. She thought she was looking at an apparition, that she had finally lost her mind. It was Henry. The tapered fingers Jane had described, the dark curls, square-jawed. He seemed a little rougher than she'd imagined, but the choirboy look of him was unmistakeable. When she spoke to the attendant, her voice betrayed her.

'Who is that man?'

'Oh, that's Mr Bentham. Giles Bentham.'

He must have heard his name because at that moment he looked straight at her. His look was initially one of curiosity, but he appeared distracted. Lydia felt him appraise her briefly. She blushed, even though she was used to feeling like an item of curiosity. She willed her hand not to swoop to her face. From this distance he could not have noticed her scar. She suddenly felt commanded to give an explanation for her presence in this room. From outside there was a sudden burst of laughter. Whalers, undoubtedly, under the influence of the cheap Mauritius rum that had flooded the colony.

Lydia turned her back, pretending to busy herself with Lemprière's diaries. Out of the side of her eye, she noticed Bentham had returned to the book he was reading. She went back to her seat and began to go through the diaries methodically. He was sitting next to the bay windows overlooking Argyle Street, one of Lydia's preferred reading spots, although she sometimes found the vista distracting and noisy.

For the rest of the day, each time her mind wandered, she found herself looking at his back. He was always absorbed as she should have been. He had stopped reading and was writing instead, or sketching; she found it hard to make out. She saw his elbow rise and fall, and a quill scratch in front of him, or was it a pencil? From this distance, she could not tell. The implement seemed to fly across the page.

After returning from a short trip to purchase some writing paper, she found that he had gone. His chair was neatly pushed against the table, the books he had been reading in a pile to the right of the desk. On impulse, she engaged the younger attendant in small talk about the weather, the new shingles on the old thatched roofs and her dislike of that modern iron, the material used for the steamships on the Derwent. He seemed taken aback – she had been visiting now for almost a week and had barely spoken a word to him. Then she inquired in what she hoped was a casual tone whether the gentleman who visited this morning was local.

'I haven't noticed him here before,' she added.

'No, Mr Bentham hasn't been in for quite some time, Madam. He's visiting from the old country.'

'He's a researcher?'

'You don't know who he is?'

'No.'

'Mr Bentham's great-uncle was Jeremy Bentham. He designed the Panopticon, you know, Miss Frankland – the Model Prison. We have many valuable papers in the museum dealing with convict history, particularly Port Arthur, where we have our own Panopticon, you know. Mr Bentham finds them extremely useful for his research.' He said this last part proudly.

Lydia stared at the attendant. 'I too have an interest in that prison,' she finally said.

He seemed not to hear her. 'Mr Bentham is researching a biography of his great-uncle.'

The following day, Lydia took her customary walk down to the wharves, then, determined to finish off Lemprière's papers, she headed back to the archives.

It was wintry outside. Sleet had sliced across her cape that morning on the way to the museum and she had mud on her boots from a trip to the cove. Inside, she made her way to her reading desk, but a chair, with books, impeded her.

'Permit me . . .' Bentham gripped the back of the chair, lifting it easily over the top of his desk. Then he offered his hand and a fleeting smile.

'I'm Giles Bentham. I don't think we've met.'

Close up, he seemed older and shorter, more ordinary. His voice was not as deep as she had imagined; it was soft, modulated. His nose was a little sharp. He had stubble on his cheeks and his skin was colonial, brown from the sun. Beneath the thick dark hair, she could see his eyes were deep blue. In the silence before she spoke she felt his eyes on her face and sensed his curiosity. She wished she had put on more powder. She felt angry, thinking that he mistakenly thought she had deliberately taken that route. She kept her eyes on the desk, knowing she was flushed, wanting to dismiss him, but realising to do so would be unthinkable.

'Lydia Frankland,' she said quietly.

'A regular guest at the archives?'

She nodded her head.

She was intent on getting back to her seat, but she caught sight of a sepia painting on his desk. It featured a strange Gothic construction that looked like an illustration from a child's book. It was intricate, as though sketched laboriously – a dome on top of a building like an old bandstand, which sat oddly supported by six pillars. There were layers of floors like a tiered cake dissected neatly in half. The effect was of some strange fantasy wedding cake, and it seemed eerily familiar.

'The Panopticon,' he said. 'My great-uncle's design.'

'Jeremy Bentham.'

'You have heard of him?'

'I have read *An Introduction to the Principles of Morals and Legislation*.'

It was the sort of response Jane would have given – confident, wanting to create the effect of intelligence. She could remember virtually nothing about the work. She bit her lip, hoping he would not ask further questions, but after chatting about the colony, he asked her if she would have afternoon tea in the Government House gardens. Much later, she remembered he had not allowed her any time for her usual diffident response, as though he knew she might refuse if permitted time to consider.

That afternoon, in the heat of the gardens' glasshouse, she felt like a wilting begonia. The dress she had on, close to the throat with loose sleeves, was of inferior quality and should not have been worn in public. For months she had taken too little care about her appearance. She was glad at least that she had donned her petticoat. In the phaeton on the way to the gardens, hurtling past the landmarks she knew so well, she had felt more aware than ever that they were strangers. As they trotted through the wide, paved streets, she thought how often she had watched other couples ride past on an outing.

Inside the glasshouse they were seated formally, each watching the other. The light flooded through the glass ceiling as the sun chased the clouds across the sky. She saw that his brown velvet frock coat matched the mustard-coloured cravat around his neck. The formal attire seemed to suit him, yet she could imagine he would be comfortable dressed more casually. His hands were clasped in front of him as though he was waiting for her to speak. She wanted him to take charge of the conversation as she could think of nothing to say. Besides, he might find that she could not remember his great-uncle's works after all.

She was saved by the arrival of the afternoon's offerings. He surveyed the cakes on the silver trolley with enthusiasm. She reached for the closest sweetmeat. As she bit through the thick white icing of a sugary cake into the sickly marzipan, she felt nauseated.

'The way you looked at the painting I had,' he said suddenly. 'I thought you might . . .'

'It is strangely familiar.'

'Oh?'

'It reminded me of the Model Prison at Port Arthur.'

She placed the sweetmeat on the plate in front of her and closed her eyes, seeing the narrow corridors leading into the centre like a man-made spiderweb; the light flooding in from the ceiling it did in this room; the corridors in contrast dark and cold; the men in hoods.

'You've been there?' he was saying. 'It may seem foolish, but I had no idea they welcomed holidaymakers. I had expected it to be out of bounds. For what purpose did you visit?'

Lydia could not answer. Her fingers were sticky with the cake and she clumsily picked up the fine china cup, sipping her scalding tea. She placed the cup back on the saucer.

'You did seem alarmed when I first saw you at the archives,' he continued, ignoring her silence. 'Forgive me if I am rude in saying so.'

'Alarmed?' She had recovered enough to speak. 'You reminded me of someone, that's all.'

'What did you think of Port Arthur? I have heard it was supposed to be a place worse than death.'

And her father had helped create such misery.

'It *is* a peculiar building,' she said, as much to cover her discomfiture as anything else.

'What?'

'The Model Prison. Why did your great-uncle design such a place?' She struggled to regain composure.

He did not answer her directly. Instead, he asked, 'Do you know why we fear ghosts?'

'No.' She swallowed, wondering, absurdly, if he knew her dreams.

They were like dancers, their words complicated manoeuvres, each watching to see the other's reaction to the last intricate step.

'Because we know they don't exist.'

'I don't understand.'

'Ghosts are purely fictitious, mere figments of the imagination, but we are still afraid of them, you see?' he said.

'Well . . .'

'It is precisely the intrusion of something unknown and strange into our world that makes us scared. My great-uncle was pathologically afraid of ghosts. He tried to rid himself of the fear by telling himself they didn't exist, but it made his terror intensify. Do you believe in ghosts?'

'I can't see what this has to do with the Panopticon.'

She hoped her tone would give her time to examine what his curious statement meant. She looked at his fingers again, curled around the handle of the cup, his left hand rested on the table. He wore no wedding ring.

'Well, Miss Frankland, if you can fear something that doesn't exist, then you could use that psychology to control prisoners or, in this case, convicts.'

She was finding it hard to concentrate.

'Why not introduce fear to control their existence? That painting, the sketch, you saw on my desk?'

'Yes.'

'The dome is where the inspector was housed.'

The inspector. The spiritualist. The two had merged into

one for Lydia. The absurd little clown of a man talking of séances and inspectors. He had believed in ghosts and he had told her something about her future. Her hand was trembling as she lifted the cup to her mouth. She did not believe in such things.

'The Panopticon was a prison,' Bentham was saying. 'The inspector, who sat in the centre, was never seen by the convicts, but the building was set up in such a way that the convicts believed they were being watched at all times. None of the prisoners' movements could ever escape the eye of the inspector.

'The inspector, like the ghosts, did not need to exist, but the convicts needed to believe that he did. They wore slippers so their feet made no sound; they wore hoods so they could not see their fellow captives; they were kept away from the privileges of the free. Even in their prayers, they were boxed away from each other. And what did they see through the slits in their hoods, and as they walked to the chapel and looked straight ahead? They saw the inspector.'

'Or thought they saw him,' she said.

'For what purpose, do you suppose?' he asked.

She shook her head.

'To subdue the criminal, to reform the criminal mind.'

Her father's wish entirely. She looked at the man opposite her.

'Mr Bentham, your great-uncle and my father pursued similar interests.'

'Your father?'

'Was governor here.'

She saw him digesting this information, appraising her differently. She continued in a rush, not wanting him to misinterpret why she had told him this.

'He used classification to control the convicts, dividing them up into boxes like plants, like Linnaeus. He used their tattoos to identify them in the same way you might describe a stamen on a crocus. And their punishments were dispensed accordingly.'

There was silence. There, it was out. In that moment, she saw surprise in his eyes.

She added: 'I can hardly say I am proud of that fact.'

She felt she had been entirely honest, not hiding behind words as Jane had taught her, not presenting herself as the governor's daughter for recognition and praise. She'd said what she believed was the truth. At the same time, her face was flushed. She had criticised her father to a stranger.

'Sir John Frankland? I never knew he had such an interest, Miss Frankland.'

'No, he is not generally known for that.'

'How peculiar. Our ancestors were preoccupied by the same thing. So this is why you are in the archives? Is this what took you to the Model Prison? I'm afraid I cannot quite believe a woman such as yourself would travel so far from home to visit a place like Port Arthur. You are travelling alone?'

He was altogether too interrogatory and too familiar. As Lydia struggled with her conscience, his questions blurred together and she found it hard to decide which to answer.

'No, my father wasn't exactly the reason for my visit, not at first. Originally, I wanted to research my stepmother's past.'

'Why your stepmother?'

Lydia found that question even harder to answer.

'I suppose I lived so much of my life with her and . . .'

But Giles had returned to the topic she now would rather avoid.

'If your father was governor, then surely he would have known of the Panopticon? He must have been responsible for overseeing its foundation?'

'I am discovering some aspects of his governorship that I knew nothing about,' Lydia said quickly.

'So this explains your interest in the Model Prison?'

'I visited Port Arthur after reading my stepmother's diaries. Until I visited, I had no idea about its true purpose or my father's role in its foundation. What is your view of such punishment?'

'Cruel, although our forebears might have disagreed,' he said. 'It was like a laboratory in which to carry out experiments. I am fascinated by its major effect – that inducing the inmate to believe himself to be permanently visible ensures an automatic function of power. It is a form of control. Much like the way you described your father's preoccupation with classifying men. My great-uncle wanted blinds on the windows of the Panopticon, so the prisoners could be watched at all times.'

He was studying her again, leaning back slightly, his hands resting on the table. Strangely, she felt empathy with his words. She forgot about her disfigurement.

'So both your great-uncle and my father wanted the same thing,' she said.

'I think they felt that by imposing order on men, they could control them. But you cannot control people that way.'

She told him then, because she had to tell somebody, about Henry – a victim of the penal system at Port Arthur. She desperately needed to talk to someone who could make sense of these strange dream-like worlds she had inhabited.

'I had no idea they transported boys,' he said.

'They were the colony's future labour force.'

She could have said much more but did not trust herself. There were too many unresolved feelings.

'You never visited Port Arthur as a child?'

'I did, but I didn't realise.'

Lydia had become used to keeping secrets but she was not used to being the subject of attention. She felt exhausted and flustered.

Outside her guest house at Battery Point, Bentham helped her down from the phaeton and kissed her gloved hand. She refrained from asking if she would see him again.

That night, lying on the muttonbird feathers of her bed, Lydia knew that the afternoon had given her strength. Merely speaking to someone else about the incidents that had preoccupied her for so long legitimised her thoughts. Besides, it was a relief to talk to someone who could understand them. Bentham was the first real company she had had since leaving England other than curious mortals like the ferryman and Wellard. Both of them were delving into the emotions of ancestors long dead, attempting what? To discover more about themselves? When she fell asleep, Bentham's face merged with the other ghosts. But when she awoke, she couldn't remember any details of her dreams.

CHAPTER TWELVE

The following morning Bentham was nowhere to be seen in the museum. Lydia refused to demean herself by asking the attendant whether he was expected. Instead, she began sorting out the loose pages in her stepmother's collection, determined to place the documents in some sort of order. Her patience was rewarded when she saw Jane's handwriting on the familiar lined paper of her diary, buried among the colonial secretary's correspondence.

30th July, 1841

The side of lamb, tender and juicy, was a present from one of the settlers – our first of the season. And the Naples finger biscuits – the second attempt from Lydia – did not crumble when you picked them up.

Lydia was a young girl again, still new to menstruation, clumsy around men – or so Jane had always said. This was the five-course Tasmanian Society dinner held to celebrate the advent of one of the first microscopes in the colony; the dinner where the lizard had been dissected. Carts belonging to Tasmanian Society guests had lined up in the overgrown laneway outside the kitchen. They had all been there: John Gould, Ronald Gunn, Count Strzelecki, Johann Llhotsky – the men in Jane's sphere of influence. Lydia had stood at the top of the large stairs with the mahogany railing, which led down to the large front door, so she could see the guests when they arrived.

Jane had begun dinner with a toast to Charles Darwin, noting what he had written about the Galápagos: frying hot islands, a paradise for giant reptiles including giant tortoises, some weighing eighty pounds, she reported, adding that he had poked his gun at one of the large reptiles and it hadn't moved. They had ridden one up a mountain. Then the guests had begun the entrée, tiny poultry pies with leeks. In the praise for the dinner, Jane had announced that her stepdaughter had finally mastered the art of baking. Lydia remembered her embarrassment.

She was allowed to attend the meal, but not the Society's business to be conducted after dessert. What possessed her, then, to disobey her stepmother? Creeping back into the hall, unseen amongst the festivities, she had hidden behind the velvet curtains, watching while two men carried to the table the Overhauser microscope which had been delivered in a large wooden crate.

They had taken the blood from the platypus and had cut up the blue-tongued lizard to compare their cells in a bid to find out whether the platypus was a mammal or not. Jane had written:

We were creating history that night. The platypus has been described as a bird without wings. Dr Edmund Hobson, the scientist among us, explained to our group that the blood resolved itself into two parts – serum, or water of the blood, as it is vulgarly called, and the clot, or solid matter. He said the shape of the blood globules in the two great divisions of the vertebrate classes was remarkable. It is one way of determining to which category the animal belongs. We were able to compare the blood – specifically the composition, the colour and shape of the blood globules, searching for grand divisions in the animal kingdom – to find out whether the platypus, the *ornithorhynchus paradoxus*, is indeed an animal or a reptile.

Lydia could see the drops of the creature's blood on the table.

Hobson deftly trapped a drop of blood on a thin plate of glass, then covered it with a scale of mica. We could see clearly the globules were not elliptical.

They conducted the same experiment on the lizard and concluded that the platypus was not a reptile. Jane had recorded the conversation, presumably to copy out the details for a later Tasmanian Society paper.

Lemprière told us how fossils were the product of geological change – the slow, ceaseless action of wind and water – and about a relic of ancient times he had uncovered near the boys' prison – silicified wood, the colour of agate – and what it might tell us about the age of our planet. He asked whether anyone agreed with Lyell that the Earth is considerably older than stated in the Bible. He said he had been troubled in part by what Lyell had said. No one else spoke. Everyone, I saw from my position at the head of the table, was listening. I was fearful of what my husband would think, he being such an observer of the Scriptures.

Lydia put down her stepmother's pages and gazed across the room. Two decades before the publication of *The Origin of Species*, the Bible's authority was already being challenged. Lydia knew how much her father would have hated such blasphemy. It was clear that Lemprière, too, was battling with the contradictions he had encountered. Jane had said in her letter from Marlborough that they were engaging in heresy, so they certainly knew the risks they were running.

We talked about birds and, on impulse I invited him to Ancanthe, my vale of flowers, to see our collection for himself. I decided to bring Mathinna, for she always enjoys a ride in the carriage.

Ancanthe, ten miles north of Hobart Town, was the colony's first Greek temple and Jane's dream of civilisation in a wild colonial outpost. Lydia had not intended to visit Ancanthe, but now the temple beckoned and so did a day outside in the fresh air.

As her chaise rattled along the new macadamised road, she was assailed by painful memories. There had been no room for her in the coach going to the opening of the temple. Jane had told her this in the tone she used to signal there would be no argument. The day had been warm. Mathinna had been sitting in the rear of the carriage, impassive in a yellow dress. On her feet were white shoes with embroidered daisies and in her hair she had a yellow wattle.

Ancanthe was going to become a museum, a collection of the finest pieces from Van Diemen's Land – part of Mathinna's heritage, Jane said. When they left the colony Jane had taken much of the Ancanthe collection with her. Lydia remembered the pandemonium that accompanied packing six years' worth of crates: the marsupials and platypus in glass cages, the grasses from the colony, penguin eggs, lizards, and paintings Jane had commissioned. She remembered how much of Jane's library had been discarded. Much of the furniture had been left behind in Government House.

Now, more than twenty years on, the man in the chaise looked perplexed when Lydia told him her destination. She struggled to give directions, but as soon as she mentioned it was past the Newtown Racecourse the driver remembered.

'The old temple they store apples in? I know the one. Never in all my years of driving 'ave I been asked to visit that place. Now there y' go.'

They headed north out of Hobart Town, past the botanical gardens and Government House, past all the new houses that had been built since Lydia last visited these parts. Almost an hour later they were there.

In the native bushland of wattle trees and blue gums, the temple still looked absurd. It had been abandoned to the wilderness, that much was clear. It had a Parthenon-style entrance, sculpted stone walls and a pathway of stone steps leading up to its entrance.

Lydia pushed open the creaky wooden gate, delighted to find the same small white daisies that she had once made into chains for her father so long ago littering the grass. Sir John had also been absent at the opening of Ancanthe. She wondered what he had thought about the place. Jane had bought the land with money that she had received from her father, a silk weaver in England. She had spent months choosing a name, consulting with the Tasmanian Society members, insisting it must have classical roots. Jane and her projects. Lydia often thought she herself was a project to be moulded into shape – from a wilful child to submissive adult, her unorthodox edges to be smoothed into compliance. Jane seemed to view motherhood as an educational project to be undertaken with a minimum of emotional attachment. Perhaps the storekeeper had been the only person to see through her impervious façade.

On impulse Lydia bent over and picked a handful of small daises. Sitting down on a tree stump, she absent-mindedly scored the stems with her thumbnail, threading the next stem through the hole.

She walked slowly around the outside of the temple to the front door, which was flanked by four sculpted pillars. It had been boarded up and she could smell the unmistakable pungent sweet fruit. She tried to peer in through the door, but it held fast. The sandstone walls bore the marks of convict picks. They must have carted the blocks so far from town.

On the ridge above the temple she chose a clear patch of grass and spread out her cape. The grass was a little damp but the day was warm. A breeze stirred through the yellow wattle as she fossicked through the wicker basket packed by Anna and found smoked pork and crusty bread. She lay down, tilting her chin so she could see behind her. At first she hadn't noticed Mount Wellington but now she could see clouds swirling around its dolerite peaks. Every time you looked the mountain appeared different. The sun shone strongly, a red glow behind her closed eyes.

I took my place, as etiquette dictated, in the rear of the carriage. She sat in front, behind the driver. We jolted down the pebbled driveway and into the traffic of Macquarie Street. She was wearing a carriage dress of deep plum with a darker-coloured auburn shawl trimmed with lace around her shoulders. It made her skin more pale and I noticed, perhaps because of that, a mole on her neck.

Beside her was an Aboriginal child called Mathinna, solemn and wide-eyed, in a yellow dress. She was talking to the child, her head bent slightly, her shawl askew. Mathinna, back straight, hands clasped on her lap, did not respond. I speculated at the strange couple they made. What made her adopt such a child? She displayed none of the attentive motherly touches Charlotte would administer, yet, as a couple, the effect of the two was mesmerising: the pale-skinned aristocrat and the dark-skinned little girl. It left me uneasy, but I'm not sure why – a fear perhaps that she was using the child for her own ends in the same way, I suspect, she uses me. I thought of the polished performance of the previous night, the sumptuous repast, the formal conversations, the experiment, conducted like a grand finale to the evening. I wondered, as the carriage clipped through the newly paved streets of Hobart, why she had never had children. It had never occurred to me before. She married late, perhaps that's why.

I could see her profile as we passed the busy market place. Indeed, I had ample time to study her before we reached our destination, to identify, the way I do with my specimens, a meaning from her existence. Her features are pleasingly symmetrical. Her languid grey eyes are perhaps too far apart, but when she is excited I feel embraced by their fervour – they ease any harshness in what she has said. A face of intelligence, alluring. Her mouth is almost too perfect. A cupid bow, small and dainty as if she has painted it that way. It's usually set in some expression of preoccupation.

I wonder how old she is. She does not have the weary, worn look Charlotte sometimes has, dealing with our offspring. She embodies so many contradictions: her candour – that childlike innocence – conflicts with her confidence. She handles herself well, too well perhaps, particularly in the bosom of men who listen to her so intently. But those who know her seem to realise there is an edge to her banter. It's as though she is leading them through innocent remarks to a place they might not wish to go. Is that what she is doing to me?

Outside the carriage window, fishmongers were displaying their wares. She turned to point out something to Mathinna.

'The rest of our little group will join us at Ancanthe,' she called above the rattle of the wheels.

She turned, when I least expected it, saying she would like me to paint her portrait. I was too surprised to reply but I must have muttered something because she seemed to think I was happy to oblige. The prospect, I must confess, fills me with delight, even though I resented her expectation that I would obey. I have not painted any women, not even Charlotte, never grappled with the curve of the female breast on the canvas. I spent the next five minutes imagining my eye travelling across her body and lingering . . .

She turned to speak to me again. She was telling me that Mr Gell is making an inscription for the foundation stone of Ancanthe. The carriage was quieter now we were out of the traffic. I imagined sipping fine madeira after dinner, indulging in intellectual discussions, nibbling on foie gras. Afterwards, in the intimacy of the drawing room, we would talk about Balzac, Alexander de Tocqueville and the French Revolution. We could discuss fossils and Lyell's theory of how they evolved.

I asked her who else would be attending? She mentioned

Captain Ross, Francis Crozier and Mr Joseph Hooker, the son of Sir William Hooker, who's just been appointed the director of the Royal Gardens at Kew. Hooker has recently returned from the Antarctic with Ross and Crozier, where he collected a plant from Antarctica – fossilised wood, even though the continent has no forests. He is calling it the *Flora Tasmaniae* and he is greatly excited by his find. He wants to compare it with vegetation found in Van Diemen's Land, to see if the two continents are linked.

She asked me then what I had meant at dinner when I asked whether the Earth might not be as old as we believed from the Bible. I did not want to say much more on the subject and in many ways regretted what I *had* said, but she seemed unperturbed and chattered on. As the scenery whistled past, a kaleidoscope of colours and smells, I was drawn into this privileged world in which she lived, with so much at her disposal. There were so many people in coaches, phaetons and on foot, and we caught glimpses of bush between racecourses, houses, a steeple of a church and a mill when we crossed near a stream. My senses were assailed with colour – the winter sun bright overhead, the sky taut with brilliance. Her voice was full of exuberance as she flitted from reciting the poetry of Wordsworth to talking of the death of Coleridge. 'Alas, a loss like Byron, but their words are our inheritance.'

She asked me what I thought of Coleridge's dying words – that Christ's miracles did not withstand historical and scientific scrutiny. Why will she not leave this alone? I told her I considered these words blasphemous. I reminded her he had also said that the Bible maintained its spiritual authority.

Twenty minutes later, we were outside a small building resplendent with Doric columns. Mathinna had been silent for the whole journey.

The building was a most unexpected sight so far into the bushland. The temple is a feat in engineering. Each sandstone column
is more than sixty feet high and three feet wide — she rattled off the
measurements even as we began to dismount.

I almost laughed out loud because the building is so typical
of the sort of oddity she would champion, further proof of her
single-mindedness. I could travel in the wake of her energy, which
seems to know no bounds. I could achieve the things I have not yet
achieved. If I had met her twenty years ago, perhaps on one of her
trips to the Continent . . . I deliberately did not think of Charlotte.
I was enjoying the play-acting, the sense of the bizarre I'd experienced since entering the carriage.

She accepted my hand on alighting. It was gloved and felt cool
and small. Captain Ross, Joseph Hooker and Francis Crozier
were waiting for us. She had planned a cold luncheon, she told
them — potted tongue, bread and red wine — to be eaten at Upper
Ancanthe. She spread her arms like a child welcoming guests to a
tea party.

I stood in the dusty clearing at the bottom of one of the pillars
and looked skyward at the dark shape of Mount Wellington. She
told me she has climbed this mountain. I imagined her walking
in her crinoline, determined to reach the summit. I examined the
columns again, constructed in segments, and the ornate carvings
under the roof. A white cockatoo with a pale lemon crest flashed
past, screeching outrage.

It was a day that ushered the imagination to journey forth, a
day close to perfection that invited only thoughts of the present.
The smell of hay and manure was in the crisp air. Green pastures
flowed from the mountain — I could make out turnip crops in the
distance. Here and there was a small cottage tended by emancip-
ists. A herd of goats grazed on the hillside, their bells tinkling on

the distant horizon. A woman came out of a barn, leading her cow behind her, its hot breath suspended in the coolness of the air. In the distance the Derwent sparkled and ships bobbed, specks anticipating the open sea. Surely this is paradise, this island at the end of the Earth. A garden of Eden. I felt happier than I had for a long time.

Mathinna was close by. She had kicked off her shoes and was scuffing her toes in the dust. Lady Frankland saw me watching her. I turned my attention to the vista before me. The whole valley and the mountain stream were to be her own botanical garden. She asked if I approved. I told her she was the luckiest woman in Christendom.

She seemed to be playing a game that we were the oldest of friends. It took the greatest restraint not to take her hand as we began to walk up a rough track.

She called back to Mathinna not to forget her shoes.

We finally caught up with Hooker, Ross and Crozier sitting on lichen-covered boulders under the shade of a stringy bark. A convict servant produced water in a pitcher from the mountain stream and we drank thirstily. We talked about magnetic observatories and the men's most recent trip to the south pole. I will find ways to visit Hobart Town more often – to be with such people gives me purpose. They are inquisitive, like me. Lady Frankland adroitly steered the conversation, putting me at ease. Hooker, the botanist on Ross's voyage, spoke of finding silicified wood in Antarctica, which proved the chilly continent must once have had forests growing where now there is ice. He said the fossil was similar to some of his botanical collections from Van Diemen's Land. Lady Frankland suggested Hooker might want to donate the fossil to Charles Darwin, who was collecting specimens from all around the globe. Darwin, after all, she said, was trying to make sense of why he had seen shells embedded in marine mud on the summits of mountains in the Andes. It seemed to prove the mountains were once on the bottom of the ocean. He had also observed coral atolls in the Indian Ocean with lagoons in the middle, perhaps because they had surrounded islands which, over a long period of time, had sunk out of sight.

After the others left – picks in hand, intent on collecting more fossils – and Mathinna had also disappeared, Lady Frankland asked me about the fossilised wood specimen I had discovered at Safety Cove. I told her I believed it was a species of beech and she became quite excited, saying that Darwin, too, had collected beech trees in South America – of the *nothofagus* variety – as well as a fungus that grew on them. Perhaps my fossil could be compared with Darwin's collection? She asked me whether I believed any theory about the continents being linked. I said I was not sure. She remarked that we were studying plants that no one had seen before and I agreed we were indeed at the forefront of the discovery of so many new species.

We spoke of Linnaeus and she questioned why he had not considered, in devising his catalogues, the diversity of species in such far-flung places as Van Diemen's Land. I, too, had been wondering this about the creatures I have dissected. I thought of the pouch on the kangaroo rat, the duck bill on the platypus. We also spoke of Darwin's work and discussed the reasons why many of the species he found in the Galápagos were related to those on the main continent of South America, yet each differed according to which island they came from. She did not know the answer, but she said Darwin had told her he met an English governor on one of the islands who knew which island each giant tortoise came from by the patterns on its carapace. Darwin had speculated that these creatures adapted to wherever they were living. I said perhaps that was why some of the animals we saw here appear to have adapted this way, like the platypus. Taking in my interest, she declared her hand. Darwin apparently wants collectors from Van Diemen's Land to continue on this side of the world what he had begun in the Galápagos.

I realised immediately that the invitation invites a degree of trust, but at the same time, I am uneasy. Darwin's theories go against many of my deepest-held beliefs, especially that God is the designer of all things. As we were talking, a dark cloud passed across the sun. I realised we had crossed some sort of threshold. Rebellion is part of her nature, but is it in mine? She extended a gloved hand to end the conversation and moved swiftly to her feet as if she, too, had experienced the shift. She walked up the track in the same direction as the others. I remained, dazed, uncomprehending . . .

I hardly heard the first scream I was so engrossed in my thoughts. When I did, I ran towards it urgently and as I rounded a corner, I saw her prostrate on the ground, face down, sobbing, her skirts awry.

She was pushing herself up and half sat, a dirty smear on her face. I was sure she must have fainted. Her pupils were large, dilated. She looked up at me and said: 'A snake.'

We were alone in the clearing. As I eased her into a more comfortable position, she told me she had a phobia of these creatures. I was on my knees and I had one arm around her waist – I was so close I could smell her scent. After a while, her breathing slowed. I could hardly make out her words but she seemed to be saying something about evil and slimy, cold bodies – not knowing where they might slither. After a while, I proffered the other arm to help her to her feet.

She stood on the path, breathing deeply, stating flatly that she had never seen one out in the open like this, but that for so many months she had imagined doing so that at first she thought the creature on the path an apparition. I tried to comfort her, saying that they meant her no harm, speaking to her as though to my children. I could see her bite her lip and tears came to her eyes. I was surely privy to a side she rarely displays. I thought of the woman in the drawing room supervising the collection of blood for the experiment, so confident, so calm. She was crying now. I placed my hand on her shoulders. Her eyes were downcast, her shawl slipped from her shoulders. Once, she then told me, she was sent a Valentine with a dead snake attached to it. She could not continue the story. She said she was not wanted here like her husband. My hand rested on the back of her neck and she lifted her head to look at me. Her grey eyes swam with tears. I ached to hold her, then. Mathinna appeared further up the track. She stood silently watching us, barely discernible in the shade of a she-oak. I wasn't sure how long she had been there. I was unable to think of anything to say. Lady Frankland said quietly that we were on our way and that Monsieur Lemprière was assisting her.

The child did not move. Lady Frankland pulled her shawl across her shoulders, covering herself, and the three of us walked in silence, our earlier ebullient mood dissipated. A few drops of rain fell. We found the others. Ross was saying there was so much to discover, but his voice was dulled by the mist that had suddenly arrived.

On the trip back to Government House I imagined that the snake was a serpent, an omen. Temptation . . . I tried to shift my thoughts away from her, but I could not seem to. When I watched her with Mathinna it now seemed obvious that any closeness between them had been illusory. The girl retreated into herself as soon as she set foot in the carriage and it became clear to me that our etiquette and ridiculous rules of behaviour must seem to her like a pantomine. I thought of my own new baby, strong and healthy, her plump wrists and blithe smile. How uncomplicated my life with Charlotte is.

I will not collect for Darwin if he questions God's word. Doubt, I have read somewhere, is a divine contrivance for testing men's faith, enabling the staunch believer to stand by his beliefs so he may qualify for heaven. By questioning the Scriptures, I am exposed to doubts. I have walked in the Garden of Eden and been tempted by the apple and all that Eve offers. I will return home at once. Painting her portrait is out of the question.

Lydia lay on the hard ground under the wattle tree, the sun hot on her cheeks, her fingers tracing her scar. As the wind stirred through the trees, she slowly stretched her legs and sat up, scanning the horizon.

The temple lay below like a figment from her dream, a Grecian icon in an Australian wilderness. There was no one there. She was slipping into other worlds – she no longer knew what was real and what wasn't. One thought seemed uppermost in her mind. In the time her parents had been together, she had never seen them touch.

After a while, she walked wearily down the hill to the cart track where the chaise waited under an oak tree. The driver was impatient to be off. As the wheels clattered across the dirt track, the horses' hooves dislodging stones, Lydia felt she was becoming an intermediary for subterranean lives.

CHAPTER THIRTEEN

Back at the guest house Anna helped her with her cape,
brushing off grass that she had not even noticed. Lydia was
touched by her kindness.

'You don't look well,' Anna remarked.

She obeyed Anna's motherly instructions and headed for her
room, allowing herself to be pampered. The bed was inviting
with its white linen quilt and fluffed-up pillows, the oil lamp
lit beside it. She felt drained. Dressed in a camisole, she slipped
under the sheets and almost immediately fell asleep. She dreamt
she was back on the *Fairlie*, gazing up at the shark dangling on
the end of the hook, blood splashing onto the deck, blood
from her face splashing onto ears of maize, blood on Jane's
petticoat. Henry was there – his mocking smile evolved into
Giles Bentham. Then the spiritualist appeared, urging her
to take part in a séance to discover a pathway through this
labyrinth of the dead. Did Giles Bentham believe in these
spiritualists?

She awoke and it was still daylight. She fell asleep again, this time dreaming of a story she had read in *The Harbinger of Light* about a nun bricked up in the cellar of a Victorian house. The séance group had experienced a chill in the room and a figure in grey had appeared, emitting no sound, lit by a supernatural light.

When she awoke again late in the afternoon, the first thing she saw was the wooden box. Henry's papers.

10th December, 1841

He was a coward at the end, the Bundock we all knew, lips like steel, a three-day growth on his chin, standing in the middle of the muster ground in an oil-cloth coat, his stomach protruding like a shelf. In the light from the oil lamp it was like a scene from hell itself. Bodies, blood and underneath it all, a low horrible moaning. I had seen many a 'crowning', the first at the rookery of St Giles, but none that had gone this far. With the rest of them, I scrabbled with my bare hands at the bricks in the fireplace. Without mortar they came out easily. Bundock, the victim, his mouth full of shit. He must have pissed himself in fright. I could smell it. He knew he was going to die. We were in it, one and all. Then I heard voices outside. Hawkins. Bundock was lying face-down on the ground, not moving. Thomas was standing close to the door, a brick in his hand.

How ridiculous Hawkins looked the next day at muster with those whiskers and that balding head. Hateful, superior, sneering, waiting for us to break rank. We stood about ten deep, four hundred of us. In the men's prison, they would shop each other given any chance, but not us.

Thomas was the only one he could prove had taken part in the crime. He was the first boy to be flogged in the men's prison. We stood assembled before breakfast on a square of grass next to the hospital. The triangles were like a wooden tripod, secured to the ground by strong pins.

He was stripped to his trousers. The flogger was a sturdy man, barrel-chested with powerful wrists and blank eyes, cat o'nine tails in his hand to break the spirit, his soul long since departed. I saw Thomas put the musket ball I'd given him in his mouth. No one else noticed. Two overseers grabbed his arms, stretched them over the triangle, fastening them with rope, then his legs, first tying them at the knees and then the feet, till he was pinned like a butterfly on a board. We have no choice in this, Father, no choice at all.

I closed my eyes but I couldn't block the sound of the whipcord slicing through the air and his screams. The cord soaked in salt water and dried in the sun so it's like wire when it reaches your back. They say you care, Father. We must believe that. Eighty-one knots sawed through Thomas's flesh. At each blow, the flogger passed the whip through his left hand. I heard him saying so softly, 'Damn your eyes. This will open your carcass.' Thomas's blood dribbled from the whip, the colour of red wine. A boy's unscarred back, not a man's.

Hawkins was watching me as Thomas was carried past, half conscious, his shoes filled with blood, his back – still bare – like a side of freshly cut meat. Even his chest was streaked red.

As an adolescent in Van Diemen's Land, she had known flogging for the men was commonplace, but not this type of punishment for a boy. She and Boardman would have been the same age. She thought of Lemprière, who had witnessed this cruelty probably thinking of his own children. Her stepmother had meted out education and morals as though this would deliver boys from hell itself – had she done anything to stop this degradation? And her father . . . He must have known.

Lydia stood by the French doors looking into the descending darkness. A wallaby hopped across the lawn, feeding from the scraps Anna had thrown out from the kitchen. She brought her a light supper, which Lydia picked at without enthusiasm in her room in front of the small fire. She lit some more candles and forced herself to continue reading.

There were pages with prayers praising the Lord; writings about the crucifixion; more of John Donne's poems; words of violence that penetrated Lydia's pretence at calm. Then another diary entry.

Thomas didn't speak to me much, didn't speak to anyone. I had visited him in solitary, smuggling in damper at the risk of a flogging, for which he thanked me. It's two weeks since his flogging and we've been assigned to the vegetable patch to mulch the new seedlings with seaweed. It's Christmas Eve but it doesn't feel like Christmas. I've been watching him move in such a way that his skin does not touch the cloth of his shirt, a sign of his suffering.

I had been considering my plan all morning. We would never get this chance again. As we distributed the rest of the kelp over the seedlings, I straightened up and pointed to the track that left the vegetable patch and meandered across the hillside and down to the rocks. His eyes were questioning. I told him we would visit my refuge where we would be safe. Thomas has never been to my cave. The only way anyone could be seen would be from the ocean as it's not visible from above. It would have been unlucky for Hawkins to be passing in a whaleboat.

He stood at the entrance. I saw his eyes dart around, peering fearfully into the depths. Then he turned and looked at me as though he had known this would happen all along. I placed my arms around him and pressed my face to his. It was cold. He trembled and started crying. The smell of the seaweed and shriek of the gulls that morning will stay with me forever. I placed his head on my shoulder and, with my other hand, gently traced my fingers over his face down his nose, across his cheeks and over his jaw. Shifting his head from my shoulder, I turned him to face me, and tasted his tears, then moved down to his mouth, prising it open with my tongue. Carefully I unbuttoned his coarse shirt, all the while offering sounds of comfort. Then I carried him deep into the cave and laid him on his side. His eyes were a mixture of a childish curiosity and resignation. I unbuttoned his trousers, reaching the last button, pulling at them gently. His eyes were closed tight shut and his knees curled up to his stomach.

I resisted the urge to hurt him. Pulling his knees down firmly, I was surprised to see his cock, hard, in the gloom. Seeing him so aroused I pulled off my clothes in haste, my bare knees on the gritty wet sand. His fingers were in my hair. I showered his belly with kisses, then nosed the soft skin inside his thighs and my mouth was on him. He exploded with a ferocity that merged with the thunder of the waves. Afterwards, I held him by the shoulders and drove myself into him. He screamed most terribly and began whimpering.

Later, we lay skin against skin on the damp floor of the cave. He had not spoken, but nor did he move away from me. I stroked the hair that curled at the back of his hairline and kissed the nape of his neck, turning him towards me. I saw he was crying. I lifted up my arm and he turned awkwardly and nestled there.

Surely an hour went by and I knew we must get back. I wanted him again. I quoted him a line of Donne: 'a sin, or shame, or loss of maidenhead'. I had to know if he had lain with a woman. He shook his head. He asked if I had and I said one or two, but assured him the first time I saw him, I wanted him. I told him how I had first noticed him lying under that tree when we were working on the railway, had watched the way he raised his arms to swing the pick. I told him I wanted to possess him then. I'd been watching him for a long time. I asked if that scared him. He shook his head, but I knew he did not trust me. The cave's shadows lengthened and we pulled on our clothes, shivering, and crept down to the shore, scrabbling on to the rocks, picking handfuls of kelp. I removed his shirt, bathing his wounds carefully in the salt water as he sat on a rock. My cock grew hard again, but there was no time.

Back at the barracks we folded down our hammocks. No one noticed that we were half an hour late and our clothes were damp. His voice, or did I imagine it soft on the night air, asked me if it was a sin to be loved.

From that day Lydia saw the world differently. Truth, she thought, is a strange thing. It was what she sought, yet now she had found it, she no longer wanted it. In the early morning she felt as though life had seeped from her. She was disturbed by Henry's descriptions of male love; wished that she had not read the filthy words, but it was more than that. She knew now it could have been anybody. It was her innocence Henry Belfield had wanted to possess, the same way he had wanted to own Thomas. She remembered her furtive fantasies in early adolescence that stemmed from this episode in her stepmother's cabin, how she had imagined him making love to her, even though she barely knew what that meant. If Jane had not returned to the cabin when she did, she might have lost her virginity. Belfield had become entangled in her early desires of sexual awakening while she battled with the shamefulness of her thoughts, praying to the Lord to rescue her, thinking of herself as possessed by the devil. Only through sheer willpower had she refrained from touching herself, praying to be rescued from such sin. Finally, the memories had faded, but now Henry's words had aroused her from this inertia, leaving her, a woman in her forties, vulnerable, untouched and unloved.

CHAPTER FOURTEEN

The following morning there was a note from Mr Bentham in the visitors' box at the guest house, inviting her to the zoo. She responded with enthusiasm, pleased at the thought of seeing him again. Besides, she was delighted at the prospect of being outdoors in a warm morning of sunshine after the sleet.

She spent the early part of the morning reading newspapers, novels – anything to take her mind off Henry's diary.

Beaumauris Zoo was in Battery Point, not far from Lydia's guest house. It was not really a zoo in the way Lydia thought of London's Regent's Park, but more a private collection, a suburban menagerie in the grounds of a mansion belonging to a wealthy Hobart woman. The grounds sloped down towards the harbour. Inside a marquee English tea and scones were served. The entrance to the zoo was through a wide lobby with a sweeping staircase. Following the wooden sign, guests walked to the end of the lobby and out of a glass door into the garden. Beyond, rows of chrysanthemums flanked the walkway to the cages whose floors were swept back to bare earth. In each there was an exotic beast.

Under the protection of her parasol Lydia felt poised, no longer ill-at-ease as she had been in the glasshouse on their first outing. Her senses were heightened by the creatures around her and the proximity of Giles Bentham by her side.

They saw zebras, antelopes, polar bears and an elephant. But it was the animal that prowled around the long dusty cage that had them mesmerised. It looked like a large, elongated dog with short brown hair and about a dozen or more stripes from the base of its tail to its shoulders; it had a big head and a lopsided gait. They stopped in front of the wire enclosure and read the sign. Thylacine: a Tasmanian tiger.

'It looks as though it has been patched together by a child who is unaccustomed to drawing. Look at the size of its head and its enormous jaws,' Bentham remarked.

'As though the hind legs don't belong to the body,' she added. 'The tail looks like a ruler, protruding so awkwardly. And look at those stripes. It's as if they've been painted on the wrong animal. It is indeed like an animal imagined by a child.'

Lydia was thinking of her stepmother and Lemprière coming close to challenging God through their own experiments, even though they could not have known then that strange beasts like this one must have evolved over perhaps millions of years.

She remembered Louis' words about how privileged they were to be visitors in this far-flung part of the world. She had a sudden sense of the vast wealth of knowledge that lay within their reach; of the people she had known in her lifetime who were at the brink of discovering so much about the world in which they lived. She thought of the astronomer John Herschel, Jane's friend, who had gone on to discover how to fix photographs on a negative, had indeed coined the new name photography; of Ross seeking discovery of the south magnetic pole. And even earlier in history: the discovery by Copernicus that the Earth wasn't at the centre of the universe. Then Darwin had come along and discovered so much more. What would he have made of such a beast? Since he first committed heresy, scientific and religious belief had been shattered.

Lydia could not imagine God creating such a creature as the tiger, but she could imagine this animal adapting over time – what other explanation was there for its peculiar characteristics? As she stood there on the gravel path, the sun pleasantly warm on her back, looking at the animal pacing back and forth, it seemed undoubtable that it had evolved, although it looked as though it had stopped in the process. She was startled when Bentham spoke, for it was as though he had read her thoughts.

'To think people criticised Lyell in the end for not grasping the nettle on that "mystery of mysteries" – the successive appearance of new species on Earth. Yet, so many people like Lyell knew there was irrefutable proof that landscapes changed gradually. Why couldn't we accept that this could happen to humans and animals, the animate objects? Isn't the birth of new species just as natural?'

'So you are a believer of Darwin's "heresy"?'

'My father was like my great-uncle. He taught me to question everything I see, hear or read. How could you not ask: "Why?" when you see such an animal. What did God mean by putting together such a beast that is never mentioned in the Bible? Why does he have such large jaws? Why is he a marsupial?'

Bentham had not taken his eyes from the cage. In certain lights, such as now in the dappled sun, his profile had the look of a Grecian boy, innocent and alluring, not as handsome as she first thought, but more real because of that. She guessed he was approaching forty, or perhaps older. For the first time, she noticed a small scar on his left eyebrow and wondered what had happened. She knew so little about him, but how easily they fell into conversation. She had to remind herself they were strangers. She grappled with the familiar before it registered. Was this how Jane had felt when she talked to Lemprière?

'This beast was once all over Australia and now it is only found on this island,' he was saying. 'Why do you suppose that is?'

Jane listening to Lemprière, spellbound.

He continued: 'The species has adapted to its own environment and elsewhere has died out. It's much like Darwin's tortoises, only there are no other animals like this to be found anywhere in the world. If we speak in Darwinian terms, this species has survived as long as thirty million years, a period disputed by what we know from the Bible. To be here, Miss Frankland, and able to observe these things firsthand . . .'

His excitement was palpable.

'You have read *The Origin of Species*?' he was asking. 'I savoured every page. He is a fascinating man.'

'I went to the launch with my stepmother and yes, I read it then. She encouraged me to believe it was true but I didn't know why at the time. I have also read some of the diaries he wrote during his journey on the *Beagle* which he is supposed to be releasing publicly,' she said. 'But he was not the first to hypothesise that species adapted and evolved. Well, he wasn't the only one to do so. The world was ready for Darwin.'

'No, the general idea of breeding racehorses, finding the best mix of characteristics to get the best horse was not new. But the idea of natural selection accomplished by an eternal struggle for existence was, was it not?'

'Amateur historians were already questioning the number of species, especially here in Van Diemen's Land. My step-mother and . . . an amateur collector, a storekeeper at Port Arthur, they too questioned and dissected different species – speculated. I think they both came to realise more than a decade before Darwin published his theory of natural selec-tion and survival of the fittest that God did not create the Earth in seven days.'

'What?' he said sharply.

He had turned his head towards her but his expression was hard to read in the shadow of the she-oak. She thought he was hostile, but as her eyes became used to the shade, she was surprised to see his eyes soften.

'How so?'

'I have been living with their ghosts,' she said.

Why, she thought later, did she choose that moment? He ushered her through to the tea-rooms at the rear of the old building, from where they could still see the animal pacing up and down in his cage. He had his arm around her as he shep-herded her to a seat. She let herself be led and began to tell him the story. Right back to the beginning: the folded yellow note in the glass cage to everything else that had led her here. She blushed and stumbled when she mentioned Henry Belfield's name, and there were some things she did not tell – the forni-cation on the ship and in the cave; Henry's lust for Thomas;

her own buried secrets; her stepmother's true feelings for the storekeeper. Could he detect the heat rising from her body and diffusing into her face, the emotions over which she had no control?

Later, they walked through Battery Point, her hand on his arm, the other holding her parasol. His arm felt strong but she felt otherworldly. She grasped him tightly as they walked across the uneven cobbled streets downhill to the wharf and the warehouses at Salamanca. She was still talking. After she finished, he was silent. Throughout her life she had been a listener, a receiver of information. She felt guilty, then. She must have bored him. Perhaps he thought her mad?

'There is much we keep hidden,' he said slowly, the first words he had uttered for some time. 'And I feel privileged you have chosen to tell me, Miss Frankland. You have been living alone with this for too long.'

They began walking back up the lane, away from the wharves and the warehouses, until they were standing outside a tiny church opposite the guest house, an Italianate construction with multi-layered terracotta roofs.

'You are an extraordinary woman, Miss Frankland. Your life has been full of exposure to many wondrous things.'

She raised an eyebrow.

'And not many women with whom I have been acquainted have read as widely as you have.'

She felt irked by his comparison, as though she were a racehorse and he was checking pedigree.

'Tell me about your great-uncle,' she said. 'You said he taught you to question. Perhaps,' she added, 'that's why you are also impertinent.'

He feigned hurt then smiled.

'I was about five or six when I first remember seeing the Panopticon, the painting you saw on my desk at the archives.'

'Why is it called a Panopticon?' she asked him.

'It means "taking in" or "showing everything in a single view", from the Greek *panoptēs*, meaning "seeing everything". It was actually my grandfather, Samuel, who thought of the idea in Russia while he was building amphibious ships for Catherine the Great. He was responsible for the factories and workshops on Potemkin's country estate, and he had to supervise a large workforce. So he designed the principle of central inspection: a Panopticon building that would embody the principle. His brother, Jeremy, my great-uncle, is generally credited with the idea since he worked on the principle back in England as a solution for the reform of criminals. He was fond of my father, George, who helped him with much of his work.

'By the time I first saw the painting, my great-uncle had lost his mind, or everyone thought he had. Now, I am not so sure. His body, you know, is in a cabinet at University College, London. That's how much he feared burial. He gave directions in his will that after his death a friend of his had to give a lecture and use his body to demonstrate an anatomical dissection, then his skeleton was to be wired together in a sitting position – he wanted to look as though he was in contemplation – and the rest of his body was to be padded with straw. He was to be placed in a glass cabinet clad in a black suit he was fond of wearing, sitting on a chair he had occupied while alive. My great-uncle called this idea the auto icon – a man in his own image, preserved for the benefit of posterity.'

Giles Bentham chuckled. 'He thought that way he would be free of ghosts who might plague him in his coffin under the ground.'

'Surely you can't still see him?'

'Alas, his plans went wrong. In spite of everything, they failed to preserve his head. He'd ordered that it be preserved following a tradition carried out by the Maoris in New Zealand, which meant getting rid of all the moisture, but his face ended up being expressionless. They had to make a replica of wax. And they had his real head embalmed and placed in a box next to him.' He laughed again. She was surprised he could see humour in such an incident.

'You would be amused by this,' he continued. 'He is still supposed to attend college council meetings – they bring in his body in a wheelchair and in his hand is the stick he always used – called Dapple. He is said to be present, but not voting.'

Lydia was thinking that his past was as complex as her own. She hardly knew whether to believe him.

Out loud, she said: 'So you can visit your great-uncle whenever you wish?'

'The first time I was scared, terrified.'

'Do you think he had meant you to be?'

Bentham shook his head. 'I don't think so. He took a great interest, as I said, in my father, George, and later in me – even though I was only young.'

'So he is a ghost who does exist?'

He smiled again. 'You remembered.'

They were still standing outside the church. Neither of them made a move to cross the road to the guest house.

'I find your story fascinating, Miss Frankland, especially the story of the boy prisoners. My great-uncle wrote of children, too, and the abuse of them in the name of progress. I have no idea what he might have thought about the prospect of transporting boys. I was thinking while you were talking of

Henry and . . . who was the other boy? Thomas? You said one murdered the other?'

He had been listening to her.

'Do you know why?'

She too had been puzzling over the motive, but upon hearing him speak the words she had only voiced inside her head, she felt she might already have told him too much. It was better to shift the focus. She shrugged her shoulders.

'Not yet.' She paused. 'What was your reaction to the Panopticon when you first saw it?'

'I thought it was a fairy story about a kingdom of elves that inhabited the towers.' He laughed. 'They were fighting against a wicked warlord with wild white hair and a terrible temper. When he was in a rage the mountains trembled. He had dwarves who cast spells to fight for him. I used to write the spells, or draw them, for I was too young to write.'

She imagined him, a young boy full of imagination with a relative who fostered his make-believe world. She had a sense he was sharing his past to ensure she would feel less vulnerable for sharing hers. She was grateful. He talked about his gradual realisation that the Panopticon was a horror story of a different sort, and how as an adult he had felt compelled to explore his great-uncle's work, even travelling across the world to do so.

'What do you make of these murders? The murders at Port Arthur. There seemed to be so many of them? Were they linked to the boys' murders?' he asked suddenly.

'I have to finish Lemprière's diaries and Henry's scribbles. I cannot answer that yet.'

The sky had clouded over and a pale yellow light had transformed everything with its eerie glow. At last Bentham graciously took his leave, doffing his hat. From the window of the parlour she watched him stride back down towards the wharf, a solitary figure – the only person she had trusted with her story. Why? He was asking a lot of questions and had only offered some solace. She wanted to be alone to recall some of the caution that characterised the old Lydia.

The next day at the museum she began working through some small drawers labelled 'Crimes' underneath the large window looking out on to Argyle Street. The crimes were catalogued under 'Port Arthur penal settlement' – not categorised according to crime, but listed chronologically.

By the end of the day she had a list of victims, the accused and details of their trials. None of the murders had taken place in the boys' prison, except for the killing of Bundock, who had died some thirteen days after he was stoned. No one had been charged with his murder. In all, seventeen murders had occurred in the three-year period, which included Thomas's. What Lydia found peculiar was that every one had been witnessed by other convicts.

It was mid-morning before she discovered two more strange facts: the same convict names kept appearing as witnesses and in each instance, the man accused of the killing had confessed, and had rarely disputed the evidence. The hanging of the accused seemed almost a foregone conclusion. She looked across the room. No one appeared to notice her state of distraction. She kept returning to the words in Lemprière's diary. Why did he believe he could have prevented more murders? Lydia wondered whether she should tell Bentham about the patterns in the murders, or perhaps she should keep this discovery to herself. For most of her life she had rarely trusted anyone.

Hawkins' handwriting was on each report and when she checked the colonial correspondence file using the same dates as the murders, she found letters from him to Frankland. Hawkins would often use the words 'motiveless murder'. She was sure this was the same phrase Lemprière had used in his diary.

6th November, 1841

I beg to assure His Excellency that every possible means are adopted on the settlement to check such crimes. I trust that the proceedings of the inquest will be found to be correct.

As if he was apologising for their frequency, he had added:

In reference to the prisoner Bell's character, I find that he was forwarded to this settlement for stealing His Majesty's sheep – a poacher of the worst kind. Sentence of 'Death Recorded' was passed upon him for that offence in April 1833.

She scanned the pages of the ledger. Some words jumped out at her:

Every possible precaution is taken to prevent these abhorrent unnatural acts from occurring; the places you allude to such as the vegetable gardens, the rocks, seashore etc. are continuously watched and only the boys who are devotionally disposed are permitted to visit the former. I, myself, keep watch. As for the boys' sleeping quarters, despite the fact they are crowded, lights are kept burning all night in different rooms and overseers are on watch constantly. The boys are visited at uncertain hours. In addition, I have taken the precaution of securing bolts on the outside of the doors, which permits me to enter their dwellings at the most opportune times . . .

Hawkins had every right to be watchful over the hundreds of prisoners, including the boys, but somehow Lydia suspected such diligence served Hawkins in other ways, allowing him perhaps to prey on the boys for other purposes. How much had he known about Bundock's abuse of power? Hawkins had written some comments on his death:

I have not enough evidence to charge someone with this unfortunate man's end in spite of one boy being caught armed with a brick. That does not prove he committed the crime; indeed, I believe it was not this boy who plotted poor Bundock's demise, although I had him flogged as an example. It is no doubt the handiwork of some handful of boys, ringleaders in this deplorable act. I found Bundock to be a trustworthy lieutenant. His absence will be sorely missed. I have taken some stringent measures to ensure such an episode will not happen again. Bundock kept the boys impeccably clean, supervising their hygiene frequently. He often called me in to inspect his steadfastness. It is the best way to ensure the spread of syphilis does not occur.

She thought of the remains of the foundations of the tiny huts on the lonely promontory. Who had ensured the boys' welfare was looked after? Why had her father relied on Hawkins? He was obviously malevolent, from what Jane had said about him and Henry. He had collected the boys' escape vessels as trophies. The boys who had been prepared to risk death to avoid prison. Hawkins had absolute authority at Port Arthur. He could punish men and boys on a whim. He had dissected those unfortunate enough to be hanged. If Jane had observed such cruelty about the man, why had her father continued to employ him?

The next day Bentham was back at the archives. He approached her as she stood by the desk, for the first time unsure what to request. He was excited, his cheeks flushed. He had made progress, discovered some original plans of the Model Prison. The drawings he showed her were almost identical to the bandstand illustration she had seen on his desk that first day. His great-uncle's dream had been transported across the seas and he wanted to see it, to visit Port Arthur. Would she come with him and be his guide? Was he being presumptuous?

Bentham's blue eyes were shining and his enthusiasm was difficult to counter. She paused, however, feeling under siege at his insistence, knowing they shared different experiences from their research. They were at different stages of their journey. Unlike her, he still saw the penal colony in abstract terms, underestimating the depravity, the bleakness of the place where men had been reduced to beasts. Pretty drawings in a picture book did not do justice to the reality of those cold corridors, heartless jailers; prisoners robbed of all human dignity – treated in the same way as animals. Even their bodies were desecrated.

'You are quiet,' he said, finishing.

'What would your great-uncle make of such imprisonment of boys, barely into adolescence?'

He paused before answering.

'Some philosophers have thought that children ought not to be subject to the caprice and ignorance of their parents. They believe the state ought to educate them. The systems of Sparta, Crete and the ancient Persians, for instance, are supposed to have supported this plan, but my great-uncle always believed it was the right of the parent to discipline and rear their children. The state does not have that right.'

He was so cerebral. Did nothing affect him? Lydia was thinking of how, as a child, growing up in Van Diemen's Land, she had been a sightseer travelling through a landscape that may have seemed exotic, but on magnification was cruel and reprehensible. The worst part was that she had not noticed. Or had she built up a shell to protect herself from what she'd encountered?

'What of the murders? Have you discovered why they happened?'

He had misinterpreted her silence.

'Not exactly why . . . except that there were so many of them. The commandant, Hawkins, refers to them as "motiveless murders". It seems too grotesque to contemplate it but it's almost as though he organised to have these convicts killed . . .'

'The commandant? What makes you think that? I wouldn't have thought so. It wouldn't be in his interests to have such violence breaking out under his regime.'

'A lot of things don't add up,' she said. 'Lemprière knew something, but he could not reveal what it was. Some of the witnesses mentioned at the scene of one murder are also mentioned in other murders.'

'That does seem strange, I must confess. And didn't you say one of them had a towel inside his cap, as if he expected to be murdered? If my great-uncle had his way, whatever they were up to, the inspector would have been able to see them.'

He always came back to *his* research, *his* great-uncle. But then he did not know what she had been reading. She hadn't told him the entire story, about Henry's diaries, nor Hawkins' reference to unnatural crimes. She felt contaminated by what they contained. It was not the sort of material a lady should be reading and it had evoked a strange turmoil within her. Nor was this the proper sort of conversation to have with a man, especially a relative stranger. How could she possibly begin? She knew she was blushing again. She had paid money for those papers as if she had procured them for her own pleasure. She saw Wellard's face, mocking.

Bentham, looking concerned, helped her to a seat. Was it his fault that he didn't understand because she had not taken him fully into her confidence? Besides, she too had once been like him. Unknowing, unsuspecting.

'Will you come with me to Port Arthur?' he said, as she sat down.

CHAPTER FIFTEEN

Lydia opened the wooden box, plagued by questions. Why had Henry murdered Thomas? Were the other murders linked? Putting aside her fears about what she might find, she devoted the next two days to reading the remainder of the papers.

22nd January, 1842

I got the gunpowder after I exchanged a tobacco chew with one of the corporals at the stores. Now I could work on a great image for our tattoos: a crucifixion scene. Our covenant. We would both wear the same design. I'd copied it from a book I borrowed from Hawkins.

When I began marking his flesh he screamed and I smothered his voice with my hand. A small trickle of his blood ran down my sleeve onto my arm.

If in thy little book my name thou enroll.
Flesh in that long sleep is not putrified,

But made that there, of which, and for which it was;
Nor can by other means be glorified.
May then sin's sleep and deaths soon from me pass,
That waked from both, I again risen may
Salute the last, and everlasting day.

I read him Donne's poem on resurrection while I cradled his head against my chest. Two days later, when we were lying on the floor of the cave, I saw that some of the puncture marks on his arm were infected. I picked up a damp eucalyptus leaf from the floor of the cave and placed it over the wound. He said he didn't have a fever so I concentrated on bandaging his wound with crude bark. He trusts me.

Near the mouth of the cave, I have hollowed out a bed from the sand on the floor. We can see anyone approach. The bush is our audience. The first time I felt a salacious thrill performing in the open air. Later, as we basked in the sun's warmth, I thought of the way old Tom used to lie at his master's door, soaking up blue skies and birdsong. In the afternoon we faced our lengthening shadows and the cold muster yard. One day when we lay on our stomachs and I propped myself up on one elbow to see the sun fill the hollow on his back, we talked about Bundock's inquest. Then I asked him the question I've been wanting to ask him. Had Bundock ever touched him? He sat up and turned away from me. I placed my arm around him. He struggled. My fingers closed on his wrist. With my other hand, I put my fingers under his chin and forced him to look at me. I said quietly: 'He had you, didn't he?'

I wanted to hit him. He had never warned me. The surf crashed below. Perhaps I already had syphilis. My mind examined all the possible times, but I had watched over him. I wanted to know how he had him, all the details. When? I wanted to ask him, how? But he had turned away from me, his back towards me. My Thomas, contaminated. I told him Bundock was in hell, embraced by the flames of Lucifer. I walked across and sat in front of him. His head was bowed. I could have made a fortune from those looks, those curls. He looked up at me. I knew then that he did not want me the way I wanted him. He never would. I asked him what he thought of God and he told me he thought He was the Almighty. I told him we were like the penitent thief in the Bible. As long as we confessed to our crimes we could still go to heaven.

I told him about the signs I have been sent already – the dead bird on the beach washed up on the sand yesterday morning; the shape of the clouds over the moon last night; the misshapen rock I picked off at high tide. I told him, my Adonis, we had nothing to fear. The time was right.

We had already committed a sin by doing what we had done, but I told him that in the Scriptures God approves of man lying with man as it says so in the second book of Samuel when David says: 'I am distressed for thee, my brother Jonathan: very pleasant hast though been unto me: thy love to me was wonderful, passing the love of women.'

I told him our love could surpass the love men have for women and that I loved him with my own soul, in the same way Jonathan loved David. He cannot abandon me now. Jonathan gave David his robe, his garments, his sword, his bow and his girdle, and I would have given Thomas all of these things if I had them. I told him we must make a covenant until death do us part. I told him again we would both go to heaven. He asked then if we were going to die.

There were pages missing from the exercise book. Lydia could see the evidence close to the spine. What had Henry planned? Thomas should have feared for his life, yet he trusted him. She was powerless to change what had already happened, to jump into the page of the diary she was reading and warn Thomas. The writing began again, the last fragment, with no date as though it were in the middle of an explanation.

He has faced betrayal from all who knew him. James, on board the *Frances Charlotte*, who broke into a wine cask before they arrived and then blamed him. When he arrived at the settlement, he was already labelled a troublemaker. He told me about his drunken father who'd beaten him with an old brown leather whip. When he cried, his father told him, he reminded him of his mother's desertion and that made him hit the boy harder. At seven he'd been tied to the bed and left without food. He had gnawed on the wooden legs and eaten dirt, kicked a missile at the rats that scampered across the floor. At night he'd woken to their scratching and scuffling. He believed he would die where he lay. When he and his brother finally left their father, he was fourteen. They earned money labouring and learnt to be men, but his brother vanished one night. Thomas had been thieving for more than a year when he was caught and sent 'across the pond'. Three weeks at the hulks and the ship set sail for Van Diemen's Land.

The betrayal of the other boys hardened his heart. After the wine cask, and by the time they were within sight of the cliffs of Cape Raoul, he had learnt again that signs of friendship were not to be trusted.

On the way back to the muster, halfway down the hill to the bakery, he wanted to know who I had murdered. I said it was my uncle who had disinherited me, that it was just on dusk and we were alone in his study when the old bugger came into the room. I described how he went down the way Bundock had, flailing like a bloody partridge, that I'd represented myself at the trial at the Old

Bailey. Had a big turnout from my home village, but the judge was agin me. I told him about the death rattle and said it was all true, that's what it did sound like. He wanted to know why I'd killed him and I said that my uncle had sold our family home and used the money to pay off his debts. My uncle was a gambler, I said, and my father's death was his windfall.

It was my uncle who coached me in the ways of the military. Being initiated into the ways of promotion, he'd called it. The smoothness of his shaved cheeks and the smell of talcum powder, his rounded belly: 'You'll have to learn fast, lad. Learn how to be a man.'

'And here I am,' I said, and just as well he couldn't see my face.

We were within sight of the bakery, scrambling down the hill over loose rocks, staying close to the ground, waiting behind one tree, then the next, to ensure there were no guards. We almost missed muster but I knew then, he was with me.

Lydia walked through the streets of Battery Point and down to Sandy Bay, but this time, instead of visiting Nutgrove Beach, she walked quickly along Sandy Bay Road, her head down to the passing traffic. That afternoon she covered many miles, walking up into the hills of Dynnyrne, where she passed some of the more sumptuous homes that graced the lower slopes with their large white verandahs and long sloping lawns. Here, near an orchard and cowshed, she rested awhile and looked down on the streets of Hobart, her eye following the path of the river from whence it had come: westward towards Bridgewater and the convict bridge, then further again to the mountains in the distance and finally — many miles from here – to its source in the high country. Its path was through the glacial mountains, the wild country her parents had crossed so long ago. Lydia thought of Bedford Place. She recognised how little she understood about her life and how much she had learnt since Jane had died. She no longer felt able to judge any of them, least of all Henry and his misguided desires. They were all victims of sorts. Perhaps she was too.

24th January

Hawkins didn't want to see me. I'd sent him the letter I'd written Lady Frankland, asking her for more books. I wanted his advice on what I'd written in the letter. I imagined him reading over my words, receiving them with pleasure. They would give him an opportunity to summon me. Could I discuss my letter with the commandant before it was dispatched? A simple request.

But I was told that he had decided there was no need to meet. In retrospect I should have realised something was amiss. This had never happened before. But I asked via a note whether I could have his permission to go to the library at the main settlement, that I would appreciate his guidance on my reading choices.

This time he relented. Powers, his manservant, explained as he led me down the hallway that the commandant was not well.

He looked like a man possessed, his hair wild, his eyes vacant and his skin deathly pale. He would not look at me; instead, he twisted his fob-watch and paced across the wooden floorboards looking out of the window to the Isle of the Dead.

I enjoyed the fact that he was suffering. I was in no hurry to leave. If I had only read the signs then, I should have held my peace. We quickly exhausted my questions about some of the books Lady Frankland had recommended. He granted me leave to attend the library. I could tell he was about to summon Powers to draw our meeting to a close. I watched him rub his nose distractedly with his forefinger. He looked so smug.

I told him then that I'd been keeping up my reading of the Scriptures too. The large mahogany desk lay between us. He told me in his dismissive way that I could talk to Monsieur Lemprière about that. He was the convict chaplain, after all.

'Isaiah 1:10-17, Jeremiah 23:14, in reference to Sodom,' I said. 'The sin of Sodom had nothing to do with men fornicating. Even Jesus understood the sin of Sodom as the sin of inhospitality.'

He sat up straight in the chair with military precision. If I had a moment of doubt it was drowned in a wave of hatred for him. I thought of Bundock taking Thomas, probably with Hawkins' permission. The words rushed forth. Words I know now I should not have said.

'I saw you watching.'

The fallen stone had given away his whereabouts. A splash of colour in the undergrowth – a scarlet tunic – at first I had thought it was a common soldier. Then I saw his face. He was witnessing a crime punishable by death or, at the least, the maximum flogging. Instead of arresting us, I saw his filthy sweat of excitement. I thought of my uncle. I decided to give him a performance.

He sent his fist crashing down on the table. After that everything happened quickly. The sound sent Powers catapulting into the room. A china cup fell onto the carpet, a brown stain of tea spread onto the rug.

'Out!' His rage was unstoppable. Spit flew from his mouth and his face was crimson as he scattered papers and files everywhere from his desk. I thought he would have a heart seizure. Above the hubbub, Powers called for the guard, who was ordered to take me away even though I did nothing to resist. For the first time since arriving here, I felt vulnerable. My heart beat with real fear. The guard had been waiting for me to fall out of favour and he gripped me with pincer-like intensity, even though I did not struggle. I had crossed some line. I had miscalculated. I had expected Hawkins to throw himself on my mercy, promise anything to ensure my silence – that he would always protect me, perhaps that he would free me, that I would be safe. I was his loyal subject, he must know that. I've done so many favours for him. In his twisted way, I thought he cared about me.

I was taken by whaleboat back to Point Puer. As I saw the settlement loom before us, the cluster of timber houses, the boys on the shore, the smoke rising from the cookhouse, I felt ill.

The writing stopped in the middle of the page. There were more loose pages in the box, but Lydia did not have the heart to read them. Instead, she sat for a long time looking out on the street below until the gas was lit in the streetlights.

CHAPTER SIXTEEN

Lydia knocked on the small wooden door at the entrance to the cottage. She could smell jasmine and roses. Shells – tiny button swirls she had seen at the beach on Nutgrove – and abalone, gleaming turquoise and pale oyster pink in the morning sunlight, were piled in small mounds on the porch. Large, flat, dark green swathes of seaweed were draped from the rafters, wet straps bearing the smell of the ocean – native kelp – probably part of Charlotte's seaweed collection. The salty aroma mingled with the small scented white flowers. Lydia inhaled deeply.

This time no one responded. Lydia was deliberating her next move when she saw a figure in the distance walking slowly up the hill towards the cottage. She recognised the large-boned housekeeper, shoulders bent homewards.

As the woman drew closer, Lydia searched for an explanation that would justify her second visit. She saw onions, fresh spinach and strawberries piled inside the wicker basket and noticed the woman's worker's hands, chafed and soiled, and her face – unsmiling, hostile – underneath a cotton bonnet.

'I was looking for Mrs Lemprière.'

'For what reason?'

The woman had reached the gate. Behind Lydia the front door opened, creaking slightly on its hinges. She spun around. Charlotte was there in the gloom, her large eyes reproachful, her hand small and dark on the brass doorknob.

'Miss Frankland.'

Her voice was higher than Lydia remembered. The words were spoken with resignation.

Lydia breathed deeply, forcing calm. Behind her the housekeeper pushed past, bumping her with the basket. Some onions dropped to the ground. The woman bent to pick them up, grunting annoyance, scooping up the skins that had fallen. Then she disappeared along the side of the house as though to signify her disapproval. Charlotte did nothing to correct the woman's manners.

'Madame Lemprière.'

Lydia stood on the porch, waiting for an invitation, a clue as to how she should respond.

'You've read his diaries?'

'Most of them, Madame.'

'And?'

'I would appreciate your advice.'

'My advice?' Charlotte laughed, a small laugh. She had loved him – that much was obvious. She must know that he had loved her. If he hadn't been such an ardent scribe, his infatuation with Jane would have remained his secret. Lydia was sure he would have been mortified that he had hurt her. She was thinking that once secrets are revealed they can change destinies irrevocably. This woman may have lived a modest widowhood unblemished by imaginings of her husband's apparent infidelity. How many secrets she had discovered on this journey.

'You are wondering why he left so much for the living to find?' Charlotte asked shrewdly.

Unsure how to answer, Lydia heard herself say: 'May I come in? Would you mind?'

Charlotte seemed almost relieved at her request. Walking up the hallway Lydia looked at Lemprière's portrait. Those eyes, smiling, so sincere, yet concealing so much: his real feelings for the governor's wife, the truth behind the murder Henry had committed, Hawkins' culpability, her father's unedifying governorship. He had been present through all the scraps that made up the fabric of the past.

Charlotte could have sent her away. This time, though, it seemed as though she approved of Lydia's audacity.

Lydia sat on a small ottoman patterned with mauve petunias, next to the window that looked out onto the front garden. Here she was better able to take in her surroundings. Ignoring her housekeeper's behaviour, Charlotte had rung the small silver bell on the sideboard and directed her to bring them refreshments. The parlour was modestly furnished with a hearth and a large black kettle on the stove. On the walls were the portraits bearing his trademark, the thick oil paint gleaming luminous from the light of the fire. Other paintings depicted creatures of the colony: there was the kangaroo rat, green rosellas, a swift parrot, a platypus and an echidna. Suddenly she recognised one of the portraits: the sitter was dressed in the same scarlet tunic Hawkins had worn, but instead of his hawk-like stare, a child's face sat above the uniform, with the same disembodied look she had noticed in Hawkins' portrait.

'Isn't that Captain Hawkins' uniform?'

Charlotte was caught unawares.

'Ah, Hawkins,' she said bitterly. 'Yes, and that is Edward, our eldest, who sat as a model while Hawkins was in Hobart.'

She paused.

'Hawkins abandoned my husband, you know, even though it was Louis who saved his life.'

'His life?'

'He found him half dead from frostbite. Never fully recovered. Strange, as there was no medical cause – for his death some time later.'

'When was this?' Lydia interrupted.

Charlotte continued as though she had not heard her.

'He died about seven months after he resigned as commandant in order to organise the running of the Queen's Orphan School in Hobart Town. Lost his will to live.'

'Your husband didn't mention that in his diaries.'

'But, you don't have all the diaries, do you, Miss Frankland?'

Up until then they had been exchanging pleasantries. Now they had moved on to different terrain. Charlotte's tone was bitterly mocking.

'You may consider yourself an old maid, but I truly believe the path you have chosen is an easier route than mine. I was a girl of nineteen when I first met Louis. So little experience of life and he so charming. He was a good husband, mostly . . .' Her voice trailed off.

Lydia was stung by Charlotte's personal attack. This visit was causing more pain. She masked her embarrassment when the housekeeper arrived with tea in Royal Doulton rose cups.

'I fear I have intruded. It is not my place to be asking these questions.'

The housekeeper departed, leaving the door slightly ajar. Lydia spoke again.

'Madam Lemprière, I don't know exactly why I came. I lived with my stepmother until she died six months ago. I found something in our house in Bedford Place that made me realise my past was not quite how I believed.' Lydia's voice broke.

'I have decided to let you read them, Miss Frankland,' Charlotte said quickly. Her voice was edged with mistrust, but a little softer. Lydia dared not speak.

'I had planned to burn them. I had picked out a place behind the cottage where we rake the fallen fruit. Over the years I have imagined those pages smouldering. You might have realised your life was a lie. We have something in common then. I have never read all the diaries properly. You will know why if you have read anything of them at all.'

Lydia looked at the rose vines curling around the verandah. She watched a bee settle and fossick for pollen.

'In a way, I welcome your visit,' Charlotte said. 'I have wondered how I could live to the end of my days – knowing so much and telling no one. I have read those in my possession, and they have helped me understand pieces of the puzzle – my husband's obsession with the boys, Belfield and Boardman. You would know we had our own children, but my husband's heart was as big as the ocean. He was acutely aware of our comparative affluence.'

Charlotte smiled wistfully.

'We had food to eat every night. Education. But above all freedom. Do you know when he changed, Miss Frankland?

It was after the boy's corpse was washed up at Safety Cove. He found the body. The boy's little chest was bloated and his eyes had been plucked out. The escape vessel they'd made was in the shape of a coffin. You see, he found the boat as well and later they found the other boy. They both had logs tied around their legs. Louis cried that night in my arms. Nothing I could do would stop his tears. He kept talking about Hawkins' vessels like trophies on his verandah. He insisted on attending the postmortem. I told him not to go. I could see he felt responsible, the same way he felt responsible for his father's death.'

There was silence. Lydia stared at the blackened kettle on the hearth. She could think of nothing to say.

Charlotte continued: 'It was a miserable place to live, Port Arthur. We were prisoners ourselves. Hawkins was fond of whist and spoke in the military code, which I often didn't understand, nor did Louis, as French was his native language. He never liked the commandant. Hawkins collected skulls, did you know? Of his victims. Well, those convicted of murder who were hanged. He was permitted to do so. He kept their skulls in his glass cupboard like the specimens of those poor stuffed creatures in Louis' museum. All that cutting up of animals and humans in a bid to understand science.'

Charlotte looked at her then, large-eyed, animated. There was impenetrable silence in the room.

'It's hardly a wonder we all lost touch with what life was about. The hardest thing for me to face – do you know what it was, Miss Frankland? I doubt whether you would, for it's not what you might expect.'

'What?' Lydia cleared her throat, willing more power to her voice.

'He died without his work being noticed. He sent so much to that fellow, Darwin, who published *The Origin of Species*. And all those tidal records he made on the Isle of the Dead. Ross claimed credit. Yet it was Louis who recorded everything so meticulously. He was a meteorologist, a painter and a taxi-dermist, as well as a doting, loving father who worked under extremely difficult conditions. In the end, all he had was a small skate named after him.'

Charlotte recovered her composure and sighed.

'Lady Frankland — she never helped him. I know she spent the last years of her life ensuring her husband — your father — was a hero, sending ships to find him. She was always in the limelight. Yet it was your father who should ultimately have been held responsible for placing Hawkins in such control. He gave the orders to make the place "worse than death". Louis showed me the letter your father wrote to Hawkins. The misery they had to endure. For what?'

This woman had just articulated what she had known for some time. Her father — gallant Sir John, whose bust was housed in the place of heroes, Westminster Abbey — had led the colony to adopt new forms of cruelty experimenting with human beings, treating them like specimens. Lydia felt her breathing quicken.

'Lady Frankland did nothing for Louis. I was told he left some of his official papers to her. She visited me before your family left, asking for his sketches. I did not know what she was talking about. In my view, he should have destroyed all his papers, but he wanted to help all those convicts who were still suffering, particularly the boys. He didn't expect me to inherit such a legacy.'

Charlotte's face was hard, her eyes penetrating, accusing.

Lydia wished with all her heart she was anywhere but in this small parlour.

'That's why I have decided to give you all I have from him, in the hope, Miss Frankland, that you will do more than your stepmother; that you will use your connections – and I have no doubt you have many if you can afford to travel across the world on a whim – to ensure my Louis is finally commemorated in history, in the annals of the Royal Society of London, at the least. You will not show any intimate sentiments he writes of to anyone – such words are best left unread by me and others. I am sure, for your father's reputation, you too would rather they remained hidden. It is for this reason that I trust you. I give you the diaries, in total, so you can see for yourself the truth of the woman who brought you up, whom you lived next to day to day, and so you may ask yourself: "Does she deserve loyalty?"'

As Lydia walked once more down to the quay from where the little red steamer would take her back across the water, Charlotte's words reverberated in her head. In her right arm she held a bulky parcel containing the rest of Lemprière's diaries. Charlotte had told her not to come back as her visits were too taxing on her health. She told Lydia to leave the diaries at the guest house when she had finished. She would have someone pick them up.

Across Charlotte's words came a series of nagging questions for which Lydia had no answers. Can someone love one person and, at the same time, be married to someone else? Had Lydia ever loved anyone in the way Jane had expressed love? She thought of Giles Bentham. Their paths had crossed in an improbable way. She doubted whether, in her old life in England they would ever have met. But in spite of being so well travelled, he could not understand her discoveries, nor did she intend to share any more of them. And now he was asking her to travel with him to the penal settlement. She had no one to ask about the propriety of such a request. Besides, she was not sure whether she wanted to go back to that place of nightmares.

In the guest house Lydia slipped into a white cotton nightgown and fell asleep reading a history of Regent's Park Zoo. She dreamt of Tasmanian tigers and devils with yawning mouths and teeth like scissored cheese. Downstairs, the scales of a piano thundered through her dreams. Outside, cockatoos screeched alarm like ambassadors of portent. She was a child again, eight years old, peering inside cages with domed roofs and spires, walking haltingly among vibrantly coloured turquoise humming birds, craning her neck and squinting to see the heads of four Sudanese giraffes, dark diamond shapes against a dazzling sky. The animals were walking in pairs through a tunnel of wisteria in the zoological gardens.

'It has only a seven-vertebrae neck.' She heard her father's voice and she tried to count them, although she knew it was impossible. 'The tiny wren we see in the garden has fourteen.'

'Why were they made in so many different shapes?'

'Who decides how many vertebrae they had?'

'How many of them fitted in the Ark?'

'How did Noah choose them? Did he have to take the striped quagga and the great anteater with its long freakish nose?'

She had hoped to impress him with all these questions, but her father did not answer. Then one of the giraffes turned its swaying neck, beckoning her to follow.

'An escape,' someone cried. Behind her a zookeeper carrying feed chased a kangaroo with a baby in its pouch. As the animals filed past, she recited poetry:

A curious kangaroo,
Who stands upon the strangest tail
The tale, though strange, is true.

'Why does it have a pouch, Papa?' she asked her father.

He squeezed her hand. 'To carry its baby.'

'If Mama had a pouch, would I have died in her pouch when she died?'

He laughed, and she began to cry.

'I don't like you, Papa. You didn't care about Mama. You cared about nobody but yourself.'

Then she noticed a group of people standing patiently under the shade of an elm tree. Lemprière was there, his hand on Charlotte's arm. He was frowning. Charlotte, the same Charlotte past middle age, was staring at her. Her lips smiled, but not her eyes. They were all waiting for her to say something.

Jane appeared next to them out of the shadows of the elm tree.

'This is my collection,' Jane said to Lemprière, who shook his head.

'I think not, my Lady. You are a long way from home now. You may not know what to do.'

Without warning, he seized Jane by the shoulders and pulled her towards him, kissing her on the mouth.

The dream stayed with Lydia in all its details, leaving her frightened and desolate. It was as though they were all having a joke at her expense.

CHAPTER SEVENTEEN

Early one morning, with a fair wind, they left the comfortable shores of the Derwent River on a clipper and crossed Storm Bay.

'We are at the bottom of the civilised world. Imagine those who were exiled here in perpetuity,' Bentham said. 'We can return to the old country whenever we wish.'

At the mouth of the river they battled a south-west rain squall and Lydia experienced a familiar bout of seasickness. He encouraged her to return to the deck, where the fresh air revived her and he showed her how to look at the horizon to steady her gaze.

He was absorbed in all that he saw. She enjoyed showing him this barren landscape, pointing out the landmarks she remembered: the fortress of Cape Raoul with its basaltic prisms and cliffs that slashed the skyline like steel razors. He exclaimed aloud as they passed a colony of seals flopping into the water like lead pellets and together they watched them disappear from view. It was as if she was giving voice, at last, to what she had experienced alone; that by talking about what they saw, her life began to exist again. For once, she wasn't trawling a subterranean past in which she had played an unwitting part. She had been right to make this journey, if for no other reason than she had lost her way and needed to remember she had her life in front of her. Giles Bentham existed in the present.

The waves crashed onto the deck. She smiled at him. When she felt queasy, he held her arm protectively and helped her back through to the saloon, ordering her tea. But when the weather took a turn for the worse once again, she returned to her tiny quarters and lay on her bunk, enjoying the solitude. She had brought with her the rest of Lemprière's diaries, hoping to match what she might see at Port Arthur with what he had written. She began leafing through those she had read. Charlotte had included the book he had written in 1839 about all three penal settlements where he had worked: Sarah Island in Macquarie Harbour on the wild west coast; Maria Island, a windswept island on the east coast of the colony; and the third penal settlement, Port Arthur, which remained open after the closing of the other two in the early 1830s. Lydia enjoyed the immediacy of his writing, imagining that she was standing there next to him. She felt comforted by his speculations about life and was sure she would have liked him had they met, despite him loving the same woman as her father. She sensed why Charlotte had remained loyal to him.

14th January, 1842

Went for a walk after dinner of salted pork and bottled gooseberries with cream. Charlotte was already in bed with our new baby, Fanny.

I was a hundred yards from the shipyards when I looked up at the moon that scattered shards of silver across the inky black water. The stars were like untarnished jewels, brighter than any I have seen in the northern hemisphere. The eclipse was already well under way by ten past nine according to my watch: the unmistakable shadow across its surface, too symmetrical to be clouds. A moment in history. I had the feeling I could reach out and touch it.

The letter was inside the breast pocket of my coat. I have almost memorised it. Darwin's enthusiastic if ponderous prose. I still feel a thrill when I think of his words. He is interested in my silicified wood from Safety Cove and says he is going to compare it with the discovery from Ross's expedition in the Antarctic. I must confess it was discussing Hooker's discovery that day at Ancanthe that prompted me to seek Darwin's advice.

He is extending Lyell's earthquake-cause of mountain uplift and is even more convinced that coral reefs are the last relics of disappearing mountains. He is still unsure of so many things and is anxious about Henslow judging the merit of his words. If Henslow disapproves, he writes that he will give up science, for science will have given him up.

I tried to imagine Mount Arthur, lit by this half moon, as a mountain under the ocean.

I plan to send him skins and plants, against my better judgement, but he is so appreciative of my contribution. I will also tell him of my discoveries about the marsupials from my dissections. He will be particularly interested in the one we call the tiger.

Some of what he writes continues to concern me, however, like the fact that he does not believe in Paley's assertions. Why, Darwin asks, if God is such a good designer as Paley says, are there insects with tiny wings that cannot fly and snakes that show fragments of useless limbs? Why are so many species in the New World similar, but not identical, to those in the old?

These questions stir more within me. Why do I dissect animals? Why am I interested in biology and geology? Why study the tides and the weather? I need to make some sense from my results and progress from these deductions. I need to be confident about my calculations, but I do not feel confident or happy about some of the conclusions I'm tempted to reach.

I know I should be wary – I still feel that Darwin's speculations are suspect. He is, after all, the grandson of Erasmus, the man who suggested species were the result of biological change. Erasmus was a member of the Lunar Society, and its members were well known to have criticised Christianity. They only met when it was a full moon. Perhaps they were possessed by Satan.

While I sat reflecting about the universe, with such a monumental thing happening above, she came unbidden into my mind, her hair and bodice wet with rainwater. Her face looked so anguished in the clearing. Now I have settled back into my work I feel more disposed to paint her. It will be another chance to visit Hobart Town and that taxidermist.

Lydia wondered whether Charlotte had given her these extracts as a sort of penance. Even now, more than twenty years later, she clearly blamed Jane for being the temptress, taking Louis away from his family and undermining her marriage. Perhaps Charlotte wanted someone to share her pain, for surely no one else would ever know of her husband's feelings for Jane. Or she had simply not read them. Lydia could imagine the pain these words would have caused her. She was glad Charlotte had not seen the letter Jane had written Lemprière.

If I had the same telescope as Galileo, what would I see? The Milky Way, hot balls of gas held together by gravity, some invisible to the naked eye. As a boy, I visited Stonehenge with my father. Four thousand years ago people were already using those huge stones to predict eclipses. Ancient civilisations have read their calendars by the advent of an eclipse: when to plant and when to harvest and when to celebrate religious feasts.

I reached into my cloak and undid a button on my jacket, slipping my hands inside to reassure me. I shivered from the contact of my cold hands. My heart beat strongly. I am right to care about my life. No matter how insignificant I am in the face of the universe, I am a living and breathing entity. Besides, I have responsibility for all these little bodies up in the house, not to mention Charlotte. In the darkened cluttered room we share, I kissed her on the eyelids, but she was sleeping the sleep of a mother recently out of childbirth. Exhausted.

Lydia spent the rest of the overnight voyage in her cabin. When she emerged, long after the sun had risen, she was surprised to find they were passing the cliffs of Point Puer. From the water it held nothing of the magnetism of being on the promontory, imbued with the tangible presence of all those boys. From the sea it looked innocuous. She could see some ruined buildings, eucalypts and a small beach, and it was hard to imagine eight hundred of them running around there. Then the Isle of the Dead came into view and around another bend the commandant's cottage. The wild lupins had proliferated since her last visit. There were marigolds with vermilion centres; in the middle of the garden the sundial. The penitentiary with its windows like eyes staring out to sea, and the old church where they once worshipped, its spire askew from a fire. In spite of the warm weather and the pleasing colours, Lydia was filled with dread. She wished now that she had not come back. Her optimism from yesterday dissipated as she took in the scene before her, as though revisiting a recurring bad dream.

'I never realised it would look so civilised. Quite like a piece of old England,' Bentham remarked.

Lydia was reminded of the couple she had met at the commandant's cottage on her last visit, exclaiming like holiday-makers at a Brighton resort. She was expecting too much from him.

Fresh from reading Lemprière's words, she imagined him emerging from his store as they pulled up alongside the wharf. She recalled Jane's description of the bewhiskered man in a short coat and Charlotte in the out-of-date hat ornamented with flowers and ribbons. In contrast to her silence, Bentham was excited by all that was around them, full of anticipation like a child on an outing. Lydia thought his enthusiasm inappropriate but she tried to shrug off her mood, remembering he had seen none of this. Unlike her, he did not have ancestral ties here. Besides, he had spent so much time in libraries reading books about what he was to see. They began to walk along the wharf past the store and up some steps to the commandant's house.

'Darwin never visited Port Arthur?' he asked as they walked up the sandstone steps.

'I don't think so.'

'I'm sure he would have found it fascinating. He had his twenty-seventh birthday at Secheron House in Battery Point, did you know, not far from where we boarded this ship? His monkey was buried in the back garden, but its skeleton has only just come to light. Strange man. He also kept a pet turtle from the Galápagos, which he shared with his servant.'

She was silent, imagining all those who had walked up the steps under her feet.

'You told me your stepmother knew Darwin,' he said, determined to draw her into conversation.

'Yes.'

He looked at her with a perplexed expression.

'You are uncharacteristically quiet, Miss Frankland. What more have you discovered?'

She sighed and made a conscious effort to include him in her reveries. She knew she was being unfair. Trust would not come easily to her.

'Further proof of infidelity.'

The words were out, unchaste words, improper between a woman and a man who were relative strangers. A deep pink suffused her face, but either he did not notice, or kept talking to cover her embarrassment. They were standing next to the sundial in the garden.

'Between?'

'My stepmother and the storekeeper, Louis Lemprière. Well, perhaps not exactly infidelity, but disloyalty – the straying of the mind.'

'And his wife knew?'

'Undoubtedly. Well, she knows now.'

She felt a twinge of conscience that she had betrayed Charlotte, but it was out. She told him what she had read the night before in her cabin, about Lemprière's notes on the eclipse, his views on the insignificance of his life and his comments about Jane.

'I know what he means about insignificance. Each of us is like a grain of sand under such an endless sky,' he said. 'I feel the same way when I look up at the heavens and try to evaluate my life.'

He had put it so simply, and his shrewd assessment of events set her at ease. Why should she feel such guilt about the actions of people long past?

'When I look around us, everything will remain here, no matter what happens to us.' He paused and she saw he was struggling to put his thoughts into words.

'The waves will continue to crash on the shore long after we've gone and the stars will observe our death as they have so many others. It's probably the reason I wanted to follow in my great-uncle's footsteps. He wanted immortality – went to extraordinary lengths to ensure he would be seen as immortal, to ensure his physical presence would be around for years after his death, centuries, he hoped. Yet . . .'

'What?'

'Even though he made all the preparations, immortality, Miss Frankland, is an illusion and something, in my view, we should not seek.'

'Jeremy Bentham contributed greatly to mankind,' she said. 'He challenged all laws, ancient and modern, saying they should be evaluated according to the single ethical principle of "utility". A law is good or bad depending upon whether or not it increases the general happiness of the population.'

He smiled at her.

'You surprise me by your knowledge, Miss Frankland. I do not mean to sound patronising, on the contrary,' he laughed. 'I often thought that the fire that destroyed the old Houses of Parliament two years after his death might have been his revenge.'

He was looking at the small whaleboats moored up alongside the jetty. She watched him for a few moments.

'Are you married, Mr Bentham?'

'Are you, Miss Frankland?'

He began to smile again and in that moment her trust evaporated. She immediately felt belittled, looking down at her feet, avoiding his eyes. His tone seemed mocking. Then, in an abrupt change of subject, he was talking about the onslaught of an early summer. Tasmanian weather was like that, he assured her. Cold one minute, freezing the next, and then hot northerlies. She had turned away quickly, ensuring he did not see the hurt in her eyes. Instead of climbing the steps to the hotel with him, she told him she would continue walking.

Leaving him at the hotel entrance, she wandered through the neglected gardens with its profusion of marigolds until she came to Hawkins' fig tree outside the room she had occupied when she had visited alone. Bentham was playing with her and seemed to gain pleasure from tormenting her. She was beginning to feel their friendship was about proving who knew more and that she was rewarded if she came up with the right answer. She did not need his approbation, nor should she have accompanied him here. He probably had a wife and several children, but chose not to wear a wedding ring. She was a distraction, far away in the colonies. Women may now be permitted to take degrees at the University of London, but as a man he could never know the solitude of the spinster, cursed forever to sit alone near the hearth, chastised if in pursuit of anything more stimulating than embroidery. Even this journey she had undertaken to the other end of the world was hardly seen as a lady-like endeavour. What did he truly think of her? He had to be mocking her.

When she entered the hotel lobby, he was standing at the counter talking to the hotelier. She saw right away that the hotelier recognised her.

'Perhaps you might like to explore the settlement yourself,' Lydia said as their luggage was dispatched to their rooms. 'The sea journey has not agreed with me. I'll spend the afternoon recovering.'

'Certainly.'

He was at all times polite. He smiled at her and she wondered whether she had been too abrupt. Had the hotelier said anything untoward? She was sure he was friends with Wellard. Lydia was conscious of the beginning of a headache. What did she fear? She had nothing to hide, only the voices of ghosts tumbling around inside her head. She had done nothing wrong. But what if Bentham met Wellard and he told him about the content of the documents he had sold her? What would he make of her then? She was allowing her imagination new flight and her heart beat faster with anxiety. She closed the door of the cold, empty room with its whitewashed walls and sat on the edge of the narrow bed, pulling out Lemprière's diaries. She would leave Bentham to make his own discoveries.

31st January, 1842

Where to begin? I write these words with a heavy heart. Before dawn I was awoken with a loud banging, a message of urgency that catapulted me out of bed and set the baby crying, a voice telling me that they had found Captain Hawkins. My mind was befuddled with sleep. Then I remembered Hawkins had been visiting the whaling station in Blackman's Bay. I opened the door and saw Powers, Hawkins' manservant, hooded against the cold. ''Tis thought he is near death. Came through the semaphore in the first light.' I began immediately to write to the governor, as who else is in charge now but me?

We found him by the barking of his kangaroo dogs, in near impenetrable scrub in an isolated part of the peninsula where no one, probably not even convicts, has been found before. He was chattering incessantly about how Venus and Tartar had shown him how to lick the hoar off gum leaves in order to survive. He wanted to know where his boxlock pistols were with the spring bayonets. He had no other weapons, not even a knife. The pistols, which were found near him, were not even primed.

When we placed his frozen feet near the flames of the fire, he screamed like an animal, telling us God had saved him to punish him further. He might die still. He behaved as though he had confronted the devil himself.

He had been one hundred hours without food. His lips were so cracked he could hardly open them. His face was emaciated, his eye sockets clearly visible, his sharp nose even more pronounced and his eyes clouded. I thought he had lost his faculties. I repeatedly raised a pannikin to his mouth but he moaned, then lapsed into delirium again.

We took him by whaleboat to Eaglehawk Neck, to his convict railway, on which he was transported like ordinary cargo while still inside the whaleboat. Throughout the trip he lay pale, with his eyes closed. At one point I thought he was dead, his breathing was so shallow. I remained inside the boat with him, covering his form so that when the rail-carts began to pick up speed on the descent he would not be injured. I am not sure whether he recognised me. At the top of the hill, the cart clung precariously, while the convict pushers jumped on board. He gave such a terrible cry. I pitied him then.

I pitied him less later, when I began to make sense of the strange utterings he was making.

I cannot commit his words even to this diary. He spoke of a cave and boys. His breath was foul. He had watched a boy fornicate with another. I was sure one was Belfield. He wanted to confess that he had spilled his seed onto the rocks at the sight of their nakedness. He told me he was evil and should be hanged until he could no longer draw breath. His talk was dirty, filthy. He blamed the devil tempting him this way. To think he has been alone with my children. I thought of his compliments about Charlotte's cooking, how he had permitted me to open the museum, assisted me in setting up a tidal gauge. He played a good hand of backgammon. We were on the right side of knowing him.

What was he doing in such remote bushland? Why did God let him survive? A convict had accompanied him, a man he'd had flogged the week before, and he had not killed him. But I suspect instead he led Hawkins deep into the bush, hoping he would die. Maybe the convict had planned to kill him and the plan had gone awry. Belfield would understand, he said. He mentioned his name many times; that the strong survive and the weak are eliminated. Then I knew it was Belfield he had seen in the cave.

Back at the settlement, I left him under the charge of Dr Casey and walked wearily back up the hill. In the parlour Charlotte was cradling Fanny. How I was glad to be home. How I long to have life returned to me the way it was before the governor's wife entered my sphere; before Charles Darwin's chatter about two creators – one creating species in the old country and one in the new, before I was burdened with all of these confessions from dying men.

9th February

I did not find out what happened to Belfield right away. Each time I asked, Hawkins gazed out of the window as if he either didn't care or wasn't able to care. As soon as I found out the truth, I visited the coalmines myself, on horseback that same morning. The youth was brought to the surface half an hour later. He had been buried in one of those cells deep underground. His long limbs were bent and could not support him, and they had to hold him by the arms. He cried out in pain whenever he was moved. Matted and filthy, his hair was plastered to his brow and his eyes were screwed up against the light. His tongue lolled from his mouth and his head, unconnected with his body, hung loose like a rag doll. He cringed as I tried to touch him. I could smell his excrement. He consciously willed his head towards me, his eyes stared wildly and he babbled − not a human sound, but high-pitched, directionless. I have heard this sound before from men who have spent a month in total darkness in isolation. I felt a deep hatred for Charles Hawkins.

I asked the overseer how long Belfield had been kept like this and he said fifteen days. There was shiftiness in his eyes. I asked how deep underground the cells were and he told me thirty feet. The cells, he said, measured five by three feet. No one could stand in those dimensions. He said that he had instructions that even when food was delivered to the prisoner it was only to be bread and water, and that no candle was allowed. At the beginning the boy had begged for one. He didn't like the dark, the overseer said, adding that Captain Hawkins knew that, but there was nowt he could do. He said he hadn't had a boy in there before, but he stressed that the commandant himself had given the orders. I told him there was no need to let Commandant Hawkins know about

Belfield's release and that due to the commandant's illness I was now in charge of the boys' settlement.

I ordered him to be placed under Dr Casey's care in the hospital and to be kept well away from the commandant. Hawkins was punishing Belfield for his own sins, that much is clear. These boys were committing sins because they had lost their way. Temptation strikes us all, but Hawkins' behaviour is reprehensible. He is meant to be the moral guide of these boys.

12th February

My work at Point Puer is my focus now. I have seen first-hand what damage has been wrought under Hawkins' leadership. I am here as the boys' saviour. Reforming their souls is a penance for my earlier neglect. I present my sermons on Sunday in the chapel to restore their faith. Too late, I have realised that the boys probably killed Bundock to punish him for the unspeakable evil he inflicted on them, and that it may well have been supported by Hawkins. I may never know. God help these poor young souls. I will do my best to serve Him.

Each morning I walk from my house to the jetty and then travel by whaleboat to the Point Puer promontory. I read them the Scriptures with a suitable morning prayer before their bread and gruel. Often I return to the settlement in the evenings for hymns, to read another gobbet, and to give the final prayer. As I read the Lord's words and take part in confession about my own adulterous thoughts, I feel cleansed.

13th February

Last night, when I was trying to minimise a smudge of ink on the store's ledger, I became aware of someone in the doorway. It was a boy. I did not recognise him first, then remembered that he was the one who was flogged for killing Bundock. Thomas Boardman.

I ushered him inside and offered him a seat on the bench against the wall. He flinched as his back touched the plaster. I engaged him in conversation, asked him where he was working. He said he was bookbinding and that he was seventeen years old. Then, I asked him why he had come to see me. He raised his eyes to the windows. To talk about God, he said. What specifically about God would he like to talk about, I wondered. He asked: Was it a sin to be happy? He said another boy had been talking to him about sin and he knew they had committed one.

His hands were like live eels in his lap, moving incessantly. He was not much older than Edward and quite clearly deeply troubled. He said he wanted to confess. At first, I thought it was about Bundock's murder.

I told him I couldn't give confessions. I no longer feel able to take on the responsibility, but I didn't tell him that. He said that Henry had told him they could only be freed from their sins if they offered themselves to God. That way they could go to heaven. The words were all too familiar. I thought of the broken body brought up from the shaft in the mines. I asked him, with a sinking feeling in my stomach, if he meant Henry Belfield. He stood up suddenly and pulled off his shirt. I caught a glimpse of the deep welts on his back and thought it was those he meant me to see. Then I saw it – a crudely rendered tattoo – a scene from the crucifixion.

He and Henry, he told me, had done things that were supposed to be performed between a married woman and a man. He talked of their covenant, the tattoos, Henry's promise of escape.

It is time the governor knew about all this. I should send a message via the semaphore to Hobart. How much does Frankland actually know about this place he has deemed should be worse than death? Does he turn a blind eye to the goings-on of Hawkins? What would he make of the fact that he appointed a man with such evil propensities? It was Hawkins who led these boys on a path to the underworld. They have strayed from the fold.

The boy was still talking and I was barely listening. He was telling me that if they repented before they died, Jesus would allow them into the gates of heaven. Henry had told him that it was so much better there.

Henry had said they would be like the penitent thief on the cross with Jesus. They had done their time on Earth, where they had lived in hell. It was their time now to live in paradise. Henry said their tattoo was the sign for St Peter to recognise them. Hell would be for the likes of the commandant and the lawmakers who tried Christ.

I placed a hand on the boy's shoulder. I told him sharply that he was not to say such sacrilegious things and he began to sob. Perhaps I had been too harsh. I reassured him I would look after them both, but as I said the words, I felt how inadequate they were.

CHAPTER EIGHTEEN

Lydia left a note for Bentham to say that she was indisposed.
Her room was at the back of the house near the stables and
had probably once been servants' quarters. If she stood by the
tiny window she could see the semaphore, a tall pole that had
been the trunk of a tree, with spider-like wooden protrusions.
She remembered from childhood how its arms would jerk
into action, spitting out letters from the alphabet, announc-
ing an escape. Now it was silent, a lame, strange neglected
apparition at the back of the hotel. For the rest of the day
she sat in her room eating junket and drinking tea, with the
curtains drawn and the whale-oil lamps burning, not wanting
to step on to the ground outside, nor to wander among those
buildings again. She was in a dream-like state. She wanted no
interruptions, not even from Giles Bentham.

There were more papers in the parcel Charlotte had given
her, some bundled up in string, which she opened carefully.
Lydia sifted through them. Lemprière's sketches. She recognised

more of the settlement: the promontory of Point Puer; Champ Street, the main thoroughfare of the settlement. The chapel. God's presence – how important He was to this tale. The boys lived with a constant reminder of Him. Her father carried out punishment in His name, so too did the commandant. Lemprière and her stepmother were challenging His word.

She thought of the pick-marked sandstone blocks in the ground, the foundations for the dank cells where the convicts spent time in solitary, the dumb cell where they were locked in the dark for a month at a time and Bentham's great-uncle's design which kept them under surveillance like animals in a zoo. So much of the colony had been an experiment based on cruelty as a cure for evil, yet, at the same time it had abandoned these boys to evil itself.

Here were Lemprière's original sketches of Hawkins, Edward in Hawkins' scarlet jacket, sketches of the ships in the moonlight, an early attempt at an eclipse, some quotations from Copernicus and Galileo.

Then Lydia found a pen and ink drawing with some watercolour, hastily contrived, the bold lines conveying urgency. The woman staring at her, her hands clutching a fan, was at first not recognisable. Then she realised. In the forty years she had lived with Jane, she had never seen her look so wistful and coquettish, but it *was* Jane, without doubt. A woman past middle age. The characteristic mask Jane adopted, a veneer of distance, was not there. Lemprière had captured a yearning for youth. Her eyes – warm, hinting at intimacy – beckoned, but the most surprising aspect of the portrait was the clothes she wore. Lydia felt ashamed. The dress was low-cut, a rich peacock hue. Unlike most of Jane's apparel, worn up to the neck, the neckline was scooped, revealing the beginning of the curve of her breasts.

Her hair was loose and hung around her neck and down to her shoulders. Lydia had only seen her like this occasionally when she was getting ready for bed. Jane always ensured that even Lydia saw her only after of hours of preparation, powder, pampering. She forbade Lydia ever to mention her age. Perhaps the painting was an imagined scenario? Surely the sketch could not have been posed. Had Charlotte seen it? She turned over to the next page.

20th February, 1842

Yesterday I had the exquisite luxury of being able to watch her with the easel between us. I could have adjusted her mantle, slipped it from her shoulder, the momentary warmth of her skin under my fingers. She was close enough for me to bend and breathe on her bare shoulder. I could see her chest rise and fall. Her eyes are not pale grey as I imagined, but dusky grey/brown. How to capture them, to do them justice: every line from her finely boned nose to those lips . . . The turquoise dress . . . imagine what lies beneath. To feast upon her boldly, which etiquette dictates so firmly against.

I retreated behind the canvas and I think she sensed my distance. Did I imagine hurt in her eyes? She has given me no reason to suppose we have any kind of relationship other than that of governor's wife and protégé. She is so charming when her feelings are in disarray.

The allure of being so close to her, yet not being allowed to touch her, disturbed me greatly and probably contributed to my dream. Last night, the devil sent her to me, luring me away from my family. In the darkness, I could hear her wooing voice telling me there were many types of love. Walking towards the face glowing in candlelight I could smell the faint scent of lavender in her hair. She was dressed in a pearl-coloured nightdress and on her face she wore the same expression as she had in the carriage. The lines on her face spoke of experience, intelligence, of power. I felt intoxicated. She raised her hand, palm towards me, as if to stop me. Then she pointed to an old door raised above the floor with a big wooden latch, beckoning me to follow. Her fingers grasped the latch. Water gushed in and filled the room.

She told me the Lord hath commanded that we should follow and, still holding my hand, she kicked with her small bare feet. Seaweed fronds like garlands were in her hair. I wanted to taste the salty water, to possess her in this ocean. Then I saw an ark overlaid with pure gold glinting far below us. On the deck was a seat with gold cherubs carved on the back. Their wings, spread high, were facing each other. On the table were candlesticks and four bowls, like huge almonds, with flowers. I pulled her towards me and began to envelop her in my arms.

When I woke, the room was hot. I lay there for a while unable to sleep, praying that I would never fall into temptation like this. The devil taunts me with carnal desires. I remembered how provocative she was as she bent to pick up her fan yesterday, a blend of brittle and tender, like a fruit that one breaks in half to suckle the moist softness inside.

I must listen to His commandments, not follow the idle passions of my heart, for what good could ever come from fulfilling them? By agreeing to paint her portrait I have been a consenting player in this drama. I am a fly in a pot of honey, lured by greed, my wings clogged, unable to move.

Our paths are so different, hers and mine. She is privileged where I am a working man supporting my family, never mind that I was once descended from judges and jurats. We are both driven by our hunger for knowledge. Apart from that has she ever given me any reason to doubt she loves her husband? He takes her to exotic locations, bestows upon her the authority to name valleys and rivers and mountains, and funds her fancies to build Grecian temples in the wilderness. He provides for her, sates her appetite. She does not know poverty. I am play-acting in this old weatherboard building called Government House, rubbing shoulders with those in power. I do not belong here.

She can afford to question Christianity, to flirt with her beliefs, the same way she plays with me. It began in the storeroom when we were locked in handcuffs at Port Arthur. It's all a game to her: the way she speculates on Darwin's theories; the way she supports that buffoon of a husband who appoints despicable creatures like Hawkins and Bundock, and helps support this brutal regime.

21st February

I have to leave this house immediately, close myself to temptation and return to my rightful place by my wife's side. I have decided to finish the portrait at home. Charlotte will sit for me as Edward once sat for Hawkins. I should be home with my family. The path I am treading is not one I want, or need, to follow.

Dear God, please give me a chance to return to be your servant to give up these foolish thoughts. I beg your forgiveness and atonement for my sins.

> *And the man said: 'The woman whom thou gavest to be with me, she gave me of the tree, and I did eat.'*
> *And the Lord God said unto the woman: 'What is this that thou hast done?' And the woman said: 'The serpent beguiled me, and I did eat.'*

We met in the dining room an hour after I had decided to leave. She poured tea from a large china teapot patterned with white roses, her lips fixed and disapproving. She said her husband would be disappointed he would miss my visit as she had told him much about my museum. He was looking forward to talking to me over dinner. She uses words as a weapon. I apologised for upsetting her plans. Then she asked me about her portrait. I said I had almost completed the sketch and that with her permission I would have no problems finishing the painting at home.

She said she wanted to see the sketches before she made the decision to proceed to the painting and as she and Sir John are to leave for Transylvania on the west coast soon, she would like to see something before then. I am, once more, the servant.

When we both heard the wheels of the carriage approaching, I saw her realise I had already made arrangements to travel. That whatever she might have said, she could not have prevented me from leaving.

I reassured her that it was my fervent wish that my endeavours bear a resemblance to what might please her. In truth, the sketches leave much to be desired. But there is a certain raw power about them, as though desire had imbued me with confidence.

Lemprière's own handwriting declared his preoccupation with her stepmother. Lydia debated whether to tear up the drawings. Charlotte had chosen not to destroy them. Even though no one else knew of their existence, she had preserved this physical evidence for so many years rather than banishing these pages to the flames, or raking fallen fruit over them; destroying the siren, the temptress, an immortal reminder of the fragility of her marriage. Lydia knew then Charlotte had taken a certain amount of satisfaction unleashing this description on Lydia, hoping to provide proof of Jane's disregard for Sir John. Or had she meant to use these words one day as blackmail against her stepmother? If Lydia had not appeared at her cottage, they may well have gone with her to the grave, for who else would read them? Lydia was sure Lemprière would never have wanted Charlotte to see and read these pages, to be exposed to such private thoughts, and that he had meant them to be destroyed. He used his diaries as a method of confession, to unburden his feelings. Presumably, given that these were in Charlotte's possession, Jane had never seen them.

Lydia wondered how many marriages suffered from illusory lust. How little men could be trusted. She felt a flicker of anger towards Charlotte, remembering those large eyes using her in the way Jane had used her, a vehicle through which to channel past lives. Then, unbidden, the clown-like face of the spiritualist swam before her. She now sensed why he had been attracted to her. She'd been communing with the dead since she got here; with all those disparate souls.

CHAPTER NINETEEN

Giles was sitting in the dining room, head in hands, his fingers pushed into his hair, eyes downcast. For a minute or two Lydia had time to observe him before he saw her. She watched his expression change from contemplation to pleasure as she walked across the room.

'We should get out of this place, go for a walk. If the weather holds, we can go this afternoon,' he said.

The words stopped her in her tracks, sending a shiver up her spine. The words Lemprière had said to her stepmother in the museum before their walk to Stewart's Bay. For a wild moment she suspected he had read the diaries, but she dismissed this as absurd and managed an ordinary response.

'It will do me good to get some fresh air.'

He seemed genuinely pleased to have her company and apart from inquiring about her health he made no other allusion to her brusque behaviour the day before. He began giving her accounts of his sightseeing, snippets and anecdotes from the guides. He had spent most of his time at the Model Prison.

'It is quite something to see such a building incarnated, not as a picture in a book, but built as my great-uncle always dreamt.'

'Should it not have remained in a picture book?' she answered.

'We might think that in hindsight, but back then the authorities believed it was an effective alternative to flogging prisoners. Your father, for instance, was always battling with how to reform the convicts.'

'And *he* was above being judged,' she said. 'My father turned a blind eye to what was going on. If you saw the tiny confines of the dumb cell, that heavy door sealing out the daylight . . . Did you try standing in it in total darkness? That's why the lunatic asylum was built. The Model Prison made men submissive, but too mad for reform. The idea never worked.'

'There is no proof of that.'

'Oh?'

Perhaps he was right, Lydia thought. She felt suddenly tired of the burden she was carrying.

'My great-uncle spent most of his life devising a better system of political thought. He viewed the functions of law and law enforcement from the perspective of incentives: that by raising the "cost" of crime in the form of punishment, self-interested individuals would choose to commit fewer misdeeds, and the public interest would be served.'

'He never lived to see the results of the Panopticon,' she countered. 'My father believed that he could convert vagabonds, useless in one hemisphere, into active citizens in another. He thought he would be able to give birth to a new and splendid country – a grand centre of civilisation. That doesn't mean to say he achieved his aim, nor even that the aim was noble.'

Giles was silent then, as if he had inadvertently discovered the reason for her hostility. She had tarred both their ancestors with the same brush. Seeing his comprehension, she softened a little and told him she would accompany him that afternoon. 'Have you a destination in mind?'

'Destination?'

'For our walk?'

'Yes, Stewart's Bay, the forest just north of the settlement, around the point from the shipyards.' Bentham smiled then, appreciating her change of subject. 'You can tell me more about this storekeeper, Louis Lemprière.'

As they crossed the causeway from the penitentiary to the other side of the bay, Lydia imagined Jane walking along the beach in the company of a man whose hobbies included dissecting animals; free for an afternoon without her husband. What had she been thinking? She hadn't really been playing with him. Had he ever received the letter she had written from the west coast?

They walked past the shipyards, now deserted, reaching a small beach washed with coiled green ropes of seaweed. When the raindrops fell the pearly sheen of oyster shells could be seen scattered across the sand.

'After a heavy gale the beach here is probably covered with these shells,' he called to her, but his words were snatched by the wind that had begun to howl around them. The brim of her bonnet flapped hopelessly like a wounded bird. She gathered her mantle close and, tightening her bonnet, bent her head into the wind. They saw the storm only minutes before it hit, a dark brooding force hovering behind the Isle of the Dead. It was upon them like a driving force, a living being venting its rage. The rain was more like hail, piercing their faces with tiny needles. They were nearly blinded by its fury.

'The woods,' he mouthed, his voice barely audible. He raised an arm, pointing ahead, his cloak an encumbrance. For a moment she thought he might fly. She raised a hand in acknowledgement, quickening her pace, but she seemed to make little progress. Battling the wind, Lemprière's and Jane's faces appeared before her. Had they walked this way?

Then, barely realising it, they reached the shelter of the forest. Lydia's face felt as though it had been boiled in hot water. His too was red and flushed. She was surprised when he began to laugh, but she caught his mood, her mouth releasing a bellyful of laughter. She held onto a branch for support and they succumbed to the hysteria and laughed until their stomachs ached, gasping for breath. She felt exhausted, relieved that the tension that had been between them since they had arrived at the penal settlement had suddenly dissolved.

She began to shiver. Bentham took off his cloak and spread it on a log. Her laughter spent, she looked at him. His face had a pale sheen lit by the eerie light from the forest canopy. She had a strange sensation he was a vision, a ghost like the rest of them. She had never spent so long in the company of any man, apart from her father.

Underneath his cloak his quilted olive-grey waistcoat was dry. He removed his cravat, rubbing the material in his hands.

'To dry yourself, your hair.'

She hesitated, her hands hovering near her bonnet strings. It was true the rain had seeped through the material and the bonnet now clung to her head. What a sight she must look, her face powder probably streaked down her face. The familiar feelings of inadequacy returned. By now she knew he was used to looking at her face, but not without powder. She reached for the cravat, placing it on her cheeks. It was still warm and smelt of scent, at once unfamiliar, masculine. She rubbed her hair.

'It's the only thing I can offer . . .'

She smiled. 'Thank you.'

The rain had become fine drizzle, but under the canopy of the trees they were protected.

'Pull the cloak around you,' he said.

She sat carefully on the log on the proffered cloak, drawing the weight of the material around her shoulders.

'*Carpobrotus rossii*,' he said. She looked up. He was pointing to the beach they had left behind. In the distance purple flowers with hearts of yellow stars grew in abundance on the dunes. They seemed quite beautiful to Lydia, and in that moment she felt absorbed into the landscape, experiencing a feeling of connectedness to her own sense of being, the same connection she had felt after taking a bath in Bedford Place in a distant life, so long ago.

'The Aboriginals used to eat it. The leaves act as water storage organs, allowing the plant to survive in heat. We call it pigface.'

'Did the convicts know about that? It may have helped those who tried to escape to survive.'

'I read about it yesterday in that old library – it's still standing, you know, your storekeeper probably visited there often. I was also reading that the convicts wore forty-five pounds of leg fetters riveted around their ankles. Their flesh was worn down to the bone, even though they had leather gaiters to keep the irons at bay.'

'Oh?'

She looked at him, interested in his apparent change of heart. He had always been adamant that his great-uncle had a social conscience and had never previously engaged with the brutality of incarceration. Perhaps his social conscience, too, was more developed than she suspected.

'On Sarah Island in Macquarie Harbour over on the west coast, if a man wasn't broken by working under icy water in chains on the slipways or rolling logs, he'd be left overnight on Grummet Island,' he said.

'Lemprière – the storekeeper – worked there, too,' she answered.

'He must have observed much cruelty.'

'It was the fate of the boys that disturbed him the most.'

'You said you had got much of the material on the boys from the man in the general store, didn't you?'

'Wellard?' She shuddered and then looked at him sharply. 'Why? Have you spoken with him?'

'Maybe you should visit again while we are here.'

She sighed. 'Mr Bentham.'

'Giles.'

'Giles. I don't know if I would be able.'

'Able?'

'To read more.'

She was looking at her hands, not at his face.

'Miss Frankland . . . You must allow me to help. It sounds as thought the subject matter is too disturbing to be encountered alone.'

She began to tell him about Henry and Thomas as they looked out at the splashes of purple in the dunes towards Stewart's Bay. She still could not tell him the boys were lovers, or that the commandant had preyed on them. There were some things she could still not say.

'These boys were abandoned to the sadistic practices of the commandant and the overseers, Giles. It is little wonder they killed a man. The system has a lot to answer for.'

'Why did Henry kill the other boy?'

'I still do not know the answer,' she said.

'I have a great deal of respect for my great-uncle, who was trying to change things,' he said.

'He still had some responsibility for the way they were treated,' she said quickly.

He did not reply. He was sitting at the other end of the log but he had turned towards her and was looking at her. She saw hurt in his eyes. How could she expect him to pay penance for what his ancestor had done? Why then was she carrying guilt?

'My stepmother, Lady Frankland, once wrote that the convicts knew no pleasure beyond sensuality,' she said, to cover the silence. 'She was told that the character of the convict population was one of arrant cowardice. My father's opinions were no more enlightened.'

'And you carry the burden of both your parents' views?'

He was right, but she would not admit it. Their shared intimacy had begun to dissipate. They now stood in the clearing, as perhaps her stepmother and the storekeeper had stood so long ago, locked in their own worlds, a chasm between them, formal once again in spite of their bedraggled demeanour.

'We should be returning. The storm has eased off,' she said stiffly.

'Of course.' Her words galvanised him into action. 'You must put my cloak around you.'

He bent to pick it up from the log where it had fallen.

'That won't be necessary.'

They walked back in silence, quickly. The rain had abated as soon as it had begun.

He escorted her to the lobby and bowed farewell.

Back in her room, she immediately considered apologising. He had been nothing but a gentleman and she could find no rational explanation as to why she was punishing him. Besides, as they'd been walking, it had occurred to her that their forebears had been themselves puppets of another distant regime. Certainly, they had inflicted suffering, but to what extent had they – even Jane, for that matter – actually witnessed the effects of their actions?

She had supper in her room alone and the next morning she skipped breakfast. It was mid-morning when she walked downstairs to the lobby and found a note. The handwriting was recognisable from Bentham's other missives – clear, legible and confident. There was no reference to their journey into the woods. In the quietness of her room, she reread it:

Miss Frankland,

In a way, we traverse the same path, although I appear to have difficulty convincing you to believe this. An act was passed in 1819 prohibiting children under the age of nine to work in cotton mills; the first of a series of parliamentary bills passed over the next forty years in a process of law reform that was prompted by the writings of my great-uncle. What you have told me about Henry and Thomas I do not treat as lightly as you might suppose.

I must leave in a matter of weeks. Please, permit me to enjoy your company. Besides, we have much to discuss.

Yours, GB

The note was an invitation of sorts, but his words provoked a contradictory response – a sharp pain she had not expected nor invited. He was to leave after all and he had mentioned this fact almost as an afterthought. Was he courting her? Or were they two people on the other side of the Earth seeking a distraction from solitude? She found it difficult to pinpoint why he affected her so much. She was flattered by the way he appealed to her intellect, conducting conversations with her that he would surely usually reserve for his gentleman's club in Mayfair, but that wasn't all. There was something else. The way she felt when they were together: how aware she was of his presence; how pleased she was at the prospect of seeing him. But she could not afford to get involved. She felt a wave of irritation with herself. Was that how she journeyed through life? At the edge of existence? At least she had options: a disposable income and with it, a choice of direction. Why couldn't she choose to be happy? What did it mean to be happy?

Picking up a small hand mirror on the dressing table, she stared at her face, her eyes, as usual going straight to the scar, a thin jagged line as if drawn by a fine red crayon, more evident as she was unpowdered. What did he think when he looked at her? The lines around her mouth where she smiled were not unattractive. Her nose was at least refined, spared the disfigurement from the accident in spite of Jane's fears. She had Eleanor's small pointed chin and her father's air of calm.

A woman of middle age. She focused on her eyes, also inherited from her mother, large and hazel-green with thick lashes. Her father had once said that they were a mirror for her soul. She had learnt early in life that they revealed too much. As the years went by, she created a mask she hid behind. Never beautiful, Jane had said about Lydia's lack of physical appeal to a suitor, as though Lydia had deliberately selected her appearance. Lydia realised that for all those years she had accepted Jane's pronouncement.

Her fingers traced the scar again and rested on her lips. Kissing the tips of her fingers, she ran them down the top of her bodice and then, cupping her hand inside, caressed her nipple. Her eyes responded. Intimacy. She could not imagine sharing such an emotion with anyone. She was terrified of it but at the same time intoxicated. The giving of herself to another. Her experience with Henry Belfield was her only encounter with male desire, and his motivation made her shudder. That was probably why she had banished Belfield's behaviour so effectively, why she felt so uncomfortable reading words of love. She was resigned to being denied pleasure.

In this wild landscape, she could travel unchaperoned with a man in a lonely land where anything might happen. Surrounded by ghosts, she had abandoned her usual reserve. She thought of their shared laughter, how he might have thought her gullible. She placed the mirror back on the dressing table. Here, they could play out their roles without rules of etiquette. Their relationship had flourished in the same place her stepmother and Lemprière's relationship had developed. She picked up the mirror again. Her brows frowned and she thought of how stern she must look when she admonished him. Even if he was unmarried, he would not be attracted to her. In her former life, Giles Bentham would play no part. Apart from the indiscreet question about his marital status, she was glad she had not betrayed any more feelings.

Lydia sat at the writing desk, dipping her quill into the ink. It took several drafts to reach the right tone. When she finished the third attempt she reread what she'd written and felt pleased that the note achieved what she sought. It was both clipped and impersonal. She wished him a safe journey, informing him she was deep into her work. On impulse, she wrote a postscript. With his great-uncle's knowledge of the lives of disenfranchised children in England, perhaps he could assist her to put the colonial case into context if she were to publish any of the diaries. She rested the quill on the inkpot. It had never occurred to her to make them public before, nor had she given much consideration to what she might do after this journey ended. After she deposited the letter behind the desk in the hotel lobby, she regretted her offer. Her more cautious side had counselled against it. Besides, she was not the owner of the diaries. She did not know what possessed her to suggest such a thing. He would surely not interpret the request as an interest in him. They shared similar intellectual interests, that was all.

Well, it was done. She could hardly ask the man behind the desk to return it. An hour later, still in a state of confusion, she walked in the drizzling rain down Champ Street, her feet level with the roof of the penitentiary, whose doors were at sea level. Stepping close to the sandstone wall, she avoided the puddles and took the long flight of worn sandstone stairs down to the building. The cricket ground stood empty and the settlement felt more like its original purpose: a jail.

She was walking past Wellard's store when Bentham's words came to her. The familiar array of convict wares, the broad arrow carved into a block of sandstone, an old pick, some leg irons and some new additions lay outside the shop. Lydia also noticed daguerreotypes, some blank-faced men she presumed were convicts. She could see Wellard inside in the gloom, bent over some ledgers. On impulse, she went in. He did not register any surprise at her visit.

'Thought you'd be back, Miss.'

He engaged her in banter about the weather, the tourists, his booming business. Then he said: 'Just so 'appens I 'ave somethin' for you. Some missin' bits. P'rhaps the most inneresting bits of 'em all.'

Lydia's mind said 'no' but she heard her voice say, 'Yes?' Wellard's eyes were on the small kid-leather purse she had tied around her wrist. The familiar feeling of being exposed that she experienced when she was around him came over her. The man was bad. She should have asked Giles to accompany her. It had been his idea after all . . .

'Why didn't you include this with the rest?' she asked, mustering assertiveness.

'Well, now. I din't know I 'ad 'em 'ere, now, did I? Amazin' amounts of stuff in the back of this shop.' He gestured behind him and leered at her and his face was repulsive with its chapped lips and rotten teeth.

This time she refused to part with a guinea and began to walk towards the door. In the end he accepted eight florins. He disappeared for what seemed to Lydia an eternity, then returned and handed her an envelope, tattered and filthy. She looked inside.

'It's only half a dozen pages,' she exclaimed.

'Oh, yes, but what pages they are too. 'N' he writes small. A real gentleman, that Belfield. That's the boy you mentioned, remember, Miss, when you were 'ere last. Not that I can read, but I've asked people who can and they've told me wot's in these pages. Turn your 'air, t'would. Those poor brats. I've been 'ere too long 'n' all.'

She was counting out the money, suspecting as she did so that it was the hotelier who had helped him read the pages.

His hand hovered over the coins.

'Matter of fact, I wuz lookin' for you,' he said, 'but they told me you left, sudden, like.'

'I will not be back again.'

He smiled a gap-toothed smile. 'That's what they all say.'

She walked up to the Model Prison, unfolding the pages from the envelope, breathing deeply, unsure whether she wanted to read the contents. She may have paid for nothing. She sat smoothing her skirts on an old stone wall near an unused barn and surveyed the scene before her. A mist had settled across the hill. The honeyed colour of the penitentiary glowed in the overcast light. Which house had been the Lemprières'? The paper rustled in her hands, which were pale with the cold. She began to read.

19th February

Sweet Jesus and the Holy Ghost, I see signs everywhere. The milk I spilt on the table before breakfast, the dead bird under the water tank. Old Tom would've had that bird for sure, but Old Tom's gone now. I have to wait until the signs change. At night, I still piss myself, thinking again of my tomb, terrified they will foil the plan. Let me be sent to the timber gang, please God. Every night I pray, waiting for an answer. The covenant will protect us.

She was almost too distracted to continue, but forced her attention back to the page, filled with a sense of foreboding.

Yesterday, I knew the time was right. I'd been first in the queue for gruel, hungry as always. God had sent the sun to shining after so many days of rain. The overseer called my name. I was assigned with Adonis, his sweet flesh that I have not touched for months so close to me at muster. We were to help build a barn to house the animals, about three-quarters of a mile from the settlement. Part of the carrying gang, the leading working party, divided into teams, some carrying planks, others carrying beams, others shingles. I was to be on light duties as my foot is still twisted. Inside the privies while we were alone, he held my head in his hands to stop it from shaking and kissed me on the forehead. Later, we walked across the yard and I jumped a puddle to see if I could clear it. But my good foot crumpled and instead of clearing it, I fell heavily. Thomas helped me up. He could not know we were doomed. Yet I am spurred on by Frank MacNamara's poem:

> *For he is thoroughly purged from sin,*
> *And although in convict's habit dressed,*
> *Here he shall be a welcome guest.*

21st February

The day was clear, that much I remember. I awoke early. We ate our gruel, then collected up the tools, assembled in the muster yard. Then we began to walk away from the settlement. The overseer was a grumpy man named Daniels. He'd be one that'd watch us if we strayed, and a hard one to fool. What if the ball was hoisted at the flagstaff at the end of our day in the bush and we had not had the chance to be alone?

But it worked like clockwork, as though fate was with us after all. After lunch Daniels propped himself against a tree. I called to him that I had a dreadful thirst and that Boardman knew of a stream not so far away. He barely responded, so sleepy was he. We walked into the edge of a eucalypt forest. We were alone in the bush in its midday heat. No animals anywhere. Two wattlebirds rasping and croaking. Out there more of the same forever. No escape, not across this terrain.

I led the way, changing direction several times. I could tell he was behind me from the sound of his feet crackling on the ferns. When we reached a clearing, I heard the rushing of a waterfall. The ground was then damp underfoot after the heavy rains. We disappeared deeper into the rainforest. Tree ferns grew, huge canopies choking out the light. Our feet made no noise on the wet earth, after the dry crackle of bark and leaves. A dragonfly whirred past.

I told him this'd do.

Now the moment had come, my heart beat faster. I had never before been appointed the killer. He had drawn the shortest straw. To be murdered would be easier for him, he said. I remember thinking he did not understand what he was saying. But he said he feared the rope around his neck more. We were like boys playing a game of soldiers. He put his arms around me as we stood in the clearing, and placed his hands on either side of my cheekbones, stretching my skin. He told me that my eyes had changed the most. We lay down together, the way we used to. Ferns and bracken and damp leaves. He knelt above me. He wasn't used to being the initiator, he said. But neither of us was up to the task and he collapsed on top of me. I began stroking his hair as he sobbed. I was aware of him in my arms, of my responsibility towards him. If we could stay here forever in this peaceful place . . . I listened for sounds, for Daniels' voice. I must act. I turned towards him. There were words that must be used. Why didn't I give up then? Because I believed it to be right in God's eyes – that God had spoken to me and was waiting for us. That we could be together forever.

I told him we should walk towards the stream and waved my hand. We got up. The shape of our bodies in the bracken was a flat space in the wildness that surrounded us.

I began with the familiar words:

'Now, to business. You know the plot. Are you against it?'

But he interrupted. 'How would they know to hang me,' he asked, 'if there was no one to say I'd done it? We should have asked Jem and Biddy,' he said. But this is our journey, no one else's.

I told him it was no matter and continued reciting the words I knew so well, telling him he had to repeat them after me. I made him say out loud he wasn't against it. I was remembering the first crime we had committed: the killing of Old Tom before we stoned Bundock. Then, as now, he was following my instructions. He looked at me solemnly. I kept reciting that he'd have the chance of giving them the go-by 'cause they'd never know what happened. If anything goes wrong, he must make sure and tell the judge that it's his own free will. Then I spoke more quickly, telling him to say he was ready. He said he was.

I pointed again in the direction of the creek. As we walked towards the water, the ground sloped away. I bent to pick up a large stick. I walked behind him. He balanced himself to walk down the bank, his eyes on his feet. I began to raise the weapon, but at the last minute he spun around and our eyes locked together. I had not expected this. He had tears in his eyes and was saying that we hadn't said goodbye. Curse him. He wasn't making it any easier.

My hands were sweating. His words mingled with the blood pounding in my ears. He was talking too loudly. He had to stop shouting. I must already have begun to hit him as my hands were wet and sticky with his blood. I could hardly look at his beautiful face. One eye was half closed. This boy never doubted me, loved me in spite of who I am, he believed in me, he believed I had the strength to deliver us to heaven . . . I was seized with panic about what to do.

Above me a strong wind brushed the tops of the blue gums, the noise competing with the rushing water. In desperation I pulled from my pocket the knife we had used to mark our tattoos. I had no choice. His blood was between my fingers and the knife was slippery – I couldn't grip it properly. Rusty, none too sharp, and too wide a blade. I held it high above my head. The knife met its target, but I had not used enough force. It had lacerated his skin, but bounced off. It lay on the ground next to him.

He had fallen forward onto his stomach. I dragged him until he was half propped up. He was muttering quietly. I could hardly bear to look at him. I bent closer. His words bubbled through saliva and blood. He was saying he'd had enough – to kill him, kill him. Sobbing, I put my arm around him, my half-butchered boy. I dragged myself up and, picking up the knife, I got behind him, imagining he was my uncle, taunting me with money. I concentrated on the nape of the neck I adored and raised the knife again as high as I could. The terror of being locked up and buried under the ground again drove me and I brought the blade down with all my might. God would look after me. This time, the tip embedded at least an inch beyond the blade. I cannot remember the sound he made but he was still sitting up. I tried to pull the knife out and then I screamed at him. It was his fault. I'd be caught and hanged.

I no longer wanted him to die. I heard rushing water. I thought I heard footsteps. I could no longer hear him.

I prayed to the dear Lord to help me, but bad omens appeared before me in succession. The crow I'd seen when we were lying in the bracken dismembering a bird; the puddle into which I fell the day before. He was lying face down now. Using both hands, I pulled on the handle. It broke off and I fell backwards. The blade was in his neck. I turned him around with effort. Blood smeared across his face, his mouth was open but it was his eyes – I will never forget their expression.

I screamed.

I wanted to tell him it was all right but instead I told him I'd lied to him, that I'd never killed another man. Not even my uncle. That I'd been trying to impress him, that I was a coward, a failure. Even though my uncle had wronged all of us, I'd lost the courage to pull the trigger, it had gone off accidentally.

I told him about my racket exchanging boys for favours to save my own skin, that my uncle had taught me the value of boys. Hawkins knew what I was doing, I was sure. I told him I knew I didn't deserve his love. Words came and went. At some point I discovered I was running blindly, wet tree ferns slapping my face, my leg dragging behind me, running as best as I could to escape. To have one more chance at life.

There were only two more pages and the words were barely legible.

Rushing in the undergrowth, clawing at the branches grasping me, tearing my clothes and refusing to let me pass. Screaming, not caring whether anyone heard me. I thought of Hawkins, of Bundock – anything not to think about my Adonis. I splashed my face in the stream, ran my hands under the water, trying desperately to get the blood out from under my nails, washing away the facts, trying to wash him from me. I examined my hands, the hands that killed him, but it was too dark under the forest canopy to see clearly.

How long before I heard voices? It was my gang sawing with a big cross-saw — two men either end, cutting into a large eucalypt under Daniels' watchful eye. I pushed my hands into some moist soil at my feet, smearing it on my face, gulping air. Then I walked slowly into the circle, dragging my leg behind me.

I told Daniels that Boardman had absconded while I was drinking after he had showed me the creek. He was suspicious, but then he seemed to believe me. I pointed in the opposite direction to where we'd gone, but as my back was to him, his fist slammed into my head and I reeled sideways. As I picked myself up, he ordered the men to search the bush. He said that I was mealy-mouthed scum and he didn't believe me. Why hadn't I gone too?

When the men returned, empty-handed, he ordered one of them back to the settlement to send a message on the semaphore.

The last page was soiled with dirt, the ink smudged, and Lydia had even more difficulty reading it, the writing was so small.

Two days later, I stood summoned before Daniels. He told me a man called Sedgewick was cutting brooms in the bush when he heard groans coming from under a giant gum tree. The sight that greeted him caused him to call God for mercy, Daniels said. Because the thing was human, he told me. Daniels was smiling. It was flyblown and clotted with gore. Boardman was still alive.

Lydia was thinking back to the written words in the Old Sessions House in London. The entrance through an ancient archway with its gargoyle lions and dragons. Words that only partially conveyed what had happened. Words that would haunt her for the rest of her life.

CHAPTER TWENTY

In the privacy of her room, Lydia opened a small oval container and engaged in something she rarely did. Inside was some snuff. Her father had taken it regularly. It left her feeling light-headed and she dozed fitfully. Eventually she sat up, shaking herself out of the stupor that consumed her, forcing herself awake. Dressing mechanically for supper, each gesture felt leaden. She chose a dark blue serge dress and a black woollen shawl to match her mood, reflecting that her maid at Bedford Place would have disapproved of such dark shades as they made her face too pale.

What would she tell Bentham? She knew he would notice. He had asked to help. Lydia contemplated ripping the pages into little shreds and scattering them in the stream behind the Model Prison, together with the diary entry and Lemprière's sketch of her stepmother. But she had no right to dispose of these items of the past, they were not hers to destroy. Yet no one, surely, needed to carry this burden.

As soon as she walked into the parlour she saw Bentham seated by the fire. He was reading one of the Hobart newspapers. Light from the flames softened the lines on his face and he looked boyish, comforting. Her heart skipped a beat.

'Miss Frankland. Whatever is the matter?'

He put his arm around her. She struggled for composure, starting at the weight of his arm on her shoulders, the touch of a real human being. He shepherded her through to the dining room where another fire burnt brightly. Apart from three others, the room was empty. A smell of burnt custard filled the air. She had no appetite for the local skate with hollandaise sauce.

Seated opposite him, she could not bear to look into his eyes. She knew her nose was red and she wiped it distractedly with a handkerchief.

'I must return to Hobart Town.' She spoke so quietly he had to lean forward to hear. In a rush, she told him: 'I've found out why he killed Thomas.'

'Wellard gave you something?'

She nodded bleakly.

'You must share it with me.'

She did not say anything.

'Come. You should eat. I know it's not the best fare.' He picked up her bread roll and began to butter it. Something about his gesture reminded her of the many times she had performed the same role for Jane. Always looking after others. Overcome with his kindness, she felt tears prickle behind her eyelids.

'I will book our return voyage immediately.'

He stood up. 'At least try the broth. After that, you must show me what Wellard has given you. For a woman of your disposition, I fear he has done you a disservice. I should never have suggested it. I must also thank you for your note. I would enjoy helping you in any endeavour to have your stepmother's work published.'

After he left she nibbled on the bread, spooning up soft carrots and onion from the steaming hot bowl. In a few minutes he returned with news that due to an impending storm the clipper hadn't sailed, but that it should depart in the morning. After supper they farewelled in the lobby, formal again in the mahogany surroundings.

As they boarded the boat the next morning, she handed the pages to him after a fitful night of deliberating the consequences. He would know the boys were lovers and that she had concealed this fact from him. She was unable to articulate her feelings.

Mist enshrouded the Isle of the Dead and she could not even make out the promontory of Point Puer. As the ship picked up on the breeze she stood on the deck, drawn by the darkness enveloping the desolate place that had caused so much turmoil in her life. In the rain and mist the buildings floated like disembodied pieces from a sandstone jigsaw: the church with its wooden spire, the rampart of the military tower next to Hawkins' cottage, the hospital on the hill with its statue of Hippocrates. Then they rounded the corner and it was gone, vanished as though it were a mirage: Point Puer, Port Arthur, the Isle of the Dead, all signs of civilisation. The clipper hugged the shore. Rounding Cape Raoul they encountered a wind of such force it made the vessel pitch. Thrown against the handrail when she went below, Lydia bruised her arm. The seas were the roughest she'd experienced, with a nor'west gale that had the ship bucking and heaving, waves lashing the deck. She only just reached the privacy of her cabin before she expelled the contents of her stomach into the privy. She wished she could also eject the violent images that swam before her eyes. She lay down, weakened by the retching.

It was not until they reached the entrance of the Derwent that she saw Bentham again. She was standing at the bow gazing at the approaching town, drained emotionally and physically, when she heard his voice behind her.

'I am so sorry that you have struggled alone with all of this. Please, let me help somehow.'

'You cannot undo the past,' she answered, half turning towards him.

They were passing the Iron Pot, a lighthouse built by convicts in the early years of the colony and now used by whalers. A large iron cauldron had been abandoned there. Once they entered Storm Bay the weather became calmer, but the clouds were still dark. The hills that flanked the river were bathed in the sunlight breaking through. Three rainbows slashed the skies in brilliant, dazzling colour.

'There was much you have not been telling me.' His voice had an accusatory tone.

'How could I?' she asked.

How could he be concerned about his own ego after what he had read?

He looked at her, one arm on the railing, his eyes confused. Walking two steps towards her, he stopped. Something in her solitary figure repelled comforting.

'You might wonder what a woman of my position is doing seeking such unsavoury truths,' she said, not seeking sympathy, instead providing an explanation because she thought it necessary.

'On the contrary, Miss Frankland. I, too, am seeking my own truth from the past so I, of all people, might understand. Perhaps, like you, I have not fathomed my own reasons. We are alike in that way. Besides – and I know this is a delicate matter – but my great-uncle wrote an essay arguing to decriminalise sodomy which, in his day, was punishable by hanging. I can understand, however, how abhorrent this material must be to you.'

She looked at him standing there in his frock coat. Would she have noticed him if he had been a passenger on the voyage, she wondered? She felt hard, distant. He was a middle-aged man, not the boy she sometimes saw, passably handsome, his brown skin declaring his difference to the more pallid passengers. He was wearing the same cravat he had worn that day in the forest and he held a black felt hat in his hand. She wondered if the cravat contained her scent.

He would never understand her sense of failure, however similarly he tried to paint their experiences, nor the sense of inadequacy that had dogged her all her life. Jane had continually cast her as a disappointment. Why should she not still believe her?

He went on. 'What's been written in this letter should be reported to the authorities.'

She lifted her head defiantly. 'To what avail?'

'This, and much of the other material you have told me about, are historical documents,' he said. 'Perhaps they should be published. What will you do with them?'

'That is my business.'

How could she publish something that damned her father? That was too much pain to bear. She saw his expression change to one of resignation.

'I leave soon,' he said.

'Then I must bid you goodbye.'

She returned to her cabin. When they had disembarked on the wharf amid the familiar smell of rancid oil, rotting animals and fish, he wordlessly handed back Henry's pages. They both watched as their luggage was taken up from the berths below. Above them she could see the organ pipes near the summit of Mount Wellington shimmering in the heat. Lydia boarded the phaeton almost immediately, waving farewell. She saw him watching, glad she had left with her dignity intact. In minutes she was delivered through the chaos and up the hill to Battery Point.

Anna's familiar neat double-storeyed white-painted guest house, with its box hedge gardens and marble statue of an angel in the garden, was a welcome sight. There was something clean and pure about the smell of wax in the hallway, the polished hatstand, chairs positioned neatly around a small table. Anna emerged from the kitchen, wiping her hands on her apron and welcoming Lydia in her guttural German accent – strong, positive, sure:

'Why, Miss Frankland. Good to have you back.'

In the week that passed she heard nothing from Bentham. Her sense of containment vanished as the cold settled in once more. For the first time she felt sympathy for her step-mother's plight, as thoughts of Giles consumed her. All week she had watched the ships from the verandah of the guest house, wondering if he was on one of them. Each morning she began the day by checking the visitors' box. No note arrived.

After six days she decided to revisit the museum and check whether there were any execution records for Henry Belfield. If Bentham was there she would maintain a polite distance, but as least she would know if he was still in the colony. Whatever emotion she may be experiencing, he must not know. She was in control.

At the museum he was nowhere to be seen. She forced herself to concentrate on the task at hand, resisting the urge to ask the attendant any questions. He had remembered her, and like a conjurer producing a rabbit, he appeared behind the desk carrying a small maroon book. It was not unlike the diaries Lydia had discovered almost a year ago in the attic at Bedford Place. She felt her heart quicken with excitement.

'Your parents' journey to the west coast of Van Diemen's Land, to the penal colony in Macquarie Harbour,' he said. 'I knew it was here somewhere. In your absence I have been recataloguing some of our original items. It was in the wrong file.'

She opened it immediately, experiencing the now familiar thrill at reading a new document. The front page was entitled 'Trip to the west coast of Van Diemen's Land, March 1842.' The trip that had begun this journey. She had come full circle. Lydia smoothed back the pages, stiff from lack of use, probably never read. Pages were missing at odd intervals.

Marlborough township

26th March, 1842

We have left too late in the season. At the end of March we face the abrupt changes of weather. When the native beech turns brown, winter has set in. But Sir John is anxious to see for himself the first penal settlement of the colony on Sarah Island, which was closed in 1829. It will also give him an opportunity to map this terrain – much of it is unnamed. The rest is known as Transylvania, a name I thought full of foreboding when I first heard it. I will take my specimen boxes so I can examine the local habitat.

We are only a small group. A free settler, David Burn, a play-wright of tragedies – a diminutive man with a sharply drawn sense of humour; John Barnes, a slightly built, red-headed young man, and a fountain of knowledge who was a surgeon at the penal settle-ment in Macquarie Harbour before it was disbanded; and James Calder, our leader, the deputy surveyor-general, a neat military man, shaved and perfumed. He personally beat our path as far as Frenchman's Cap some six months ago and is accompanying us to help map the terrain. Stewart, my maid, is also with us, as well as a band of convicts freshly released from Port Arthur. They do not say much but they seem prepared to carry my luggage and are willing enough. I sense, though, they are not used to taking orders from a woman.

Yesterday, Stewart told me word had got around that my specimen boxes are hatboxes. I suspect Calder was the source. They think me frivolous and arrogant, my explorations a rich woman's fancy. Seventeen hats, one for each day?

For the first few days we rode through cleared pastures of scorched hills. The only living things I saw were a few scrawny sheep grazing and a party of convicts building a probation station. The weather was unseasonably dry due to a prolonged drought. After five days of riding from Hobart Town, we reached a finger-post nailed to a gum which pointed to Marlborough.

This frontier settlement is my last chance to send or receive mail. I have posted the letter, mechanically, not allowing myself to dwell on the decision, nor its consequences.

I was shocked by the news about Henry Belfield, which reached us as we were packing for this journey. I cannot believe that he would be so malevolent. To think that I presumed I could save him from moral corruption. He will surely be hanged, I tried to intervene, but even as I did so, I knew that Sir John would have none of it. Instead, he chided me for becoming involved in his plight.

We have forded the Dee River. Such English names for an un-English landscape. The trees were like dried-out grey ghosts; in the prevailing wind, their fingers pointed in the same direction as if seeking water. Ten years ago they were vibrantly green, Calder tells us. Killed by frost, some say, but he maintains it is an act of God. We can never hope to understand this territory we traverse.

Tomorrow, after breakfast, we shall set off on foot to attempt to find Lake Echo, journeying further into the interior, heading for Frenchman's Cap, crossing the River Nive, only horse-ankle-deep. I am not sure why, but I feel plagued with despair. Past travels have been fraught with danger, but for some reason I feel particular foreboding about this journey. The darkness up ahead, both in the sky and land, the craggy mountains clothed in mist . . . Perhaps it's because I'm remembering Calder's descriptions of *Paradise Lost*, as though this is indeed hell itself and the end of the earth. Beyond is Transylvania.

29th March

On the banks of the Derwent, about a mile below Lake St Clair, we were met by Calder, who had prepared the night's camp. There were bark huts for Sir John, myself and Stewart. Calder shared his miniature bell-tent with Burn. The headache that has plagued me since we left Marlborough has gone. I was moved by the sight of the native golden autumn colours reflected in the lake. Sir John said it was the most beautiful sheet of water he had ever seen. I feel as though I am a member of an audience watching a play but unable to engage.

Burn commented on the fact that the mountain behind us, Mount Olympus, looks down on Lake St Clair, named after a Scottish family from Loch Lomond. I have become fond of this small man already. He plagued us with letters leading up to the journey, requesting that he be allowed to accompany us, telling us he was always on forty-eight-hour alert, ready to pack his bags at any given moment.

The next morning our washbasins were covered with ice. When I pulled back the door of the tent, the scene that greeted me was breathtaking. The sky was an intense blue, the atmosphere of the purest ether. Mist wreathed the mountains, draping them like a silk shawl.

From here to Macquarie Harbour we have only a foot-track. Calder has erected temporary huts along the way for the vice-regal party. Provisions left at the huts are kept to a minimum in case they are used by escaped convicts.

We have entered Transylvania, having left the horses with some of Calder's men on the last of the cleared land before the bush begins. In the afternoon the sun broke forth with dazzling brilliancy, the promontories of the distant mountains glorious against the azure vault of sky. I experienced the thrill of the explorer, walking where few have walked before.

Tonight we are camped on King William's Plains under the majestic peak of Mount King William. The tents are pitched in such a way that we can view the grandeur of the landscape. As the sun slipped down this evening with a lurid, murky glare, the horizon gleamed wild and watery, perhaps an omen of what is to come. I am writing this while reclining on my fern mattress.

31st March

Ah, for the comfort of that early ride. I have not had the heart nor the inclination to keep this as a daily journal. I force myself to write in case I forget what has gone before. Besides, everything is damp and the ink smears across the page, making my writing illegible. Today I found some dry paper, loose sheets, which I will copy into my journal upon our return. I say that with optimism, for who knows if we will even make it through this journey. These pages may be discovered lying next to our prone bodies.

It blew a gale during the night and by daybreak there was drizzling rain. This morning, Sir John read the morning service with a short sermon on the edict of Darius that consigns Daniel to the den of lions. We took shelter under some rocks. I wonder how my husband would react if he knew I am questioning the Old Testament?

All day the sun has barely shown itself from beneath the clouds. Much of the bush cleared last year by Calder and his convict working party has grown back. I am forced to walk now, and the convicts carry the palanquin empty − all but useless against the impenetrable scrub. I have scrabbled like an animal with the rest, digging at the earth, clinging to branches, slipping and falling in the mud that is everywhere, squelching around my feet, smearing my hands, my clothes, between my toes. Every dress I packed has been splattered. My feet are perpetually wet. I hate that the most.

3rd April

Everywhere I look we are surrounded by trees and darkness. I am left mostly with my own thoughts as we walk in single file.

Yesterday I began to reflect on my life. In the silence of the forest I realised that I have carefully constructed security, not happiness. In the past few months, the scaffolding of my world has begun to collapse. Now that we face pressure from the government, we may well be recalled. And what then? Piece by piece, the dust and mortar is falling around me. Is it since meeting him that I have felt this way? Each step I take is uncertain. My eyes are forever on my feet and the undergrowth beckons me to its bosom. My hands are scratched and torn from grappling with horizontals that grow everywhere, like barriers across our trail. Those trees peculiar to this island, whose spindly branches straddle our path, reclaim the work of Calder and his grim-faced men. They have cut on average more than a third of a mile a day in this wild territory.

The rainfall, steady at first, has become thick and turbulent. Water is everywhere, rushing past in the many streams we ford, louder still in the rivers, which threaten to spill unchecked over the banks and drown us all. We are like waterlogged beetles, clinging to the barely discernible paths, wedged in rocks against the current. Tonight, we stay inside our tents; no doubt tomorrow morning we shall be greeted by the water drumming on the canvas. I'll have to fight the desire to stay there, avoiding damp clothes and shivering in the early morning air.

To the west of Lake St Clair the swamps turn into miniature lakes. We cannot yet sight the top of the grand mountain. Frenchman's Cap, with its quartzite peak which stands between us and the west coast like an ancient natural guardian. This afternoon Calder ventured forth, but returned defeated. Some unforeseen arm of the mountainous mass impedes us from exploring further. The weather cares not for our schedules. My husband had told me this journey would take no more than a week, but we shall soon enter our second.

There was a space of a page, where Lydia presumed Jane had planned to write more. Then the writing continued.

We never see the sun. The water has ruined our timekeepers. My calves, my whole body, ache as the damp rises from the earth. It pervades everything: my wet dresses taking up valuable space in the tent, my sodden walking shoes, the light, too dim to read by. I have collected nothing in my specimen boxes. Private ablutions are carried out not far from the settlement. We eat as the convicts eat — on blankets spread around the fire, sharing the same fare: salt pork, damper, black tea with sugar. To think it was a fortnight ago that we lunched at some of the grander properties at the Ouse, a few days' ride from Hobart Town — sumptuous pork pies and vegetables from the garden.

At mealtimes I notice the convicts' dirty hands grasping at the food, no pretence at manners. Calder told me that at first they did not understand what it was to be treated kindly. It took some time for them to realise they were not to be beaten at regular intervals. At mealtimes food is fuel for them, so I cannot judge them on manners alone. Gradually I have begun to address them by name. More than once while climbing through this wild land, I have grasped the hand of the one I call 'the bargeman' for assistance. Calder told me this was his occupation on the Thames before he was transported.

Today my burst blisters caused me to wince with each step. The trees grow ever stranger, darker and more sinister — beeches and pines of so many varieties no one can name them. Perhaps the strangest sight is the cabbage palm, a spiky porcupine-like plant with no branches, standing higher than two men — indeed, some rise to thirty feet. It has a headdress bunched out at the top, the trunk curved under its weight. We climb over fallen myrtles, past stringy barks and fern trees heaped, jumbled and woven in tortuous gestures after plunging into a deep, gloomy, woody dell. It is, as Calder has said, as if we have entered hell itself. In each curved branch I imagine a coiled snake waiting to spring at me. They would be unused to humans in this Godforsaken place. I travel in the middle of the party. It is an unspoken agreement that anyone who sees a snake does not alert me to the fact.

5th April

We have finally reached the confluence of the Surprise and Franklin rivers. The bridge across the Surprise was a fallen beech, which thankfully reached the other side. The Franklin proved harder. We spent hours scrambling down its banks through a forest of sassafras, unable to find a crossing. Eventually we left the river and emerged at what Calder calls Painters Plains.

Sir John told us when we stopped to boil the billy that the last time he was here he found two native bark huts and some crude bark paintings. There was an outline of a dog, an emu and some other designs. The artist, by a strange oversight, had forgotten the animal's tail and had made the forelegs twice as long as the hind ones. He couldn't make out their exact meaning and left them to be reclaimed by the elements. The huts are long gone – the natives do not build structures that will last. They are forever moving on.

I waited for the tides, the moon. Last night I dreamt of this land before we came, where phosphorescent creatures flitted across the river and shadows built and rebuilt houses that were washed away. I awoke to more rain on the canvas. By now, he will have received the letter.

We are to go nowhere today, so I write up these notes. The rain has turned every tiny rill into a stream, each stream into a river. The Frenchman still looms above when the clouds clear, but instead of filling me with joy, its presence reminds me of our lack of progress.

Burn is reading the second volume of *Master Humphrey's Clock*, sighing constantly over the fate of 'noble Nell'. His pessimism, from one usually cheerful, is enough to cloud our fate.

In his sermon voice tonight Sir John imparted the news that the *Breeze*, which awaits us at our destination on the west coast, has been instructed to sail on 25th April. We have many more swollen rivers to cross in that time. If we don't make it, what will befall us? Calder said he believed we should turn back, but my husband has already decided to continue. I saw Calder's expression at this announcement. Sir John began to recount some familiar anecdotes, saying he had been in worse situations in the Arctic. I asked him what happened if we reached the coast and the ship had sailed, a question I was sure was on the others' lips. He frowned at me. Now that I know the truth about his Arctic expeditions, I have grown bolder. Is he really capable of leading men? Where once I could depend on him, I am no longer so sure. I think Calder doubts his reasoning, but he would never say anything. I remember the first of the two journeys my husband made to that frozen continent. He had left at the wrong time of the year and the expedition was an unmitigated disaster. Nine of the twenty-one men never returned from the first voyage in 1819, and two of them were murdered. Yet these facts are not generally known. What is known is that he wrote a best-selling book as the hero who ate boots to stay alive. His second voyage was a success, but in spite of that he waited almost ten years to be made governor in Van Diemen's Land.

For so many years I have thought him a hero, but I have only ever had his word for it. He has become a stranger to me, obsessed with ideas about building a grander colony than New South Wales.

He wants to map it himself, name its rivers and mountains and conquer it all. Has he never cared for others but himself? I am thankful we no longer need to share quarters. He seems callous to me now, especially when I think of the picture Lemprière painted for me and his stories about the cruelty of the place. Why should I not believe him?

The newspaper clippings she had read in the archives in Hobart Town had accused her father of stupidity, of irresponsibility, of pig-headedness. She had hoped they were scurrilous and sensationalist. They said he preferred an occupation as explorer to that of governor, pointing out that when he chose to journey to the west of the colony, traipsing over mountains for his own interest and glory, the colony had been left with no one at the helm. She had read, too, about his first journey to the Arctic, where some naval officer was quoted as saying Frankland's expeditions were the worst-planned in the history of polar exploration. She had skipped across most of the articles, closing her eyes to the words. She hadn't wanted to believe them. Now, as she read Jane's diary, her stepmother's words of denigration confirmed what she had feared, and she could see now that their love had not been what she had imagined.

But if Jane suspected her husband was such a failure, why had she been inconsolable when each ship returned from the Arctic without him?

She read on with increasing dismay.

7th April

It has finally been decided today that Calder and some of the convicts will return to Lake St Clair for more supplies. We wait, in what Sir John has called Detention Corner, for an improvement in the weather. The winds roar and the rain continues to fall in torrents. This land resents the intrusion of human beings.

9th April

Fifty-four hours later Calder has returned, carrying packs of eighty pounds. The rain has turned to sleet and snow. My cheeks ache with the wind, and my eyes and nose are streaming. Melting snow has swelled the banks of the Frankland, which flows a few feet from our tents. The water hurtles around rocks with a power we cannot contain, threatening to drench us all. Last night, lying on a bed of damp green fern on sheets of stringy bark, my dreams were accompanied by gurgling water. This morning the damp had seeped to my undergarments. My teeth chattered and I could not control them. Dawn broke and the sky was wild and lurid. We could die here like escaped convicts and our corpses, like theirs, would remain forever undiscovered. I know, by midday, with only hours to warm up before nightfall, I will be shivering.

10th April

Today the ground was treacherous underfoot so I was always seeking the high ground between the icy pools of water even if it was muddy. Not a patch of ground was dry. Sir John told his troops we would laugh at this one day. He spoke with his jacket, full military, strained across his chest in spite of us being reduced to rations. But it was his face, that pampered babyish complacent pink face, like a newborn ready for the new day, which annoyed me the most. I have begun to despise him. Outwardly, I show a brave face. How little I know him and how little, by default, I know myself.

Lydia flicked through the pages of the small maroon book. There were more ridges in the spine, more absent pages. Where were they? She came across some blotting paper with Jane's handwriting in reverse on it. She imagined Jane closing the book as she finished copying out the journal each day. Where were the other words that would never be read?

Lydia left the museum avoiding the eyes of the attendant, masking her vulnerability, before heading out to the traffic in Macquarie Street, narrowly missing a young boy rushing past carrying bread. Outside in the fresh air she stared for a moment at all the activity – carts, broughams and farmers in for market day – her mind still in the wet landscape of Transylvania. Across the road from the museum she slipped into a tea-room and ordered some tea, and ham and tomato sandwiches.

Afterwards, instead of returning to the museum, she walked down towards the wharf. She hardly noticed she had turned into Macquarie Street until she saw the high brick wall. Bentham had pointed it out to her once as they passed in the phaeton. A few decades ago from the windows of the treasury, citizens would have had a good view of the men dangling at the end of a rope, he said. Between the iron spikes on top of the jail wall, the sinister silhouette of the gibbets would have been visible. The wall was still there, but the sandstone had weathered. Crevices had appeared, some as wide as a fist. Henry had died there, she was sure of it.

CHAPTER TWENTY-ONE

Back at the guest house Lydia found an envelope waiting for her in the visitors' box with her name on it in Giles Bentham's handwriting. She carried it to her room, not wanting to open it right away, savouring what might be inside. The envelope contained something other than a note. It was bulky. She closed her bedroom door and sat in the chair by the window overlooking the box hedge. Spring daffodils bloomed in the garden below and in between them grew tiny flowers of powder-blue. Inside the envelope was a sheaf of papers filled with handwriting she recognised immediately. As her eye travelled down the first page, she caught the word Charlotte. Sipping Russian caravan tea brought by Anna, she carefully removed the rest of the papers. He had written on the first page.

L,

I believe you will find this interesting. I need to have it back intact as soon as you have finished. I hope this helps you in your journey.

Best wishes, GB

She turned to the last page but there was nothing else, nothing about his proposed date of departure.

29th April, 1842
England-bound

Finally on board the *Neptune*. We have been sailing for two weeks now. I have my volumes of books and half the money I deposited in the treasury, holey dollars – Spanish coins I had hidden away from the days when Father and I owned the shop. The weight was almost more than I could carry, although the coins were not worth as much as they were when we were merchants. Then they were four shillings and four pence apiece. Now they are half that. I have left Charlotte the rest. She will be well looked after while I'm gone, until she and the children are ready to join me. Then we'll start life afresh.

How had Giles come by this? He was full of surprises. He had reached out to help her. She wanted to see him, to thank him. More than that, she wanted to show that she trusted him. What had he done to deserve her rudeness? She remembered the unaccustomed touch of his arms around her, how he buttered her bread roll as though she were a child. How it felt to be comforted.

I will use these notes I am writing when I give evidence. Belfield's story came to me in fragments during my visits to him in the tower at Port Arthur, where he was kept prisoner before being sent to Hobart Town. The boy was skin and bones, even though I made sure he received good rations. When I first told him he would go to the gallows, he said: 'Yes, yes,' grasping me around the ankle in such a grateful manner I had to be careful not to step back in disgust.

Each day I spent hours with him, as though by absorbing his madness I could do penance for my previous neglect. Gradually he told me the story. The more he told, the worse I felt. I recognised the phrases and words he used, the same words I had heard before in confessions – part of the ritual, or 'the game', as they call it, carried out in front of the nose of the commandant. When I asked where he came by these words, he said he thought they had been handed down from prisoners transported to Port Arthur from Norfolk Island.

Between sobs he told me that he was not fit to live. In the six days before he was due to be hanged his only request was that I offer him salvation in another life. How could I do that? What should I have told him? That I would fail him too? I should have prevented them from playing their game. When Boardman came to see me, clearly troubled, I ignored him. I was the only one who knew about it, yet I had told no one. Would God have wanted me to be silent when a boy's life was at stake? And the other victims? All these men telling me how they had killed their fellow humans in God's name. I released them with my blessing, telling them they would go to heaven, for that is what the Bible teaches. They believed God would forgive them.

I should have intervened as I guessed deep down Bundock's evil intentions, although I never admitted it, even to myself. I suppose

I hoped that by not confronting such matters they would cease to exist. Besides, I felt powerless confronting Hawkins who gave the man nothing but praise.

I sit with my notes before me, trying to collect my thoughts. I shall write all that I remember in a report and include it with the confessions that I have finally committed to paper, from those men involved in ritual suicide pacts to escape the abominable situation in which they found themselves. This will be vital for any evidence I give when I get to London. Writing this diary helps me examine my thoughts and assists me to practise redemption. Weak to the last, I allowed my father to die. And I did nothing to protect two boys not much older than Edward – what's worse, under my protection.

I can still see him crouched on the floor of the cell, defeated. One morning when he was rational, I told him of my plan: that the abolitionists had organised a Select Committee into Transportation and I was going to England to give evidence that boys are electing to die to escape their prison on the other side of the world – and we call this reform.

He laughed in my face.

In between the visits to the tower, I spent time at Safety Cove. Hot days, the sun bouncing off dazzling sand, even the chill wind in the shade absent. That first afternoon, using a flint rock the size of my fist, I tackled the sandstone bank, hacking at the soft rock until my hands blistered, I was breathless and my chest ached. My hands were slippery with sweat. I sat on the shore, breathing pungent kelp air. The bizarre image of my son Edward inside Hawkins' jacket came to me, his tiny shoulders inside the clothing of the man I once trusted. Then another image – Boardman's hands on his lap. The innocence of youth. The bush hummed as if interrogating me.

The next day in the museum I accidentally knocked over a jar containing the foetus of the Tasmanian tiger and the acrid smell of formaldehyde filled my nostrils. In the mid-morning light, it shattered on the floor. I stared at the lump of the unborn reefed from the womb. I thought of Cuvier and his shattered specimen jars and all that he must have confronted. I did not have his resilience. What did I care of Darwin? I vowed there and then to give up dissection. To give up my life here and return to the old country. My wanderings on the way home took me past the church. I looked up at the new wooden spire atop the sandstone walls. The heavy brass bells were chiming for the evening service, an age-old sound. God, for whom they carried out their orders . . .

3rd May

How could I have left Charlotte and the children to go to England? Am I abandoning them the way I have abandoned others? As we bid each other farewell, Charlotte's expression wounded me beyond endurance. At the end I almost told her, but I must keep the real purpose of my journey secret.

It was Sir John Frankland who gave Hawkins the power – to be the executor, arbitrator, as well as the judge. He propped up a system that had no heart – that persecuted men and boys. He will surely be dismissed after they find out the truth. And what of Lady Frankland? I wrote to ask her to save this boy from being hanged, but what hope can come from such a plea? They were leaving for their journey across the island. I did not even say goodbye . . .

5th May

The trial was just before I sailed. It took no more than an hour. Sedgewick was the man who found Boardman's battered body. Before passing into unconsciousness from which he never recovered, Boardman apparently named Belfield as his killer. The verdict was no surprise to anyone. To be hanged by the neck until dead and his body to be prepared for dissection. I watched Hawkins' face. It was impervious.

Some two days later I sat in Belfield's cell. He handed me a wafer of a coin, ground and smoothed. I turned it over in my hand and saw it was inscribed with their names. A love token, the date and the words: Point Puer, Thomas and Henry. On the back was the same drawing I had seen on Boardman's arm – the crucifixion. He pulled up his sleeve and showed me the matching tattoo.

On an unseasonably warm morning in March, the day before he was due to die, I gave him the condemned sermon. Half an hour later Reverend Bedford's corpulent figure filled the doorway. After each hanging, Bedford breakfasts at the St David parsonage with the captain of the guard and the sheriff. He likes to hang as many as he can at one time, otherwise his breakfast gets cold. The sight of the man filled me with despair.

His eyes were shining as Belfield confessed his sins. He let forth a torrent of condemnation, jabbing his finger skyward, telling the boy that since he had killed and fornicated with another he had brought himself to sin and therefore death. He told Belfield that he should pray for forgiveness, and that he doubted he could offer him salvation from his sins. He must repent. After Bedford left Henry sang hymns. I had assured him that the Reverend's word counted more with God, but I saw at once this was a mistake. Belfield plainly would not trust him. Once more I had let him down. I still behave as the system expects me to behave.

At eight o'clock the next morning, as the bells of St David's tolled, his face was pale and glowing. He told me he could see a light when he closed his eyes. Thomas's battered face had appeared before him like an angel and told him he was forgiven.

The twelve-inch bolt swung open. Bedford, the deputy sheriff and the executioner entered the cell. Behind them in the draughty corridor were four 'javelin men' — convict police from Port Arthur. The executioner presented him with a rose and then pinioned the boy's hands behind his back. Belfield fell to his knees. He began muttering:

Our two souls therefore, which are one,
Though I must go, endure not yet
A breach, but an expansion,
Like gold to airy thinness beat.

I wondered whether Bedford had ever heard of John Donne. Hearing him say those words gave me comfort as well, as I knew the boy gained solace from the poet's words.

Two Aboriginals — one a boy, the other an old chief — found guilty of murdering a shepherd were also to be executed. Peletegu, the old man, I had seen earlier carrying out spectacular stunts for a small bit of sugar, clapping his hands and rising four or five feet into the air, and taking up a broomstick lying in the jail yard, which he threw like a spear so it disappeared through a small hole in the side of the sentry box.

Walking down the corridor between the chaplain and the deputy sheriff, Belfield still held the rose in his pinioned hand. He was quiet, resigned. As we entered the execution yard, and walked further into the quadrangle, I heard the noise swell from the crowd. Reporters from the press stood nearby. Could Henry smell the muffins still warm at the baker's? He'd wanted to know whether the rope around his neck would feel heavy or light. Did the hangman know he no longer weighed as much? He'd heard the tales of a hanging going wrong. He'd told me in his cell that the rope must be lengthened to dislocate his neck so he did not die of strangulation.

Trust in God, trust in God, trust in God. I urged him to say these words, even though I was beginning to doubt them myself. On the platform, the old blackfella, no longer playing stunts, lay like a bundle of clothes discarded in an untidy heap, an exposed leg showing lesions on his skin. Nearby, the young black boy, about ten years old, stood watching. The crowd jeered. The old chief uttered a scream, a guttural sound, shattering my thoughts. The crowd went silent. Some pushed forward. The young boy was smiling. I noticed the coffins piled on the cart. Three black boxes. The executioner moved towards the chief and hauled him up the steps. He screamed again. On the platform he fell face down. The tension from the audience was palpable. But the old man did not move.

The executioner went to the corner of the stage, picked up a wooden stool and carried it across to where the old man lay. He placed him on the stool and put the noose around his neck. He pulled down the cap. I had never witnessed a hanging. I tried to close my eyes, to will myself away from this. A clatter as the stool fell, the trapdoor bouncing on the floor, released of its load. The old man's body swung jauntily above it. He had made no sound.

The crowd collectively strained further forward. The Aboriginal boy's eyes were travelling around the square, darting here and there. He was more agitated now. He fell to his knees. The executioner masked the boy's head and the rope was hung around his neck. He struggled, colt-like limbs flailing, uttering words in broken English.

As the trapdoor opened the cord slipped halfway up the boy's neck. I saw his hand, spider-like, grasp at it wildly, then a small amount of red blood seeped through the cover over his head. The crowd gasped.

The executioner pulled on the rope to drag him back up. For a moment the cap slipped back and his eyes stared out wildly, blood trickling from his nose. Every minute the boy breathed seemed an eternity. He gasped, then came a shrill screaming. The executioner dropped the rope again. The screams stopped abruptly.

I watched Belfield and saw him close his hands tightly around the flower the executioner had given him. The doctor often does not inspect the bodies until an hour after the hanging. That he might lie there that long waiting for death to claim him. I felt sick. The executioner now moved towards Belfield. He was led up the ladder to the platform, his feet placed over the trapdoor. I could see the executioner's hand grasp his shoulder, the weight of those large hands, and the coil of rope as it landed around Belfield's neck. The white cap was placed over his head. By his side Bedford was mouthing prayers.

Blindfolded now, his hands free, Belfield reached out to the world he was to leave behind. In one hand he still clutched the rose. When asked if he had any last requests, he said he had nothing left to live for. He asked that God forgive him and that he would go to heaven. The chaplain's voice incanted slowly, 'Christ receiveth sinful men.'

The mountain, a dark brooding presence, was behind us. Amen, trust in God. Amen, trust in God, I said silently. Did Belfield hear the bells that began chiming? Was a light still shining within? As the rose fell from his hands, he swung into the darkness that awaited him.

7th May

I have recorded all that I remember from that dreadful day. Watching the moonlight on a dark sea already hundreds of miles from Port Arthur, the deck sways under my feet and the wind buffets me hither and thither. Two weeks ago the children were helping Charlotte decorate the sitting room for my forty-sixth birthday, hanging the biggest branches of tree ferns from the low ceiling of wattle and daub. When I returned from the stores Edward was standing on the wooden table with a wreath of flowers. There were jokes about the serving girl sacrificing too much to the 'rosy God'.

I was thinking that this was my farewell, for I did not know if I would return. I congratulated Charlotte for the feast she had produced from our small kitchen: soup followed by trumpeter, a goose, a round of beef, rabbits, wild duck shot by Casey the day before, two chickens and some ham. Next to Casey sat Reverend Turner. We talked of Hawkins' slow recovery – it is expected he will resign – the newspaper coverage of the Franklands and their journey westward. It seems the tide has turned against them – his days as governer may be limited, she may be homeward-bound.

Casey, the good doctor, will manage affairs here while Hawkins' future is decided. I drank too much. At midnight, I was in tears, sobbing in Casey's arms. He was at a loss as to how to respond, his unruly red hair bobbed alarmingly. Charlotte came to his rescue with a glass of madeira, putting me to bed with soothing words, bidding the guests good night. I fell asleep hoping that Belfield had seen me in the crowd and drawn some comfort from my presence.

10th May

It has taken me days to come up on deck and eat properly. I thank the Lord again for the forthcoming inquiry, my chance at redemption. I devour books to understand the new country to which I sail. Much will be different since my father and I left. Not since the

Great Fire of 1666 have there been so many changes there – the Victorian Age they are calling it, named after our young queen. The first regular Atlantic steamship service has begun. Railroads now reach into the metropolis: one has been built between London and Birmingham. I imagine the surprise back home at the concept of Hawkins' human-powered railway. Men as beasts.

Viaducts, bridges, trails of steam, smoke, sparks cutting across land that was unchanged since the Middle Ages . . . The inns have vanished with the mail coaches. Instead, I gather massive train sheds like iron cathedrals, brassy and shameless, have taken their place. Factories are shutting down because of rallies about conditions in London, Birmingham and Bristol. There are mobs in the streets. It's said the monarchy is to be dethroned, the House of Lords abolished and private property confiscated. Sir John Frankland always said he feared another French Revolution.

Darwin's package arrived the week before I boarded the ship. I did not open it until yesterday. My life seems unstable enough already. It was, however, with some joy that I eventually did so. I feel a growing connection between us. But I had feared that he might have given me up as someone who doubted him too much. After all, I came close to accusing him of blasphemy, though I did emphasise that I was deeply honoured at the idea of collecting for him. Now I have read the contents of his letter, it's like a missive intentionally hurled. Firstly, and importantly, he appears not to hold my criticisms to heart, saying my sentiments are understandable. Five years ago, he might have agreed with me.

He writes that he has been busy cataloguing and distributing the specimens he sent home during his voyage on the *Beagle*: primitive sea creatures, shells, fish, and then perhaps animals on land. Since returning from his voyage he has been elected to the secretaryship of the Geological Society because of his work on the coral reefs, on volcanic islands and the geology of South America. Of most interest to me, and probably Jane, are the notebooks he has written on the transmutation of species. He has sketched out a thirty-five page outline of his theory and left instructions that it be published in the event of his unexpected death. Lady Frankland and I are named among the beneficiaries of his notes 'should any unfortunate event come about'.

The biggest surprise is his declaration that we have helped him reach some of his conclusions — living, as we do, in a bright and savage land where everything is waiting to be discovered. He is convinced that the emergence of those new species so painstakingly dissected by us and the other collectors in the Antipodes are the result of descent with modification. Like Jean Lamarck, he believes biological change has been shaped by alterations in the physical environment, with plants and animals progressively fitting themselves to the changes in the physical world.

His theory is simple: the globe has undergone such far-reaching changes — as suggested by Lyell — and, indeed, proved through Darwin's own travels on the *Beagle* — that it is not unreasonable to assume that life, too, has undergone a comparable transformation. If not, the passage of time would have brought about a lethal maladjustment between living things and their environment and in the long run, the earth would have depopulated itself.

He urges me not to let his words fall into public hands, as he is probably some years off publishing.

I have read his letter over and over, and am struck by the simplicity of what he is proposing, as though it has been obvious to me all along. I am waiting for the impending storm, trapped as thunder builds in a house I fear will collapse. Everything I read increases the torrent. Lyell's *Principles of Geology* and Thomas Malthus's work on population: if the population goes unchecked, it will continue to double every twenty-four years, increasing by geometrical progression. This will outstrip resources such as food, air and water and there will be a struggle for existence.

The more I think of Malthus, the more sense Darwin makes, the bigger the crisis in my faith. In the inky black nights, with the slap of the waves loud on the wall of my cabin, I speculate on what he has said. I have many weeks ahead of me to compose a reply. Sleep brings no relief. I suffer from old dreams and am threatened with blasphemous thoughts. I fear my sight will once again be taken from me.

I shall write to Lady Frankland to tell her that the confessions and my report will be left to her should anything befall me. When I look into her eyes, I see into her soul. And me, the curer of souls. Yet I cannot cure myself.

CHAPTER TWENTY-TWO

Lydia needed help navigating through the shoals, avoiding the currents that would drag her under. She needed some distance from the torrent of words that beckoned her back to the past. Jane's actions seemed to her now to be more complex. Perhaps she had tried to remain immune to the challenges of being human – being vulnerable, suffering in love – and for some reason Lemprière had pierced that confident exterior, stirring the real Jane to respond. Keeping her emotions in check had always helped Jane survive. Her marriage increasingly seemed a loveless affair, one borne out of convenience rather than passion. Sir John had suited Jane's purposes: she had been looking for a husband when the newly appointed hero returned from his second Arctic expedition. Lydia thought of Lemprière's sketch of her stepmother, of the emotional declaration from Jane in the letter she wrote from Marlborough. She could not imagine Jane writing such sentiments to Sir John. Then she thought of her stepmother standing on the wharf at Southampton, tearfully bidding her husband farewell.

She was thankful Giles Bentham had not seen Lemprière's sketch, nor his scribbled fantasies. Where had he come by this diary? What had happened to Lemprière?

While she owed Giles thanks and was still touched by his attentiveness, she felt that he had trespassed; that he possessed a hidden part of her, only newly realised to herself. Besides, there was nothing to indicate that he wanted to see her. Perhaps he had already left, a rebuke for her rudeness.

Her fingers closed over the polished sharpness of a ruby she wore around her neck, which had once belonged to Jane. Jane had died alone and never fulfilled her dreams. Was that how she, Lydia, wanted to live? Bentham's address was on the back of the envelope. He had taken lodgings near Wapping, a dilapidated part of town near the rivulet, where Lydia remembered her stepmother had once visited a taxidermist.

She spent some time considering her response, then wrote back thanking him for the diary entries and asking where he had come by such material. She suggested an idea that had come to her that morning. If he had not already departed, then perhaps he might consider journeying to Ancanthe before the ship sailed?

You may remember I told you I visited Ancanthe, she wrote. It's quite an evocative place, a temple in the wilderness only ten miles north of Hobart. My stepmother had it built and asked members of the newly formed Tasmanian Society to come up with a name. It had to be classical. Ancanthe is Greek for vale of flowers.

He replied the following day. His ship was to sail at the end of the week so there was little time, but he could meet her that afternoon. He would come to her guest house with a coach in preparation for the journey, but if that was not convenient could she respond by the return post? He had found Lemprière's words by accident. He would explain when they met.

He arrived in the lobby at the guest house, a smile in his eyes, his hands crossed in front of him, and she felt excitement at seeing him.

'I am glad to renew our acquaintance,' he said.

'And I, too.'

As they clipped in the chase, past the racecourse, he told her that Lemprière's papers had been in the possession of an old friend named William Gourlay, a Hobart Town lawyer, whom he had known from his youth in London and who had emigrated to the colony as a free settler. He and Gourlay had met at the Masonic Club in Macquarie Street after Giles had returned from Port Arthur. Giles had mentioned the storekeeper during their conversation about the penal settlement. Gourlay said he had thought the name was familiar and a couple of days later he had summoned Bentham to his office. Lemprière's papers from his England-bound voyage were in the vault of his legal firm. They had been there for many years, untouched as far as he knew, and he had no idea how they came to be there. He had permitted Giles to peruse the documents and allowed him to borrow the first few pages, which he had promised to return before he departed for England. Gourlay said that once the pages were returned he would leave instructions that the rest of the material be made available to Miss Frankland.

Lydia was silent, watching the familiar landmarks, aware of his presence and listening to his story. When she looked up, he was smiling at her.

'I see what you mean about the significance of their discoveries,' he said. 'To impress a man such as Darwin in the way that Lemprière describes . . .'

'Yes,' she said, at last. 'I never knew Lemprière had diaries from the ship. Presumably Jane didn't know either, nor even Charlotte.'

She told him then about her journeys to visit Lemprière's widow across the Derwent, worried about the pain she may have caused Charlotte. He reassured her that he believed Charlotte would have understood.

He held her parasol as they strode from the road up to the temple, Lydia managing to keep up, in spite of her crinoline and heavy skirts. As they walked she talked more about her parents' desires to introduce the colony of Van Diemen's Land to civilisation; Jane spoonfeeding culture to the free settlers. Ancanthe had been part of that dream for her.

The sculpted steps – the grand entrance – impressed him. Lydia gave him the measurements of the pillars. He wanted to know how it had been built; what she remembered from her childhood.

'She must have been an unusual woman, your stepmother,' he said when she had finished.

'Unusual, yes. Taxing, also. I always felt, somehow, that I didn't live up to her expectations,' she answered.

She saw him digest this. Below them the Derwent snaked through the valley, widening as it prepared to open into the ocean. Shafts of light pooled around an inlet on the opposite shore and a rainbow arched across the sky. She felt a sense of déjà vu. She was thankful he did not ask her to explain to what expectations. Instead, he changed the subject.

'You never told me that she and Lemprière were in correspondence with the great man himself,' he said.

'I have only just been discovering this myself,' she said slowly. 'Looking back, I always wondered why Jane wanted to leave Darwin's launch of *Origin*. I think now that she feared that Darwin might mention her connection to Lemprière if he saw her there in the audience. Not that Darwin would have suggested that there was anything improper in their relationship, but he knew how close they were to uncovering evidence that supported his theory of evolution. Interestingly, my stepmother always played down Darwin's collections from Van Diemen's Land as her contribution would have greatly upset my father who was a staunch believer in God. Her contribution has never been cited in his work to my knowledge, nor indeed has Lemprière's. Perhaps Jane wanted it that way. Jane only mentioned she had done some collecting for Darwin that evening at the launch. Darwin did come to her funeral as a mark of respect, which I thought was a great honour for her. What he felt for Lemprière, I do not know ...'

'Nor did you explain the love affair between your stepmother and Lemprière,' he admonished quietly.

'I ...'

She was embarrassed, as if by uttering those words he had unwittingly legitimised their relationship. She was acutely aware of her father's place in all this and she was discussing a secret with a man who was not even a family friend.

'I am not sure if it was an actual affair,' she said sharply, but added: 'Though it is true, they appear to have had strong feelings for each other.'

'But what about your father?'

'What about my father?'

'Did he know?'

As they walked up to the door of the temple, she felt dizzy from the proximity of him.

'I have asked myself that question many times. I expect I will never know the answer.'

They stood on the steps. Lydia, one step above him, was level with his eyes. She felt an urge to discard her accustomed position of strength, to rest in his arms and take comfort from someone who knew so much about her complicated life. But he was telling her that his research was taking him back to England, he did not know for how long. He seemed distant, preoccupied. She felt acute sorrow. She wanted to ward off the past, to delay the present. She wanted to tell him she was grateful to him for being there, for showing her Lemprière's words.

'Thank you again,' she said, looking into his eyes.

He looked at her for some time.

'I am concerned about your welfare, after what you have been through,' he said. 'What will you do now?'

She breathed into the silence.

'I do not deserve your concern.'

'Who has looked after you, Miss Frankland? You have spent your life in the shadow of others, caring for them. Your stepmother and father had plenty of support and approbation. I saw your father's statue in the square. Your stepmother is also well remembered here and the ship built in her name still sails.'

'I am not sure all that is entirely accurate, Giles. Their name was not as well regarded after the trip to the west coast, to Transylvania. My stepmother never spoke much to me about this after they returned. The trip represented failure, you see. They – she and my father – were castigated for making the journey and leaving the colony to govern itself for over a month.'

'A serious concern, considering the colony was only forty years old,' he said. 'And considering it was still a jail with the majority of its inhabitants convicts.'

'Exactly. I didn't know that at the time, but we left the colony, it seemed to me, with some haste, after months and months of stalemate – waiting for the news of the recall we knew would occur.'

She was remembering their hurried farewells as they boarded the ship to sail back to England. Compared to the fanfare when they arrived, the contrast could not have been more stark.

'My father was not quite the . . .'

She felt a surge of emotion trying to put into words what she had discovered these past few months. She was aware of the warmth of him and his solidity as he placed his arm around her. The smell of cigars, an unfamiliar scent of masculinity.

'I don't know what to think any more.'

She struggled, looking for her handkerchief to combat tears.

'I have read words my father has written. I cannot recognise him as the man I knew. Why was I so blind to what was right in front of me?' She paused. 'Perhaps my stepmother had reason to resent him.'

She pulled away from him and walked down a step.

He was standing behind her but she couldn't face him. 'I find I can't trust anyone any more. I can't trust the memory of my own father, nor my stepmother . . . Mr Bentham, forgive me for some of my behaviour . . .'

'Giles. Come . . . Lydia?'

He held out his hands to her in an almost fatherly gesture and, her fingers in his, led her to a stone seat at the bottom of the steps. Sweeping away the leaves on the seat with his hands, he cleared a space for her to sit. Then he sat down beside her and, taking her hands again, turned her towards him.

'There is nothing to forgive. You are a remarkable, courageous woman. I have said so before. You are far too hard on yourself.'

All around were the sounds of the bush and the gurgling stream. She thought how often Jane had described this place as Arcadia. It was paradise, she'd said. Lemprière had called it a Garden of Eden, a paradise tinged with temptation. The temple was behind them. In front was the mountain, looking less sinister than that day when she had visited alone, but still a presence. She knew her face would be ravaged, her scar inflamed. She had her hands in her lap and dabbed at her nose, aware he was watching her. How high the mountain was. From here, she could not even see the organ pipes near the summit.

'In spite of everything, I think she probably loved the storekeeper, or thought she did. Now I think I understand why.'

Her handkerchief was a tight ball in her hand.

'I wish I could have talked to her.'

'But she spent so much money searching for your father when he disappeared in the Arctic,' he said. 'She must have loved him.'

'Perhaps she felt she should behave the way she was supposed to behave. Jane was always concerned about appearances.'

'Are you?'

She turned around to face him in surprise.

'I . . .'

'You do not need to answer that, Lydia. I had no right to ask such an impertinent question.'

She gulped, knowing that previously she would have chastised him. Instead, she allowed him to lead her up the slope at the back of the temple, where he spread his cloak on the grass near the brook – the same cloak she had worn in the woods. He motioned her to sit. She did so awkwardly, feeling more vulnerable than she ever had, her skirts spread out before her, one arm supporting her from behind.

He walked down to the stream and returned with his handkerchief wet from being dipped in the rushing water. She dabbed it onto her face. They sat looking at the mountain in silence.

'If your stepmother was concerned about appearances,' he asked, 'why did she keep the letter she wrote to Lemprière from Transylvania? Come to think of it, how did she come to have the letter if she posted it to him?'

'Charlotte must have returned it to her and she would have known then that he'd never received it. As to why she kept it, maybe she wanted it to be found, or perhaps she intended to destroy it but wanted a reminder of how life might have been, of the intensity of her feelings for him, that she was capable of harbouring such feelings? I don't know. She always cherished Van Diemen's Land and told me she would return one day. She said she had many memories here. In the days before she died, she talked of the place incessantly. How much it changed her. Do you understand, Mr Bentham?'

'Giles.'

'Giles.' His name still sounded strange on her tongue.

'If only I had been able to ask her some of these questions before she died. When I first found out she loved another man, I felt so sorry for my father, and ashamed for him, too. I was angry with her. I blamed her for much of what has happened to me through life, but it was my choice to stay by her side. I put myself in her shadow. Perhaps their marriage wasn't always easy. He was an arrogant man and could be heartless, besides. Classifying the prisoners in the way he did; introducing a system that inflicted punishments that turned men and boys into madmen as a macabre experiment; and all the time believing he was God's servant. It is no wonder he was recalled to Britain in disgrace. I don't know if he ever understood the consequences of what he instigated in Van Diemen's Land . . . There, I have said it.'

She paused. 'I'd prefer to believe that he didn't realise rather than believe he didn't care.'

'So, if you were a convict in Van Diemen's Land you might elect to die rather than survive. It was far from survival of the fittest as Mr Darwin saw it,' he said. 'Some of them were not electing to survive.'

She sighed. 'The fittest ones *did* survive; indeed, the government officials, the despots in the old country who controlled Van Diemen's Land from afar, survived.'

'And you?' he asked. 'Are you a survivor?'

Lydia sighed again. She felt beholden to justify herself not just to him, but also to herself. She had lived in Government House where her father had signed decrees and death warrants and devised punishments, and she had closed her ears to what was going on around her. She had returned to England, abandoning Mathinna who was as much a pawn as the convicts, at the whim of her parents' desires. Mathinna's searching brown eyes came to her again, her lips curving upwards in a forced smile. When they played together, she had not looked like that.

Sensing her distress, Giles placed his arm around her and this time, she cradled into its crease. The earthy smell of him was reassuring, helped her feel less worthless. Neither of them spoke. She laid her head gently onto his shoulder. Looking up, she could make out the unshaved bristles on his chin. She looked down at the buttons of his coat, resisting the urge to pull away from him – she felt vulnerable, unsure, wanting to maintain a distance, but also to open herself to intimacy. She wondered if he could hear the beat of her heart.

'You can't blame your father entirely for all of it,' he said.

Her voice was barely a whisper. 'He loved me, as much as he was able.'

'He did.'

The prickling of tears prevented her from speaking more. Then, from below, the coach driver appeared through the swing gate at the bottom of the hill where they had left the phaeton. She sat up, straightening her hair, moving slightly apart from him. The driver was carrying a hamper. Bentham began to unpack the picnic, laying out a linen cloth next to his cloak: bread, potted tongue, the new season's apples and claret. She watched as he smoothed the cloth and laid out some napkins. When she could finally speak again, she said: 'The strangest thing . . .'

'What?'

'I feel as though I am living her life.'

'In what way?'

She was too embarrassed to tell him about Jane and Lemprière at Ancanthe . . . The sketches he'd done of her. Intimacy. Henry Belfield's lips and hands on her so many years ago. The closeness of him by her side.

They ate in silence, but she had little appetite and soon began to shiver.

'You are cold,' he said. 'We should return to Hobart Town.'

He helped her to her feet and she stood up shakily after being seated for so long.

She was acutely aware of every move he made.

'I haven't seen inside the temple,' she said suddenly, realising that this might be the last time she would ever visit Ancanthe.

At the entrance he forced open the wooden door, removing one of the boards. Inside, she stood in the semi-darkness surrounded by sandstone walls. Hay was on the floor and there were apples everywhere, stored in crates in the coolness of the interior.

'Jane would have been so upset to see this. All her dreams of a museum of culture came to nothing,' she said.

As she finished speaking, she heard him walk up behind her, then his hands were around her waist. Turning her towards him in the shadows, he kissed her. His mouth tasted of claret and the sweetness of apple. Her heart beat against her chest so hard she thought she might swoon. For some moments she lost track of everything except him, then slowly she extracted herself, but not before she looked into his eyes and thought she saw within them the same depth of feeling as her own.

She held his hand on their way back to the carriage, concentrating on her boots as they clambered down the hill, objects that suddenly seemed foreign to her. Pink clouds gathered at the summit of the mountain, wreathed around the organ pipes like a veil, bringing with them the familiar Hobart chill. The light had changed to an apricot hue. As they journeyed back to Hobart Town she was overcome with the events of the afternoon. He did not speak either, nor acknowledge what had transpired. Once, when she looked into his eyes, she caught an expression – alluring, unfathomable.

Dusk folded in around them and the lights of the town slowly came into view.

'Do you think she knew he loved her?' Giles asked.

'I don't know,' she answered slowly. 'Nor whether he knew she loved him.'

He left late one squally morning in December, when the wind blew from the south-west with a chill off the Antarctic that felt more like winter. They were surrounded by people. His hand and lips were warm on her gloveless skin, a gesture that appeared so formal after the intimacy at Ancanthe. He had told her he planned to mount a homage to his great-uncle – a panorama of landscapes on the Strand of the Port Arthur penal settlement, including the Model Prison. She had given him some letters by inmates in the Model Prison, which she'd found amongst some of the original documents from Wellard. They would form part of the display. His blue eyes contained excitement, a desire to be off, of which she felt she was not part. She maintained her familiar defence: a cautious distance. Life was strange, she was thinking. He had asked her when she might be back in London, but she had feared he was merely being polite and she had been evasive, unsure how to respond. As she watched his ship sail down the Derwent, she decided the best course of action was to accept their meeting as a special encounter – nothing more. Why, then, did she stay in the biting wind, until the afternoon light on the Salamanca warehouses began to fade and the mast from his ship was like the silhouette of a tree on the horizon of Storm Bay?

That evening, she felt an unfamiliar, unquenched longing.

Lying in bed staring through the French windows at the garden outside, she considered this ache for some time, before admitting that it was probably love. Thoughts of Giles Bentham came to her throughout the following day. Anna sensed something was amiss and tended to her with even more care than usual, but Lydia's mind was elsewhere as she relived, in minute detail, their day at Ancanthe for the umpteenth time, remembering things he had said, the picnic they had eaten, his hands sweeping the newly fallen leaves off the stone bench, but most of all the taste of him. Delight at those memories was quickly followed by a conviction at the futility of it all and, as the day wore on, melancholy descended.

After three days, she made a concerted effort to reclaim her life, taking short walks around Battery Point. It was not until almost a week later that she returned to the museum for the last time, to her stepmother's words. What would Jane think about Giles Bentham? By now, Lydia had come to believe that she might well have understood.

12th April

We have arrived in the Acheron Valley, at a place that the convicts call the Glow Worm Forest. It's a multitude of sparkling lights which Calder says are caused by phosphorescent fungi. I imagined Darwin in such a place, collecting funghi: white and luminous orange, some wet blue, the colour of laudanum, and others with large brown feathery clods like elephant's ears. Darwin, scribbling notes, divining. Those furrowed eyebrows imparting concentrated enthusiasm, his eyes communicating knowledge.

Above us are dark trees: gigantic myrtles, native laurels and more natives, celery-tops and Huon pine. Some are dead, their trunks and limbs strewn, criss-crossed and twisted in their own kingdom of hell. The monotony of the landscape . . . The forest extends for six miles, beginning with slimy, reedy scrub that clutches at my ankles trying to drag me earthward. Mud clings to the hem of my dress. My hands are tougher now, though they still bleed when I grab hold of boulders and trees as we scramble down slippery hills.

The palanquin has long since been abandoned, except on the rare occasions when we follow the river and the ground is flat. Conversation is limited as we are usually in single file – Stewart is always behind me.

Once or twice, when we stopped to drink from a stream, I chatted with Mumford, the bargeman – square-jawed with a nose like a broken cucumber. He served two years at the old penal settlement on Sarah Island in Macquarie Harbour. His hands are like hams and his wrists sinewy. He is rugged and solid, and that is comforting. I have begun to question him and he is a natural storyteller. His words, spoken with a Cockney slang, penetrate my exhaustion.

The harbour where we are headed, he said, is thirty-seven miles long and about nine broad, with two miles between its heads. It's known as Hell's Gates and is one of the few bodies in the world to have tidal water with a bottleneck entrance that faces west. Ships can easily get trapped because a sandbar sits across the entrance. When the tide is against the wind, millions of tons of water a minute boil through the entrance into Hell's Gates. He is a man whose livelihood depends on the weather – like Lemprière. Mumford's life has been dictated by the tides. His tales lead me into a world that is both foreign and familiar, and help keep my mind off the arduous journey.

Macquarie Harbour, he said, looks directly into the roaring forties and the waves of the southern ocean crash with a fury on 'that pitiless coastline'. I stood in my wet clothes shivering, contemplating more bleakness. I find it hard to imagine ocean after all these trees.

At night, we now sleep in open tents but feet apart, n'er a weapon or firearm close at hand, trusting our safety to these mens' hands. Mumford and the other four convicts possess axes and tomahawks. What if they turn against us?

13th April

I can no longer remember why we came to this decaying place. Burn has nicknamed our camp the Valley of the Shadow of Death. The sun never shines. As we slither down embankments only to find yet another ascent, I have become convinced we are making no progress. Beside us, the dark brown, tea-tree-stained Acheron River flows like an artery of this interior. Several times, we have had to cross it. The last time, my blisters began to bleed. They stung in the icy water, red hot needles, making it agonising to walk. I have come to dread the rain. Never before have I felt so waterlogged. The moss, a brilliant green, is slimy underfoot.

Today, the sound of the rushing water changed, and then, around a bend, the river suddenly plunged twenty feet into a waterfall. I stood with Burn, Sir John and Barnes, and peered down the abyss.

Calder built a flight of stairs from the trunks of tree ferns, fastening them with stakes almost perpendicular to the sides of the precipice. We began the ascent. I grasped the slippery grass next to the makeshift staircase. Below us, the river raged fearfully. Stewart followed behind while I hitched up my skirts, the men waited respectfully behind. What a sight I must have been – mud-smeared, my hair loosely pinned, sweat on my brow and under my arms. I smelt my own body odour and imagined scented lavender baths, my hair soft again from washing.

We eventually reached the top of the falls and sunshine. But after the watery promise of a few filtered rays, it disappeared behind the dark clouds that gathered ominously. Before us was a miserable plain. We trudged across it, our footsteps soundless except for snapping twigs.

Out of the impenetrable reainforest, we were exposed to cold winds. Having climbed on top of one of the bare hills, we saw yet more dark forest up ahead. Leeches, fat with my blood, clung to my legs. I thought of the hedgerows of England, the measured fields with welcoming inns and hot cider. I cried easily that day.

This morning we were greeted with the same indifferent grey sky. The rain has not abated. The next forest was even denser than the Acheron. We have long since stopped naming the peaks, rivers and valleys we cross. Instead, we walk, stumble, scrabble and suffer in silence. Rations have all but disappeared. In spite of the unappetising food, I tackled the morning's fare, always hungry . . .

Mumford was up ahead, the kangaroo knapsack strapped to his back. He never complains. Always the same – stepping, striding, sidestepping obstacles easily. He has probably seen much worse, though it is hard to believe. But then he talked more about Macquarie Harbour. Grummet Rock, a low point almost level with the sea, was the place of punishment. Just above high-water mark was a planked gangway one hundred yards long. By the side, in the centre, were the triangles. Convicts were tied in such a way so that the commandant and doctor could see their face or back. He said it was their custom to walk between each lash. This meant anyone who got one hundred of the best was tied up from between one hour to an hour and a quarter. The convict was then sent immediately back to work. He wouldn't be allowed to go to the hospital until the next morning, when his back would be washed by the doctor's mate with a little hog's lard spread on a bit of flax so, if necessary, he could be flogged again the next day.

Over dinner, I quizzed Surgeon Barnes, who surely must know if Mumford's tales are true. Barnes confirmed what Mumford told me. As a surgeon, he said, he had witnessed floggings and cruelty in Van Diemen's Land by what he called the most inhuman tyrants since the reign of Nero. This had the effect of demoralising them and they became even more desperate characters than before. They simply lost hope. Some of them even murdered their companions as they felt 'weary of life'. When I suggested that they deserved punishing if they had killed another — they surely needed to see the error of their ways — he laughed loudly. Most, he said, had not been transported for murder, but theft, drunkenness, disobedience of orders or petty thefts. It was the system that produced murderers. To think I had not realised this.

I was stung by Barnes' tone of unexpected bitterness and couldn't help feel it was aimed squarely at me. On Sarah Island, he said, they used a much heavier instrument than the ordinary cat-o'-nine-tails, which soldiers and sailors received. Convicts were subjected to 'a thief's cat', or a 'double cat o'nine tails' — each with a double twist of whipcord and each tail with nine knots.

For once I had no questions. After his stories, I was left with an increasing sense of disquiet. That night around the campfire I told Burn. When I said that this place was a dark place filled with sadness, he pointed out it was not the place, but the men who were vile.

14th April

After these exchanges I feel consumed by guilt and anger. These stories belong to the past. After all, the convict settlement was closed nine years ago.

Around the fire that night Sir John read another sermon. I watched his face in the firelight. When he'd finished, I asked about criminal reform. Whether we had learnt from the mistakes of Sarah Island, or whether convicts without wives, children or homes were as badly off as slaves used by the Empire to expand its interests. He looked startled, particularly as we had an audience. Hush, he said.

In such a small company every exchange is noticed. Burn looked uncomfortable, caught in a domestic space. I knew this was about Sir John's livelihood, but I was remembering the exchanges we'd had on the *Fairlie*. Sir John's private secretary had argued for more humane treatment of those who were jailed, but my husband had not listened. Perhaps it was easier not to question these things but to accept that we were here as Queen's servants to perform our duty, I had said.

Even Mumford shifted uneasily. Sir John told me firmly that there was a better time and place for this discussion. He called me Lady Frankland, which he rarely does.

I pulled myself to my feet and stumbled to my bell tent.

16th April

Today is Sir John's birthday. I brushed down the ferns from my petticoat and, with the help of Stewart, retied my hair, horribly lank from lack of bathing. At the top of one of my bags was the plum cake I had carried from Hobart Town.

When I opened the flap of the tent, my husband was talking to Calder and two of the convicts. They had a map in front of them.

Above the roar of the river I produced the cake. Mumford's eyes were dazzled. No one spoke. Sir John looked faintly embarrassed. With the smoke of the breakfast fire and some black tea and sugar, the sweet taste of the raisins was like manna from heaven.

Lydia looked up from the pages of the journal. Jane was more real to her now than she had ever been. She was struck by how similarly she felt towards her father, how little Lydia could respect him now. Perhaps she was misjudging him, but then she remembered the correspondence, his signature at the end of the harsh edicts, the Model Prison, which had operated under his jurisdiction. And she remembered Jane telling her that Van Diemen's Land had changed her life forever. Now the place was having a similar effect on her.

18th April

We spent last night in a tiny clearing, the large river beside us a formidable barrier. During the previous three nights, more rain has fallen and the river is as high as ever. Mumford and Wilson are working on a raft. Wilson is a shipwright by trade.

We are eking out the dwindling provisions Calder retrieved from Lake St Clair. I have become accustomed to eating with my fingers from the pannikin, sitting awkwardly on the ground, failing to resurrect the taste of plums and raisins.

As we were finishing lunch, Calder came to tell us it was not safe to cross, not even in the raft that was being built. They are going to try to construct a canoe out of Huon pine. Sir John said that with Mumford's bargeman skills we would be across the river in no time. More false hope, I was thinking. Is this how he talked to his men when they were dying in the Arctic?

Here, the phosphorescent fungi blooming around us in the thick darkness is the only difference between night and day. As darkness fell, I imagined myself in the sitting room of our London home drinking coffee and eating sweetmeats.

Burn spoke unexpectedly into the gloom, saying he agreed with what I had said the other night – that this system has driven men to depravity. He began then to relate a bizarre tale that I will recount here. If it had not been Burn telling me, I would scarcely have believed it.

This, he said, was Pierce country. Apparently Pierce was a convict who, with seven companions, escaped from Sarah Island. Burn said he had read Pierce's own testimonial and that Pierce claimed that their cannibalism idea had begun as a joke – one of the convicts had said he was so hungry he could eat a man. All around them were kangaroos and emus, game of all kinds, but they didn't even attempt to hunt these creatures. They began by killing the weakest of their party and drying their flesh. They rested for a day, then took it with them as provisions.

I stared at the cold water that flowed between us and freedom, and glanced at Mumford, who was frying damper in the campfire. Burn told me Pierce was the only one to survive. After he had eaten the last victim's thigh and arm he took off his leather belt and decided he would hang himself, but just then he came to a clearing where there was a fire with pieces of kangaroo and possum in it. He took it as a sign from God and ate hungrily. He killed two young ducklings and walked until he could see Mount Wellington in the distance. It was while he was eating a lamb raw that he was caught by a shepherd. Of course, no one knew what he had done. The shepherds gave him rum, food, a musket, a pistol and a knapsack. He was, however, eventually recognised and apprehended.

He wasn't executed. Instead he was transported back to Sarah Island, from where he soon escaped again with another man. A short while later a ship bound for Hobart Town saw smoke on one of the beaches nearby. Pierce was caught – this time with half a pound of human flesh. He was even wearing the murdered man's clothes.

Apparently he had lit a fire to deliberately draw attention to himself. He told his captors he was 'horror struck' at his own inhuman conduct.

I stared into the glade, weighed down by the terrible story. The air in the tree-fern clearing where we sat seemed filled with menace, as if at any time a savage would appear in our midst, blood smeared across his person. The wildness of this place turns men into inhuman, degraded brutes . . . But is it the place or what has happened to those in it?

I thought of previous dinner-party conversations, debates over supper, intellectual prattle about transportation and captivity, reform and punishment. As if sensing my thoughts, Burn added that transportation would never cease because it supplied the colonies with labour. Yet this mild-mannered man, in spite of his views, would not have defended me in front of my husband. How many people disagree with the governor in private?

Lydia shuddered at the desperation in this tale. It was little wonder Jane had thought they would never return alive. Why had her parents never told her of the trials of this expedition when they returned home? She looked up from the journal and noticed there was hardly anybody else around. She half expected to see Giles Bentham, and tried to shake off the thought of him. She was more than ever ready to begin her journey home.

These weeks of traversing the island had transformed her stepmother. Lydia clearly remembered how uninterested Jane had been in the convicts' plight, except to take a charitable interest in their moral wellbeing. Confronted with the reality of their punishment, lost in the wild terrain of the west coast, instead of taking the high moral ground she had become conscious that they were human beings after all. Lemprière would have approved.

CHAPTER TWENTY-THREE

Lydia packed her belongings and paid a visit to Gourlay's office. The chambers were in Macquarie Street near the burial ground of St David's Park. Outside, dark clouds chased across a sunless sky. She wondered, as she looked at the busy street filled with horse-drawn buses and carts, whether she would ever return to Hobart Town.

The clerk had been expecting her and directed her to a large rosewood table in the lawyer's library, where she was given a slim file.

'I believe that is all there is,' he told her.

Lemprière's handwriting was barely recognisable. It was not the orderly hand she was accustomed to. Instead, the words were scrawled across the page.

Another letter from Darwin was waiting for me when my ship finally berthed in Cape Town. Dear Charlotte has written several pages in her rounded girlish handwriting, bringing me tales of home, ordinary stories that seem so far away. The house cow has given birth to two calves, one chestnut brown, the other black and white. Edward is working at the store with a new storekeeper, who sounds amiable enough. The older children are still learning French. Fanny has cut three teeth. These words once would have made me homesick, but I read the letter as though it were composed for someone else.

I sat in a tavern at the docks reading Darwin's letter with great pleasure. He has been noting every sort of fact that has any bearing on the nature of species. After reading so many agricultural and horticultural books, he is increasingly convinced that species are not immutable, and he says he has finally found the simplest way by which species adapt. Now, more than ever, he adds, he needs evidence for his postulations. He again urged me to keep our discussions secret until he serves up in his magnum opus what he knows cannot be refuted.

He has much to say about a book that is yet to be published, *Vestiges of the Natural History of Creation*, written anonymously but, he suspects, by Scottish journalist Robert Chambers. I have heard nothing about this book. Darwin says it is anticipated to sell tens of thousands of copies. In his book, Chambers apparently speculates that if people can accept that God assembled the heavenly bodies by natural laws, what is to hinder us supposing that organic creation is also a result of natural laws? They are accusing Chambers of declaring religion is a lie and say that he has made 'human law a mass of folly and a base injustice; morality . . . moonshine'. Darwin confesses the whole thing leaves him more determined than ever to go to print with his theories, but Chambers' book will make him extremely careful in any publication he embarks upon.

Darwin's discoveries are attacking the very nature of society, the nature of religion. There is no escaping that. Yet, after rereading Lyell, Cuvier and especially Lamarck, what he has said indisputably makes logical sense. All my old stalwarts and beliefs – marriage, religion, the penal governance – have been shaken.

Darwin wants me to come up to Kent as soon as I arrive to meet him and his wife, Emma.

25th June

Having left the great Cape, I've had to resign myself to my cramped cabin once more. For the first two weeks back at sea, we have been plagued by adverse winds and searing heat, without a cloud in the sky. The buzzing of flying insects wakes me daily. Lumps have appeared on my upper arm that I am always scratching. One has become infected.

Lady Frankland must have returned from her travels by now. At the bottom of my portmanteau, I have some of my unfinished sketches. One in particular catches an expression I know well. Whenever I look at it, I feel the guilt of a man committing adultery.

27th June

The weather has worsened, as though to punish me. Gigantic rollers bear down on the ship, threatening to smash her, throwing her off the wind. At one point this great sea took her right abeam, turned her so far over that the lee bulwark was two or three feet under water. The sea poured into the poop cabin and below deck. For half an hour I thought we were all to be cast into the depths. Then, slowly, like a cork out of a bottle, she righted herself. Another wave like that and the barque would have been my coffin and all this writing would have been lost. My sketches have become water-logged, the ink merging into a muddied mess of lines as though replicating my blurry memory. I have been drinking whisky in my cabin. My world is losing perspective.

? June

I have contracted a fever. When did I first feel it? Was it the morning after the storm when the ship was becalmed? Upon waking I felt as though I'd had no rest. Since then, I have had to be careful where I place my feet as my head is spinning. My bones ache. I have taken to my cabin and keep lapsing back into sleep. Dining times come and go. I have lost my appetite and cannot even pick up my favourite Lyell.

When I stood up on deck yesterday, the light hurt my eyes and my head throbbed. The ship's doctor is a shifty little man with arms like a spider and fingers that poke me with distaste. He is more concerned, it seems, with his welfare than mine. He scuttles this way and that, avoiding my questions. Instead, he asks me some of his own, which I barely have the strength to answer. How many times has he administered to me?

This morning I woke drenched in sweat knowing only by the lightness in my cabin that it was day. I have banged on the wall of my cabin. My voice I hardly recognise. This diary is my life-raft to sanity.

'Yes, that is all of the material we have,' the clerk answered Lydia. When she inquired as to whether Mr Lemprière's wife had seen these papers, the clerk said he didn't believe so. He had no idea, either, how they had come to be deposited at this office. Even more confusing, the clerk added, was that there were no instructions. Perhaps he should have passed it on to his widow, but due to the delicate nature of the contents . . .

It was still early. Lydia walked slowly towards the museum, only two blocks from the solicitor's office. She was on the final leg of her journey. Lemprière had never recovered, of that she was sure. Lydia imagined him dying alone and helpless; of Charlotte's discovery of his death and the grief of widowhood; his children growing up without him; his collections of animals; his records of dissections and all his patient recording of the tides and weather – to no avail. What had happened to the evidence of the men's confessions that had compelled him to abandon his wife and children?

At the museum, Lydia was given the last of her stepmother's journal. While Lemprière battled the sea voyage, her stepmother had also been under siege.

19th April

Burn, Mumford and the shipwright Wilson have produced a canoe in four days. It's built from the sturdy ancient pine that grows here in abundance and has turned out to be the most seaworthy of vessels. I have named her *Lydia*. This morning I stepped from the bank onto it as it tossed around dangerously in the current. Mumford held the bow and gave me words of encouragement. I struggled to find somewhere to sit onboard, holding my drenched skirts, staring down at the tannin-stained water. I thought of the convict boys building their makeshift escape crafts in complete secrecy, risking a flogging, and the boy who built the coffin-shaped vessel to take him to his maker. I was convinced we too would go to a watery grave. Eddies like whirlpools ready to swallow us; boulders visible below the surface. I imagined being trapped beneath one of those rocks in icy cold water.

Displaying his bargeman skills, Mumford pushed the vessel away from the side. Burn sat at the bow. Stewart and Wilson were beside me. The current tugged at the tiny craft and it took all Mumford's energy to keep us on target. We zig-zagged across the eddies. When we reached the reeds on the other side, Mumford and Burn helped me up the bank.

None of us could have forecast what happened next. Mumford was chopping down some young saplings to make a fire. Stewart and Sir John were searching for a campsite. I heard a blood-piercing scream and Mumford stumbled through the under-growth towards me, Calder and Wilson already at his side. Mumford's arms were thrashing like a bird falling out of the sky. Blood soaked through the rags Calder was holding up to his face. A bent stick he had been chopping with his axe had flown up and hit him in the eye.

They carried him to a makeshift fern bed in front of the unlit fire. Calder began administering to him. Mumford was Calder's right-hand man during the two seasons of labouring on the track to Transylvania. Calder is clearly fond of him. In all the years Mumford has been with him, Calder said the convict has never had an accident.

When I returned from fetching water from the river Mumford was whimpering. He began to scream when Calder, using tweezers from our medical supplies, removed a splinter. There was blood everywhere – his eye was a gory mess, the eyeball visible.

In the absence of my maid and husband, I was the nurse – bringing brandy and holding Mumford's hand. There were only a few hours of marching through the Gordon Forest before we reached the coast, but it was clear we would not be going anywhere.

Calder tied a bandage of coloured linen around Mumford's eye so now he resembled a child's rag doll. I ferried basins of water back and forth and bathed his forehead. Sir John and Stewart returned. He appeared more concerned with my welfare, admonishing me not to overtire myself; that I should leave this kind of work to Stewart. Then he promised to grant Mumford and the other men a ticket of leave when we returned to Hobart Town. That is at least some consolation, but I can't help reflecting that he clearly believes loyalty can be bought and money can solve everything.

20th April

Today Mumford sat in my palanquin while I walked beside it. He hardly spoke. The able-bodied men have donned kangaroo knapsacks and are carrying his load. I have a persistent headache and I am gripped by fear, even though this morning was full of sunshine and promise and we were nearing an end. Lemprière's face floated across my vision, his expression one of distress.

The Gordon Forest had some of the most beautiful scenery we have yet encountered. We stopped often to bathe Mumford's wound. He is becoming feverish. I caught a few words: Grummet Island and a woman's name, Fiona. He will never regain his sight in his injured eye. I am not sure whether he knows this. As we walked I was wondering quietly out loud about Darwin's theories. I spoke of Lemprière's tidal gauges and meteorological tests. Species of animals – something to cheer me up.

'You know so many things, my lady.' The convict's voice, quiet for so long, shocked me. I stared at him. He turned his seeing eye away from me. I told him then about my museum at Ancanthe; how interested I was in collecting. Gradually we exchanged conversation. He told me about himself, of his life in London surviving on the proceeds of petty crimes. He began as a 'buzz-gloak', a pick-pocket, and soon became experienced at 'fogle hunting', drawing out handkerchiefs, before progressing to 'bung-diving', taking purses. He was transported for stealing a writing desk. He did not even know how to read or write. The thought of leaving England did not concern him; in fact, he was pleased at first to be plucked from London's streets. But after four months in the stinking hulks, he longed to return. When he arrived in the colony he was assigned to work for a farmer on the road to the north of the island. There he was accused of stealing a farmer's chicken and he was sent to Sarah Island, then the only settlement for those reconvicted after arriving in the colony. Despite three separate lashings, he survived. After the settlement was closed down, Calder selected him to work on the road to the west coast.

I asked him if he had ever married and he said he hadn't; that there had been a pretty girl called Fiona with chestnut hair, but after he'd gone 'across the pond', as he called it, he had no contact with women.

We had been walking for some hours when I heard excited cries. The river came upon us suddenly, wider and tamer than the inland rivers we had crossed, and dappled in sunshine. In a few miles, it would flow into the ocean.

'The ship, the ship.'

Indeed, it was the *Breeze*. Once I thought the barque small; now, floating in the harbour, she looked much larger than I'd remembered. I turned to the palanquin and smiled at Mumford. We had finally reached Macquarie Harbour. Across the water was the dreaded penal settlement, Sarah Island. I looked out to sea, towards Hell's Gates. There was no wind. We had exchanged our forest prison for the ocean, and the sight of the expanse of sea and our ship brought exquisite relief.

1st May

Almost two weeks have passed since we arrived at Macquarie Harbour. I am sure that back in Hobart Town, Lydia and Mathinna will believe we have perished, not to mention the concern for Sir John and the fate of the governance of the colony.

On board the *Breeze*, I have seen less of Mumford. He spends much time below deck as he cannot face daylight. Three or four times a day I take him fresh water and Burn's copy of *Master Humphrey's Clock*, which I have begun to read to him. It pleases him. Slowly, though, we begin to slip back into our separate routines.

Sir John is writing to his private secretary that the journey has been safely accomplished although the captain of the *Breeze* informs us that supplies are frighteningly low. He was about to set sail when we arrived with barely enough food to return to Hobart Town. Now, there are extra mouths to feed and we have no way of getting past Hell's Gates as the wind is not right.

We have been dining on fish heads thickened with oatmeal. On Saturday we had gull soup, which we feasted upon as though we were one big family. Mumford is still in much pain – his eye has begun weeping and we are fearful of infection. I take his temperature regularly, change the bandage and clean the wound.

He shares an interest in collecting, although he doesn't call it that, and we spend many an hour discussing the difference between native plants and European ones. I have learnt much from him.

There are few other distractions on board. In the tiny library in the captain's cabin, there are the *Quarterly* and *Edinburgh Reviews*, Tocqueville's *Système Pénitentiaire* and the *Statistics of the Orkneys*. An odd collection, not calculated to raise drooping spirits. Most mornings, I help Sir John work through some of the correspondence that came with the *Breeze* even though we have no surety the letters will reach their destination. He has commented more than once about my changed demeanour. I realise how much he relies upon me. He is used to me dispensing advice, guiding him through the quagmire of colonial politics, taking an interest in his doings. I have little appetite for it now, though. There is a growing distance between us. He cannot understand my preoccupation with Mumford, which I know exasperates him. I see now why he wasn't concerned with Belfield's fate.

3rd May

Yesterday, we landed on Sarah Island, the penal settlement disbanded after Port Arthur was built, where Lemprière used to work as a storekeeper. The summer scent of sweet briar, clover and mint assailed my senses. The houses and jail were on the more sheltered side of the island. I found his house easily as there were not many: one belonging to the doctor, the other the superintendent.

Standing alone in the doorway of the deserted cottage, I imagined Charlotte cooking at the stove, a baby to her breast, the warmth of the hearth, clothes drying. But as I turned to leave, I saw an apparition: Lemprière in the doorway, his eyes like a man demented – water rushing in to take him away. I felt an unbearable emptiness.

6th May

Two nights ago it blew a hurricane. We heard the thundering ocean outside the harbour like the enemy battling down the armaments. When we awoke, there was an eerie silence. We climbed up on deck to greet the pearly sheen of the new sun. The ocean glowed, luminescent in pale yellow. Gradually the wind has veered to the east.

This morning, the captain ordered the anchor to be pulled up and the ship began to whirr and clank into life. An hour later Sir John stood on the deck, the sun agleam on the dome of his head, and read us a sermon. We were going home. I felt a mixture of relief, but also concern about returning to my old life.

Early this afternoon, the *Breeze* crossed Hell's Gates. We raised a cheer as the ship narrowly missed the rocks and floated into the open sea. We are free, sailing on the smooth ocean, a steady wind propelling us northward. After a few more hours of hugging the coastline, we came across the *Eliza*, our rescue ship — a schooner of one hundred and fifty tons, a mammoth compared with the *Breeze*. We transferred to this luxurious vessel before night fell.

The *Eliza* brought us news, a copy of the *Launceston Advertiser*. My fears have been confirmed. It seems we must not expect public sympathy upon our return. I feel stung by the sarcasm the words contain after the struggle of the past weeks. Sir John has undertaken a gross neglect of important public duty. According to the editorial, we have suffered the natural consequences of an indulgence in folly, procured at the expense of the whole colony.

What awaits us in Hobart Town? Sir John said nothing when I showed him the article. Instead, playing the explorer, he continued his surveying of the coastline as though the words were of no matter to him. I cannot stop re-reading them. They have even printed details of his failed Arctic expedition, describing how he led men to their deaths by choosing the wrong time to venture north through the pack ice, and abandoning the ship when they should have stayed.

What will this mean? The secretary of state will be sure to find out about this scandal. I imagine arriving back to Government House; how we will be shunned by the Hobartians. Perhaps these cruel accusations are right. Has my husband ever really understood what responsible governorship means?

Lydia remembered how the wharves had been almost deserted at Sullivan's Cove the morning the *Eliza* docked. How ashamed she had been standing there, waiting, and how angry that they had risked so much. She had spent weeks in despair, believing they were dead. Looking back, she thought of how little she had known both of them. She did recall hushed recriminations from Jane in the following months at Government House, which she had not dwelt upon until now; her father's tense moods on the voyage back to England a few months later.

A cutting from the *Van Diemen's Land Chronicle* was pasted into Jane's journal: an editorial accusing him not only of lacking leadership qualities, but of being slow and ponderous, a buffoon. The article even claimed that behind his lacklustre governorship, the real power lay in the authority of his wife, Lady Frankland.

Within four years, her father would be dead, or as good as dead. Lydia was glad she'd never had to confront him with what she knew now before he had sailed on his last voyage, relieved that the last time they embraced he'd been a hero in her eyes, and that was how he would be remembered by posterity. After he had been deemed dead in the Arctic, Sir John Frankland had been elevated once again, the notoriety from his earlier journey forgotten.

Was the truth important? Lydia battled with the question.

How much had her father contributed to the brutality of the regime, or had he inherited a mantle of leadership, where punishing governance was expected of him?

The select committee's inquiry had gone ahead, Lydia remembered, without Lemprière's evidence, as far as she knew, pushed forward by the abolitionists who likened the outcome of transportation to slavery. The evidence given by government officials who had witnessed the barbarity first-hand had underlined these failings. Lydia wondered whether people like the surgeon, Barnes, had given evidence.

The committee had recommended that transportation be abolished in New South Wales and Van Diemen's Land. In spite of being aware of the committee, at the time she had never connected the failures it highlighted with her father, as she believed it was the system that had been wrong, and that he was merely an administrator of that system. Now though, she felt that her father was essentially weak, heartless, with little understanding of or empathy with the suffering of others.

Van Diemen's Land had strengthened Jane, even if she had not been brave enough to play any role to prevent the horrors that were taking place on the island. She had shown sympathy for the convict, Mumford, albeit belatedly, and if it had been possible for her to intervene further for the life of Henry Belfield, she would have done so.

And what of Belfield? They had all been victims of their own demons. She shut the last of the Transylvania diaries.

CHAPTER TWENTY-FOUR

Summer 1866

London no longer held the same anxiety or allure for Lydia after her travels. On her return, she had decided she would begin life afresh, even if she did not know exactly where or how. Imbued with growing confidence, however, she knew her first project would be the publication of Jane's diaries. She had already written to the Royal Society in Hobart seeking its consent. Giles did probably not realise that with his quiet words of support he had given her the confidence to undertake such a project. She still thought of him often – wondered how he was faring, whether his panorama on the Strand was going ahead, whether he missed her? She was glad he would have approved of her new project and agreed that Jane Frankland's life deserved to be preserved for posterity to stand alongside her husband's bestselling book about his heroic voyages.

During the months at sea travelling back from Van Diemen's

Land, she had time to think about the past. There would be an appreciative audience for Jane's words: her work at the Female Factory; her observations of colonial life and transportation; and, of course, the work she had carried out for the Tasmanian Society. Then there was the matter of the emotional content. Truth, she had concluded, was a fine thing as long as it didn't damage others. She had begun already to edit out the sensitive parts.

There was much to be done in the first few weeks after her return. In the mornings she worked in Jane's study; in the afternoons she supervised the dispatch of furniture from the unoccupied rooms to the auctioneers, dispensing with remaining servants and having meetings with the family's accountant. Her father's relatives visited, but she had few other callers. She enjoyed the quiet that had settled around the house, gradually being emptied after all its years of occupation.

Lydia was working on Jane's journal of the overland trip from Melbourne to Sydney when the maid announced his arrival. Through a crack in the door, the bustle of cabs and the glare of the street behind him, at first all she saw was a silhouette. Then he was inside, the soles of his leather boots squeaking as he crossed the marble hallway and up the stairs towards her. In front of the servant on the landing they embraced. Her heart beating fast, she led him to Jane's study away from curious eyes.

For all these months she had tried to forget Giles Bentham. Now, all thoughts of composure deserted her. She felt the familiar conflicting emotions – resentment that he had caught her unawares, but delight at being close to him again. They exchanged pleasantries, drinking tea in the room where, a year ago, she had read Jane's letter and where, upon her return from Van Diemen's Land, she had uncovered more secrets.

She had searched the glass cages again, more thoroughly this time, taking out each one and patiently levering the animals from their cages. Underneath the brush-tailed possum, glued onto its wooden stand, was a compartment and inside a tight wad of paper.

As he waited at the window, she brought the pages to him, knowing he, of all people, would understand their significance.

'Lemprière died on the ship some time after Jane had returned from the west coast,' she said. 'Can I read this to you?'

He nodded, gazing at her, his eyes that strange intense blue she remembered.

23rd December, 1864
Russell Square

Well past middle age, I finally discovered love and all that went with it. I must see that as an accomplishment. This is my confession.

I betrayed Louis. I owe it to him to record what I have never admitted. First, that I loved him. Second, that I still love him now, and always will. Not to have known him would have been worse. To go to my grave without acknowledging him would be a double betrayal, although these words may never be found so perhaps, after all, I am still choosing the safe path.

To think of those difficult few weeks after we arrived back on the *Eliza* . . . Reunion with Lydia and Mathinna, and the relief of finding them well. The silent carriage ride from the wharf to Government

House; bathing in lavender water and dressing in clean clothes. Then attending to my mail and finding nothing from Louis. Waiting for weeks, until finally my solicitor paid me a visit with a letter that he said related to an employee of the colonial government who was deceased, but had directed some documents be sent to me. He had thought the matter urgent. For some strange reason I can see the scarlet rhododendron I planted outside Sir John's study window and I remember the man's embarrassment at my tears as I rushed to my boudoir . . .

Louis Lemprière, late of Port Arthur, has requested Lady Jane Frankland be directed to contents in her name left in a safe at the lawyers Dougal and Allport. The particulars can be sought from Mr William Gourlay, solicitor, who awaits instructions from Lady Frankland.

How I wished I was back on the *Breeze* then, protected from the winds of fate. The announcement of his death brought more grief than the news the following year that we were to be recalled. With Louis gone, I no longer had any reason to remain there.

All these years later, I realise I have shut out the essence of life. I am left knowing I have only grasped a tiny part of what might have been. I die knowing that while I did not betray my husband, I betrayed my one true love. I never showed the confessions to anyone.

Lydia's voice was clear and low as she finished reading. She looked up. Giles Bentham sat in the old leather armchair near the window, his teacup forgotten on the table next to him, leaning forward slightly, his chin cupped in his hands like a child waiting for the end of the story.

'My father may never have known about Jane's feelings for Lemprière,' Lydia said. 'I must say I had no idea she still thought of him so much after all those years.'

He nodded.

'And I found this letter.'

10th May, 1842

My dear Lady Frankland,

I trust you will understand why I have left these documents in your possession. If you receive this letter, some accident will have befallen me – an eventuality I did not expect, but in this world, as Mr Darwin has often said, one must always be prepared.

I leave these papers to you, as you alone, I trust, will furnish them to the right authorities. My mission upon leaving Van Diemen's Land is to deliver these notes to the Select Committee on Transportation. They are confessions taken from the convicts over the period of time I was convict chaplain, and from the boy Belfield, with whom you were acquainted.

'The confessions were also concealed in the glass cage. They must have been collected by Jane from Gourlay, but she was not given his diary entries – the ones Gourlay gave you – though they must also have been sent back to Van Diemen's Land after Lemprière died,' Lydia said. She described how he had collected the confessions over a year. He had written these records in secret, struggling with the notion that as the confessions of dying men, they should not be made public. His troubled conscience was clear to see from remarks in the margin.

Each murder had been planned with chilling attention to detail. Some of the victims, however, had died lingering deaths, because the instruments used to kill them had been far from adequate. At least fifteen men had confessed as to why they had murdered their fellow prisoners. Each expected to go to heaven. Lemprière had commented on the ritualised language they had used, as they challenged the authorities by committing a crime no one understood. Particularly disturbing was the fact that those who confessed were more than ready to be hanged.

The notes on Belfield that he had made on board the ship were even more comprehensive as he had thought he would be using them as evidence.

Lydia continued:

I have thought long and hard about my reasons for this course of action. I know it is unlikely you will ever read this letter, but should it end up in your hands I know, too, I am placing you in a near untenable position. However, given our friendship, which I greatly value, I believe you will rise to this occasion. Given, too, that we already share our knowledge of what some would call 'heresy' with Mr Darwin, I feel you are better placed to share this confidence. I hope this is not a presumption.

My wish is that these confessions from the condemned men become public knowledge. I want the British government to understand the effects of its poisonous legislation relating to transportation. I understand this might be extremely awkward for you, but the criticism is less aimed at the men appointed to carry out the rules than to the architects of the legislation.

In our previous conversations, you have defended your views on transportation, but if you read this material, you may change your mind. Some of these words have come straight from the heart and were not meant for publication. I hope, they speak, nevertheless, of authenticity.

I have not discussed these matters with anyone, not even with my wife, Charlotte.

I remain your esteemed companion in your memories of me.

Yours truly,
Louis Lemprière

Lydia glanced at Giles again. 'They were carefully hidden, and you can see why. There's a little more from Jane.'

Charlotte was surrounded by the noise of his children in the crowded cottage and the ordinary smell of life: newly washed clothes and boiled cabbage. I dallied longer than I should. That we both loved the same man bound me to her, except she, not I, had a right to grieve. I did not mention the papers he had left me, nor did she say anything about them. I had no right to him. That was never clearer to me than that day. His place was here. I was acutely aware that she wondered why a governor's wife was taking such an interest in a storekeeper. I asked for sketches he had done of me, but she did not seem to know what I meant. She said he had drawn many people. Instead, she gave me one of his still lifes, beseeching me to show it to collectors in London. I took it gladly and went to some lengths to reassure her that I would see his work was recognised.

I never showed Louis Lemprière's papers to Sir John and it was some time after I returned to London that I received the letter I had sent from Marlborough, unopened.

When we got back to England I was pleased that Sir John finally received a commission to seek the North-West Passage. In the end, that remained his passion — after all, he left his first wife near death to map those icy lands. That he died doing what he loved, in the end, became important to me.

I never gave up hope at first, travelling to the Orkneys and Shetlands, attending clairvoyants in summer and then in early autumn returning home to be closer to any news that might come. I sent letters, increasingly passionate, begging for financial assistance for the rescue. We had public prayers in sixty churches throughout the country. I spent almost all my funds sending ships to find him, as if by trying to save him, I could do for him what I had not done for the man I truly loved.

When the *Erebus* and *Terror* wintered in the Arctic in 1847 they told me they found three graves, a pile of empty cans and the remains of a magnetic observatory. The Eskimos found spoons and forks with his crest on them and his order of knighthood. They confirmed his death after finding the official letter buried under stones at that bleak cairn so far north. They tried to tell me his crew had resorted to cannibalism. Perhaps I will never know how he died. Was he thinking of me in his last moments?

I wrote to the Home Secretary requesting that a place be set aside for my husband at Westminster Abbey for a bust to be made of marble.

He was questioned little at the committee's inquiry, for which I was thankful. Much of the blame shifted instead to the Secretary of State. Apart from Barnes and other petty officials, there were few to connect the Frankland regime to the brutality.

By the time he was ready for his final trip to the Arctic, my husband's reputation had been resurrected. By then, I am ashamed to say, I could not bear to besmirch his name. I am as guilty, then, as my husband, having lived the rest of my life as the widow of a gallant hero who perhaps never was.

After more than a decade of widowhood, I face my deceit every day. My only salvation is the publication of *The Origin of Species*, Charles Darwin's worthy tome selling for fifteen shillings. Thirty years after I was first aware of the man, Darwin's ideas are fully formed, yet once he had written that revealing what he knew was like confessing to a murder. Neither of us, however, is mentioned in his final work. I am not hurt on my own account, but I am for Louis, who once again has been overlooked. His fossilised collections undoubtedly contributed to Darwin's deductions in linking one continent to another.

Darwin is now a semi-invalid, after devoting his life to the theory that has caused such schisms in the religious fraternity. Unlike me, though, he spoke his truth. Commuters have been buying the green-clothed book in droves outside Waterloo station. The world is ready for Charles Darwin.

'That's it,' Lydia said, looking up at him. 'She stops there.'

Giles had left the armchair. He was standing with his back to her, looking at the street below. At the nape of his neck his hair was darker and curled slightly. She was conscious that her family – strangers to him – had become part of his life through her.

'An incredible story,' he said softly.

'Jane was weak in spite of all of her adventures and bravado,' Lydia said. 'I find it hard to forgive her in some ways. She did not defend the man she loved when he had implored her to do so because it might have brought my father into disrepute. But Lemprière went to his grave believing she would help him. And she loved him, there's no doubt about that.'

'And love conquers all?' he said.

She glanced at him swiftly, thinking he might be mocking her.

'I am working on publishing some of Jane's work,' she said quickly. 'Have you showed your work at the Strand yet?

'No, but I will shortly. That's one of the reasons I liked your idea of working on your stepmother's diaries. They are – like my great-uncle's work – a record of history, whether we agree with what they have done, or not.'

Lydia placed the pages back inside the bureau and closed the desk, locking it with a small brass key she had in her purse.

'If I hadn't discovered that first letter,' she said slowly, 'I would have lived my life constructing a past based on distorted memories.'

'And a piece of history would have been sent to the auctioneers . . . and who knows what would have happened to it. Now, how do you feel?'

'Not so confused,' she said. 'I feel more at peace than I have ever done.'

'Didn't Lemprière call himself the curer of souls . . . remember?' Giles asked.

She nodded.

'You too are a curer of souls, Lydia. You have laid them all to rest.'

She searched his face again, still not quite trusting.

'Perhaps I have laid the ghost of my family's past to rest, but there are some things I cannot undo. My stepmother died without knowing what Lemprière felt for her. The diary entries that you found in the laywer's office in Hobart Town must never have been seen by anyone. Perhaps he hadn't meant them to be preserved? They may have been filed separately from the confessions. Who knows?'

'From what you've told me, Lemprière always loved his wife,' he answered.

'Yes, indeed, but there are many types of love. He may just have been infatuated with my stepmother. He certainly felt a deep fascination for her, but was it love? I suppose we'll never know. Jane probably loved me too, after all, but she couldn't tell me. Or she wasn't able to love me in the way I needed to be loved.'

In one step, he was before her. His arms encircled her waist and she remembered how secure she had felt being held by him. He drew her towards him.

'Lydia, I must tell you. I have not been able to stop thinking of you. I love you and have the deepest respect for you.'

Her face was buried against his coat, but he pulled back from her and looked into her eyes. She felt in disarray. He was smiling.

'Did you ever read what Darwin wrote about blushing in *The Expression of the Emotions in Man and Animals*?'

Lydia shook her head and swallowed.

'That a pretty girl blushes when a young man gazes intently at her because she immediately thinks about the outer and visible parts of her body and this alters their capillary circulation.'

She laughed out loud. She felt a great burden had been lifted. Her life sprawled before her: a living, breathing thing, filled with sadness, but delight, too – and for the first time she knew how to enjoy it.

AUTHOR'S NOTE

My original intention in writing *The Curer of Souls* was to write a work of non-fiction, but there were too many gaps in the primary sources to tell the story; too much that was left unsaid.

In the ten years I lived in Tasmania I embarked on many walks through its impenetrable forests and mountains; visited the 'Tench's' hangman's apparatus in Hobart; lived at the Port Arthur penal settlement as Writer in Community for the Australia Council; walked the windswept, craggy promontory of Point Puer, which pre-dated the Parkhurst boys' prison on the Isle of Wight by four years; and visited the desolate seclusion of Sarah Island on the west coast. I was seeking words that would describe the melancholy of the place as I restlessly searched for meaning in its past. Tasmania seems to me to be an island where the recording of the past is secondary to expunging it: after Port Arthur was closed as a penal settlement, letters were written in the colonial press asking that it be razed to the ground. More recently, Walter Mikac, whose wife and children were killed during the 1996 Port Arthur massacre and whose story I co-wrote, was asked immediately after the massacre to pull the crosses out of the ground that he had erected in his family's memory.

Fiction can map silences, reflect voices marginalised by the more traditional historical telling and explore issues that might otherwise be taboo. Fiction can also reconfigure the archives and reshape the lived experiences of actual characters within the hybrid possibilities offered by a contemporary lens.

I drew the characters of Lady Frankland, Charles O'Mara Hawkins and Louis Lemprière from the diaries of Lady Jane Franklin, Charles O'Hara Booth and Thomas Lemprière. Reading about their daily existence heightened my imagination and helped me to bridge the gap between the past and the present. I practised their mannerisms, speech and viewpoints, their prejudices and desires in my sentences in the way actors might immerse themselves in a particular character.

In the finished work primary sources have merged into fictional accounts; bona fide characters sit alongside fictional ones. I, as the author, cannot always say where the real begins and the imagined ends, but the genesis of this book began in seeking facts in the same way that I researched my other books.

I discovered Thomas Lemprière's diary in 1995 at the Mitchell Library in Sydney, followed closely by the published diary of Charles O'Hara Booth edited by Dora Heard, and the photocopied versions of Lady Franklin's diaries, which were housed at the Archives of Tasmania in Hobart. Later, I travelled to England to the Scott Polar Research Institute at Cambridge to view the originals.

All three diarists knew each other, but they offered widely different perspectives of the isolated outpost that was colonial

Van Diemen's Land in the 1830s. They provided me with a chance to tell individual accounts of history. I enjoyed the fact that they were private documents recording public history and therefore provided a refreshingly different view to the traditional histories of the colony.

Thomas Lemprière was the author of *Penal Settlements*, first published in part in the *Tasmanian Journal of Natural Science* (Hobart Town 1842–46). He was born in Hamburg, Germany, into a family from the Channel Islands and, like his fictional construct Louis, was descended from the island's wealthy inhabitants, including judges and jurats. In 1822 he immigrated to Van Diemen's Land. Destitute by bankruptcy, he became commissariat at the three penal settlements in the colony: Maria Island (1826), Macquarie Harbour (1827), and Port Arthur (1833–48). Lemprière defined himself as a dilettante and his interests encompassed meteorology, painting and natural history.

Charles O'Hara Booth, who provides the basis of the fictional character O'Mara Hawkins, oversaw the Port Arthur penal settlement during the period of its greatest development between 1833 and 1844. Booth had the characteristics of a mad inventor. He built Australia's first passenger railway drawn by human power, which ran from Eaglehawk Neck to the penal settlement. Booth also established telegraphic communication to Eaglehawk Neck. In 1838 he became lost in the bush in the Forestier's Peninsula and was almost dead by the time he was rescued. He never properly recovered from the ordeal.

My depiction of Lady Frankland is drawn mainly from Lady Jane Franklin's Van Diemen's Land diaries and letters, which form part of the collection of 168 journals and 2000 letters she penned until shortly before her death in 1875. The Franklins founded the Tasmanian Natural History Society (the first

Royal Society to be set up outside the United Kingdom). Lady Franklin built a Grecian temple named Ancanthe on Hobart's outskirts as a cultural museum to exhibit a collection of the colony's natural history. Ancanthe still stands today in Lenah Valley. She was accused of meddling in governmental affairs in the colony, and often advised her husband. She also adopted an Aboriginal girl, Mathinna, who was left behind when the Franklins returned to England in 1844.

Diaries may dupe the reader into believing they are true confessions, but how many of us write the truth in our diaries (although perhaps we believe we are telling the truth, or our version of it). Apart from the perceived insincerity of this form, I struggled with the fact that all three diaries were tampered with after their authors' deaths. Some of Lemprière's papers were burnt late in the last century; Lady Franklin's diaries were scattered across the globe and have pages torn out, sometimes a hundred at a time. Many were copied by Sophy Cracroft – Sir John Franklin's niece, and companion to Lady Franklin for almost forty years – who selected some for publication and had illegible letters copied, often inaccurately. These copies were then corrected and edited. Booth's diaries were also copied and errors and deliberate omissions were made by an official in London, according to Dora Heard.

In the novel I have created a fictional unrealised affair between Lemprière and Lady Frankland. Reading Lady Franklin's diaries and letters, I found myself questioning the words, 'My dearest love', a mode the Franklins used when they addressed each other in correspondence. So many of their letters seemed impersonal, dealing with the colony: the cost of bushels; the estimate questions in the Executive Council and the advantage of supplying barley and peas as a contract price. Did Jane Franklin's heart and mind stray during her many self-imposed solitary journeys in and out of the colony, even if she remained physically faithful? And would there be evidence if she had strayed? Her husband was clearly not her intellectual equal. Scott Cookman, in *Ice Blink*, his book on Franklin's last voyage to the Arctic, writes: 'Polite society could not, in fact, imagine why she married him in the first place or why she remained so devoutly committed to him.' There have been many questions about her devotion to her husband after he disappeared and here I present my interpretation of her apparent loyalty.

The real Lemprière and Jane met on more than one occasion, due to Lemprière's keen interest in the Tasmanian Natural History Society initiated by the Franklins. I felt Lemprière would have been Jane's intellectual equal. On 29 August 1838 he notes that he called on Lady Franklin 'to see whether she would go round the workshops [at the Port Arthur penal settlement]. Too wet [but she] gave me some rare seeds'. Lemprière did a preliminary pencil sketch of Sir John Franklin in 1838 and coloured a sketch of Cape Raoul in 1837 for Lady Franklin, for which he received 'a pretty note' in thanks. The scene of Lemprière and Lady Franklin being handcuffed in the storeroom is based on an episode from Lemprière's diaries.

Sir John Franklin's most negative characteristic was that he was dull. The fictional Sir John Frankland is a more Machiavellian character. If Sir John Franklin was guilty of anything, it was ineptitude. William Gates, a Canadian patriot transported to Van Diemen's Land, wrote that when Franklin made a speech before them he '. . . made more blundering work of his business than a dullard'. There is no doubt that the real Sir John was more humane than his fictional counterpart.

His fictional character is a composite of Sir John Franklin and Lieutenant Governor-General George Arthur. It was Arthur who introduced the Linnaeus-like classification of convicts and who developed such an evangelistic vision for the island jail, decreeing that Port Arthur should be 'a place worse than death'. It is Arthur's words I have used in Sir John's letter to the Home Secretary about how essential classification was in bringing about the end of transportation. Nor was the Model Prison introduced during Franklin's regime, although the concept was developed in Philadelphia in the United States in the late 1830s during the time Franklin was governor, so he may well have been aware of it. The building, modelled on Pentonville jail in England, was, in fact, begun in 1848 and completed in 1852.

As both commandant and magistrate, Charles O'Hara Booth had absolute control over the prisoners and could order punishments summarily without recourse to a court of law. He was responsible for inventing some of the most brutal punishments inflicted at the settlement. This more vindictive side contributed to my creation of his fictional counterpart, though I have no evidence for his homosexual tendencies. But he did express his abhorrence for the crime it seemed to me to a point of obsession in his diaries, where he would refer to 'unnatural crimes' (homosexuality was not invented as a word at this time).

Both Lydia Franklin and Giles Bentham are fictional creations. Lydia occurred to me as I held one of Lady Franklin's diaries at the Scott Polar Research Institute and imagined Sophia Cracroft working on Lady Franklin's words after her death. She is loosely based on a composite of Sir John Franklin's daughter, Eleanor, and Sophy Cracroft. Sophy Cracroft became one of Lady Franklin's would-be biographers.

I discovered only while completing the final draft of the novel that Jeremy Bentham was particularly fond of his nephew George, who became a famous botanist, and to whom he gave his inheritance, but I have no knowledge as to how he felt about any great-nephew or whether one ever existed. Jeremy Bentham never had children of his own. The details about the treatment of Jeremy Bentham's body after death is factual, however, as is his preoccupation with ghosts.

Other changes I have made include the time and location of Thomas Lemprière's death. The real Lemprière died at sea en route to Europe from Hong Kong, probably from dysentery, but some ten years after his fictional namesake. Although Thomas Lemprière sometimes performed the role of convict chaplain, an occupation commonly described as 'the curer of souls', I have no proof that he heard confessions or that he travelled to England to tell the authorities of a 'game' involving suicide among the prisoners. The real Lemprière was a deeply humane man, however, and often wrote about the difficulties he encountered living in a place such as Port Arthur. He was also deeply devoted to his wife, Charlotte, with whom he had twelve children.

I can thank Dr Stephan Petrow for drawing to my attention a letter from Chief Police Magistrate Matthew Forster to Governor Arthur, which discusses the 'drawing of straws' at Port Arthur. Marcus Clarke, who visited the penal settlement in the 1870s, where the original film *For the Term of His Natural Life* was made, also notes a discussion about straw-drawing with an old timer who was still captive there. Suicide pacts are documented by Robert Hughes in *The Fatal Shore* as taking place on Norfolk Island. There were many 'motiveless murders' documented in the settlement's records. After years of research into the inhumane conditions at Port Arthur, I did not find it hard to believe that convicts would choose an option such as a suicide pact.

I have not been able to prove that the murder of Thomas Boardman involved such a pact. However, the account of the murder was based on actual inquest papers from 1842 and there has been speculation it was homo-erotic. Boardman did linger for two days at the foot of a gigantic gum tree 'clotted with gore and fly-blown', according to the playwright David Burn, who visited Port Arthur shortly after the murder and described the murder as 'motiveless'. Boardman did identify his assassin before he died, Belfield was hanged for the offence and orders were given that his body was to be handed over to Dr Bedford at the Colonial Hospital for dissection. It is also true that Bedford liked hanging prisoners in lots so he could get to his breakfast on time. The account of Belfield's hanging is partially recreated from an actual account of a hanging reported in the *Hobart Courier*.

The characters of Boardman and Belfield are entirely invented. Their criminal records are the only way to glean evidence about their lives. I have used primary source material such as F. C. Hooper's *Prison Boys of Port Arthur*, and I also had access to a database study conducted by local historian Irene Schaeffer and Dr Robin MacLachlan, who was then at Mitchell College of Advanced Education in Bathurst.

The scene involving the stoning of Bundock was based on an account in the Brand papers from 1842 when 'Frederick Augustus Adolphus Bundock, a convict overseer, who was disliked, was set upon with bricks'. Although Bundock did not die from his wounds, in July 1843 another overseer named McGuire died from a wound inflicted by two boys, who were sent to different stations on the peninsula. Two other boys also killed an overseer's cat and for this I drew upon an account by Robert Darnton of the 'Great Cat Massacre' in the rue Saint-Severin in Paris in the late 1730s, which involved printing apprentices torturing and ritually killing cats. Dr Hamish Maxwell-Stewart made this known to me.

The existence of paedophilia at Point Puer is the resounding silence in the traditional historical documents, although *le vice anglais* as an act between two males was known of and was reported in British Parliamentary Papers in 1846. One of Booth's diary entries does detail that 'a certain very revolting offence' was a 'frequent occurrence at Point Puer'. This occurrence was apparently not proved, but Booth was concerned enough to write that in the future he would appoint 'free, rather than convict overseers'.

Peter MacFie, a historian at the Port Arthur penal settlement in the 1980s, wrote that although the sexual practices of the boys were rarely reported, 'It seems likely that . . . sex was yet another commodity traded on the black economy. There can be little doubt, however, that many sexual encounters were far from consensual.'

The Select Committee on Transportation was headed by Sir William Molesworth, but it sat in 1837, five years earlier than in the novel. It was during these hearings that officials such as the surgeon John Barnes, who had been posted to Macquarie Harbour, gave graphic evidence of the brutality involving the convicts. The findings of this commission resulted in transportation to the colonies eventually being abandoned and such a practice being likened to slavery.

The tale of the convicts escaping Macquarie Harbour and engaging in cannabilism is true, as is the account told to Lady

Franklin of the surviving member of the escape party, Alexander Pierce, who was eventually hanged after a second escape where he also ate his fellow escapee.

The real Snakey Wellard was born in the parsonage at Port Arthur in 1900. He was a popular man with a much happier disposition than his fictional counterpart. Snakey drove coaches around Port Arthur. The general store next to the penitentiary, which included relics of the convict days, was actually run by William Radcliffe.

As to the Darwinian references, Charles Darwin celebrated his twenty-seventh birthday in Hobart Town in 1836 while Arthur was governor. There is a story that his monkey is buried in the grounds of Secheron House in Battery Point. Darwin left Van Diemen's Land on the *Beagle* carrying fossils from Eaglehawk Neck and other parts of the colony, although I have no evidence that Thomas Lemprière or Lady Franklin collected for him. Darwin was one of the many luminaries to visit Hobart Town around this time, a list that included Joseph Dalton Hooker (later director of the Royal Botanic Gardens, Kew) James Ross and Francis Crozier, and the ornithologist John Gould. The Tasmanian Society met regularly and did indeed conduct an experiment that involved examining the globules of a monotreme's blood to see if it was related to a reptile or a bird. The real Sir James Clark Ross died in 1962 and, although he was a friend of the Franklins and helped Lady Franklin search for her husband, his character in the book is fictional.

In 1859, while correcting the proofs of *The Origin of Species*, Darwin read the introductory essay to Joseph Hooker's *Florae Tasmaniae*, a book on the collection of Hooker's plants from his earlier journeys to Antarctica, Tasmania and New Zealand.

He was greatly influenced by the work and remarked that he expected it would convert botanists from the doctrine of immutable creation. It was through Hooker's collection and the comparisons that he made with plants all over the world that Darwin was able to speculate about why so many botanical species had so much in common despite being oceans apart.

The Expressions of Emotion in Man and Animals by Darwin about ape ancestry, sexual selection and human expression was published in 1872, seven years after the date in the novel.

After ten years of research and writing, I have written a story that presents a possible world based on the actual. As Aristotle once said in *Poetics*, it is not the function of the poet to relate what has happened, but what *may* have happened. I hope in imagining this world and pursuing this dialogue with the past I have illuminated some of the shadows of Van Diemen's Land. Ultimately, however, it will be the reader who determines how this book is read.

ACKNOWLEDGEMENTS

There are many people I would like to acknowledge in my writing of *The Curer of Souls*. Most of all I would like to thank my husband, Grant, for his thoughtful comments and faith in the novel, and our children, Elliot, Phoebi, Oscar, James and Jess, for their patience, love and support. Also I am grateful to my father, Charles Simpson, who believed in the book from the beginning.

The Australia Council supported me by giving me a Writer in Community grant in 1995, which allowed me to roam the Port Arthur penal settlement for three months as I lived just outside of the grounds. Also thanks to Arts Tasmania for a small grant to help in my earlier research; and the Varuna Writers' Centre for a regional fellowship in 2002, which included the best gifts a writer can have: time, nourishment and the spirit of Eleanor Dark – and some mentoring with Carl Harrison-Ford.

Thanks to my two Tassie writing buddies Heather Rose and Rosie Waitt for our lunchtime get-togethers to support each others' prose; Dr Debra Adelaide, my supervisor from the University of Technology, who helped and encouraged me through the drafts for my doctorate of Creative Arts; Dr Heather Jamieson for some early proofreading; Martin Ball for fleshing out some ideas about the imagined love between Lemprière and Lady Frankland; Ronald Allen, who helped me turn an early draft of the novel into a screenplay; amateur Tasmanian historian Irene Schaeffer, who gave generously both her time and research on the boys of Point Puer; Annick Thomas, Tony Phillips, Maggie Best, Heather Rose and Cameron Forbes, who gave me their homes in such beautiful parts of Tasmania in which to write. Anthony Lawrence, whose poems I greatly admire, helped on an earlier draft, and Richard Flanagan shared his insight into the correlation between the nineteenth-century natural historians' obsession with classifying the natural world and Lieutenant Governor George Arthur's attempt at classifying humans – the convicts.

My gratitude goes to Dr John Hunter from CSIRO, Hobart for allowing me access to his work on the tidal benchmark at Port Arthur, which gave overdue recognition to Thomas Lemprière's painstaking work at Port Arthur; to the staff of the Archives of Tasmania in Hobart, particularly Margaret Glover and Brian Diamond, who have since retired; to the staff of the Scott Polar Research Institute at Cambridge University, and the Parks and Wildlife office for access to the Brand papers. Staff at the Mitchell Library in Sydney also helped me during my early days of research, as did those at the Royal Society of Tasmania and the Tasmania Library at the State Library of Tasmania. I would like to give thanks to Jenny Parrott, who painstakingly transcribed Lady Franklin's Van Diemen's Land diaries; to Annie Warburton for lending me *Darwin* by Adrian Desmond and James Moore (1991) and *Where Worlds Collide: the Wallace Line* by Penny van Oosterzee (1997); to Dr Hamish Maxwell-Stewart for his knowledge of convict tattoos, particularly the importance of the crucifixion as a symbol; and to Geoff Lennox for lending me his transcript of Lemprière's Maria Island diaries.

I must extend my appreciation to the descendants of Thomas Lemprière, particularly Andrew Westbrook, who lent me *The Penal Settlements at Van Diemen's Land*, and the late Miss Marjorie Westbrook, Thomas Lemprière's great-granddaughter, whose grandmother was Thomas Lemprière's daughter, Fanny Westbrook, whom I interviewed in Dynnyrne, Hobart, in 1996. Thanks, too, to Michael Lemprière, a descendant of Thomas Lemprière, who sent me – more than ten years ago – the monograph *The House of Lemprière*, an early family history.

Lastly, I would like to thank Catherine Hill for her enduring thoughts and care in editing the novel and helping to deliver it into the world; Jane Palfreyman for her inspiring enthusiasm; and Gayna Murphy for her visual representation of my fiction.

Several books were important to me in writing this novel. Frances J. Woodward's *Portrait of Jane: a Life of Lady Franklin* (1951); *Sir John Franklin in Tasmania 1837–1843* (1949); *Charles Darwin in Australia* by F. W. & J. M. Nicholas; Charles Darwin's *The Voyage of the Beagle*; Dora Heard's edited work *The Journal of Charles O'Hara Booth* (1981); *Port Arthur: a Place of Misery* by Maggie Weidenhofer; *A Bright and Savage Land* by Ann Moyal; Ian Brand's *Penal Peninsula: Port Arthur and Its Outstations*

1827–1898; Victorian People and Ideas: a companion for the Modern Reader of Victorian Literature by Richard D. Altick.

The following convict narratives were also useful: *Experiences of a Convict* by J. F. Mortlock; *A Burglar's Life* by Mark Jeffreys (1893); Martin Cash's *The Bushranger of Van Diemen's Land* (1843); Chartist John Frost's *The Horrors of Convict Life* and William Derrincourt's *Old Convict Days*. Carolyn Stone and Pamela Tyson's evocative images in *Old Hobart Town and Environs* were also helpful, as was the detail I gleaned from Elliston's *Hobart Town Almanack and Van Diemen's Land Annual*. I also acknowledge George Mackaness's historical monographs of private correspondence of Sir John and Lady Jane Franklin. I am grateful for David Burn's account of the Franklins' journey to the west coast of Van Diemen's Land.

I am indebted to a more contemporary work – *Possession* by A. S. Byatt – which remains my favourite novel and gave me the courage to continue writing. And finally, my thanks to the diarists, whose legacy of richly rewarding words made this book possible.